I0598228

INHERITANCE

THE LEGACY SERIES

MARIANNE MAGUIRE

ALSO BY MARIANNE MAGUIRE

THE LEGACY SERIES

BORN

INHERITANCE

BEQUEATH

DEDICATION

I can be a complicated, dorky, emotional mess, I can go from zero to sixty in a blink of an eye. It takes a certain kind of man to handle my kind of crazy, and for me his name is Scott. For over 20 years he has been my strength, my rock and my inspiration. He believed in me even when I couldn't believe in myself. He has supported, encouraged and pushed me to be the confident woman I am today. Not many relationship can make it through as many storms as we have, but I'm grateful that he knew how to build an umbrella for two to weather them all.

Thank you for being my family, my inspiration, my human and my heart, you complete me and I will forever love you.

"To the world you may be one person; but to one person you may be the world."

-Dr. Seuss

CHAPTER 1

"Hurry up, September! What part of, *I have a surprise for you,* didn't you understand?" Gage is as excited as a puppy with a basket full of toys, as he paces in and out of the bedroom door.

"Hold your horses, I'm putting on the boots *you told me to wear.*" I bark back teasingly. It is hard to be mad at him for rushing me, after all, he does have some kind of surprise for me. "You know, this might be easier if you asked me to wear my rubber garden boots instead, at least they just slip on."

With a groan, he approaches, "Not on your life, would I ever let you be seen in public with those hideous things." Kneeling on the floor beside the bed, in front of me, he brushes my hands aside and says with a smirk, "Here, let me help you or I will die of old age before I give you your surprise."

I laugh at his words as I watch his long lean fingers make quick passes, back and forth from eyelet to eyelet, across the front of one boot from toe to thigh. In the eight months that Gage and I have been lovers, he has helped dress me more than the others in our polyamory relationship. From the simplest of zippers on the back of a strapless cocktail dress to the straps and buckles on the most bizarre bondage-style outfits, and now to these soft leather riding boot. It dawns on me that Gage, likes to wrap me up and show me off to the world, and that is not such a bad thing.

At the top of the last boot, he finishes tying the bow up and asks, "They aren't too tight for you?"

His question becomes blank air from his lips, it never really reaches my ears when, his hand motions move roughly from the laces at the top of the boots, to push their way up the outer jean clad sides of my thighs. From there he grabs handfuls of my ass cheeks in each hand and pulls me with aggression towards him. He is firmly planted between my thighs, and I wrap my legs around him so I can feel every inch of his all male body, especially the hardest part between us.

With his right hand, he releases my backside only to replace it with a good handful of my long trusses, that he pulls my head back with. Swiftly, he leans forward and captures my lips with his own and that question he asked, no longer matters.

Out of my four lovers, Gage has always been the most accepting of the relationship, and the most aggressive of my lovers. Always the first to suggest we try something new, whether it be position, toy, or tie-up. Always the most patient in showing me how far to push my limits, and he's the most willing of my partners, to share the bed with another partner. Gage loves sex and he loves control, I believe this is the Alpha werewolf part of him, and why he was such a playboy for so many years. He could never find someone as open and willing in the bedroom or playroom as I have become.

Even now, after months of sharing my body with him and the others, I can still go from zero to sixty in a heartbeat when it comes to Gage. His kiss has me limp as a rag doll, his touch makes my heart pound wildly and uncontrolled in my chest, and his body pressed against mine has me so feverous my skin glistens with a sheen of sweat. At this point, he can ask me to do almost anything if it means that my reward is him pleasing me. I love that about Gage, whatever he gets me to do, ends with my pleasure, because Gage is a giver.

Our kiss grows deeper when he parts my lips and starts to worship my tongue with his own, sucking and nipping, he is driving me mad. His left hand, still on my ass, spreads my cheeks apart so he can finger my rosy hole even through the denim, while he rubs the hardness of his cock at my fly. The fever I have on my body moves directly to my middle, and a great pressure starts to tickle in the most delicious way. I can feel my wetness pooling in my jeans and I want to rip them from my body so that he can have his way with me.

Sadly, as fast as he turns me on he is even quicker at shutting me down, leaving me wanting, begging for more. I'm at the point where I can feel the orgasm so close and intense, if I can't release it I fear I might die. He pulls my head back by my hair to separate our bodies, I only then realize I have been holding my breath since I don't have enough air to scream my displeasure at him.

He holds me in place, his hand gripping my hair, his body dominating my space, and his other hand still stroking my ass. I focus on his face, his eyes so blue that they are their own shade, but deep within them, I see the fire that burns, for only me. I smile at this small victory; I too can turn him on just as much as he turns me on.

With one of his signature smirks he whispers, "I swear on my life before this day is done, I will have your ankles tied to the bedposts, your thighs spread wide enough for me to eat that delicious pussy of yours until it weeps from pleasure. Only then, will I allow your greedy cunt to devour my cock until I fill you with my seed."

I gulp air and try to speak but he has won this round, rendering me speechless and his to control. I can only anticipate our later when he will no doubt follow through with his vow, and I can't wait.

He releases his hold on me and stands up leaving a cold vapor between us, and the last of his words evaporate from my thoughts. I feel a pout coming on. "Mmm, that pouty face is sexy, but quit playing around and let me show you your surprise." He reaches out with his hand to help me up.

He's back to being excited, while I'm still hormonally on edge, so unfair of him to leave me all worked up, but I also know it will be worth it in the end. With a smile on my lips, I mentally switch gears, trying to get my head back into the present. Damn, this is so hard when the eye-candy is so mouthwatering.

He pulls me out of the bedroom and down the hall to the garage door, where he stops to grab our leather jackets and helmets from the back closet.

"Are we going riding?" I ask, suddenly realizing that my attire is more in tune with a Sunday bike ride and not a walk in the park.

I'm dressed in the soft leather boots, jeans, and a fitted tank top, but add the heavier leather jacket and helmet, it's a good indication his motorcycle will be a part of our day. My excitement increases for a whole other reason; I absolutely love to ride.

Gage introduced me to motorcycles this spring, once all the snow had melted, and it was finally seasonal enough to bring his bike out of storage. At first, I was leery; motorcycles seemed so dangerous but once I realized that, even if I fell off, I'm immortal and can't die from the fall, then I reveled in the feel of it. Much like driving my jeep with the roof off, but faster and more freeing.

With a chuckle and a shake of his head, he says, "You will see in just a minute but I'm happy to see you're on board with me now."

"Not my fault, you worked me up back there. It always takes me a minute to wrap my head around a game change." I try to sound angry but who am I kidding, Gage can see right through me. "You do have my curiosity piqued, especially if it means we're going for a ride."

He helps me into my jacket, and as I turn I see a big toothy grin spread across his face. *This is going to be a good surprise.* He doesn't speak as he watches me twirl my hair up into a loose bun on top of my head so I can put on my helmet. When I am ready he steps back towards the door but takes a pause, "Are you ready, September?"

"Oh, am I." My excitement bubbles out in my words.

Gage opens the door and walks into our newly expanded three-car garage. After my big transition from human to the Queen of all Supernatural races last fall, Gage started a huge reconstruction of my house in the country. We needed some extra rooms for all my lovers, as well as, the guards. Being a Queen means I will have threats from the Overlord, who currently rules the kingdom that I am to inherit.

What was once my modest home, that I first bought for my parents, is now a giant mansion, for all the people of my court. Gage not only added room in the garage, but also added an extra level on top, and an addition on the backside. Outside he built another garage for four more cars, and in the far corner of the property sits a new log style cabin, this is where my two best girlfriends, Lilith and Jamie, live.

The renovation didn't, however, stop there, underground, much like the underground of the hotel, that I once bartended at. Gage burrowed a tunnel from under my house, back into the forest beyond, to connect to a bunker between my house and his brother Garo's cabin. In the bunker, we have enough room for a few hundred more supernatural, in small hotel style rooms. Almost every room in my house, the bunker, both cabins, and the hotel in the city are filled with Supernatural beings who have come for many reasons.

After being reborn as a supernatural myself, making many of the races prophecies come true, rumors and stories flew through all the different communities. Some came to our city to see for themselves if what they heard was true. Some came for the safety in numbers factor, the Overlord is known as a vile and nasty man that has no time or patience for lesser beings, and he has killed many of the weaker beings. Others came for support and in anticipation of the battle that will one day happen between myself and the Overlord over our kingdom.

That last one always dumbfounds me, why do people support me? I'm a human turned supernatural, with no experience or clue as to what I am doing. If I didn't have Gage, Sabre, Magennis, and all the others in my court, I dare say we'd have no hope in hell of defeating this evil Overlord, Lazarus. He had, after all, been powerful enough to take away my parents magic and make them human.

These are all things for another day, but I think a lot about it. It consumes my thoughts all the time and at the most inconvenient times. Like right now, when I should be thinking about what Gage has in store for me. Sometimes I wonder if I can ever stop being a worrier and start being the warrior.

Gage stands blocking the doorway with his buff body, and even when standing on my toes in heels I can't see over his head. I hear some whispers, but I'm unclear on the voices when the outside door slams and Gage turns back around to look at me. With a big smile that makes his eyes sparkle, he takes my hand and escorts me across the threshold of the door.

I walk with trepidation. My heartbeat suddenly speeds up a few levels, and I'm all kinds of giddy. I let my eyes wander around the room, scanning the walls for any clue as to what might be in store, but find nothing new or out of place. In the center of the garage sits my Jeep and Gage's sports car, the last stall is empty, but usually, it is occupied by the SUV Sabre drives.

I'm disappointed but of what I'm not quite sure until the big overhead door suddenly starts to roll up. Gage loops my hand through his arm, to escort me down the stairs, between our cars, and out onto the pebble driveway. There in the summer sun is his beautiful Harley-Davidson, a Fatboy in all of its chrome sheen and red detail inlay glory, sparkling in the sun's rays. The bike looks as tough and masculine as its owner, I can't wait to get on the back and feel the bike's power between my legs, and Gage's body pressed against mine.

We walk a little further and at the end of my Jeep, the whole driveway opens up into my view. I'm able to see, not only Gage's bike but another even more spectacular Harley-Davidson, a Soft-tail Slim series with a low slick look. This one is finished in a charcoal satin with vivid black shiny inlay on the tank and the two fenders. The motor and exhaust are chromed and polished to perfection to shine between the black steel laced tires.

"Happy Birthday, Baby!" An enthusiastic Gage cheers from beside me.

"What?" I stumble out. "I thought you didn't celebrate birthdays?"

Laughing at my obvious shock, Gage explains, "We don't celebrate our birthdays because after the first hundred you tend to lose count, but in human years you are only twenty-seven, and still remember what it's like to have a party and gifts."

I walk around the bike, taking in every hard angle and beautiful line, stopping to quietly add, "I've never had a party or many gifts, nothing like this," I look up at him to show off a huge grin, "You bought me a bike? This is for me?" I'm over the moon with excitement.

This is the most extravagant gift anyone has given me, ever. Running the seven-foot length of the bike, I jump at Gage to wrap my arms and legs around him for a big hug. I'm screaming, shouting, and even crying a little. "Oh, my God, you bought me a bike! This is so awesome! Thank you so much!"

"So, does this mean you like it?" Chuckles Gage, while I smother his face in wet kisses, hitting him in the forehead with my helmet.

"Are you kidding me? No, I hate it. Of course, you silly man, I love it, and you may never get me off of it. Can we go for a ride?" I babble out with anticipation of getting on the road.

Gage looks as happy as I feel, while he gently places me back on my feet. Digging into the front hip pocket of his jeans, to produce a beautiful shiny silver key. Attached to the key is a chain, and at the end is what appears to be a rabbit's foot.

"Is that a bunny foot?" I ask with hesitation, slowly reaching with pinched fingers for the key.

"Well, of course, it is. A werewolf can't have a bike without a good luck rabbit's foot from her last hunt, now can she?"

Laughing at the thought of this being a real foot, from one of the poor bunnies I have hunted and killed, over the last few months. "You didn't really get this from an actual rabbit? No, skip that, I don't think I want to know."

Pinching the key gently between my fingers, and holding it up to sniff at the evidence. Yup, sure enough, it really did smell like a rabbit. Unsure if I should be grossed out or oddly fascinated at how Gage managed to, not only find a foot from one of my kills but to also preserve it somehow to make it an accessory. In truth, I'm more surprised with this gesture than his gift. Gage obviously thought this through to incorporate it into the gift. Only a werewolf would show you how much he loves you with a mutilated animal part and that alone, as strange as it is, melts my heart.

"So, are we going to stand here all day debating the origin of the keychain or are we going to try out the bike?" Gage asks before my mind can wander down the weepy romantic road it is starting to head toward.

With a happy burst of glee, I turn, without having to be asked twice, and hop onto the cushioned leather seat of my new shiny toy. "Let's go!" I shout as I place the key in the appropriate slot.

After a quick run through of all the bells and whistles, I kick start the badass machine into action. I start out with a trial ride around the driveway circle, to get my bearings before we head off to the open highway. The early morning sun warms my body but the cool breeze, whipping around me, keeps me from overheating as we drive towards the city. The engine purrs smoothly between my legs as I become more comfortable with the way the bike handles. Smoothly and with ease, the bike guides me without much manipulation on my part. It gives me the opportunity to take in my surroundings and enjoy the journey.

For the better part of the morning, we tour open roads lined with wheat fields, driving through the concrete city, and west towards the massive Rocky Mountains. Stopping in the small tourist town of Banff, for a light lunch, at the top of Sulphur Mountain. To get to the top of the seven thousand plus elevation, we park our bikes and ride in an enclosed glass four-person gondola. The view is spectacular all the way up and once we reach the restaurant at the top we enjoy a three-hundred-and-sixty-degree view of the Bow Valley area, which includes the town of Banff at the bottom and the surrounding forest, bow river, and the enormous mountain range.

"This is so breathtaking; I feel like a bird looking down from the heavens." I'm in awe of the splendor surrounding me from the top of an observation deck. A sign in front of us explains in great detail that this was once a meteorological station on the summit.

Gage makes a throat clearing noise, and I glance up at him, he is staring at me with a look I can't quite place. "That is how I feel about you, Baby."

"Are you getting romantic on me?" I tease.

"If that is what I am feeling, then yes." He reaches for my hand and pulls me towards him, embracing me for a gentle but loving cuddle. "I love showing you new places and seeing them again from your eyes. You amaze me September, you embrace the world with an innocence so pure and honest, it is so refreshing. You make me love the world again, to see the good in people again, don't ever lose that."

I meet his eyes with my own and smile, my insides turn to mush for this man, "Then don't ever stop showing me this beautiful world and never stop loving me." To capture this moment, I roll up on my tiptoes and reach for his lips with my own.

I mean for our kiss to be soft and sweet to speak for this touching moment. It starts out that way, but as usual, every time Gage and I are near we turn into hot and heavy quickly. He has the most sensual and kissable lips, soft and thick, so tasty that I'd love nothing more than to nibble on them all day. Our mouths dance together in a synchronized routine of licks and nips. He likes to show his love of worshipping my mouth with his tongue, lapping at me like I'm his favorite flavor of ice cream.

My body instantly heats up, even at this high elevation with the cool breeze caressing my skin, I'm burning with an internal fire. I press myself closer into his hardened muscles, and freely run my hands up under his jacket and shirt so my fingertips can seek out his hot flesh. Between us, a static of energy grows along with his cock pressing against my stomach. Being of a magical and demon nature, I feed from emotions that build my powers, lust is the most powerful of these emotions. When I get too worked up, an energy builds that needs to be released, and the best way to do that is through sex or blood lust. I have been working with Andras and Lilith to use other forms of release but right now, sex is what I want, and I think Gage is on the same page.

With a groan, however, he breaks our connection, for the second time today. "We need to stop, Baby. This is too public, and we need to get going back to the city."

I too groan, between brief pants of breath, "But no one is out here, we can make this quick." I give him a devilish grin for good measure.

"You're killing me, September," he moans in angst then adds, "later, I promise. We have to get back to the city, Sabre will be waiting for us. Then maybe we can both give you the pleasure you need." Seeing my disappointment, he gives me another kiss, this one is a simple joining of our lips to seal his promise before he slips away.

I grumble as he takes my hand and leads us back to the wood slatted path that takes us back to the lift and our ride down the mountain. The line to catch the gondola down is smaller than it had been coming up. I notice the tourists come off the gondola in droves then bustle around the shops and restaurant, but not many go walking the wooden paths to take in the views. Humans are always in such a hurry.

Gage pulls me to the back of the line to wait for the gondola cars to fill before descending the mountain. As the line thins and it is soon our turn, we luck out with our own private car. Stepping into the glass vessel we sit on a tiny metal bench before the lift operator locks us in, and propels us along a thick cable down the mountainside. It's only an eight-minute ride to the bottom dock, but Gage is about to make this worth my price of admission.

As our car slides out of the docking station, Gage wraps his left arm around my shoulder while his right-hand caresses my thigh. Once we begin our slow-motion fall, his motive is perfectly clear when he quickly goes down on his knees. Pushing me gently back to lean against the glass wall, he spreads my legs open in front of him.

"And you said the path was too public." I start to lecture him but stop short when he unzips my jeans in a blur of motion.

My pants have a convenient wrap around zipper in the crotch that makes it easier to go to the bathroom without having to pull off the thigh length boots. It also makes it easier for Gage to gain immediate access to me. A bonus situation any way you look at it.

"Ssh, just enjoy the ride, Baby. No one will see you up here," he whispers while pulling the two halves of the material apart to run one of his long lean fingers through my slit.

I moan at the instant heat of his skin on my own then groan when he leans forward, and softly follows the path of his finger with a lick. He kisses his way leisurely around my folds before sliding his tongue into my wet pussy. "Mmm, Baby, you taste so good," he mumbles against my clit, the vibration adds to the incredible feel.

"More!" I cry out.

"Feeling greedy, baby girl?" He says between laps to my clit with his whole tongue.

I wail out some sort of response as I watch him devour my sex with just his tongue. Over and over he licks at me, tasting every inch inside and out. I start to feel the heat, and I'm inching towards the edge of pleasure, slowly he dips his fingers into me. The first one, he teases me with, then two and three to stretch me wide. My hips buck in time to the rhythm he's creating with his tongue. I'm so close, the heat burns in my core, I don't want him to stop until he makes me cum. To ensure this isn't another one of his teasing moments, I grab fistfuls of his hair to hold him over my pussy.

The rhythm of his tongue picks up speed on my clit and his fingers push inward, stretching my opening and allowing him to manipulate my sweet spot. Unidentified words spill from my lips through gulps of cool mountain air. My eyes never leave his mouth and what he's doing to me, for me. He knows what I want, what I need, and now he is giving me my heart's desire. His wild gaze flickers up to meet mine and it sends me over the edge. I orgasm into his mouth and still, he keeps licking me until my juice is dripping down his chin.

His speed increases as he goes for a double, I have no intention of stopping him.

I feel the car jolt up and then ease down as it passes the last cable connection before the bottom docking station. We have mere minutes until the car stops and I'm just getting started. Mentally, I picture us riding each other, up and down the mountainside, for the remainder of the afternoon.

Abruptly, Gage changes his motions knocking me from my fantasy. His tongue tickles the head of my clit with fast fluttering passes, two fingers now turned at an angle sweep back and forth through my wet opening, while the other two fingers on the same hand slowly massage my other passage. Until I met Gage, I had never once thought of having anal sex but in the past eight months, he's shown me I can't ever see having sex without it. It adds a whole other element to the intimacy we share and the orgasm is undeniably the most intense that I have ever experienced.

His ring and pinkie fingers break over the outer ring of my asshole and I begin to feel the dam about to explode out of me. With one hand, he is able to control me, manipulating me from the inside while his thumb works my clit on the outside. He moves up to take possession of my mouth too, owning every part of me. The first taste of myself on his lips makes me scream my release into his mouth and he laps up my sounds like he lapped up my juices until I'm out of breath.

In the final minute of our ride, he continues to slowly sweep his lips over mine to allow me to catch my breath while his fingers slide from my body. I feel his other hand shift to his jacket pocket to produce a handkerchief, which he gently pats up my mess then zips my pants back together.

"Better?" He ends our kiss to ask, but then adds a couple last quick peck.

"Yes, much, thank you." I sigh with content and sit back up to adjust my clothing just in time for the car to bounce into the bottom dock. "Excellent timing, Mr. Blackwood." I wink at him.

"Ah, thank you, Ms. Rae, but I can't take all the credit." Gage winks back while rising to his feet, holding out his hand to help me to mine.

We exit the car when the operator opens the door and I'm positive the guy gives Gage a knowing wink. I feel my cheeks instantly redden and I want to dive under the platform to hide but Gage strolls with purpose down the steps and across the exit as if he's proud to show me off. By the time we reach our bikes in the parking lot I'm feeling just as confident and sexy. God, this man is good for my ego.

The afternoon summer sun is hotter on our backs as we mount our bikes and kick them into gear. I put my helmet on and take one last look up the mountain, a tranquil feeling floats over me. Gage leans to my side to give me another quick kiss adding a smile that lights up his whole face and takes my breath away. One last look up the mountain then back at me before he revs his motor, releases his clutch, and takes off. I happily follow him down the winding road, through the quaint town, and back to the highway that will take us to the city.

It could be the post orgasm energy talking, then again Gage does make me feel special, but today, I feel like I can do anything. His support and especially his encouragement gives me courage and confidence to reach new heights. Not that my other lovers are lacking in this department, they each have their own way of boasting me when I need it most.

In the last few months since my change, I have grown and learned so much about myself. I have not only become a Queen of the Supernatural, but also a strong and confident individual. On this bike, I feel free to do anything, strong enough to take on the world and that, I'm sure, is exactly what Gage is trying to accomplish. He sometimes is at a loss for the right words but he more than makes up for it with his actions. Today, he's giving me lessons, don't be embarrassed about anything you do, don't take everything so seriously, try to enjoy the ride, and most importantly always believe in yourself, and you can do anything.

I open up the mental link of communication I share with my men and my court. In the beginning, I was only able to communicate nonstop with Sabre until Andras, the Demon God of the Underworld, showed me how to turn it on and off. Through this connection, I can speak to one privately or all the members of my court at once, in times of battle this will be handy. Today, it helps me talk to Gage, without having to yell across the road over the whirling wind and roaring engines.

Glancing across the space of road between us, I meet his eyes for a brief second and speak from my mind to his, *"Thank you for a great birthday, I had a great day. I love you."*

He grins back and not his trademark smirk but the genuine smile he only reserves just for me. Instead of a loving sentiment, however, he teases me back, *"Just pay attention would you, I don't want you to crash your new bike on the first day."*

Typical Gage, and I begin to laugh to myself before I speed ahead, starting a race back to the city limits. We are heading for the hotel to pick up Sabre, to join us for dinner, this gives me enough time to show Gage, I'm every bit of the rider he is. As I twist the throttle to give my bike some haul-ass gas, I tell Gage in my mind, *"Pay attention my ass, I'll beat you any day, see you at the hotel, sucka."*

I leave him behind in my exhaust fumes as I push the engine wide open and put this baby to the test. The speed helps to build up my adrenaline and makes my heart pump my blood wildly in my veins. A few months back this kind of energy would have prompted me to feed from anyone within an arm's reach, siphoning their life energy and then having sex to release the power it created within me.

Again, thanks to Andras, I can control my magical cravings, I now have a balance of both my magic and power. This means I can enjoy fun adventures without the fear of my excitement draining the people around me. I can be more relaxed and enjoy the simple things like pulling into the parking lot ahead of Gage; I just beat his ass.

"WHOOT!" I scream as loudly as I can to be heard over the revving motors.

We both pull into a space behind the hotel reserved for staff, Gage is only seconds behind me and I'm sure he could have beaten me if he really wanted to. We shut down our bikes and slide off our helmets.

"Are you quite pleased with yourself?" His tone makes me look right at him.

"Oh, don't go getting all pissy because I beat yo ass." I huff back.

He swings his thick leg off the bike and stalks towards me. The look on his face tells me I am in for trouble. I jump off the other side of my bike away from him, throwing my helmet as a block, and run for the back door.

He catches up to me quickly, picks me up and swings me up and over his shoulder. My butt in the air, legs and arms dangling down on either side of his body. With his hand, he winds it up and smacks me hard on my ass with an open palm, making me giggle.

"You like that, do you? What a naughty girl, you are." He spanks me again.

I'm giggling so hard; I don't hear the voice behind me. It's only when Gage swings around quickly that I see a blur of a person before he slides me off his body, and pushes me behind him. The motion is so fast that I become dizzy and have to grab his jacket to remain standing.

"What are you doing here?" I hear Gage growl out, while I try to control my stomach from rolling. Now is not be a good time to lose my lunch in front of whomever this is. Especially since Gage already sounds angry, no need to irritate his beast more.

"Hello, my Darling," an obvious higher pitched female voice answers. "How have you been?"

She must be stepping forward to maybe give Gage a handshake, or even a hug because he knocks me over when he jumps back. This puts me flat on the ground with my face meeting asphalt. "Jesus, September, are you okay?"

"I'm fine, just don't step on me too," I mumble into the pavement before he bends down to pick me up.

"This is the infamous, September Rae?" The female remarks snidely while measuring me up with her eyes.

My now throbbing head stops spinning enough for me to see who is talking to me. With one glance, it stops me in my tracks. The woman is stunning, from her completely natural, long, red curls, grass-green eyes, perfect smirk, and down to her expensive fitted skirt outfit and high heels. I take a quick sniff of the air and realize this she-wolf has a thing for Gage, instantly my hackles are up, and I growl under my breath.

"Oh, she's feisty, just how you like them, isn't she, Darling?" Her tone is exceedingly snide, and I have a sudden urge to hit her.

Who is this redhead bitch? How is it that she knows Gage, and for the love of God, why the hell does she keep calling him *Darling*?

"Cassandra Kline, this is Queen September Rae, my mate." Gage offers the introduction as if this will help, but he also steps exceptionally close to me and wraps his arm around my waist. It's like he knows when the shoe drops it's going to get ugly.

My heart speeds up, and I feel uneasy when Cassandra steps forward. Instead of making a move to cause me harm, she simply extends her hand and adds words dripping with distaste, "How nice to finally meet the girl that stole my life. May I ask how are you enjoying my husband?"

The world turns red around me, and the last clear thought to flicker in my brain is, *what the fuck?*

CHAPTER 2

"September, are you listening? You have to calm down. September?" Sabre's deep rumbling words are calm and full of concern, but they also sound so far away. I'm lost in a river of red haze, and I can't for the life of me remember why I'm so mad.

"Sweetheart, can you hear me?" Sabre pleads, and I get the feeling this isn't the first time he's asked.

I jerk my head up, from the spot I have apparently been burning into the floor, to see his handsome face and summer-sky eyes, clouded with worry.

"What happened?" That seems like the right question for me to ask.

"You had a red moment." This comes from my other lover, an Irish vampire that resembles a California surfer.

I sway my head to the left towards his voice and see him smiling at me, but the smile is not his usual carefree and fun toothy grin. Instead, it is the cover-up smile he plasters on his lips when he is worried for me.

"Why do you both look so stressed, what did I do?" I ask, still trying to remember the events of my day that could have caused me to have a demon blackout.

I don't get blackouts often, in fact, I've only had them twice before, and both times, I had just cause. The first, a human biker tried to rape me in the bathroom at the Silverclaw club, a couple of nights after being reborn into this world of supernatural. The second time, was when our old manager of the club, Tony Styles, had tried to trade me to a vampire council so they could use me for leverage against Lazarus. Both times did not end well for either man.

My rage triggers the demon part in me, the evil part that truly scares me because when I get like this, people end up dead, for I tend to kill them.

"You didn't do anything too serious," muses Magennis, but his smile is still guarded.

"But, I did do something? How bad?" My heart starts to race from the stress of the red moment, this adrenaline helps clear the red haze from my vision. "My eyes, are they red? My demon came out, how bad?"

"Yes, but Gage stopped you before you went too far." Sabre quickly explains.

"Barely," adds Magennis.

"Gage, where is he then?" I worry as my brain starts to open up. I remember in flashes from my day, the bike trip to Banff, the gondola ride, the race home, but the rest, foggy.

"He's okay, he just needs to...um, get cleaned up." Sabre is not telling me the whole story.

I take a minute to try to think, I just need to put the pieces together again. We had got to the hotel, Gage was not happy, but why? *Think damn it!*

"Do you want a drink or something to eat? Are you tired, do you want to take a nap?" Sabre begins fussing like a mother would over a child, it's sweet but not necessary.

"What aren't you telling me?" I glance back and forth from Sabre to Magennis. "You have to tell me," I demand, standing up from the plush couch in Sabre's office, to get as close to both of their faces as I can, to make my point.

"Right then, little Minx, we will tell you but you must remain calm. I for one do not want to be the next on the wrong side of your demon tonight." Magennis scolds as he cups my shoulders in his hands and moves me back to sit.

I flop down in a defeated state, Magennis is probably right, I can't solve anything when in a red moment. I peek up at Sabre, taking in a breath and letting it out slowly to relax and to concentrate on only his face. For some reason, this has always worked, but Sabre has been the one to rescue me in the past from bad situations. He is my pillar and strength; with him, I can get through anything.

"I'm as calm as I'm ever going to be, start talking."

Sabre walks the few steps to the couch to sit next to me on the right, Magennis does the same but on the left. They both hold one of my hands, but Magennis adds rubbing my back for extra soothing effect as Sabre begins to speak.

"You and Gage were out today, do you remember that?" He questions me.

"Yes, he bought me a bike for my birthday and we went to Banff. I got all that and I remember all the way to the parking lot, then it gets fuzzy. What happened back there?"

"Oh, spill it, this is taking forever," barks an impatient Magennis.

I turn to him. "Then just tell me," I demand.

Sabre's grip on my hand gets tighter but Magennis is the one to speak this time, "You met Cassandra Kline and tried to kill her. There I said it, end of story, now let's get on with our night, shall we?"

"Whoa, wait, that name, yes, I remember. She was gorgeous with red hair." A picture of her flashes to mind.

"Yes, yes, some would think her gorgeous, but too stick figure for my tastes and that attitude, typical evil ginger. I can say that, half my family were gingers, trust me, not a pleasant one in the bunch. Now you know, so let's..."

"Wait, she means something, what is it, tell me?" This time I turn to Sabre, pleading with my eyes. I need to understand this. "I'm fine, I'm calm, just tell me, please."

This time Sabre takes a deep breath and exhales slowly. "Cassandra Kline is from a wolf pack, out of Kelowna. She is Gage's first wife, a human marriage, not Alpha to Beta like you are to him. They were only together for six months when Gage sent her back to her pack. He didn't love her, September, Gage has never loved anyone until you." He stops to let this news sink in and it does.

The whole thing comes back to me in vivid color. She had introduced herself and implied I was his dirty mistress, that had been when I lost it. I had gone after her and got in a few really good punches before Gage had grabbed me and pulled me back. I had been so upset, however, that I then turned on him and from what I am remembering now, I messed him up bad before the security from the hotel came running out with Sabre. They had to hog tie me down and it took five of them to do it before I passed out.

Earlier, I had sex in a gondola with Gage and it didn't even cross my mind, at the time of the act, to be embarrassed about exposing myself in public but this makes me mortified. *What the hell got into me?*

Never mind that. "Is Gage okay? Is he hurt?" This question causes me to shake.

"Everything is fine, my love, stay calm." Sabre rubs his free hand up and down my leg but his body is tense, waiting for me to red out again.

"Stop worrying about me, I'm good, embarrassed but fine. I am worried about Gage; please tell me I didn't hurt him?"

"He's a bit bruised and pissed as hell, but he will heal." Sabre relaxes again and I feel bad for making my men fear me. I must talk to Andras about this, he is the only one that knows how to control these types of outbursts.

"Is he mad at me?" I screech in fear. Even though I've had rituals with a few of my lovers that bond me to them for life, I have never thought of the repercussions of any or all of them suddenly not wanting to be with me anymore. What if this turns out to be the final straw, that turns Gage away from me? Perfect timing with his ex-wife in town. Which reminds me, he never told me he was married, wait a minute, *that bastard!*

"September, what are you thinking?" Asks a frustrated Sabre. There was a time in the beginning when he could hear all my thoughts and now he has to guess at them, thank heavens for that. "He's not mad at you, sweetheart, he would never be mad at you. You know that."

"Why isn't he here then?" I ask, but in my head, I feel like I already know. He is probably embarrassed that I kicked the shit out of him, I know I'd be. He probably can't even look at me right now.

"If he's doing anything, it better be scolding that eejit. If he doesn't, then I will," answers Magennis. "Why is the scanger here, now, she had years do deal with legalities but she picks today, of all days? It's ballocks!"

I love Magennis, he has a quirkiness about him that usually makes me laugh, but right now I have no idea what the hell he is even talking about. I pivot back towards Sabre and give him a questioning look for help.

"I have no idea what Mag said, but I do know G is not mad at you. He's not here because he is dealing with Cassandra," Sabre explains what I still don't understand.

I'm growing frustrated and annoyed, then I realize what they have been trying to say, Gage is still married. My blood immediately starts to heat, and my vision switches to shades of red.

"No, no, September, no. Calm down, we can work this out. It's all a misunderstanding, we can explain." Sabre springs to action by beginning to rub my thigh, and his grip on my hand locks in painfully tight.

"Then explain, all you two have been doing is dancing around words. What the hell is going on? Tell me NOW!" I growl my anger.

In unison, both men bow their heads and answer, "Yes, my Queen."

Before either man can start another waltz with words, though, the door to Sabre's office opens and through it steps the mystery man of the hour, Gage. I glare at him with so many responses racing through my head, I am sure he can read them all on my face since he is being cautious of entering.

"May I have a word with you?" He politely inquires.

Sabre continues the death grip on my hand but queries in my head if I want to be alone. I think this over and settle with a shake of my head, but ask through our mind connection, for him to stay close and keep our link open. If it goes south in a hurry I know he'll come running. Someone needs to save Gage.

Magennis and Sabre reluctantly move from the couch and head for the open door. Sabre takes one last long look at Gage and myself, perhaps making sure we'll remain civil or trying to leave some kind of warning, for Gage or me, who knows. Then he is gone, the door closes with a click, leaving Gage and me alone in the silence.

He stands cautiously by the door, not moving but watching me. I guess he did have cause to be alarmed, I did beat him up though his bruises are fading and the scrapes are not as deep. Should I apologize for that or wait until he apologizes to me for keeping this obvious lie from me? I hate lies, and I really hate when people keep impertinent information from me, especially when they think it's to protect me. We have been over this, months ago, but obviously, Gage doesn't think it applies to him. The more I think about this, the angrier I become.

I shake my head and take a deep breath, anger will not get me to the bottom of this. I try some meditation breaths and even lean back against the couch to relax while I wait to hear what he has to say.

The room is filled with silent air for a few minutes more while we stare each other down. I can almost see his thoughts dance across his face as I'm sure he sees the same on me. Finally, after what feels like hours waiting for him to brave the storm he begins to speak.

"That's one hell of a right hook you got." He begins to chuckle but stops once he realizes I'm not laughing with him. He gathers himself and tries again, "September, I'm married, there I said it. Does it make me happy? No. Do I feel bad for not telling you, yes? Was I trying to fix it? Yes, but Cassandra is being difficult. I know that is not an excuse, I'm not trying to make any, this is my fault, I own that. I should have told you. Please, September," he comes to me, kneeling in front of me on the floor, head bowed, submitting. "Please don't be mad, don't banish me from your life. I love you, you are my mate, my Queen, the love of my life. I have never and will never love anyone the way I love you." He pauses still in his submissive pose then adds, "Please, forgive me."

I wait a moment to think over his rambled words then ask, "Why? Why didn't you tell me? For eight months, you said nothing… until she appears on our doorstep, and now you want forgiveness? Couldn't you have said something before this? If she didn't come today would you have said anything at all?"

I reach forward and place a finger under his clenched jaw to raise his head, it's easier to lie looking at the floor. I need to look him in the eyes to see if there is truth in them. What I do see shocks me, tears glisten in his pained gaze, not yet fallen from his eyelids. I can not only see his apology, but I can sense the truth of it.

"I haven't told you because I didn't know. Yes, I knew I got married, but it was years ago and for only six months, or so I thought. To be honest, September, I thought it had been annulled so I never counted it as an actual marriage. I wasn't faithful to her, for Christ's sake I cheated on her during the wedding reception, with one of her bridesmaids." He stops this time to laugh and it makes me smile, that sounds like the Gage I first met.

"What I told you last year was what I thought was the truth. I thought I loved her and planned on being her husband, but before the wedding, I knew she wasn't the one. The marriage was for title, her father is the pack Alpha of Kelowna and that would have meant I, by marriage, would be able to take that spot. It would have meant more territory for the Blackwood family, and it would have built up my business portfolio. Even I couldn't marry for such callous reasons.

After the wedding, I didn't sleep with her, the vows were never consummated, which meant we weren't married in the eyes of the human court system. We also never had a ritual mating like you and I had, where I mark her as my Beta. In our world, this too means there is no partnership. I paid her a large chunk of cash and sent her away. When she left, I gave her the divorce papers to sign and send off to be filed, she never did and I didn't think to check." He pauses to lick his lips and take a breath, but I keep my finger under his chin. He is mine to control and I want the whole story.

He continues, "I only found out about all this a couple of weeks ago when she called me. She wanted to blackmail me for more money in exchange for the papers or she would tell all that would listen. I didn't know what to do, at first I guess I panicked, I called my lawyers and they assured me it would all be taken care of. I guess when I hadn't called her back she came here to stir the pot. I was going to tell you, I swear, once I confirmed with my lawyers what to do I would have told you, but not today."

With an unhurried movement, Gage raises his right hand to my face, cupping my cheek in his palm and stroking my lips with his thumb. "Today is supposed to be just for you, a celebration of your birth. We all planned everything out to make this day special and I fucked it up. I am so sorry, Baby, I truly am."

"I'm still mad, that doesn't just go away." I think it in my mind but my heart knows the truth, he hasn't lied and I will forgive him. I did have one more question, "Is she gone?"

Gage flinches a tiny bit and I know that means no. I growl under my breath. "Wait, it's not what you think, I sent her to stay with a family across town so she won't be around you. I just need to clear this up, please give me a chance to do that. I need to do right by you, September, to show you she means nothing and never will. My heart, I promised to you, remember, but in order for this to work I have to do what I should have done eight years ago, and make this right."

I remove my finger from his chin. "Fine, make this right but if I see her, even once, I can't promise I won't kill the sneaky little twit. Understand?"

"I don't think you have to worry about that, I'm certain you scared the crap out of her. I doubt you will ever have to see her for the rest of forever." This time when he chuckles it sounds more freely, our tense moment over. "Not that it was a bad thing, to scare her, because she signed the papers ten minutes ago in Garo's office, and my lawyer is on his way to get them filed downtown. When he calls in about forty minutes, it will be to tell you that I am no longer a married man and I'm yours forever," he hesitates, then adds, "If you'll still have me?"

I sit for a minute thinking this through and letting him sweat. His hand falls from my cheek to pick up my left hand so he can intertwine our fingers. From there he waits for me to sort over my thoughts. All my men know, I like to process information before I make a decision, and there is no doubt, this is a huge one.

I have four lovers, with four extremely different personalities from four completely different races. I trust each one of these men with my life but, sometimes, these men are worse than children to handle. They each want different things in their life, but they all want me, sometimes that is hard to navigate. More for them than me. I am not going to say that the past eight months have been perfect because that would be false. I think, at times, it's as perfect as we can make it, but I also know, deep down each man wishes to be my only love. Whereas I can never and will never be forced to choose, I love them differently but equally. At the same time, I can't condemn one of my men for a relationship situation he had no idea about when every night I sleep with a combination of these four men. That would be hypocritical of me.

When facing this situation, my first fear was that Gage would walk away from me and it scared me because I can't see my life without him. Nor can I see a life, without Sabre, Magennis, or Chris. In truth, Gage helps me with all the others, he talks to them about making this work. He has helped with getting us all comfortable with sharing in the bedroom, so each man can find his own level of the intimacy in our relationship, without it causing issues.

The biggest thing is, he told me the truth, and his first words were not to banish him from my life. Gage thought the same thing I had been thinking, there is no denying we love each other. From what I understand about tonight, this is a simple misunderstanding that Cassandra, the dumb cow, created to get more money and even cause a riff in my court. That alone makes me want to hunt her down and hurt her all over again.

Another test in my already complicated life. A life where I know without a doubt, I need Gage and with that, my mind settles. "Okay, I forgive you, but know this, if anything like this ever happens again, I swear Gage, I don't know if I can control myself not to hurt you. Understand that, please, I take us seriously. All of us."

Before I finish my last sentence, Gage reaches forward and pulls me to him on the floor. He hugs me so tight I think I might suffocate. "I thought I lost you, I really did. For the briefest of moments in the parking lot, it ran through my head, and I knew if I lost you then I would let you kill me. I was so scared, September because I couldn't picture my life without you in it, and I would rather be dead, than alive without you."

"Don't say that Gage, never say that. That reminds me of my parents, my mom had other lovers too, but when Lazarus cursed her the other men killed themselves because they couldn't live without her. Except for my father, who was cursed too and Andras, who felt he needed to go on because he knew he could one day help her. That day never came but thankfully, now he is here for me. Promise me, if something ever happens, you will go on without me. Be there for the next generation, like Andras is there for me."

He pulls back from me to stare into my eyes. "I can't do that, Andras is a great man for sticking it out, but I don't think I have that kind of strength."

"But what if we have a child, would you not want to be there for him or her?" I ask hypothetically.

"Do you want a child?" He answers with a question to hide his shock.

"Do you?" I can play tit for tat.

And here we sit in the long awkward pause of silence, hanging between us. When he answers, I'm shocked for the second time tonight, "I have been hoping for the last eight months that you would get pregnant, all of us have. We talked about this in the beginning when you stopped having periods, and we thought you were with child, only to find out your reproductive cycle is more in tune with a wolf, and that means you only have maybe two windows a year for this to happen. I'd love for you to have my child but we all know that might never be a possibility. So, to answer your question, in order for me to make you that promise then yes, you will have to give me an heir. Until then, if you die then so too shall I, because there will be nothing left for me if I am without you."

I groan and fall back against the couch. "Gage, please don't put that on my shoulders, I can't deal with this kind of deep responsibility. God, today started out so great, what the hell happened?"

A knock sounds at the door before Magennis pokes his head in. "Sorry to interrupt, but I believe we have a meeting in the club to attend to. If you two are done with your lover's quarrel, Flynn is expecting us." Magennis is back to his odd quirky self, and I feel like maybe the dark cloud is lifting.

"Be right there, Mag." I smile and climb to my feet.

"I'll try if you want to," Gage says before I finish rising. "Maybe it's too late to be your first true love, but we are all prepared to be your last and forever. We will all fight for you, to keep you with us, but nothing could be sweeter than if you gave us a child."

As I look down at him on his knees, I realize we are having a pretty serious conversation about kids. A conversation I'm not quite sure if I'm ready for. "Can we maybe talk later? I don't think we have the time now and with a meeting in the club, I am going to need all the energy I have left."

"No talking required, when you want to have a baby, then we will try, everything else is good." He gives me the smile he only reserves for me, but I have a feeling my men already made their decision on this matter.

"Damn, but you guys just know how to fuck me up in the head, jeez. What happened to dealing with one issue at a time?" I shake my head at him. "I'll think about it, that is the best answer I can give, but I won't make promises so don't make it an issue and please, can we have no more drama today. I can't deal with anymore."

He hugs me, thankfully saying no more about the subject, as he takes my hand to lead me out the door, and up the stairs to the lobby. Magennis has disappeared and there is no telling whether he heard the chat about kids. I do start to relax from whatever serious shit we just experienced, and I am feeling good about the outcome, even if it means we now have a giant elephant in the room. Something else that will probably consume my every thought at the most inconvenient time.

Do I want to have a baby? Maybe someday, but not before we settle things with Lazarus. Bringing a child into a war is never good, and that might be my answer for now or the best one I can come up with to please the peanut gallery.

We pass through the lobby and the kitchen towards the back door of the club. There Gage stops me, "Before we go in, know that I love you and no matter what you may think, this does not constitute drama." With a quick kiss, he pushes me through the door before I can understand what he means by this.

As we step into a dark club, I start to wonder, *now what*, when the spotlights all click on. In a bright blinding flash of light, I'm deafened by a few hundred supernatural screaming, "HAPPY BIRTHDAY!"

CHAPTER 3

By the time the screaming buzz dulls in my ear canal, and the flash spots in my eyes finally subside, the party at the Silverclaw club is in full swing. A full capacity crowd of all supernatural, enjoying a night of drink and dance to commemorate my twenty-seventh human birthday. Something these people wouldn't normally do. If this is a strange circumstance, it doesn't seem to bother any in the crowd here. Instead, it gives them all a night to frolic, and who am I to deny them this pleasure.

At first, I am caught off guard by the surprise party, especially after the events of the day, but it doesn't take long before the energy of the crowd has me dancing right along with them. The seriousness of my day has been washed away by my current jovial mood, as I quiver and shake my way across the dance floor to the beat of the music, both Lilith, and Jamie by my side. We are having a great time laughing at Jamie's attempt at twerking, and Lilith's fail of old school mashed potato; we are just a couple of regular girls, out for a good night.

"Hey, you guys," Jamie yells over the bodies bobbing to music between us, "I really need a drink, you want to come with?"

I look over the crowd to Lilith, the shortest one in our trio, to mime with my hands, drinking a beverage then point to the bar. With a nod of approval from her, we follow Jamie off the dance floor and up to the VIP section of the club. This section has a great view of the party in the club but is also a short walk through the tunnels into the Passion Lounge. That section of the club provides live sex shows and stripteases for those so inclined.

Tonight, the two businesses have been closed to the public for my party, and the lounge sits dark, unoccupied because the dancing atmosphere of the Silverclaw is where we all want to be. Flynn, our new manager, having taken the helm from the deceased ex-manager Tony, is solely operating the business tonight, since most of the staff has the night off to play. Magennis volunteered to tend the bar as he finds watching the crowd behind the wood more amusing than being a part of it. Sabre also offered to help Flynn keep this party running, but that is more because Sabre will choose work over socialization any day.

"Mo Bandriona, uh bhuanchara, may I pour you another refreshment?" Asks my Irish sweetie.

Mo Bandriona means my Queen and uh bhuanchara is my eternal, I am starting to learn some of the Celtic words Magennis often uses.

"Why yes, we'd love another round, please." I've been kicking back on the red wine all night. It helps me control my bloodlust when I get a high from the energy of a crowd, such as tonight's.

"My pleasure, my little Minx," he purrs out and even over the music, I feel his voice tingle down my spine.

"Where's the rest of the harem, this evening?" Inquires Jamie at my side, breaking me from thoughts of Magennis.

She's looking casual-glamorous tonight in a denim skirt and black lace top. Her long multicolored hair is pulled back in a simple ponytail, making it easier to see her natural beauty shine, free from cosmetic decorations.

"Sabre is helping Flynn with the party clean up, and I believe Gage is off making plans to build a nursery." I laugh at my own joke.

"Are you pregnant?" Jamie's jaw drops as she demands, and Lilith starts making some sort of squealing noise.

"No, no, I'm joking, believe me, I'm not pregnant," I fumble out. "Lilith, for God's sake, stop making that dreadful sound. I'm making fun of something from earlier, I guess I haven't told you guys about it," I explain my mistake in word choice.

"Well, that's a relief, or is it?" Jamie's keen light-green eyes pierce me with a questioning glare.

"Um, I guess, I haven't really thought much about it myself. The guys have evidently been talking. Then with Gage still being married and everything today, I guess I'm now thinking about it, but not seriously." *Wow, do I sound noncommittal?*

"Gage is married, when did this happen?" Lilith sounds as shocked as I had been.

I tell them about the day, the incident with Cassandra and everything that followed, including a call from Gage's lawyer about an hour ago to confirm the papers have indeed been filed, and the court considers the marriage null and void. Much to my relief.

"Well, I guess you can't say you lead a dull life," Jamie snorts out between giggles.

"I know right, those days are long gone, but to be honest, I like what I have now," I say with a smile, just as Magennis drops down our fresh drinks.

"Here you go, lassies, cheers!" He gives me a little wink then returns to taking other drink orders from thirsty party goers, leaving us to our chat.

Jamie takes a quick sip of her malt scotch before speaking. "I'd like what you have too, sometimes I am so jealous. What I wouldn't give for a tight booty like his," she motions towards Magennis, "or Gage or Sabre, even that human of yours looks tasty. Gah! Your sex life leaves me feeling so forlorn."

"You act like you've been on a desert island for years, Jamie. Please, you went out with that Josh or Joe something or another just the other day, before that you had a string of men, I didn't bother to learn their names because I know by tomorrow it won't matter. Don't sound so desperate, when I know you are far from it. The problem is, unlike September, you have commitment issues, as in not having any," Lilith lectures, and I giggle to myself as they begin a round of bickering with each other.

Lilith and Jamie have been my friends for a while now. Even before my change, they had tried to go out of their way to be kind, more than I can say for some of the others I work with. However, a few months ago they moved into the cabin behind my house and the more time they seem to be together, the more I think of them as a couple. The constant arguing, finishing the other's sentences, even taking care of each other, reminds me of how my parents were before they passed away. I know they both don't play for that team, but sometimes, I honestly think they should consider it.

"What's so funny?" Lilith turns her glowing emerald green eyes on me.

I surrender with a hands up gesture and shake my head. No way am I getting involved in this one.

"That's what I thought," huffs Lilith, "besides we are hashing out this baby issue. What are your thoughts, because I think you'd be a wonderful mom?"

Damn, she's cornered me. "Uh, I haven't really thought too much about it. But, I'm not having kids until we figure out this whole kingdom business, and decide what to do with Lazarus. Until then, I'll stick to what I do have." That sounds kind of rational.

"Going the safe route, I see. But aren't you worried the guys might get bored... or want more. I mean if Gage is bringing it up, then I'm sure that means something. We are talking Gage, ex-playboy, and party guy here." I love Jamie, she confirms the doubts I have already been thinking.

Are my men bored with me? Do they want more than I can give them right now?

"Jamie, why do you do that? Look now, you upset her, and on her birthday, even." Lilith cast Jamie with another of her glaring looks, for such a tiny girl she does have a scary glare.

She then turns to me, softening her smile, "I think what you said, September, is practical for now. This is a big decision you can't make overnight, and not when things are so uncertain. For whatever it's worth, I do think you would be a great mom, and whatever you decide on this matter, know I fully support your decision."

My friends, polar opposites: one being practical and positive, the other being honest and straight forward, but both equally supportive. They both have merit in their truths, but this moment is not the time nor place to deal with it. "I know what you are both saying, I thank you for the advice and support, but this is my birthday party and I plan to have a good time. This issue is for another day; today is not that day, so how about we go have another dance."

Jamie looks at me then back at Lilith, some silent deal passes between them. I can sense this conversation will continue later because they're nowhere near done hashing it out. "Fine, I'll dance, as long as Lil doesn't do the robot again. The eighties called they want their moves back," Jamie jokes, making us laugh, getting us away from the conversation, and back to the strobe lights.

The atmosphere in the club crackles with a dynamic supply of energy from the emotions coming off the patrons. It's an electrical storm brewing around me, while I dance to the pounding bass beat of the music. I absorb the flow of power it rains down on me, and cast it back over the crowd like a gentle breeze. This gift of my power will keep the party going well into the wee hours of the morning.

There was a time that such large crowds scared me because I could not control this enormous power. The fear that I might give into the dark demon part inside me and kill someone I love encouraged me to learn everything I could, to make that *not* happen. I'm not saying I have a dominate hold on my supernatural side, but I am a lot less submissive than I use to be. I can now control my magic for good use, keeping my demon somewhat at bay, most of the time.

The flip side of using all this magic is I need to be recharged. A continuous supply of high protein foods and equally generous helpings of blood and sex from my lovers is how I keep that charge live. Once upon a time, I had a shy side, sex had been very missionary for me, and the partaking in bloodlust freaked me out. Thoughts of killing my partners always being my top concern.

Since then, this too, is something I have a better understanding of, but now my fears have traveled elsewhere, like: am I becoming somewhat of a harlot? I have learned that sharing blood and sex equally with my men is the perfect combination, and helps keep our polyamory relationship in check. Simply put, I love to share myself with others. On a night, like tonight, when I am absorbing large volumes of power, I can't wait to get home and share it with those I love the most, but do they think poorly of me because of this.

I open up my mental connection to three of my four men, Chris my human lover is away touring with his band,

and I relay to them that I want to go home. It doesn't take long before Sabre and Gage are standing at the edge of the dance floor, both with equally lustful looks on their faces as they watch me walk towards them. Seeing them excites me, those looks mean we will be doing much sharing this evening, and the silly thoughts of doubt flutter away for the time being.

If I saw a graph of my own emotions today, it would have a clear line shooting up to an extreme high, followed by a plummeting stock market crash, and every squiggly blip in between. I can use a moment, to level out the chart and end this day back on the upside.

I wave a goodbye to my energetic friends, who are still bumping and grinding beneath the laser beams of light on the dance floor. With purpose, I make my way to my men and we rush through the club towards the kitchen door.

"Is Magennis coming?" I ask Sabre once we enter the quieter kitchen.

"He's going to stay until the end to give Flynn a hand with clean up, and he'll get the girls home safe." Sabre's deep voice vibrates in my sensitive ears and along my nerve endings. I realize just how worked up I am tonight.

I grab for each one of their hands in my own, to feel a connection as we walk to the lobby, and towards the back doors. My hands feel like they're burning from the heat of our connection, starting a flow of sparking excitement throughout my body. My heart picks up speed and I find myself walking just as fast.

"Someone is eager to get home," Gage mumbles into the back of my hand while placing a soft kiss upon it, a simple gesture to make my heart flutter.

I answer him with a soft moan as Sabre opens the door to the warm summer night, that does nothing to cool my hormonally charged emotions. We reach the bikes behind the building, where Gage pulls me into a dark shadow so I face him, Sabre then moves in behind me. They encompass me with their large bodies, it allows me to feel every hard inch of them pressing into me.

Gage takes possession of my lips, pressing upon them his hungry need for me. Sabre runs his hands down my sides, nibbling his way along my collarbone, up the side of my neck, and flicks his tongue around the outside of my ear. I melt back into Sabre's granite hardness, allowing Gage to leave my lips, and travel south with his tongue, towards my breasts. Tiny sounds escape my mouth, but his kiss has left me too breathless for words. It doesn't matter much, though, in seconds, Sabre replaces the absence of that warmth with his own heated kiss. He is much rougher like he is eating me up and I let him.

My body responds without my brain telling it to. My hands reach and grab, for whatever and wherever they can. My left-hand tangles its way into Gage's long black hair, while my right grips and strokes at Sabre's firm but completely clothing covered cock. Deep inside my body, I feel the fire start to build. The more Gage sucks at my pebbled nipple through the fabric of my tank top, and Sabre presses and rubs his palm around my zippered pants, the more the fire grows, spreading wild in all the right places. Opening the mind connection, I tell them both to take me, here in the shadows or on the concrete of the parking lot, I no longer care where. I only want to be with them, as one inside of me.

Sabre chuckles then breaks apart our lips, leaving me whimpering and almost falling when Gage also slips away. "So not fair," I pout crossing my arms over my chest and even stomping my foot.

Gage takes my hand, "You want to talk fair, try riding home with this," he says, placing my palm on his engorged cock behind the zipper of his jeans. Squeezing it to guide him back to me, he groans but somehow stops me with a gentle push and backs me up towards my bike.

Sabre is waiting beside my chrome ride, holding open my jacket for me to step into. "Shall we go home, then," not really a question he asks, but more like a demand.

As frustrated as I am, I'm not so far gone that I know we shouldn't do this here. "If we must," I say with a mischievous grin because it can still be fun to try.

Before Gage starts his bike, he twists his body on his leather seat and with a bark of laughter he says, "Be still my beating heart, my baby has become a naughty siren." After a quick wink, he places his helmet on his head, kick starts the bike and shoots off.

Shrugging on the jacket I turn to Sabre to clarify, "What did he mean by that?"

Sabre has an uncomfortable look on his face. "Well, a siren is an attractive female who enjoys luring men into usually compromising sexual situations. I believe that is something Gage appreciates about you."

His obvious discomfort makes that clear but I still ask, "But you don't?"

Leaning on the bike seat he takes my hands and pulls me to stand between his firm open thighs, making us eye level. "September, each one of us is different and seeks different things, from you and each other. I won't lie by saying I don't like this confident adventurous side of you because I do, but my preference is our private intimacy, between you and me. I think we all seek that in our own minds but we have also accepted the other parts too. Some of us are just more accepting of it, like Gage."

"So, you're not uncomfortable with all this?" This had been one of the questions I thought of earlier.

"Sure, sometimes, you know I am normally a private person, and this is different than what I wanted it to be. In a perfect world, there'd be just you and me, but I know that is not possible so we make this our own shape of perfect. I am not mad about it, and I don't love you any less, it is the way it is but we all make it work. I think the real question is, are you comfortable with all this?"

The question confuses me. "Uh, two minutes ago I was willing to get gang banged in a parking lot, I think that means I'm good to go."

"Don't make yourself out to sound like some common prostitute. What you are is sexy and sensual, and the wanton attitude is a turn on because I know it is for just me, and all of us. That is the difference and why I asked this question. Sometimes, after a more ambitious lovemaking session, you turn inward, like you might hate what you have done." He places his arms around my waist and smiles, "My shy little human still gets embarrassed about these things."

I blush because I know what he is saying, after a passionate night with one or more of my lovers, I sometimes do get embarrassed by my behavior and actions. "I guess I see what you mean. It worries me, that I'm becoming more whore and less lady, especially with Gage. I mean, I love what we do and how much pleasure we all get from it, but then it confuses me when he starts talking about kids and that makes me feel dirty."

"Sweetheart, you are so much more than you give yourself credit for. Need I remind you of all the wonderful things you alone have done to make the supernatural in this city feel safe and welcomed. The charity functions you attend to raise awareness for so many needy causes. Your efforts in converting the rogue, finding them a place in our world rather than Gage having to destroy them ... that alone is amazing. It shows me your heart is big enough for everyone, this will win you the title of the most beloved Queen of all time. This is also why we, Gage, Magennis, Chris, and I choose to be in this relationship with you. You are worth everything and more."

He pauses, raising his hands to run his strong thick fingers through my hair. "Sex is something you should never be ashamed of; it is the most natural and honest thing you can give of yourself. What you give to us, exposing your sensuality, giving as much pleasure as you receive and allowing all of us to be equal partners in your heart, shows us trust from your beautiful soul. I wish you could see what I do when I look at you, one day maybe you will. Until then, I will continue to plant seeds of love where you have doubts in your mind so that in time, you will love yourself as much as I love you."

His words melt me, he's right, what he and the others do to me and for me, that's deep love. More than some cheap fuck in an alley and sometimes I need to remind myself of that. These men have never needed me, they *want* me, for the long haul, for better and worse. Giving them an open-minded variety isn't wrong or selfish, it shows them my eternal commitment of my love of them. I make a silent promise to myself, that once we finally inherit the kingdom, and Lazarus is no longer a threat, I will give them all the biggest gift from our union, an heir.

"I can see in your eyes that you have come to some kind of revelation. Care to share?" His smile is a cautious one on his lips.

I lean my forehead against his. "I think I understand what you mean, that's all." I kiss his nose, then lightly at his lips, sealing my silent promise.

"Does this mean crisis diverted?" his smile now growing in size to show his straight white teeth, "Because I have another problem that needs fixing."

I look up with concern, "What is it? Can I help?"

His eyes sparkle, even in the darkness of the night. "Oh Darling, I was hoping you were going to ask me that. See there is no problem big enough that it can't be settled by an orgasm. Right now, I am so hard for you, that I need for us to go home and solve this problem together."

I'm a good problem solver and he doesn't need to ask me twice.

CHAPTER 4

Sabre steers my bike onto the brightly lit pebble driveway, stopping a few feet back from the big overhead door. He shuts off the bike and as I take the helmet off my head, the night is silent, except the ticking of the cooling engine. The peace of my country sanctuary greets me like the warmth of a knitted blanket, it's a calm washing over me, and I'm glad to be home.

I jump off the back of the bike, having let a sober Sabre drive us home, and punch in the numbers on a hidden garage wall keypad, to open the big door. With a clunk, it rolls open, allowing Sabre to walk the bike between the cars to the front of the garage. Gage's bike is already tucked in for the night, giving me a shiver of delight, he will be inside waiting for us.

I rush up the steps but stop to wait at the door for Sabre to store our helmets. Once he's done I hold my hand out to him, prompting him to hurry up. I'm excited to see Gage but equally excited to be with Sabre, this is how love should be.

We walk through the door and I'm hit with darkness, none of the lights have been switched on. It takes my eyes a few seconds to adjust before I see tiny pin sized flickers of color on the floor.

"What is all this?"

Sabre kisses my hand then nudges me forward, "Go see."

I look back to see a smile on his face that reaches all the way up to his eyes and they glisten with happiness. Sabre and Gage have something more in store for this night.

My curiosity gets the best of me, I head with purpose towards the kitchen where most of the light seems to be coming from. The lights, I notice, are candles in every size and shape imaginable that have been spread out along the floor. The warm glow illuminates the floor, and I can see it has been sprinkled in colors of red, pink, and white from the petals of roses. The room smells amazing, not just from the rose petals, but also from a combination of vases with fresh assorted bouquets lining the countertops, the table, and every flat surface a vase can be set.

The island in the middle of the kitchen has an incredible spread of a different kind. The focal point in the center is a fountain flowing with dark chocolate, surrounded by a mix of fresh berries, sweet bread, and cheeses. Off to the side, sits a big silver bucket, holding a bottle being chilled in ice, and someone has already filled a couple of glasses with the bubbling champagne. The romantic setting is over the top, and from where I'm standing at the end of the island, it looks like is goes beyond the kitchen.

Beside me, Sabre, picks up a strawberry off a plate and dips it into the chocolate stream, before lifting it to my mouth. I greedily open my lips for him to place it on my tongue before the chocolate that hangs off the end of the berry threatens to fall.

"Mmm, so good," I moan out, biting off the stem and devouring the sweet goodness of the fruit.

He picks up a glass filled with champagne and holds it up to my lips. I lean forward to press my lips to the glass, and he tilts it for me to drink. This too has a fruity taste that mixes well with the sweetness of the berries. I'm in heaven as he continues to feed me, letting me sample selected sweets from his fingers, in between sips from the glass. My favorite part is when he licks dribbles of the chocolate off my lips and tastes the flavors on my tongue.

Time no longer matters as we stand in the kitchen with him lovingly feeding me. Seduction through food, another new one for me. He lightly brushes his fingertips up my arm, across my shoulder, and towards my neck all while tasting the sweet food on my lips. The scent of the flowers mixed with the musky scent of him, adds to the mood and flares a building passion inside me.

After another lingering kiss, I whisper, "A girl can get too used to this kind of spoiling on a regular basis."

"Hmm, does this mean you want me to stop?" He whispers back.

"Depends," I give him a wicked grin.

"On?" He prompts me with raised eyebrows.

I lick my lips with anticipation, "On what you plan to do next." My hope is to move onto something more physical, the teasing touches and soft kissing is driving me mad.

As he reads my thoughts, he immediately steps back to place the glass on the counter before taking my hand. "Let's follow the candles to see where they go, to find out what's next." He casually leads me towards the living room.

"Okay, but I don't think I can take much more of this foreplay. You better be heading towards the bed," I tease, but secretly, I hope that is exactly where he's leading me.

The candles form a path along the floor, growing larger in sizes, and some even have stands to hold them up off the floor. Between the glowing shapes are even more flowers and not the corner store variety, these are exotic looking bouquets, in cool blends of color I have never seen before. *How many flower and gift shops did they buy out today?*

We pass right through the living room and into the hall, I'm hopeful as we step into the bedroom. However, at the threshold, instead of continuing straight towards the bed, Sabre turns me into our walk-in closet, and out the other side in our newly renovated bath. What awaits me is more visual foreplay straight from the pages of a wedding magazine photo shoot.

Our oversized jetted tub is full of steaming water, mounds of foaming bubbles and handfuls of the rose petals swirl around the edge threatening to ooze over the sides. Surrounding the ledge of the tub and all along the floor, to help scent the room in an overpowering mix, are more bunches of the flowers, these are grouped together with twine. The store must have run out of glass vases.

With the overhead lamps turned off, the walls seem to move from the flickers of hundreds of small tea lights spread between the flowers. It's all completely over the top, if sweeping me off my feet and swooning like a woman completely in love is what they set out to accomplish, then they did that in spades.

Stopping beside the tub, Sabre kneels before me on one knee. As he goes down his hands run along the length of my body, making sure to brush most of my sensitive spots, sending surges of heat to my center. He leans into my stomach and rubs his face across my hips, before moving to the zipper on my pants. With his teeth, he peels the steel piece down as far as he can get it to go, finishing the work with a trail of his fingers around my undercarriage. My own hands play in the messy strands at the top of his head while I enjoy the feel of him brushing his whiskers across my skin.

With a quickness, he undoes my boots and strips them from my thighs before he pulls the two halves of my denim pants away. He lifts one foot, then the other to remove me from these obstacles, so he can be free to lick and nibble his way back up my legs. At the inside of my thighs, he stops to bite, then suck, until he leaves red marks. My breath labors watching him worship my flesh with his mouth, my mind races with anticipation of what he will do next.

Ignoring my already quivering middle, he skips over the best part to pull my tank top over my head, and once he releases it he takes possession of my fevered lips for a deep hard kiss. Sabre takes my breath away from the intensity of which he claims ownership, eating my lips like a man starved. For a brief moment, I wish he would have done this down lower only seconds ago because the need to release for him is on the verge of becoming painful.

I gasp into his mouth as his kiss grows aggressive. My hands have not left his body, as I play, grabbing his arms and back, my nails leave claw marks in their wake until I cup his firm ass in my palms to press him into me. I desire more than just his tongue inside my mouth, I want the possession of this kiss to be placed inside my wet pussy with his throbbing cock.

"Please, Sabre, take me now. Please, please, I beg you." The words mumble together against our lips.

He breaks the kiss roughly and with a pained grunt, he steps back. I cry out, then moan when I see the wet spot on the front of his pants. "Why are you stopping, you obviously want to continue as much as I do?" I say with frustration, trying to grab at him to bring him back to me.

"Uh, ah, not yet, my love, but soon. Think of how good your release will feel once you have it," he knowingly smirks at me. "First, how about a bath while I go take care of something."

With his hand, he gestures to the tub, turning to head out the door. I scream out in frustration, "You better not be going to take care of yourself. I can do that for you, right here in the tub, and you can help me bathe, while I help myself to you."

At the doorway, he glances back, the smirk still planted on his rosy lips, "For once in your life, September, just do what I ask. Please get in the bath, I will be right back," he finishes then disappears out the door.

"You have got to be kidding me!" I growl out at nothing but the ambiance.

All day Gage has been doing the same thing, working me up and walking away... except for the quickie in the gondola. Now my body feels like exposed nerve endings, every part of me stings from the burning it creates inside of me. I look at the inviting bath and give in, perhaps under the cover of warm water, I can find my own release.

With a smirk on my own lips, I step into the tub, slowly sliding into the heated depths. It feels like warm arms engulfing me in a wet hug, but does nothing in the way of helping me forget how worked up I am. While I try to get comfortable, I think of evil ways to damn the two of them, for teasing me so.

After a minute or two I do give in to the relaxation. *Okay, this isn't all that bad.* I take a deep breath, close my eyes, and let the air in my lungs slowly escape, as I allow my body to dissolve into the water. I sink down, deep into the middle, and let myself be submerged into an abyss. My mind slows to a crawl as I float under the water, the only sound is a hum of white noise in my head that I concentrate on to relax. I don't hold my breath for long, maybe a minute or two, but once I rise from the water, I do feel in control again. Enough to put my head back against the tub and rest.

Something brushes against my hip but it's only for a second. I don't bother moving, thinking it might be one of the rose petals, until it happens again. My eyes fly open with a start to find Gage, shirtless and fresh from a shower. His hair still wet and hanging down around his shoulders, glistening in the glow of the candles, his eyes dance with mischief as the smile spreads across his lips.

"Do you need a hand?" He seductively asks while his hand begins to caress my thigh.

Instantly, the calm I had been feeling, shrivels up and blows away. My heart takes a lurch against my rib cage like I just got a jump start from a defibrillator. What are these two doing to me? Their teasing behavior today is new, something I don't understand but the emotional sexual roller coaster they've been taking me on is kind of fun.

"You didn't answer me; did you not hear me?" He wants me to answer, *oh, right.*

"Yes, I need any help you are willing to give me." *Boy howdy, isn't that the truth.*

With the hand, not in the water, he reaches for the loofah, placing it on the tub edge to grab a bottle of body wash, and spreads the liquid across the porous material. Not once does he stop the hand in the water from caressing my leg, hip, and stomach.

"Sit up, I will do your back first."

I move in such a hurry, the water sloshes, some of it spilling over onto the floor, *damn...* but I am eager. It makes him chuckle as he gets to working the soap onto my back, up my neck, across my collarbone, and down between my breasts. He seems to be taking special care to not hit the most sensitive parts, and I'm sadly disappointed as he continues to scrub the day's dust from my body.

When he is done decorating my skin with suds, he takes the shampoo, pouring a good helping of the soap into his palm, and works it into a lather through my long pre-dampened hair. The nerves in my skull tingle as his strong, lean fingers massage my scalp. His pampering actions make me feel loved and cared for.

"Houston, we may have a problem," he laughs out, and I open my eyes to see what is wrong.

"There is so much soap on you and in the tub, I don't think we will be able to rinse it away. Okay, up you get, you need a shower, because you are a mess."

I look down at the water, bubbles have started to escape the edge and spill in large blots on the floor. "Oh my God, Gage. How much soap did you use, it's everywhere?" I giggle at his child like shrug, he seems to be having fun.

I lift from the water and try to shake out the bubbles, but the more I brush them off, the more they seem to multiply. The wall behind the tub looks more like a psychiatrist ink blot test than marbled tile. I'm not sure if I need to get cleaned up or less clean, but I do know one thing, all this water is going to prune me like a raisin, and that's not at all sexy.

The thought brings out a giggle but before it turns into a good belly roll, Gage appears in front of me in all his naked glory. "What silly thought crossed your mind?" The inquiring naked guy wants to know.

I no longer remember nor do I care. In a flash, I have my hands back in his hair, pulling him toward me, taking his lips into mine. I taste mint from his toothpaste as I nudge at his lips with my tongue. He opens his mouth for me and the dance begins, sucking each other's tongue tips, and swirling them round, passing the flavor back and forth until my mouth is just as minty.

During the kiss, he washes the soap out of my hair until it is squeaky clean. I don't remember moving to the shower, but that thought quickly flickers away too. My body, now free of soap, slides against his. I can feel his cock on my stomach, pulsing as it grows in size. I press myself harder into him and wiggle to help it along. He groans into my mouth and presses his own hands against my bottom to stop me from moving.

I grab a handful of his hair and pull his head back, holding him away from me, biting and licking down his neck. Two can play this control game because I realize this is what they have been doing, controlling me. I'm done playing, I want action. I kiss my way to his left nipple and suck at his hardening nub, this frees me up enough to lower my right hand and grab his girth. He's more than ready to go, the veins straining against his skin, making ridges I can feel in my palm. I stroke him down to the root, and on the up stroke he lets out a hiss.

He pulls me with force to him, leaving my hand trapped between us. "Stop doing that or I am going to cum in your hand," he speaks through gritted teeth.

I smile from this small victory and squeeze him between our crushed bodies. "I think a little tit for tat is in order, especially after what you've been doing to me all day."

He snorts, "Well, don't we seem to be in quite the predicament then. How do you propose we work out this situation?"

"I think, you should let me suck you off."

He gasps, "Oh Baby, I love that dirty little mouth of yours." His cock jumps between us as his body melts into mine. I have won this round and I'm top dog.

Pressing his shoulders so his back is up against the wall, for support, I begin my assault at his nipple. Licking the bud to the similar slow rhythm, I start to stroke him to with my hand. Droplets of pre-cum juices leak from the head and I can no longer resist the temptation to put the taste of him on my tongue.

Feet, shoulder width apart, I bend from my waist towards his cock. Stroking the shaft on the front side with my hand and lovingly licking the back side with my mouth and tongue, creating a slickness to help lubricate my efforts. As I work him up in this manner, more droplets of juice ooze from the head, before they can slide down and be lost in the mix of water and saliva. I quickly suck him back into my mouth and down into my throat.

"Ahh, Baby, don't stop. Your mouth, it feels so good." Gage praises me by stroking my hair for encouragement.

I moan out my response while continuing to work him over with my mouth, using the flat part of my tongue to apply pressure then sucking hard on his head when I get to the top. I hear his breath become short quick pants, I know I'm getting him close. My grip around his length tightens and I cup his balls with my other hand, pulling them gently forward to get my fingers under to massage his taint. I know he likes this, and I like to do the things that please him. His breathing stops for about two seconds, then I feel his hot explosion against the back of my throat. I suckle and milk every drop of it, tasting his bitter salt with my tongue but I keep going, wanting to work him back up to do it all again.

He grabs at my arms and drags me up to his lips, adding the taste of himself to the mint flavor of the toothpaste. I'm dripping with my own desire and can't wait for what will be next for us but I also don't want to tire him out. I reach for some power from within myself and direct it towards him to help rebuild his stamina.

"Ahhh!" He cries out into my mouth then slams the lever on the shower to off. "Two can play this game."

His actions speed up as he pushes the door open. He picks me up, holding me close, so I can wrap my legs and arms around his muscular body, before walking us out of the shower. As we pass on our way to the bedroom, I grab a towel off the rung, and absently start to dry his hair and any parts I can reach. My back is to the bedroom as we enter and I'm completely fixated on looking at his face. I notice his wounds have healed up completely from my earlier red moment. I brush my fingers lightly over a tiny bit of bruising on his jaw.

"I'm sorry about earlier, I hope I didn't hurt you," I whisper into his jawbone, nibbling him with my teeth along his five o'clock shadow to express my apology.

"Mmm, does this mean you are no longer mad at me?" He stops beside our custom-made double king size bed; he had designed during the renovations.

With having such large men to share a bed, it only makes sense to add a few extra feet to the bed for more comfort. Except we all seem to still end up in a puppy pile in the middle, defeating the purpose of having the bed custom built to such an extra-large size.

"Mostly, but I think you can make the rest up to me," I purr out my response.

"And what would you like me to do?" He nuzzles his nose into my neck.

"Love me."

His head bends back so he can look at me, "Always, Baby-girl, always and forever." His lips crash into mine, his embrace of softness quickly turning to enraptured need. As he takes control of my lips, he shows me how much he does need me, wants me, loves me, here in this moment, and forever into the future.

The towel I'm using to wipe away the water droplets from our shower, now forgotten as it lands somewhere on the floor, freeing up my hands to entangle in his messy hair. I love how he has let it grow these past few months because he knows I like to play with it. I have done the same because I know how much the guys like to grab my hair during play, and stroke it during a cuddle. We all mesh well together as we get to know one another on all levels, doing things with unconscious effort, simply because we want to please each other.

These thoughts only help to intensify our kiss; I suck at his tongue like I just sucked on his cock. He groans his approval into my mouth and sucks me back between swirls with his tongue, reminding me of how he licks at my clit. My body ignites with desire as the kiss becomes more like lips smacking together, the sucking sounds help flip my turned-on switch to ready, willing, and able.

I'm like a neatly tied bow, wrapped tightly around Gage's midsection with his arms tucked under my butt to hold me close to his hips. I feel the warmth as another set of hands touch down at my neck and across to my shoulders. These hands are a bit wider and stronger as they squeeze, slipping from my shoulders down to my hips, slowly moving towards my belly and back up, to tease my breasts. A flaming excitement washes over me, I know these hands belong to Sabre, and I'm finally about to have both of these men to worship and be worshiped by.

I swivel my hips in circles against Gage's belly and his swelling length to masturbate my own nub on his hardness. Sabre moves closer, until the heat of his body engulf me, as he strokes his own cock head between my ass cheeks while licking a trail up my back to my neck. Each man enticing me to their will, and I don't know which one to give in to first.

Gage is the one to direct the decision for us, pushing us into Sabre, then guiding all of us to the end of the bed. Sabre bends to sit on the edge where Gage slowly places me down onto his lap. Their hands seem to dance as they exchange their control of me between them, with Sabre having taken the wheel from Gage. I'm feeling the anticipation build when Sabre slowly lowers me down so he can enter my wetness with his erection. My insides quiver around his girth, squeezing him harder each time he pushes into me. All day I have been waiting for this, ready for them to have their way with me. After the constant teasing, I think I'm prepared for his size, but I sometimes forget just how big their cocks really are.

Sabre holds still giving me a minute to relax to allow for his entrance, but Gage is the one to come up with the better idea. Kneeling between our legs he leans into our joining bodies and uses his tongue on my clit to excite me. Stroking me with his mouth, getting me wet, and creating a rhythm in which I can gently rock my hips against Sabre with.

There is nothing more erotic than seeing these men please me. I watch with an intoxicated hunger as Gage licks at my slit, while Sabre moves in and out of my pussy. The heat that has been overflowing most of the day in my body, is now a fierce fire. This fire sizzles through my veins and heads straight to my core, attacking my dam to release in an explosive manner. Oh, how I have been anticipating this moment.

Sabre knowingly grips my hips with his hands, starting to push into me with the utmost force, hitting as far inside of me as he can go, and nailing that perfect spot of my body, that adores the manipulation of a good pounding. Fast, hard pumps combined with Gage's full, quick, passing licks over my spread open labia, I'm close to release and I ache to let it go.

The trigger that finally sends me over the edge is when a blonde head appears out of nowhere to say, "Surrender to the moment, little Minx."

Magennis interrupts my views of Gage giving face and Sabre's cock devouring my sex. He clamps his pouty lips onto one of my breasts and bites with a stinging pain of pleasure onto my puckered nipple.

My vision goes hazy, my body completely tensing as the visual in my head, audio in my ears, and manipulation of my body finally collide into one. The dam bursts and the tidal wave of the anticipated release flows from me. I scream silently into the air of the room, while my body buckles. Magennis is there, by my side, to catch me before I hit the floor.

As I recover the guys work as a team to care for me. Gage sits back, picking up the towel off the floor to wipe his face, before patting the cloth on my thighs to clean up the mess. Sabre stills inside of me, not moving for the moment while my vagina stops contracting, giving me the time I need to recover. Magennis continues to hold me up, waiting for the intensity of the orgasm to pass. I can feel the lust radiating off the three men, it cloaks me like a warm embrace feeding the succubus in me. I drink it in to let my powers blossom, like a spring crocus pushing through a snowy bed, bursting open in a colorful bloom of life.

I move my head up to look at Magennis and notice colorful strings hanging down from the ceiling. Attached to the strings are hundreds of balloons that are floating above our heads. A closer inspection of the room, tells me it has been decorated like the rest of the house, candles flicker away on the floor, dresser, and side tables. Flower petals lay across the bed and three are roses placed on top of my pillow. I slide forward to the floor, slipping Sabre's cock out of me, so I can get a better look.

"What is all this?" I send a questioning glance at each of my men for an answer, but end my gaze on Sabre. This extravagant surprise is something I can see him doing.

From behind me, Gage wraps his arms around me, "When the right woman comes into your world, it will make you want to do all the romantic things you said you would never do. Happy Birthday, Baby."

"You did this?" I'm dumbfounded, but instead of directing the question at Gage, I shoot a glance to Sabre for confirmation.

"It was Gage's idea, this whole day, to celebrate your birthday, we all helped but the details are all him," Sabre explains.

I swing around on my knees, to face Gage, his expression is somewhat guarded, and I think he's being shy. All day he surprised me time and again. Sure, the Cassandra surprise he hadn't wanted me to know, but he has more than made up for it with all the rest. He also told me the truth, he would have told me about her after today. I now have no doubts about that, not after seeing everything else he has done, he really did want this day to be all about me.

My anger has been fading, but now, knowing all this, it simply evaporates, for this is so out of Gage's box. He's the tough one, the rugged manly man, out of my four lovers. He loves to hunt and kill, race fast cars, he never shows much emotion, and he rarely tells me how he feels because those are not easy words for him. This, however, propels Gage to a whole new level of openness and it makes my heart soar. I love all of them but right now, Gage has me falling in love with him all over again.

A couple of happy tears leak out my eyes and he leans into my face to kiss them from my cheeks. "Had I known this would make you cry, I wouldn't have done it."

"These aren't sad tears, silly." I wrap my arms around his shoulders hugging him tightly and whisper into his ear, "Thank you, for this incredible day, I love you."

We stay in our embrace until Magennis breaks the silence. "You would think he is a saint or something, you know he only came up with the bloody idea, it's not like he blew up the hundreds of balloons in here."

"Now, Mag, don't be jealous, I'm sure September appreciates all the hot air you put into the plan." Gage teases Magennis, then turns his attention back to me. "Although, I do believe the guys do have something for you too. Not as great as a new bike, but I am sure you'll like it, nonetheless."

I swat Gage for being a turd but this is as normal as our normal gets, and I like that we can have fun, even during intense or sweet moments. Remembering what Gage said, I turn around to face Sabre and Magennis, settling between Gage's legs and enjoying his arms as they wrap around me. I wait to hear what is coming next because this day just keeps getting better. I can't imagine anything topping what has been given up to this point.

Sabre leans his enormous body back across the bed, allowing me to see all his gorgeous splendor stretched out. He slides his hand under my pillow and pulls it out with two small boxes and an envelope in his grip. Although, it isn't until I mentally shake myself from his body that I actually see the latter.

Once I have my eyes and mind focused on the packages and not *his package*, I ask, "Are these all for me?"

Sabre sits forward and presents the goods, "Of course, my love, who else would we go to this much trouble over?" He sends a flash through our connection, of flowers falling all around me.

Magennis breaks the mood by giving Gage a ribbing, "Tis certain none of us have another spouse that you don't know about. We wouldn't be that dense in thinking. Oh, did I say that out loud."

Gage growls behind me as a warning to Magennis, but this makes me chuckle. We all have this way of making, past or present issues, less stressful, with humor. I'm thankful it has apparently got to that stage with this latest issue. The worst of it is over, and we can move on.

"Yes, well, if you do, I will be sure to beat the snot out of you for not sharing that information with me," I tease but there is an underlining warning too.

The guys chuckle uncomfortably; I've hit a nerve maybe because I hurt Gage earlier. Did that worry them? Sabre is quick to change the subject, "Why don't you open a gift before this gets off track. I think we've had enough seriousness for one day."

I agree and jump forward to accept my presents. "Sounds good to me, which should I open first?"

Magennis sits on the edge of the bed and points to the larger of the boxes. "That one, it's from me. Breithlà shona, mo ghrà." I believe he is saying happy birthday, my love, but knowing Magennis, he might be saying something way off in left field.

I touch the paper on the gift, it's rough from different types of paper that have been mashed together but in a fancier form than just recycled brown bags and newsprint. No bow or card, just the paper wrapped square.

Using more force than necessary, I rip at the paper from the corner of the box, it's a lot tougher than it looks, but I manage to get it off. Underneath all the wrap is a simple white box, and lift the lid. Inside is a small, stunning sterling silver tiara comb, about five centimeters in width and three-

and-a-half centimeters in height. The tiara has an Irish Claddagh emblem, behind the Claddagh forms an intricate Celtic trinity knot, and along the edging of the whole piece is a thick layer of rubies.

"Magennis, it's beautiful." I run my fingers over the knot and watch it sparkle in the candlelight.

"It once belonged to a spoiled Irish Princess, centuries ago, but I felt it needed to have a home with a *real* Queen. Until today, there has never been one more deserving to wear it. I had a jeweler add the ruby birthstones to personalize it to you."

Jumping up to give him a hug, I gush with joy in his ear, "I love it! I will treasure it always, thank you."

I give him a sweet kiss, sitting on the bed between him and Sabre. Magennis sweeps the chin length bangs back from my face, taking the comb from my hand, he places it into my hair. "That is beautiful." He sighs and places his own sweet kiss upon my lips.

"I don't know what to say about all these gifts. I never expected anything like this, thank you, all of you." I'm choked up, touched by their wonderful gestures.

"You have two more to open, which would you like next?" Gage asks holding the smaller box and the envelope out towards me.

I wipe at another happy tear, leaking out my eye before taking the other box from him. Again, no card, but this one has a beautiful blue color with some type of shiny flecks ground into the pretty paper. Wrapped around the box is a thin white satin ribbon, tied up into a looped four leaf clover on top. If I had to guess the giver of the gifts, I'd have guessed this one came from Magennis because of the clover.

Again, I tear open the paper in anticipation of the contents of this box. Pulling back on the square lid, I find a dark and weathered patina colored ring. It's plain and beaten looking, except for the curly style swirls on the top of the ring, they remind me of the tops of a jester's shoes. The swirls come together, but do not touch. I think it has been designed this way to fit any finger size since it's one solid piece.

Where Magennis's gift is sparkly and fancy, this one is old yet simple. I can tell it has a history and I'm intrigued to find out the story. "This is incredible, so old and beaten, but still it has a simple elegance to it. Where is it from?"

Sabre takes the ring from the box and rolls it between his fingers, his eyes glaze over. I know he is thinking of the time and place he got the ring from. "This ring was made from forged iron, sculpted by my father's own hand, and given to my mother when they were betrothed. She wore the ring always and never took it off until the day she died when she gave it to me and begged me to give it to my own beloved. Like Magennis, I have never found anyone who I felt deserved this precious gift, not until I found you."

Good Lord, these men can play my heart strings and they do it with such meaning. I don't feel as though they have tried to one-up each other, instead, they all seem okay with the sentiment that each gift has brought to me. Tears start dripping out my eyes, falling down my cheeks when I realize exactly what this ring means.

I gasp and then hold my breath, looking from Gage, to Magennis, and finally Sabre. They're all smiling, goofy grins, and what makes this moment totally bizarre is we're all still naked, except Magennis, who is just missing his shirt. Gage has been sitting on the floor but moves up to his knees in front of me, Sabre slips down from the bed to his knees beside Gage. Magennis moves to the right to fall into his kneel on the other side of Gage.

I begin shaking and put my right hand to my mouth to try to hold my lips from quivering. Gage is the first to speak. "September Rae, Sabre, Magennis, Chris, who can't be with us this evening, and I..." He stops, glancing at Magennis to take over, "...would like to ask if you will do us the honor in..."

Magennis then leaves the rest for Sabre, who takes my left hand in his, and slips the ring upon my finger, "...becoming our wife."

Collectively they ask, "Will you marry us?"

My body is on hyper shake, I'm hyperventilating and snot crying all at the same time, I'm simply ugly, but I'm also absolutely blown away. "Oh my God, yes, four times, Yes!" I scream, falling to my knees for a celebratory group hug.

CHAPTER 5

The best things in life are usually unexpected and simple. Today has been very much that in a nutshell.

It started with a simple ride in the country, amongst the beauty and splendor of the Rocky Mountains and ended in the most romantic proposal ever. This day has been anything but simple. More like the best damn day of my life. I'm filled with so much joy and happiness that it consumes every inch of me. I'm so overwhelmed with emotions as Gage, Sabre, and Magennis, all hold me while I let out a good hearty happy cry.

It's a moment that makes me miss my parents, I want to call them to tell them my good news but they are no longer here to be part of our celebration. Maybe I can scream it from the rooftop and they will hear me in heaven and know just how happy I am. I want to tell everyone and anyone who will listen, how much I love these men and how delighted I am that they all picked me. All my worrying, thinking they'd leave me when all along they have been planning this.

I'm also a little confused as in how, legally, I can marry all four men, but I figure Magennis, the historian and oldest one of our group, would have figured this out long before they decided to pop the question.

Mostly, I feel love and I want to show my cheerful foursome just how much. Before that can happens, I first need to wash my face and blow my nose, because there is nothing sexy about boogers. I get off the floor and head to the bathroom.

Sabre calls after me, "Are you okay, my love?"

"Oh, more than okay, just need a minute is all," I say loudly to be heard over my clogged nose.

I'm swift as I wash my face and brush my ratty looking hair, making sure to replace the comb in the spot Magennis placed it earlier. Once I'm more in control of my heightened emotions and know I won't start the blubbering again, I make my way back to the bedroom.

Someone has gone to the kitchen, for the champagne Sabre and I had been sipping earlier. The glasses are flowing with the sweet liquid as the men toast each other with congratulatory cheers. Gage has wrapped himself in a towel, Sabre has put on his robe, and Magennis is still in his dress pants, I'm apparently the only member of this party that doesn't mind being naked. I've grown comfortable with my curves and this is a perfect party to flaunt them, in my opinion.

Walking to the dresser to pick up my waiting glass, I turn to raise it to them, "A toast," I say, swallowing back a few tears before carrying on, "to all of us, may we live our lives for the rest of eternity, as we do in this very moment. I love you all with every piece of my soul and I can't wait to be, um, who's name will I take?"

Taking my hand and placing a kiss on the inside of my wrist, Magennis answers, "In our world, a woman doesn't take the male's name, we believe our females are the more superior of our kind. We have all talked, though, and if you wish we will be honored to take on your family name."

I'm shocked, "That seems odd to me. You have had your titles for longer than I have even been alive. Rae was only a name my parents took when they were cursed into this human world. Did they even have a last name?" I look to Magennis for an answer.

"No, my dearest, they were only known as Livia and David, most of us older supernatural only have the one name. It wasn't until about the twelfth century that we too picked up this custom, to fit in. I, myself, have had many names over the years but I would be humbled to adopt Rae as my final name."

I chew my lip, debating this idea, "I guess, but it's not necessary." This is reverse to any human custom I know. "Besides, if we are going to continue to fit into the human world, then maybe we should keep the names we have." I turn to Gage to continue, "Maybe we could adopt Gage's, he's established with many businesses under Blackwood. Any of your names is better than mine, I haven't been around long enough for my name to be of any worth."

"Not true, my love, I think you'll be surprised with how well known you are, by just name alone. You tend to forget your importance in our world." Sabre has a good point.

"Do what you all wish, I still think it's odd, but I won't stop you from doing what you feel comfortable with. I do know that Chris may not understand this, he is human after all, and the human custom dictates me taking his name, Michelson."

"Do you think he's really going to have issues with a name change, especially when we consider there are four males in this marriage." I can't decide if Gage is being sarcastic or if he's joking, either way, he too has a point. Chris is but one out of four and if they go by ranking, he is at the bottom.

"Did he agree to this, you talked to him?" I direct the question to Gage since he is apparently the one who planned this day.

"Yup, sure did and the kid is all for it. That reminds me you have one more gift to open." He walks to the bed and picks up the plain white envelope off the floor before handing it back to me.

I can't even think of what will be in the envelope, so far, I have been given some incredible gifts and this one I'm sure, will be no different. I laugh at the envelope, again no writing and the back isn't even sealed, what do these guys have against penmanship? Although, I am loving how simply wrapped each gift has been, but so packed full of sentiment. This one is looking to be just as amazing, for inside the pocket is a ticket of some sort, for some event in Toronto but with no note to explain.

"I don't understand this one, can someone explain?" My eyes flicker around to finally land on Sabre's.

He immediately fills me in, "Chris wants you to go see him on tour, however, we noticed you don't have a passport, which means the only place we can fly you, on such short notice, is within Canada. Fortunately, he is ending his tour on North American soil, starting in Toronto this week. I think he wants to spend some time with you to celebrate the engagement since he is missing tonight."

"Really? I get to go to Toronto?" I feel the tears building again, *damn it*.

"I knew it, you've never been, have you? Mag you lost that bet." Gage snaps his fingers at Magennis in a pay up gesture.

"Honestly, I haven't ever left this city, until today, when you took me to Banff. Toronto is like a whole other world for me. Thank you, this has been, amazing." I wipe my hand over my face and take a deep breath, I'm not going to cry. I promised myself in the bathroom that I wouldn't. I do want to show them my appreciation for everything they have done to make this day the best one ever.

Gage pulls me into his arms to holds me, whispering in my ear, "I'm happy you liked your birthday. I love you, September."

"I love you too," I choke out the words into the crook of his neck, and that is where I decide to start worshipping him back.

I run my nose along his collarbone, love biting his shoulder then kissing it better. Sabre takes the glass out of my hand behind Gage's back, as he picks up on the surge of power I push into the room.

"Yay, Baby, let it go," Gage says, before grabbing my head and pressing his lips into mine. This time he holds nothing back, eating at my lips with a hunger. Pushing my mouth open with his tongue, he laps at my mouth, tasting the champagne we just drank.

He walks us back to the bed and spins us around to lay me down on my back so he can crouch over me. From the corner of my eye, I see Magennis move to the left side of the room to remove his pants. Sabre comes up on our right, pulling off his robe, giving Gage time to devour my lips. My hands slide up his back and into his hair, trying to push and pull him to my will.

Sabre kneels on the bed, shuffling down from the headboard to take my hands with his and raise them over my head. He secures them with his body as he leans forward to switch with Gage, his mouth to mine, allowing Gage to work his way down the rest of my body.

With a lazy ease, Gage laps at my skin with his tongue and teeth, nipping down my throat on his way towards my breasts. I feel my breasts swell with anticipation for the great deal of care he is about to give them. Kneading one with his hand while the other is suckled and teased with his mouth until I'm at the point I might self-implode. Then he switches sides to begin the torture again. My nipples sting from the constant assault, the burn is a welcome start and already a flame of desire is searing through me.

While Gage hungrily devours me inch by inch, working me up with a quick tease. Sabre keeps a much slower and softer pace elsewhere. Gentle tongue strokes across my lips, chewing softly on my bottom lip then biting it hard and finally kissing away the sting. I think I have the game all figured out until, Magennis runs his tongue up my leg, stopping to kiss a few soft spots along the way. Starting with the arch of my foot, nipping the skin with his teeth before moving up my calves to bite behind my knee and a trail along the inside of my thigh. I'm disappointed when he skips the best part to lick his way across my hipbone.

Magennis plays everywhere and anywhere except the one place I wish him to, while Sabre and Gage have me teased up with each one of their licks and sucks, surges of fire are pulsing straight into my core. The pulsing heat makes its way around my body to hit every sensitive nerve. I smell our lust; it has coated the room with a sweet aroma and I am hungry from it but my men know just how to feed me.

My vision has been blocked by Sabre's upside down body, so I must rely on my other senses like Gage has been teaching me when we hunt. I can taste the sweetness of champagne on Sabre's lips. His musk scent has filled my nostrils and cloaks my face, now he is all I can smell. I can hear Gage and Magennis making kissing and smacking lip sounds on the various parts of my body yet, I can tell the differences between each man.

The softness of Sabre, a whisper of his movements compared to the rough ones of Gage, while Magennis is somewhere in between. Even blind, I can tell who each man is by their touch alone. I love each one of those differences because with them comes the complex variety of the men. They keep my life grounded, sane, fun, and confusing; but open, honest and together, equally sharing as one.

Magennis rubs a quick pass of his face over my sex, and I just about buckle. I scream into Sabre's mouth and hear him and Gage groan. They are all enjoying my pleasure as much as I am enjoying them giving it to me. Magennis continues, this time, with a sweep of his pouty lips across my sex, again I scream. I'm so close to an orgasm, I feel my own pre-cum drip out of my opening. On the third pass, he uses the flat part of his hot tongue but slows right down, inching his mouth up my sex with almost no pressure. I buck my hips to gain some pressure only to have him move away, infuriating me.

There's a sudden shift as the bed dips, Sabre rolls me to my side but stays above me allowing Magennis to lay parallel to me. "Jump on top of me then, love," Magennis commands.

I roll around to straddle his leaner sculpted body, taking advantage of this position, to run my hand across his smooth chest because I love the satin feel of it on my fingertips. Vampires are hairless creatures, except for what is on their head, leaving their bodies smooth and silky to touch, as well as more appealing to look at and play with. Again, I enjoy the variety of my men, Magennis's softness to Gage's rougher exterior, and all the in between makes moments like these more pleasurable to play. I can explore the gift of what each man has to offer and I so enjoy doing just that, from head to toe.

Magennis has pulled his usually unkempt blonde locks, into a hair tie for work. I loosen the elastic band and run my fingers through the satiny strands. Like Gage, Magennis has let his mane grow these past months. I decide to take this time to show him how much I appreciate the effort while I play with the milk colored length.

I watch his younger looking face relax to my touch, if I didn't know he was a vampire, I'd believe him to be about twenty-five in human years, a male in the prime of his life. Something he takes great joy in pretending to be. It isn't until you stare into his eyes, that you discover, a wisdom from a man much older inside. Those bright aqua eyes hold so much history, pain, and suffering, but also joy and mirth. Even after such a long-lived life, he remains light of heart; the first to laugh and always see the good in everyone. I love his positive light and wish to be more like him.

Leaning forward, I place my lips over his heart, giving him a soft brush of my skin to his, showing my love. Then I let the lust take over as I run my cheek across his chest, back and forth between his nipples, licking each to stiffen it before moving back across to the other. In this position, I also have his swelling cock trapped between our bellies, this gives me the perfect opportunity to tilt my hips up and down his shaft to work him up. Once I feel his cock begin to tear on my skin, I know he is ready for me. I bite one of his hardened nipples, not enough to harm, but just enough for it to sting and I combine this with my hips. Bringing myself up to allow for his cock head to slide into my wetness, before I sink down until he is deep inside of me.

We both moan in unison as I take him inch by inch inside me, allowing both of us to feel each other's sex from the inside. With a controlled steady pace, I rock myself over him, milking his cock with my sex, the sensation is incredible and I can feel how close I am to release. Of course, with two other men in the room, I can't be selfish by thinking only of my own pleasure, I also have to think of their needs too.

Sabre is still kneeling in front of me watching the show with Gage moving beside us. I reach with my left hand to palm Gage, using the pre-cum on the head of his cock to moisten his shaft for an easier glide up, down, and around. I coordinate stroking Gage, to the rhythm that I'm fucking Magennis, to make it easier for me to concentrate on this multitasking. If I sit forward, bracing myself on my right elbow, and leaning over, I can take Sabre into my mouth. I can tease and please all of them and it heats me up quickly. Before I can stop myself, I cum with what an incredible force around Magennis's erection.

Some sort of unknown sound, gurgles out of my mouth, it's muted out by Sabre's girth, he groans and the sound encourages me to continue to stroke him with mouth and tongue. Gage, lifts my hand from his own length and places it on the base of Sabre's cock, following the strokes of my mouth, he's showing me what he wants me to do. As I add fist pumps with my mouth sucks on Sabre, Gage moves in behind me. Leaning into my back, he sucks at my neck to mark it before wrapping my hair around his fist, which he uses to hold my head back, giving Sabre better access to fuck my face. It is a quick brain spin from only seconds ago but this is what I love to get off on when Gage takes control for us all.

He knows us all well, our likes and dislikes, what gets us hot and sizzling with need and what we do to please another. I learned long ago that when it comes to sex, Gage is the master. I might be their Queen and what I say is law; in the bedroom, I have no problem with letting Gage take over and push us to our limit because the result is pure ecstasy.

My heart begins to beat with wild vigor as the reins shift, Magennis holds my hips in place to grind himself hard up into the depth of my sex. He leans up to manipulate my left nipple, pulling it into his mouth and swirling his tongue and lips to bring it to a pucker.

Sabre has my right breast in the grip of his palm, kneading my flesh and playing the skin around the areola by pinching it with his fingers. While he works my breast, I keep stroking him off into my mouth to the circular motion of his hips. With my head still controlled by Gage, I know that Sabre will soon burst his seed into my throat, and I'm salivating all over his cock head in anticipation for it.

You'd think I'd have my hands full, literally, at this point, but Gage loves to push all of us to new levels. I feel his tongue lick me between my spread ass cheeks just before he begins to massage the puckered bud with the tip of his cock. My hunger hits at this point, and my fangs drop, soon I will need blood with my lust. It also means I'm more than ready for Gage when he slips his hips forward and enters me from behind. The pressure of both men inside of me at once is at first overpowering. I try to move to fight it, but Magennis holds me in place over him so I can adjust to it instead.

Sabre and Magennis both pinch at my swollen nipples, they will be sore after this but the pain they provide now is what helps me to receive Gage's hard cock, in an easier manner. Together the men play me like an instrument to a combined beat that only they know the rhythm. Trickles of sweat escape my hairline, the flame that has been burning most of the day is now a raging inferno, sizzling with a painful hunger through my veins.

The pressure of the release builds, the dam has begun to spill over with every thrust and pump. "That's it, Baby, give in, cum for us," Gage commands.

A stream of unintelligent words vibrates out around Sabre's cock, the sensation triggers him and he begins to release his seed into my mouth. I lap it up as careful as I can, not wanting to cut his tender flesh with my fangs.

He pulls out and bends to kiss me, licking his own seed from my lips. This erotic gesture does it for me, "Yes, yes, oh fucking God, yes." I scream to the heavens.

My release is cut short by seconds when I feel the liquid heat of Magennis filling me with his own seed. The thought of his pleasure keeps me on the edge of my own, my favorite parts are getting the guys off before getting off myself. Gage pulls me up and back by the hair into his chest, he's still hard and pulsing inside of my ass. Sabre moves forward and replaces Magennis as he is still ready to go even after the blowjob. He's not gentle when he enters me with a hard thrust and I don't really care.

"Mmm, that's sweet," Gage whispers in my ear. "You're so tight, Baby, I can feel you gripping us, you want more, don't you?"

I try to shake my head but he pulls on my hair and demands, "No, answer me, what do you want, Baby?"

I mouth the words, but I have no breath to form the sounds. He pulls my hair some more and stops moving his hips. He wants an answer.

I wet my lips with my dry tongue, and swallow in some air. "More." The word comes out like the sound of a fog horn.

"More what, Baby?" *Damn, he's relentless.*

"You, Sabre, cock, I don't care," I blurt in between breaths.

Gage begins to move again, long slow thrusts. "That's my girl, so hungry you are. Then take it, Baby-girl, take us both, and give us what we need."

"What do you want?" I ask, my eyes flicker down to Sabre, his fangs are also out.

Together they both answer with one simple word, "Cum."

I groan when Gage allows me to turn my head to let Sabre feed. He's like a cobra, coming up from the waist to strike my neck. At the same time, Magennis comes around Sabre's back to do the same on the other side. I whimper, not from pain but at how wonderful this feels, attached to all three of them at once. Not only in body, but also with blood and soul. I can't hold back any longer, I hiccup in enough breath to let the scream escape. They had asked me to cum and I make sure not to disappoint.

Sabre and Magennis retract their fangs and lick closed the holes. Satisfied, Magennis falls back on the bed. Sabre, not quite done, holds me, pumping himself off deep in my core. I feel him spill his liquid at the same time as I do. He continues to hold me to let me fall into his chest as I use up my last ounce of energy.

Slowly Gage and Sabre slide out of my wetness, Magennis is ready with a towel in hand, and takes great care cleaning us all up. Gage then bends to lift me into his arms and walks me to the bed, where Sabre has pulled back the comforter for Gage to place me down between the sheets. I wiggle myself in my spot, somewhere in the middle, Sabre crawls in on left, Gage curls up on the right. Magennis lays on top of the covers between my legs, he will stay until I fall asleep then he will move to a room in the bunker underground, for his slumber during the day.

Gage gives me a kiss goodnight, "You didn't feed?" He says after feeling my fangs poking out from behind my lips.

"No, I can do it in the morning." The answer comes out groggy because I am almost asleep.

I feel the bed shake as the men jump up and begin to check me over. I giggle at the intensity of their concern. "I'm fine, we can wait, it has been a long day, and I'm tired." I snuggle into the pillow and pull the covers up under my chin.

I hear Sabre let out a low growl, he is not happy with my decision. "September," he says in that authority voice he uses when ordering his security team around or when he is miffed at me.

I smile while rolling toward him, "Go to sleep, Sabre, I promise, tomorrow. Now, please let me pass out." I crane my neck to kiss his lips then snuggle myself back in.

Oh, am I going to get an earful in the morning for be a naughty girl, no doubt about it.

CHAPTER 6

I'm standing in the center of the biggest warehouse-sized shoe store I have ever seen in my life. The brightly lit store seems to go on forever. Floor to ceiling shelving line the walls and display counters adorn the room, the whole place is packed with every designer name, style, color, and different height or width of shoe, but every pair is in my size. I must be dead and in the best heaven possible.

"This is the best birthday ever," I screech to myself because I seem to be alone.

Walking from wall to display case, I have to touch as many pairs as possible. Some shine with beautiful multicolored sequins that sparkle in the bright light of the room. Other pairs give off an attitude that I can't wait to wear to show my confidence.

Then the room shimmers, like my eyes are looking through ocean waves, blurred and hazy as the vision of the warehouse washes away. The replacement is even better, an enormous walk-in closet, bigger than my whole house. All the shoes from the warehouse have been neatly organized and staked by shades of color, to match rack upon rack of coordinating outfits.

"Now we're talking." I'm over the moon with excitement about this find.

I could wander this closet for days and never get to the end. There are so many outfits, one for at least every day of wear for the rest of my life, which will be forever. I want to show Lilith, out of all the people in my life, she will appreciate the beauty of this closet.

A loud galloping sound startles me, I swing around, taking up a fighting stance, only to find a huge wet black dog. It, no, he from his anatomy, is panting like he has run into the closet to get away from something. Water and blobs of dark mud drip from the critters coat, and there are brown paw prints caked in the cream-colored carpet behind him, from the direction he has come. A wave of panic strikes me when I realize what is about to happen seconds before it does.

"Noooo!" I scream out just as the dog begins to shake.

A slow motion, full bodied wiggle, from head to tail. Mud, dirt, water and drool are flung throughout the room, dropping soil chunks all over the contents of my dream closet, even landing a few wet droplets on me.

"Bad dog, no, bad!" I scold the ill-mannered beast.

The dog stops mid-shake to look at me, piercing blue eyes of a familiar shade stare back at me. His tongue lops out of his mouth, and he begins to pant again like he might be smiling. The beastly bugger is laughing at the mess, but I'm furious.

"You little shit!" I curse at him.

That sets him off, he stalks towards me like I might be his dinner, drool hanging from his open jaw in a long-threaded streamer. With a pounce, he knocks me to the floor, pinning my body under his enormous weight, soaking me with his wet fur. It does amaze me, though, that for such a filthy beast, he smells remarkably fresh.

The dog is sprawled on top of me, I try to wiggle out from under him but to no avail. As I move he retaliates by licking my cheek, ear, and neck with his large long tongue. With every pass, he leaves behind slimy drool, I should be grossed out, but the fur on his muzzle tickles my face and makes me giggle. The familiar eyes, that I can't quite place, look down at me, his giant head turns from side to side like he is deciding on something evil to perform. Then the dog moves his head forward and sticks his tongue in my mouth for some perverse doggie kiss.

I gasp with a startled breath as my eyes fly open. Gage is laying above me, sapphire blue eyes shining down into my amber ones, his mouth to mine, kissing me awake.

"Good morning, beautiful, where you having a pleasant dream?" Laughs the ill-mannered beast himself.

"I was ... until some giant dog ruined it for me," I grumble out in a sleepy voice.

"Is that why you were yelling something about a bad dog?" He asks with a mischievous smile like he knows my dream because he helped shape it, which judging by our current position, I'm pretty sure he did.

He has made me laugh and who wouldn't want to wake up like that. "You are seriously evil, you know that, right? I was about to have a shoegasm, it's like an orgasm, but better, and with shoes. Until this big old dog destroyed my chances." I push my bottom lip out in a pout for dramatic effect.

"Mmm." He moans before sucking my lip into his mouth, giving it a nip then a kiss to soothe the sting.

With his hands, he pushes back my hair, holding my head, then teasingly he adds, "You know, all I heard from that was orgasm because your mouth distracted me." Again, he dips his head down and sucks in my bottom lip, with his teeth he bites down and runs the tip of his tongue along the outer flesh.

I meet the action by running the tip of my tongue across his upper lip, inviting him to play. He reciprocates by opening his whole mouth for me, our tongues now free to explore each other, all mouth and teeth. A man's signature is his kiss and Gage, has an elegant one, refined with a richness of good taste and class, much like the man himself. I let myself be swept away by his experience, each swirl raising my heart rate, each nibble takes my breath away. I'm putty in his arms, willing to do whatever he wants by his seductive kiss alone.

Never parting our lips, he rolls to the left side of the bed, pulling the covers back from my naked body, and kicking them to the floor with his legs. Leaning on his right elbow, right hand still cupping my cheek, he explores my bared flesh with his left. Fingertips caress my skin lightly, raising the flesh to goosebumps, his heated touch leaving a flaming trail in its wake.

While his hands are busy seeking adventure in my curves, I too take an exploration of my own. It seems like a great idea to start with his hair, I usually do, he has amazing hair. It is still wet from a shower and I realize how I got the idea, in my dream, of water dripping on me. His locks go wavy when wet, not quite ringlets but close. I run my fingers back and down, gripping the ends to pull over his shoulders. From there, my hands are free to brush along the ridges of muscles on his back and down his sides. I move up towards his chest, stopping to play with the patch of hair that draws a line of dark, like a treasure map, down towards the winning gold.

As we play this game of mighty adventurers, seeking out forbidden fruits, I can feel his treasure buried between our hips throbbing as it grows in size. I open my legs in an invitation, but it's his hand that finds me first.

"Are you this wet for me, Baby, or the shoes?" He muses.

His question makes me giggle, and I answer with sarcasm, "Definitely the shoes."

He groans and rolls his eyes, but I pay no attention because he is on the move again. This time going over top of me like he had pinned me earlier. I grab his ass in my hands to push him towards my spread open legs.

"Are we feeling greedy this morning? Those must be some shoes; I may have to find you a pair if they turn you on this much," he mocks me.

It's my turn to roll my eyes. "I'm seriously not thinking about shoes right now, Gage," I growl at him in warning.

He inches forward, grazing my opening with his cock head, it has drops of lust from his own arousal escaping the tip. "Then tell me what you are thinking about, September?" He orders back.

I feel the extra heat of a blush, flash over my skin, embarrassed by my thoughts and frustrated at myself for still being too shy to tell him. Instead, I lift my hips enough to just poke him inside of my opening. He moves his own hips back and away, "Not until you tell me, don't make me ask you again, you will not like what I do to punish you." This time he demands from me.

I glance at his face, then stare him down because he's sporting a big ass smirk. "I'm waiting," he sounds impatient.

I bite my lip, trying to decide what to say, and coming up with the easiest plan. "You, I want you," I smile smugly.

Thinking I won when he lowers his hips back towards me, grazing my opening yet again. Using just the head of his penis to tease me, before he pulls himself away, leaving me groaning in frustration. "Try again, and Baby, it's best for you to do better than that. I won't wait all day and one more smart remark from that delicious mouth and I will put it to good use, wrapped around my cock."

I gulp, he means business, if I don't tell him what he wants, I know he will do exactly what he says he will, leaving me wanting for the rest of the day, while he is completely satisfied. I hate not getting what I want, but I also still have self-esteem issues, this is Gage's way of helping me with that. Some might think this a perverse way to overcome that, maybe because I'm a succubus it seems natural, whatever the case I know he does it to help me and it does help. I can now deal with people, with a confidence that someone in my position as Queen should possess. I owe much of that to Gage.

I dig deep, thinking the words out in my head, not wanting them to come out jumbled, taking a deep breath I look into his eyes. "I want you."

I stop to fake him out, then with a smile, I rise up to whisper the rest of the words against his mouth, "I want all of you, your body to move with mine as you possess me from the inside. Ravage me with your lips until I can't take the fire they burn me with. Heat me with a sheen of sweat as your cock teases me, devour me until even the hint of your breath has my blood boiling, then when I can't take anymore, own me as I succumb to your will."

I feel empowered by my own words, taking his lips to mine, and lifting myself up into him. He must have been as taken by the words as I am because he sinks himself deep into my tunnel, and does exactly what I asked of him. There is no more adventure seeking, no sweet romantic lovemaking session, this is about two sexually charged people giving each other what they want, a dirty fuck.

My skin does burn even covered in both of our sweat, my power crackles along my veins and out through my nerve endings. I feel so incredibly alive. My breath comes in panting gasps in between screams of passion as one release turns into another. At some point, he grabs the heavy oak headboard to use for his own leverage. The beauty of being supernatural is we have extra strength, during times like these it comes in handy for our own pleasure, but it doesn't fair well for the furniture.

Sheets, blankets, and pillows have also been destroyed or tossed around the room until we are the only thing left remaining on the bed. Gage, flips me over, under and back to the position we started in, each gives him new ways to pleasure me, either through the position itself or by using what he can to get us both there. A smack on my ass while he rides me from behind, a sheet he uses to tie me to a bed post where he brings me to release while dining on me orally. It is dirty and naughty but oh, so, glorious.

The hot sun is shining brightly in the bedroom window when I finally can't take much more. We are in a crab position, I'm propped against the headboard, he's using it for the leverage when my bloodlust hits. My fangs drop down with a painful pinch and my throat burns for the drink. There is no time for pleasantries, as I am starving.

Pushing my body up the oak wood board, I grab his shoulders and latch onto his neck, breaking his vein open with my teeth and sucking in his nectar. He tastes like the forest smells, smoky and woodsy, but so naturally Gage. As I drink, his thrusts increase, the pounding rhythm mixed with the bloodletting has me bursting yet another release this time with him filling me with his seed.

Gage collapses on me while I close up the holes on his neck, licking him softly and with care. I had not been gentle going in and I feel bad for that, my own fault for not feeding during last night's activities. I know better than to wait, although had I known Gage was going to wake me with sex aerobics, I probably would have thought twice before going to bed hungry. I will never do that again, too risky for my lovers.

I finish licking closed the wound, Gage leans us forward and up to reach above the bed into a small alcove, that is stacked with freshly laundered towels. Pulling out a couple, he opens one up and starts to wipe my face and neck. I pick up the other one to do the same for him. Nothing sings out romantic like the after-sex towel toss.

While I wipe at Gage's back, arms, and chest, I glance at the room, *what a mess*. "Jesus," I marvel then laugh.

Gage twists around to take in the room. "You are a lot of women to satisfy, September, and you do tend to make a mess."

This is usually about the time when I start to think about all the dirty things I have just done, my mind cycles through the visual of events, and that one word always pops into my mind, *whore*. My demon side has taken control and it always brings out the nasty in me. It likes fighting and fucking and when given the opportunity for either, it always wins. I let out a sigh.

Gage twists back around. "That was heavy, what's that all about?"

"Nothing," I reply, climbing off of him.

He tackles me and holds me tight, staring down into my eyes with an intense stare. "No, don't be doing that."

I push at his chest with my hands. "I'm not doing anything Gage, except maybe getting out of this bed. It has to be noon already and I've done nothing today."

"Don't shut me out, you know I hate that and stop trying to get away. You might think keeping this mind connection severed, keeps us from knowing what you're thinking but remember, I'm not Sabre. I didn't hear every thought you had when you first changed, instead, I figured you out on my own, just by the way you move, or the way you take a breath, I know what you're thinking. So, don't you dare shut me down with a nothing. I know that's a female word for a something."

He has me there and how bloody observant of him. I grind my teeth together to stop myself from crying, not because I'm sad but because I'm frustrated. I just had this conversation with Sabre last night. It all made sense then and I'm trying to get it to make sense now, but I can't talk to Gage about it.

He growls at me, he's angry, "Tell me what you're thinking, September." He uses the same tone he had earlier and the same rules will apply. Talk to him or there will be a punishment, except this time I know he won't just withhold sex, he'll also withhold himself, and that I can't handle.

He is an important part of my life, if he pulls away, ignoring me for hours, or worse, days, I will go insane. This is another lesson, to learn to share my words and feelings, if I can't do it with him then how will I be able to do it with my people. *Why must life be a constant learning curve?*

A tear leaks out my eye as I let out a frustrated breath. "I feel like a whore," I blurt, "But I know I'm not, I have a hard time dealing with what I do, we do, all of us. I sometimes feel like it would be easier if our lives weren't so damn complicated. If it could be just me and Sabre, or just me and you, this would be easier to deal with. I know that Chris has issues with the sharing, even Sabre, and do they or you think less of me because of that. Sabre said he didn't but, Jesus, Gage, none of you really had a choice in the matter."

I swipe my hand over my face then remember the towel, picking it up to wipe at my leaking nose. *What is with the mood swings lately, for fuck sakes, I'm being such a girl?*

Gage loosens his hold on me and brushes back the hair from my face. "September, baby, I think the only one that has any issue with the act of the sharing, is you. That's something you need to work out in your head, and we had a choice, you lined it up pretty well for all of us. We knew exactly what we were getting into."

He shakes his head, then continues, "What I think you might be forgetting is, I fell for the smart and spunky girl with the attitude. The one who is strong and brave when faced with this life change. Let us also not forget you kicked my ass yesterday, do you know how much respect I have for you, because of that."

He wiggles himself back against the headboard, getting more comfortable. "If I thought you were a tramp, some sleazy bar tart, there would have been no way I'd be here today." He pauses to let that sink in. "I know this shit isn't easy to deal with, your parents took a more conservative way to raise you, which is kind of odd considering who they were. In truth, the sharing with multiple men did come from Livia, it's bred into you, it's natural."

"I get all that, Gage, I do, and maybe you're right. I'm the one that has to work this out in my head. I don't think this way all the time, really, it's less and less each day, but it's also hard to change twenty some years of what I thought I should have, for what I do have now." I blow out a deep breath and realize I feel better.

Gage, like Sabre, has made some valid points, but I still struggle with my own insecurities at times. Wrestling my demon is not easy, sometimes I can have all the confidence in the world to fight it, other times my demon holds on tight and stokes the fires of doubt.

"Baby, I know this is hard, what you go through. It can't be easy being everything to everyone, all the time. I don't envy you, but I promise you this." He crawls back towards me, getting into my face to meet me eye to eye. "Every day I will let you know how wonderful you are until you finally see what we have known all along, that you are a beautiful being with the most amazing soul."

Another tear rolls down my cheek, this one not out of frustration but because of Gage's words. He doesn't express himself often but when he does, he makes statements. Like now, he is trying to explain that being his whore is entirely different from being just a whore.

"Thank you," I say because I'm finally starting to understand.

"Now, no more tears, and no more beating yourself up, there are enough people out there in the world that will do that for you. I want my happy girl back, the confident and sexy one that I love. That girl is the one I can't keep my hands off of. She is in my inappropriate thoughts ninety percent of the day. Those thoughts keep me wanting her, her presence is what keeps me aroused, and her touch nearly blows my mind. That girl is the women that will become my wife." He inches in to kiss away the tears from my cheek, then he picks up my left hand to kiss the ring Sabre had placed on my finger last night.

A knock at the bedroom door makes me jump, breaking me from the powerful spell of Gage's words. "Yeah," Gage calls out to our intruder but keeps his gaze and smile on me.

The meek voice that answers from outside the door is from my squire, Zahara, "Pardon the interruption, my Lady, but Mr. Blackwood is on the phone for Alpha Blackwood. He insists it is of a dire urgency. What shall I tell him?"

"What bloody crap does Garo need now? I just talked to him this morning and told him to leave us alone today." Gage grumbles as he paces the room looking for something to put on. In a louder voice, he responds to Zahara, "Tell him I will be right there, as soon as I find some pants. Christ this room is a mess." He stops to give me a wink.

"Shall I bring you some clothing, Master Blackwood?" Zahara suggests from behind the door.

"No, no, Zahara, thank you, please go tell Garo I will be right with him."

"Right away, Sir." I hear Zahara's steps as she moves away from the door and down the hall towards the office.

Getting off the bed I go to the closet to grab Gage a pair of track pants. "Here." I chime while tossing them to him. "What do you think Garo wants?" I inquire, leaning back against the door frame to watch Gage wrestle himself into the pants. He's still semi-erect, from being near me, like he just explained, and it's a shame we'll have to delay getting him hard. *Yeah, I'm feeling better already.*

"I don't know, but it must be important. He knew I wanted to take the day to spend with you." He works his fingers around the tie on the pants then looks up at me with a wink, having caught me staring. "Don't worry, it's probably hotel business."

He walks to the door where I am standing. "Go have something to eat, I'm sure you must be hungry. I'll join you after I take care of this." Giving me a quick kiss, and a smile before heading out the door.

As the door closes behind him I think, *holy drama Queen,* I'm not sure what has gotten into me. Already it feels like an odd day and it only just begun, *God help me.*

CHAPTER 7

A hot shower and big lunch on the back deck makes all the difference in my day. The July sun shines high above my head, the birds chirping away in the forest surrounding my house, the trickle of water in the koi pond stream, it all helps put me in a much more jovial mood. The morning's issues are at rest in my mind and my demon is silent for the time being, thankfully. I don't have to fight it as often as in the beginning, back then I dealt with more guilt and insecurity about who I was going to be. Now I still have issues, there just of a different flavor.

I am the Queen of all the Supernatural races because of a curse, that part I get and have accepted because it has been given to me and this is the part of myself I have control of. I run with that responsibility every day and do everything in my power to be the best Queen I need to be. What I have issues with boils down to sex. In the human world, sex is an intimate act, shared by two people in love, mostly to become a family unit, however that works out. In the supernatural world, it means many different things.

Vampires use sex to make bloodletting easier. When taking blood from someone it is erotic by nature and sex is the natural outcome of that. For a vampire, the blood is their survival and sex is merely the act of pleasure it provides. Magennis told me, not many vampires marry or even have relationships lasting longer than a few hundred years, for them the equivalent of a human one night stand. However, he also once said, after all these years, he still has a small piece of humanity left in him. When he first saw me, he knew he wanted to a part of my life because I have helped him get back this part of himself.

For wolves, sex is about owning your partner and showing dominance, but also to procreate. An Alpha shows his power and strength when taking his Beta in ritual, and then his strong genes when producing an heir. Most Alpha's take the strongest Beta from a weaker pack to strengthen their title, this gives them larger areas to hunt in and strengthens the power of the Alpha. This was what Gage had meant to do when he married Cassandra. He would have taken over the Kelowna pack and it would have added to the Blackwood territory. However, he never completed the ritual with her, instead, he did with me, making him the most powerful Alpha of all. The only thing Gage has not done is produce an heir, something he is now thing about, and I am still unsure of. Not that I don't want kids because I do, someday, just not for securing a title position.

The magical beings use sex as a way to share power. They believe in love and finding the right person to share their life with, but to get to that point they share magic through sex to find their perfect match. It's the magical version of an on-line dating site. This is why Jamie has no problem cycling through man after man, she's looking for the right one to enhance her magical power. For her, this is what it is about, for Lilith it is different.

Lilith has an incredible amount of magical power, she is stronger than most warlocks, which have been the strongest of the magical race for some time. She needs to find someone equal to or more powerful than her, but warlocks do not like being shown how weak they are and sometimes this can put someone, like Lilith, in harm's way. It is the reason Lilith rarely dates, but I know somewhere out in our world, there will a perfect someone for her.

The other two races are the elves and of course, demons. Both are a part of the magical race because from them come all the others. There is not much known of the elves because they became extinct, and no one really knows why. A close cousin to them is the demon, and for them, sex is nothing but collecting more power for each individual, the most powerful demon rules all. They feed from the emotions we have from sex, the dirtier the act the better, to them that is sheer power.

Andras and my mom had a connection like that, I thought he loved my mom, but what he loved was how powerful she made him, a God in the Underworld. He had wanted the same from me, but I have issues being with someone who only wants the relationship for gain. It also creeps me out that he had once slept with my mom. That being said, Andras and I still have a relationship, but I only allow him to siphon power from me through our mind connection, and because of that, he teaches me how to control my inner demon. This is a more appealing outcome for me than it is for him.

The problem with getting Andras to teach me is, demons don't have emotion. Telling him my issues with having multiple sex partners is pointless because he doesn't understand. Then again, how can he get it when I clearly have a hard time understanding it myself. All these different ways of thinking about sex makes coming to a workable solution confusing and difficult. Especially when all I have ever wanted is to simply fall in love with one man, get married, have children and live out my life.

Although, this is what I'm essentially doing, just with a few extra men. Maybe I am over thinking this, it's not about the different reasons why I have the sex I do. Yes, I do need to feed from it and use the power it gives me, I gain all the good from partaking in the pleasure and eventually, I will have a child from it. I am doing exactly what I have always wanted but I get to do it with more people.

I'm not dirty, the act sometimes is, but not me, and the intimacy I share with these men is natural. All couples do this, every day, I'm no different. I share my body with four of the most incredible men I have ever known because I want to. I see a future and it includes all of them because they are now my family. They have done whatever they can to make me feel like I'm there one and only, perhaps that's what confused me. I have been thinking it means they have problems with the others when really, it is me with the issue.

The light bulb finally clicks on inside my head, I get it. *Well, shit, that only took me a few months to figure out.* I giggle to myself, sometimes I can be so slow. No one has been judging me, I make the craziness up in my own head.

"September!" Screams an annoyed sounding Jamie, and from the tone, I sense it hasn't been the first time she yelled.

I twist in my chair to see her hanging out of the small kitchen window of the cabin at the far end of my property. "Finally, did you have your iPod on or something, I've been screaming at you for ten minutes?"

Not wanting to continue to shout I stand and begin walking towards the cabin. "Sorry, I was in deep thought, guess I didn't hear you. What's up?"

She doesn't answer, instead, she motions for me to come inside. I go to the door, open it and step into the small but well-designed kitchen. A high, barn style ceiling and skylights give the kitchen a spacious, well-lit appearance. In the center of the circular room is a curved island with a hanging pot rack over it for all of Lilith's potion pots. There are plenty of built-in cupboards for all her ingredients to be storage and inserted into the counter top itself, sits a cooktop stove for her to cook the potions on.

The rest of the kitchen wall is lined with more cabinets in between an antique farmhouse sink, as well as, the fridge and the oak table closer to the door. To the right is an archway that opens into the cozy living room complete with fireplace to heat the small cabin. On the other side of the living room is a door, which goes back into the hallway where the bedrooms and bathrooms are. This cute hideaway is Jamie and Lilith's new home that Gage built for them in the spring.

Jamie starts speaking from her seat at the tiny bistro table, "Lil is brewing and won't let me near her precious pots. I saw you sitting alone and figured we could hang out while she works." She pats the chair next to hers for me to join her.

As I sit down I hear, "If you can't stir with the big girls, then stay away from the cauldron." Lilith sarcastically fumes out from behind the island.

"If you weren't so obsessive compulsive with everything, then maybe I could help you," Jamie huffs back.

"If you could have brought home the dragon blood incense I asked for, instead of jasmine absolute, then maybe I wouldn't be thinking you are incompetent. There's a big difference in a spell for courage than one for depression, you know," Lilith spats back.

My head osculates back and forth from one girl to the other as they bicker. I take back the thoughts I've had about them acting like an old married couple, this is more like two people sharing the same jail cell.

"Do you have a spell that will make you like each other more?" I ask just to shut them up.

"What are you talking about, we like each other just fine?" Jamie gives me a wink then adds, "Right, Lil?"

Lilith gives Jamie a glare then huffs out an obvious breath of frustration, "Would you like something to drink, September? Seeing as my absent-minded roommate failed to ask." The change of subject tells me Lilith is not happy.

"Sure, please, that will be great," I answer politely as to not trigger Lilith any more than she already is.

Jamie pops up from her chair and heads for the fridge, presumably to get me that drink. Once her back is turned I open my connection to Lilith, asking if she is okay. Our eyes meet across the room and her fidget glare tells me she definitely is not. She shakes her head then breaks our connection not wanting to talk with Jamie in the room.

I get an idea. "James, will you do me a favor, can you run to the house and ask Zahara to bring us the chocolate raspberry cheesecake she made this morning. We can sit out in the gazebo and have a slice while we enjoy the beautiful day, give Lilith some room, what do you think?"

The fridge door slams with a loud thud and Jamie speed walks to the door. "You don't have to ask me twice. Meet you at the gazebo." With that she's gone, the backdoor flapping closed behind her.

"That was easy," I muse.

"Everything about her is easy," spits out an angry Lilith.

I stand and approach the island, leaning against the counter but opposite to her, close enough to talk and far enough away to stay out of her working space. Despite what Lilith will admit to, the girl does have some serious obsessive compulsive issues. Unlike Jamie, I know how to keep my mouth shut, fingers to myself, and stay the hell out of her kitchen.

"Okay spill, what's eating you?" I demand and hear how annoyed she is when she lets out a frustrating huff.

"We both know I love Jamie, but she is getting on my last nerve. She is constantly in my space. I know she wants to help, but I take what I do serious, and she wants to play around, experiment. I can't do that, not when most of the stuff I do is for you and the Organization." I nod a lot as she lets it out, best to let her vent away. "She doesn't think anything through, goes off here and there, expecting things to just work out and for her it usually does. Everything comes so bloody easy for her, it's infuriating."

As Lilith is speaking she's stirring the liquid in her big copper pot with such vigor, I fear the mix might spill over. She tosses in some eucalyptus then begins beating it to a pulp with her metal spoon. I reach across the counter to place my hand over hers to stop the action. "Lil, I don't know what you are brewing, but if you keep beating the shit out of it with such hate, you are not going to get what you want as a result. Well, unless this is to kill someone with, then carry on."

She stops her mashing and gives the pot a shocked look, "Oh, dear, you're right. I'm projecting bad vibes, see what she is doing to me."

Putting down the spoon gently she turns off the burner, gloving her hands to pick up the pot and pour out the contents in the sink. "Such a waste," she mutters under her breath.

Once all the mixture gurgles its way out the bottom of the sink, Lilith flips the pot over and begins filling it with hot water and salt. This will cleanse it of any magic left over, so it will not contaminate the next fresh brew.

"While that's soaking why don't you tell me what's really eating you. This seems like more than Jamie trying to help you make spells and getting in your way." I may not be a miracle worker with my own problems but I am great at helping others.

Lilith shuts off the tap and we walk over to the table to sits in one of the wooden chairs. I pull mine closer to hers before settling in. "You see right through me so well, you know that?" Lilith smile but it does reach her eyes.

"Apparently not that well or I'd know what this is all about, so, do tell," I prompt her.

Her smile turns to a smirk, "Jamie's dating Cale."

Those are not the words I thought she would say. "What? Are you kidding me? Cale. Seriously, Cale? As in Ronald MacDonald, that Cale?" I sputter out the words.

The first week into this new world, I was privy to my first OSU meeting, the Organization of the Supernatural Underground. The OSU polices the supernatural and in our North American chapter, run by a member of each race from the area. Magennis, Gage and his brother Garo, Sabre, Flynn and Cale are our heads at the table. Cale being the chief warlock of the magical coven in our area.

During that meeting, I had the privilege of being introduced to Cale, an opinionated man with a chip on his shoulder. I didn't care much for him and had given him the nickname Ronald MacDonald, because of his red hair, but also because he was anything but a happy clown like character. Lilith and I secretly kept the nickname and we realized after, when we talked about him, it was easier to do so with the nickname.

"I know, right, but yup, and double yup," Lilith confirms my shock.

"When did this happen?" I'm curious for the gossip.

"It started sometime last week and they hooked up here last night after Mag dropped us off from the party. Cale showed up ten minutes after we got home and stayed the night." She looks positively ill telling me this news and I understand why. The guy is not pleasant to have around.

"Cale, seriously? Jamie is so outgoing and vibrant, and he is, well, not. I just don't get it." Shaking my head in disbelief.

Lilith picks up an acorn off the table and places it on the window ledge, there is a magical belief that this will discourage lightning from striking the house, and July is storm season. Though I doubt she is thinking of lightning, this is more of a nervous tick, tidying or cleaning when upset, and what Lilith does. I think it helps her keep the world organized in her head when everything else around her is chaotic. I watch her fiddle and wait for her to continue.

It takes a few minutes before she's ready. "I get why they like each other, they have a similar energy, they will work well together magically, and he seems different with Jamie. He was actually laughing last night; I don't think I have ever seen him laugh. If you see them together, look at their auras, you'll notice they sync up, and I really think he likes her."

"Well, it must be serious enough if they are still together after a week, that's not normal Jamie behavior at all." I laugh because Jamie has a short track record with men, some have been lucky enough to get to the next morning, most don't even make it up the front step. "But, how are you with all this?" I wonder.

"Pissed!" Lilith screeches but then sighs, "I just don't get it, of all the people I know, Jamie, finds someone before me. I mean I'm happy for her but it came so easy for her. She doesn't have to worry about men being threatened by her level of energy, she can put herself out there and it works, goody for her. I'm going to be the crazy old cat person, alone with my cats and spells because I can't find anyone, and it's not fair."

I sit quietly and listen to her go on and on, my heart aches for her. It is unfair, she deserves to be happy too, like the rest of us. When she finishes her rant, I lean over to give her a big hug because she needs to know someone cares, and it's the only thing I can do right now to help.

"Oh, September, what am I going to do? I don't want to be alone the rest of my life. I've been watching you for months, collecting your happy family, living the dream. All the while, I'm over here alone, and somewhat jealous, but I took comfort in knowing, at least I had Jamie to share this with. Now she's gone, and here I am, by myself again." She slumps as I let go of her.

"Don't be jealous of the grass on the other side, it may look greener but I assure you, it's no park," I tell her, upset at her statement.

"No, you're right and I'm sorry. I'm just mad. I know it's not puppies and rainbows for you either." She deflates with another breath. "Please, don't be angry at me."

"Lilith, I am not angry at you, but you do have to stop lashing out at me, but mostly at Jamie. As odd of a pairing her and Cale are, if it makes her happy, then we, need to be happy for her, too. I also know that somewhere out there, is the perfect person for you, but you have to be patient, and you have to stay positive." I pause and she nods her head in understanding. "If you stay in this frame of mind, all you'll accomplish is driving yourself crazy, no guy wants a nutter."

We both laugh then I give her a minute to let the words soak in. "One day, when you least expect it, some tall, dark, and awesome will come riding in on his broom and steal your heart. I am sure of it."

I sense her mood shift, "I can go for some tall, dark, and awesome. You're right, Sept, and I know all this, I guess it started to add up in my head and turn ugly. Thanks for letting me vent and not hating me for it. Sometimes I don't know what I'd do without you." Jumping up, she wraps her tiny body around me, hugging me tightly.

"Yeah, well, I need you too, so let's not ever find out what it would be like to live without each other." Hugging her back, I realize this to be true. Lilith is more like a sister to me, or what I envision a sister would be since I have never had one to really know for sure. Without her in my life, I don't know what I'd do either, and I never want to experience that loss.

"Hey, why don't we go get some of that cheesecake before Jamie inhales it all," I suggest as a way to wash away the remainder of the deep conversation and possibly mend some fences.

"September!" I hear Gage's loud voice scream out my name in panic, and my eyebrows rise up in question to Lilith. "September, where are you!"

"What's that all about?" Lilith wonders aloud but through our connection, I can tell she's sensing what I'm feeling about Gage's panic.

Shrugging my shoulders in confusion just as he yells my name again, and I know I better go see what has got him freaked out. I open the back door to exit the cabin. "Gage," I call back across the yard, "I'm over here!"

He's standing at the edge of the forest, on the far-left side of the property, upon hearing my voice, he swivels. On his face, I see the look of panic but it begins to instantly fade as he gets a full visual of me. Like a bullet, he runs across the grass, cutting across the wooden bridge over the pond that meets the steps of the gazebo. He passes through the circular structure and races towards me.

"There you are, thank God." He picks me up to embrace me, holding me to his heaving chest. He sounds like he has been running more than just across the yard. "Christ, September, when I tell you to meet me somewhere, I expect you to be there. I have been going out of my mind looking for you. What the hell were you thinking?"

He lectures me, putting me down, and shaking my shoulders. He's mad, but I know him well enough to know, this anger is a front for some type of underlining panic. "Okay, you found me, stop shaking me." I put a hand to his chest, the other on his arm to stop him from giving me whiplash.

I glance at Lilith, standing behind Gage, for some kind of answer. She shrugs with her own dumbfounded look. She's just as confused as I am by his sudden panic. "September is never far, G, we've been hanging in the cabin, you know, girl chat." Lilith tries to sooth him with an explanation.

Gage, however, ignores Lilith entirely to continue lecturing me. "If I tell you to meet me in a spot, I want you there, understand? How the hell do you expect us to protect you if you're going to run around without thinking? Damnit!" He barks, putting his hands in his hair and pulling it back from his face.

"First off, whatever the hell has got into you, stop, now. You found me, right here, safe, and unharmed. Second, stop yelling at me like I'm some child, we are at home, how fucking far do you think I could have gone? Third, you better start explaining to me, right now, what this is really about because you're being ridiculous." My own anger takes control, and I let him know it by poking him with my finger to make a point, "I'm a damn grown woman, I don't need someone holding my hand every minute of the day. For crying out loud, you'd think someone kidnapped me or something."

My words hit a nerve, his face freezes into a cold hard stare. "Don't even go there."

I take a step back, Gage has never looked at me with such malevolence, it scares me. I swallow before softly asking, "What's going on? Does this have something to do with Garo's call?"

He nods his head once for confirmation, "We're having an emergency meeting at the hotel. Lilith, you need to come too."

"An OSU meeting or hotel business meeting?" Lilith questions, obviously trying to understand both Gage's behavior as well as the information he has given us.

With a deadpan voice, he answers, "Lazarus business, which involves the OSU. Now, let's get our shit together, and get to the hotel."

My eyes meet Lilith's, she has paled in color, which is saying a lot, since Lilith has milky white skin, to begin with. Her eyes have a shine to them like she might be on the verge of tears. She looks as scared as I am starting to feel. We have always known Lazarus would one day come looking for us, or more likely me. It's inevitable for us to finally meet, but we have been living with this simmering on the back-burner for far too long. It seems like we will maybe have our day with the Overlord, and it also explains Gage's enraged behavior, he too is afraid.

As I stare at Lilith for a brief second, I sense her panicked energy building, adding to the fear that coats Gage's emotions, their energy tickles my demon, but I will not allow it to wake. Instead, I let the fear fuel me; it helps me to gain control over my own mind and emotions. Like rolling the demon in a mental fight, using it to my advantage, giving me confidence and strength, instead of the usual hate or lust.

If Lazarus is indeed here, and looking for me, or getting close, I need to make sure I don't panic. I must have a level head to deal with whatever is about to happen. My people rely on me to protect them, and I must keep my loved ones safe. This is my birthright; I am their Queen. I must be ready and I will not be a disappointment.

I am calm and steady. Taking Gage's hand in my own, I pull him with me towards the house. As we walk by Lilith, I give her an order, "Get your spell kit, we'll meet you in the garage in five minutes."

We jog into the house and I am already stripping off my dress as I make my way to the bedroom closet. I grab some jeans and a T-shirt to throw on over my bikini, sunbathing is so scrapped off my to do list today. From the closet floor, I select my favorite pair of thick leather, steel-toed, biker boots. I rush to pull them on, using the two loops at the top. Once snug on my feet, I bounce on my toes to make sure they fit without pinching. If I am going to be running or kicking some ass these will be the perfect shoes for the job.

Exiting the closet from the bedroom, I find Gage waiting for me in the hall. I can smell the fear on him and his brows are pinched from stress. I walk into him to hold him tight. "Whatever happens today, Gage, I need you to stay strong. No more panicking, please. I can only keep myself together knowing you are the rock I can anchor to. Together, we can do anything that comes at us, we did it before, but for us do it again, you need to be part of my strength, okay?"

He thinks on this and his body shifts, when he's worked it out in his own mind his tone is serious, "Yes, my Queen."

He then wraps his arms around my back to pull me as close to him as he can. I know he's onboard when his breath caresses my ear with his words, "My life for you."

CHAPTER 8

We pull into the hotel back parking lot, and up to Gage's reserved spot. He puts the shifter into first before turning the car off. I want to sit in the comfort of the car's seat and prolong the chaos I know is brewing inside, but that's my nerves talking. Pulling at the handle, I open the door to get out and step back to let Lilith out of the backseat.

Gage, already at my side, places his hands to the small of both Lilith and my backs, kicking the door closed with his foot as he moves us forward. He steers us to the door, his eyes constantly scanning the parking lot and rooftop, his body tense, but alert with a cat-like readiness. His full bodyguard mode is damn sexy. We have been so relaxed lately, that I forgot how turned on I get when he is on duty. I mentally slap myself, kicking at the demon to carry on, this is neither the time nor the place to be getting my lust on.

Inside, the hotel lobby is bustling, a busload of tourists are filtering in from a day of adventure. They are milling about, some waiting for the elevator, others chatting with new acquaintances. We cut an aggressive path through the herd, no apologies made in our wake. Gage is on a mission, and he is not stopping until he gets us down to the lower-level where there is safety in numbers.

Behind the front desk, we hit the spiral staircase going down to the entertainment room, from there he turns us left towards the boardroom. At the bottom of the stairs, standing on either side of the hall are Taylor and Cody, two large werewolf sentinels. They both work security in the club and as my guards for special events when Gage or Sabre need backup. Today, their job is to guard the hall, and not allow anyone to get close to me or the leaders of the OSU.

We pass Sabre's office, continuing down the empty hall to the glass walls that show the boardroom, inside the OSU members are already awaiting our arrival. Flynn is sitting deep in thought at the back corner of the giant oval table, with Cale across from him to the left. Lilith swings herself into the seat next to him, with Garo greeting her from her other side. Magennis gives me a tight smile from his spot on the right of Flynn. Gage slides into the chair beside Sabre, who nods at us while I take up my position at the head of the table to start the meeting, "No need for pleasantries, let's start the meeting. Details, who's got what?" I demand.

Garo is the first to speak, the older version of Gage but with a short crewcut striped with white streaks. "Yes, my Queen. This afternoon I received a call from an old friend in South America, he told me five people of magical race have disappeared, three warlocks, a fae, and one witch. It happened about two weeks ago. He didn't think to tell us at first, as they are all friends, and it was presumed they had been together on a trip. The day before yesterday they found four of them, all dead, drained of any magical energy. One warlock is still missing."

Flynn responds next. He is a fae himself, tall, lean, and sculpted with snow-white hair, worn in a braid down his back, and an equally white goatee to set off his soft gray eyes. Usually, the quiet one in our bunch, when he does speak his words are well thought out and with logic. "My Lady, I have reached out through our troupe in the Underground, and have received similar stories. There have been disappearances and killings of other magical beings, not in one spot but spread throughout South America and the United States, this is why we are now joining the incidents."

"Has it only been the magical beings going missing?" I ask the group.

Garo glances at Gage across the table, a silent decision passes between them before Gage finally answers, "No, my Queen, an Alpha has gone missing as well."

I sense Gage isn't telling me the full story, so I prompt him, "Who and from where?"

He tightens his lips, I can tell he is reluctant to tell me but knows he must. I grow impatient waiting, staring him down across the table to hurry him along, he finally finds the right words to answer. "Leland Kline from Kelowna."

"Your ex-wife's father?" I ask to clarify, even though I know the truth.

"Yes," he says, and I see his throat move in an uncomfortable swallow.

"Interesting, and is the Kelowna disappearance the only one in Canada?" I think I smell a rat.

This time Garo answers, "Yes, so far we have not had any other."

My wheels are now turning; something is off. Why would there be disappearances, kidnappings, and killings throughout South America and the States but only one here; and more specifically, one who knows our pack intimately?

"Are we sure Leland Kline has been taken like the others?"

Again, I am met by Gage's defiant stare, which answers my question. "I take it from that look, Leland is about to become a big problem. Okay, let's put that on the burner to simmer while we figure out if any others are missing, or have been killed?"

Magennis takes over the meeting filling me in, probably out of pity for Gage, who is suddenly as quiet as a church mouse at the table. I'll deal with him later, for now, I need to know more about this other issue. "All this activity, makes you suspect Lazarus then. Why, may I ask?"

Magennis begins to enlighten me, "From the beginning, this is what we have been told Lazarus has always done. He began in Europe at the time of the Royals, collecting powerful supernatural to build his army. Once he had enough of them, he was somehow able to channel the collective power of that army to deceive then curse Livia and David. That's how they were brought to the human world. This is Lazarus's signature move. We know he has small pockets of armies all over the Eastern Hemisphere, but this is the first time he's ever crossed the ocean to the Americas."

"He knows I'm here and he's looking for me then." I don't ask anyone but say it as an understood statement. "How can we be sure it's Lazarus and not Kline? I think he's up to something, that's prominent."

Finally, Gage joins our conversation, "Kline's definitely up to something, but he wasn't around all those centuries ago, not many are. He wouldn't know how Lazarus pulled off what he did. We wouldn't know either if it weren't for Magennis being here to give us the details."

I am starting to realize just how old Magennis is to have been alive all those years ago. I also realize how much we rely on him. He is a huge asset for us in this war, "Then how do we know for sure?" I ask Magennis. I have a whole new respect for the wisdom I so often glimpse in his deep-blue eyes.

"He has a unique signature or aura, not like any of the other races, but similar to the energy you possess. There have been many rumors and speculation about his race, some first thought he was vampire until he channeled the powers of his army. I have heard many tales over the centuries, that he was the last of the elves, that he was one of Livia's men, some even accused him of being Andras for a time, but they were all wrong. Not many remain that even know what he looks like, never mind knowing his special energy signature. So, he can move amongst us, without ever being detected," Magennis explains.

"How will we be able to know it's him, if not many are still around?" I didn't expect my question to bring the answer he gives me.

"My Lady, the answer is clear, I am the only one that can know for sure. Therefore, I must be the one to go alone and find him." He gives me a sad and uncertain smile.

The internal wiring that makes up my emotional circuit board, connecting my brain and heart, decides to short-circuit right at this moment. I freeze, completely unmoving, like a stone statue in appearance on the outside, while inside a storm of emotions collides in a battle of epic proportions. A silent struggle for what should be the right decision, for my kingdom is being challenged by my own selfish need.

A practical monarch should understand Magennis is right, he is the only one that can identify our enemy. Therefore, he must leave to complete the task in finding and perhaps killing that enemy. Though I don't like it, it does make sense why he wishes to go alone, a hunting party will slow him down and cause suspicion. He deserves respect, for after thousands of years, Magennis, has developed serious skills that have kept him alive this long. I have to trust he knows more than anyone how to handle this situation, and make it back just fine.

To keep my people and my home safe from this evil man, Lazarus, I know it will be best to let Magennis go. Not an easy thing to come to terms with when playing with the selfish wildcard of the heart. The heart wants what the heart wants, and mine wants Magennis to stay with me; he is mine, and everyone else be damned. Emotion after emotion crash like waves from a violent storm over me, drenching me with fear and despair as thoughts come to mind. What if Magennis is caught. He can be used against us or worse killed. My mind spirals deeper as I think of a world without him, it would destroy me.

These are the sentiments of a human's mind. Sentiments, that have me frozen with a fear of my past, and what the future might hold. I can no longer afford or allow myself to have such thoughts. I may sometimes still wish to remain in that long-ago land, ignorant of this world, and exempt of my role in it, but such is no longer the case. This is where Lilith should be telling me to pull up my big-girl panties, or Jamie should be saying that life is like sex, you either lay back and get screwed or jump on top and ride it out.

The thought of my friends mentally shakes me from my tangent, these people have become my new family and they help me see the power of love. Without them to support and love me, I would never have become the person I am today. I trust in them and now, I need to use that to help me get through. I focus back on the boardroom, the faces around the table are staring at me with concern, waiting on my breakdown no doubt.

I blink a couple of times and take a long slow breath. "When will you leave?" I finally resign myself to the idea of Magennis having to go.

He hesitates. I can see him studying me, making sure I am at complete peace with this before he answers, "The Blackwood's private plane is fueled, and ready to go when you say the word."

"Where will you start the search?" I ask before making the final decision.

My questions and ease in which I ask them, seem to show the members at the table, my acceptance of this plan. I realize that there has been a collective change in postures and held breaths around the room. It makes me wonder how I must have looked going through my mental rundown. It has only been mere moments, but I sense that everyone is on edge. I suspect that Gage hasn't been the only one watching me over the past few months to get to know me better.

"I think I should start along the Gulf Coast and make my way across the South," Magennis answers as Garo gets up to turn on a big monitor attached to the wall across from me.

An image on the monitor appears; it is a map with lines at different locations. The screen seems to be operated from Sabre's phone. "I have tracked his course from the information we have received from our people. The yellow line is the approximate trail Lazarus has traveled over the past month." Sabre draws a line on his phone's screen, mirroring the one on the bigger monitor.

"A month, I thought Garo said this started two weeks ago?" I lock eyes with Garo to read his response.

Garo nods his head, "I did say that my friend, who called, had noticed the first disappearance was two weeks ago, but Flynn has talked to many others with similar strange encounters, that date as far back as last month."

"These dense jungle locations in South and Central America, are not easy to communicate through, as they have no phones. It is only in passing on boats, along rivers that some ever see each other, which makes receiving information difficult but not impossible," Flynn explains. "The timeline started approximately a month ago, on the southern tip of Chile. We believe Lazarus made his way through all the Eastern countries first, trying to locate you, and is now working his way up through all the Western countries."

"He is persistent, I'll give him that, but I'm confused. I thought after the run-in we had with the Vampire Council, he would have known our exact location by now." I make reference to the council members we fought last year, who wanted to kidnap me and take me to Lazarus to use as a bargaining chip.

Magennis shifts his eyes from the map to me. "Not all the members of the council were eager for that plan. Tony had convinced only a select few to pursue your demise, but he's six feet under, and that is no longer an issue. The remaining members are not your enemy; they only wish for you to have the throne that was once your mother's."

"I don't think they are all enemies, Magennis. I just thought someone would have said something to Lazarus by now, word does travel fast with the supernatural," I clarify.

Magennis nods, understanding I'm not questioning the loyalty of the vampire race, but there are a few who are willing to use the information of my whereabouts for their own gain with Lazarus. "The races have been hiding from Lazarus for far too long, my Queen, and they finally have something, or rather someone, to believe in again. The subs he does find, are not privy to your whereabouts. What Lazarus is trying to do is build himself a strong enough army so when he does find you, he will have the power to finally kill you. If he succeeds, then I believe he will finally try to take over the human race, and without you around he will be unstoppable."

"That won't happen," Lilith blurts out. It's unusual for her to even speak during our meetings unless asked a direct question. To suddenly do it with such confidence, I am interested to hear what she has to say. "Andras and I talk sometimes. Apart from Magennis, he is the only one that was around in your mom's time, he also knows Lazarus. Andras feels your powers alone supersede Lazarus, not to mention all of us helping, you'll have no problem bringing him down. You got this."

"Well, that may be your opinion on things, Ms. Dale, but Lazarus did manage to destroy our first Queen. We can't be so arrogant as to think he won't have something up his sleeve to take down this one," Cale lashes out at Lilith with a condescending tone. I seriously don't know what Jamie sees in him.

I ignore Cale and move on, "We can't let Lazarus get what he wants. Magennis, you have to find him. Once it gets dark start your search, I want daily updates. Find him, but be careful, please."

Magennis smiles, his eyes sparkle with an eagerness for his task. "As you wish, my Queen."

After giving my decision, I feel like I'm back in game mode, and now we need a plan. "Garo, I want you to start preparing our emergency plan for everyone in the Underground. We no longer can think *if*, but *when* Lazarus gets here."

Garo bows his head before answering, "I've already started to implementing the plan this morning, my Queen, by end of day we shall be ready."

"I want us more than ready. That means, Lilith, you will be in charge with Cale's help, to get a reinforced magical wall around the hotel, cabin, and my house. I also want to be able to know the minute a new magical energy enters our city." Cale looks angry as I pick Lilith to head up this important part of our plan. Maybe next time he'll try to be nicer towards her, but for now, he can suck it.

I continue my orders with those at the end of the table, "Flynn, please work with Jamie to update our files on every sub currently in the city. I want check-in stations set up for those not living in the Underground, then do the same for our other territories. Everyone needs to be extra cautious when out in the human world. Anyone new to the area or any odd behavior by a sub should be reported immediately. If anyone suddenly goes missing, we need to be notified right away. All of our people are important, and we must protect them. With the right rules in place, I believe we will have a fighting chance against Lazarus. Open lines of communication between the races are necessary, we will work together. If anyone thinks they are above my orders or has any complaints, they may take it up with Sabre."

"I am honored to be given this responsibility, my Queen." Flynn immediately pulls out his phone and begins punching in a text, probably to get Jamie to the hotel to start working on the plan.

Around the table, everyone seems eager to get moving. "Okay, that's our starting point, everyone has orders. I want this city secure; any questions, Sabre has the lead."

The room explodes with noise, chairs scrape the floor, feet shuffle across hardwood, conversations begin on phones and in person. A mission is in motion, but not everyone moves with vigor. Gage remains alone in his chair, waiting for direction. Once the last person has left the room he speaks.

"You're mad," he starts with the obvious.

"I am," I answer.

"Do you want me to locate Leland and deal with him?"

"No, I'll have Sabre deal with him. You are too close to the situation, and I can't trust that you'll do what I need −" I begin but he interrupts me.

He gets out of his chair, and walks to the end of the table. "That's bullshit and you know it. September, everything I do is to make sure you're safe. I've never lied to you and I will never do anything to bring you harm."

I rise from my own chair, glaring at him, "No, but you're not forthcoming with information either. How do you expect me to make the right decisions for us when you hide the important stuff from me? That's not protecting me, Gage. You hurt me when you do that; you make me look like an incompetent fool. You are constantly telling me how to be more confident and in control, and yet, your actions show you have no faith in me to do what's right."

Our anger rolls back and forth between us, but I keep myself on the level to get this dealt with fast. I am furious with Gage, but not enough to invite another red moment, and that alone is progress. Gage doesn't seem to be doing as well, his face is flush from his anger, his body tense and in a defensive stance. I can tell he feels he has done nothing wrong, as Alpha it is his job to protect what is his, but he also has to let me do my job. For all his teachings, Gage can sometimes be a huge hypocrite; he believes in me and thinks I can do anything, but at the same time I am still just a girl, *his girl*. He can be such a male chauvinist.

That's when an idea strikes me, "Fine, we obviously disagree." I wave my hand to end the fight. "I have to go say goodbye to Magennis then pack for Toronto, you can go help Garo, make sure the wolves are keeping guard of the city." I turn to walk towards the door.

He catches my arm to turn me around. "You are not going to Toronto, not now," his voice is deadpan serious.

I get in his face to make a point, but calmly I say, "Yes, I am. Chris asked me to come, and I want to go. You cannot tell me what to do, Gage. Maybe some time apart will be just what we need."

"You're punishing me!" He explodes with rage, "No fucking way."

A wicked smile spreads across my face as I free myself from his clutches to go towards the door again, stopping at the threshold to add, "What's good for the goose and all." I leave him with mouth gaping open.

This is a small, but proud moment for me; understanding that the only way to get Gage to see my side is by becoming him. The student is now the teacher, and I just schooled his ass. He is right, I can be confident and it feels amazing.

CHAPTER 9

I enter Sabre's empty office, heading for the back wall, and the door leading to his apartment. Walking into the open floor plan, I find Sabre at the bar-top island, papers spread out in neat piles beside him, and laptop open in front of him. At the sound of the door opening, he stops typing to look up and smiles when he sees me walking towards him. Turning in his chair, he opens his arms to offer me a hug. I promptly take full advantage of the affection and jump into his big, welcoming arms.

"You look happy," his words are muffled as he speaks against my neck.

"I am happy, odd timing, I know, what with everything that's going on." I shrug then laugh.

"No, I like to see you smile." He breaks our hug to pull me into his lap. "Care to share? I could use some of that positive vibe, at the moment."

"Yes, I can imagine, you must be stressed and I'm about to add to it." I place my hand on his cheek and meet his lips for a warm kiss, sweet and simple. "I'm tired of Gage keeping me in the dark. So, I have sent him to work with Garo, which means, I would like you to hunt down Leland Kline and find out what he's up to."

"Ah, you're using reverse phycology so to speak, not only are you beautiful but incredibly smart too." Sabre grins and rubs my nose with his own. "Good thing I anticipated you needing something like this. I already sent Taylor to start tracking Leland, and I have calls into some of the Kelowna pack members, maybe they can figure out what Leland might be planning."

"Thank you, you will let me know what you find out?" I ask, playing with the buttons on his plaid dress shirt.

"Immediately."

Sighing, I ponder my thoughts out loud, "I wish Gage could be as supportive and cooperative."

Sabre leans back to see my whole face. "Darling, Gage is just as supportive and somewhat cooperative, but he also takes being your Alpha seriously, and he's still trying to figure it out. You have to remember before you came along Gage didn't care one bit about any of this. Now he has a reason to care, and his nature is to control the hell out of it. Go easy on him."

"Oh, I know all that, he and I are fire and oil, that can be bad when we work with each other, we ignite into flames. We work best when we feed from one another when only one of us is in control. When dealing with this business, he needs to let me be dominant, so when it comes to our personal life, I am more than willing to submit to him. He understands the separation but has a hard time giving me control when I need it most, and I must teach him. This is why I'm using the same punishment he uses on me. It's the only way he'll understand because that's how Gage is wired."

Sabre ponders over this before answering, "You amaze me, every day. You have grown leaps and bounds, and I'm so proud of you."

"Thanks, but don't be amazed yet, wait to see if it works first. Although, I am leaving for Toronto tomorrow, maybe a couple days without me might help do the trick." I smile at Sabre, feeling proud until I notice his face.

His eyes are almost gray and his skin is pale, his arms which have been holding me loosely in his lap, are now tense. "You're still going to Toronto, alone?"

"Yes, but Sabre, I'll be fine. Defeat the Darkness is already in Toronto. Chris is sending their plane out tonight, for me to leave first thing in the morning. I will ask Garo to have some of our people there to provide security for me, along with the security the band has. There is no way Lazarus will go from somewhere around Texas to Toronto overnight. I would think at the rate he's moving, we won't see him in Canada before next month, we have some time. Besides, Magennis will find him before then and we will deal with it, a couple of nights won't hurt."

Again, Sabre takes a minute to think this through before replying, "I will not try to change your mind about going. If I could, I'd go with you, but not with our current situation. I will feel more comfortable if you could hold off on torturing Gage, for the time being, and consider taking him with you."

I sit up and away from Sabre, more on his knee than in his lap. I think back on how I had reacted in the boardroom when Magennis said he was leaving, and how I felt about it. Sabre is having a similar reaction with letting me go. "I wish you could come too. It would be fun to spend time with you, to experience something new with you. We haven't spent much time together lately, I miss that."

"I miss that too, my love. How about I make you a promise, if you take Gage to Toronto this time, I will take you to a city of your choice, just you and me." He starts to relax, and a smile begins to grow again on his lips.

I have never been able to resist Sabre, he is my first real love, and I will do almost anything to make him happy. I grin back, "Any city in the world?"

His laugh fills the room. "Any place you want to go, but you really need to get a passport first."

"A small detail." I wave my hand in the air as if to brush that off my list. "As long as you take me to your home, where you came from as a human, only then do we have a deal."

"To be fair, I would think my parents' home is no longer, you may have to settle for some rocks on the side of a hill, overlooking the North Sea," he teases, but he's also probably right.

"Good to know, all right then, it's a deal. Once this is all over, you and I are going on a trip, to see some rocks by the sea. Actually, that sounds romantic to me. Oh, my, I don't get out much when rocks turn me on." A giggle escapes my lips and becomes infectious. It is either from the seriousness of the day or the comfortable ease that I've always had with Sabre, but wherever the laugh comes from it has us both wiping tears from our eyes.

The door to the apartment opens, bringing Magennis into the room. "What are you two laughing your cacks off about, then?"

Sabre and I glance at Magennis, then back at each other. We know what Magennis has meant, but with his accent and our moods it sets us off on another giggle fit. "Jaysus, are ye piss drunk? Been tipping a few to send me off with?"

"Oh, my sides." I grab my rib cage as I try my best to calm myself before another wave hits. I'm no longer holding on to Sabre and barely sitting on the edge of his knee, the next laugh makes me lose my balance and I tip backward off the chair, landing on my back.

"Ohhew!"

Sabre jumps off the chair and bends down towards me, "Are you okay, did you hit your head?" He's no longer laughing, instead, worry lines appear on his face as he touches my head tenderly with his fingers.

Magennis is also beside me, fussing about, checking my arms and legs for bruises. You would think I have just been in a serious fight by the way these two are acting. "I'm fine, just knocked the wind out of myself."

"Sabre, bring her to the couch to lay her down," Magennis instructs Sabre, who picks me up and does as he is told.

"Guys, I'm fine, really." Once Sabre places me on the couch, I immediately sit up to prove my point. "See, all better, you can stop mothering me now."

"If you're sure?" Sabre asks, cocking his brow, seeming unsure.

"I am," I say with conviction.

"What got into you two loons there?" Magennis questions our giggle fit as he sits to my left, absently rubbing my back with his hand.

Sabre moves next to me on my right, shrugging his shoulders, "Nothing really, we were talking about traveling and just started laughing. I think the excitement over the last few days added up. Hey, why don't we have a drink, I'd say we need to send you off with one." He gets up to go to the kitchen for a couple of beers for the two guys and a coke for me.

This gives me the chance I've being waiting for to embrace Magennis, "Ah, my Minx, ta tu mo chroi."

"What does that one mean?" I'm curious of this new string of words.

He whispers into my ear, "You are my heart."

"I'll miss you," I say, but the words seem more foreign than what Magennis just said. "I've never been away from someone before, not like this."

He pulls me to him tighter, I can smell his scent mixed with fresh laundry, like home. "I shall miss you too, Lazarus could never hug me this well," he jokes but I know Magennis, he masks his emotions with humor like Gage does with anger.

I move back to look into Magennis's eyes. "Promise me, no foolish stuff, come back to me in one piece and come back soon."

His eyes are like a window; in them, I can see decades. His world was so different from mine, but now so similar that I have to wonder what others will see one day, hundreds of years from now, in my eyes. "My dear, how can you think so poorly of me, have ye no faith?"

"On the contrary, I have tons of faith in you. Earlier, I realized how far you have come and what you have accomplished. You are an amazing man and I respect you. I trust you with my life and that I don't give lightly, I know you will do what you need to, to protect our home, our people and most of all me. I only ask that you be careful, I love you and want you to come home." These are the words I have been needing to tell him since the boardroom.

His whole face lights up as he grins at me, the goofy smile that is so carefree and pure Magennis. "I will be cautious in my approach to this task because I now have a home to come back to. You are my heart, you give me life, and a reason to be mindful of my duty to protect you; and that is something I don't give lightly. In all my years, there has never been one to which I cared so deeply as I do for you, however, I will not promise you something I cannot keep."

He takes my hands to hold them in his, linking our fingers like the infinite knot of the jeweled comb he had given me. His smile fades into something more serious before he speaks again, "If I am faced with a choice of my own life to protect yours, then you must know that I will always and forever choose you. I have never said these words to another, but I say them now because I mean them, I will miss you because I too love you."

His eyes now glisten with a happiness I have never seen before; I realize I'm his first real love. To have gone through such an incredibly long life and never truly felt love, that is sad, but for me to be able to share it with him now, that is amazing. We sit and grin at each other like love-struck teenagers until Sabre brings our drinks.

"Oh no, are you two going to start with the uncontrollable laughter now?" Sabre looks us over before placing the drinks on the small glass table top.

I shake my head as my lips quiver into a smile. "No, but I think we might start some uncontrollable kissing."

Magennis adds with a wink at Sabre, "Followed by some farewell lovemaking, care to join in?"

Sabre falls into the couch, leaning against my back to speak in my ear, "Who can pass on something so irresistible."

I'm about to add some witty reply when Magennis leans forward to kiss me so hard, I forget my own name. It is the type of kiss that steals your breath, leaving you gasping for air and quivering with want. A rushing heat fills my body as my blood pumps wildly through my veins to the beat of my racing heart.

My hands have a mind of their own, making quick work of undoing the buttons on Magennis's white dress shirt. I sweep it off his arms and away, tossing it somewhere on the floor. The act allows his smooth chest to be exposed, a perfect place to start my exploration. Dropping my mouth from his lips, I work my way across his jawline and down his neck, stopping for a minute to suckle at his earlobe.

Sabre and Magennis become a team, helping each other remove the rest of our articles of clothing. Sabre removes shoes, socks and unbuttons pants, while Magennis pulls off shirts. They are extremely comfortable in each other's space, touching and caressing one another for a common goal, to provide me with pleasure. The knowledge of them pleasing each other to help please me turns me on. *How have I not noticed this before now.*

I stop sucking Magennis's collarbone to watch him palm Sabre's cock, making Sabre hard and ready to take me. "Ohh," I moan as an incredible amount of moisture pools deep in my center.

I lean back against the couch to take in the show, I am so aroused and fascinated by this new experience. "Do you like that?" Asks Magennis.

I nod my head in approval. "Are you wet, watching me stroke your man?" He asks, this time cupping Sabre's balls before stroking his shaft.

Again, I can only nod. I'm speechless. Sabre runs his hand along my inner thigh, up towards my opening. I spread my legs for him to dip his fingers into the juice. "Jesus, you're so eager for us you are dripping," he exclaims as his cock jerks in Magennis's hand.

I watch in awe, then Magennis squeezes a bead of pre-cum out of the end of Sabre's cock. I am like a moth to a flame, moving forward to lick the bead from the swollen head. As I move, so too does Magennis, his lips meeting mine at the fountain at the end of Sabre's penis. We kiss around the head. I tongue the juice and swirl it into Magennis's waiting mouth, which gives it a combined flavor of both men.

I can't stop moaning my delight over this new experimentation. I know neither man fancies the other in a homosexual romantic way, but they are willing to play to turn me on. My demon is overjoyed by this change in events, my powers surge to life from the heavy scent of lust in the air. I want to see more of the show and see how far will they go for me. I want to feel it with them through our mind connection and I open it up to them, but mostly I want to play. There are so many erotic images floating around my head, I want to try them all out if they are willing. *Oh, but the possibilities are endless.*

"I wish we had the time for all that, but I must catch a plane soon, my dear," Magennis reminds me of our limits.

"All the more reason for you to hurry back home," I say between kissing Magennis's lips and sucking Sabre's cock.

Magennis chuckles and pulls away but he doesn't go far, moving just enough to squeeze his lean body between me and the couch. He rubs at my back, moving to make his way around to my front to caress each breast, massaging the plump folds of skin after tight pulls. With his fingers, he pinches at my nipples to peak them to points, causing some pain before soothing them with circled passes of his palm. Each pained tweak of a nipple has moans spilling out of my full mouth and flutters of heat going right to my core.

Sabre doesn't miss a beat, taking control of my mouth by wrapping my hair around his left hand and cupping my cheek and chin with his right. He guides my mouth up and down his shaft with pumping movements from his hips, allowing me to cup and massage his swollen sacs. His taste grows more bitter with each stroking suck and I know he is close to a release, but he holds off with a long push to the back of my throat. This has me both gagging and gasping for air as he inches out and then away.

I lick my lips, savoring his flavor. Some people don't enjoy the taste of a man, but I find it to be quite stimulating.

Everything about sex: the sound, taste, scent, feel, and of course, the sight, are what make the experience enjoyable. When it is all combined, that's what makes it magical.

Sabre kneels before me, spreading my legs apart, exposing me to him. His left hand still in my hair to hold me in place, his right moves down my belly, over my pubic area, and to my slit. With two fingertips, he plays with my clit, rubbing small circles over it to harden it to a nub. A girl's version of a boner. With his other two fingers, he teases my opening with similar circle motions. Between Sabre's actions on my cunt and Magennis fondling my breasts, the tingles of orgasm start to build, but the men keep me from the release by changing a direction of movement or touch in a different place. It seems like cruel punishment, but I find edging the orgasm to be just as pleasurable and my powers surge from the continuous enjoyment it provides.

Magennis suddenly shifts behind me, lifting me up and back into his lap to bring his legs under me, letting his cock slowly slip into my wetness. I start to cry out words of joy that Sabre comes forward to eat from my lips. His soft warm tongue enters my mouth just as Magennis's hardness pushes deeper into my pussy. I moan against Sabre's lips, begging with sound for him to devour my mouth while I buck my hips to get Magennis to push harder. Neither one happens, and it's like torture to be so wanting but also so incredible.

With a steady slowness Magennis moves his hips, he does not use much speed or pressure as he continues fondling my breasts, and it drives me insane. My breasts ache from being groped to the extreme, and my nipples feel like they have been stung by a swarm of bees. As much as this hurts, it also provides me with shock waves of pleasure, shooting straight into the sweet spot. If I can just get a little more simulation below, I would gush joyfully all over Magennis's penis.

I scream instructions at my lovers through our mind connection, it doesn't help as they enjoy what I call torture, it turns them on more to see me get to the edge and hold me there before getting me off. This time, as luck would have it, Sabre takes pity on me. He holds my hips to help Magennis push into me with ease, then he bends forward to lick at the folds of my pussy. The first stroke of his hot tongue on my clit has my river flowing, it pools rapidly against my dam and seeps out. The more strokes he makes along my slit the closer I get.

Looking down between my legs, I watch as Sabre's tongue slides down my slit, along Magennis shaft and back up. The sound, taste, smell, touch, all intoxicating but the sight of Sabre pleasing us both with his mouth is what does it for me. I scream when the orgasm hits, Sabre laps at my cream and Magennis rides me into the next wave. There is no time to catch my breath when the second flood hits, my body goes ridged before collapsing forward.

Sabre reaches up to catch me. "We're not done yet, my love."

He lifts me up and turns me around to face Magennis, who pulls me down on top of him, my legs slide in on each side of his body. With a grip on my hips, Magennis pushes up and into me again, hitting the back of my quivering vagina. It hurts at first, a bursting spark of pain but as he lifts me up, I feel the slickness around our combined skin.

More moans slip from my throat and cascade down my tongue to escape my lips. Sabre, still behind me, is suckling lustfully around my puckered asshole, lubricating me well enough for him to enter with the spit from his lips.

"Someone needs a cock in her mouth to stifle those moans." Gage appears from somewhere behind me, with being so busy I didn't hear him come in the apartment.

His fingers trail a path down my left side, from armpit to hip bone, causing a burn of extra heat in the wake of his contact. I shiver from his light touch, thinking about taking him in my mouth and having him join us.

Sabre slaps my ass cheek, crashing the mental picture in my head, into tiny pieces. "Ohh!" I moan with surprise.

He flashes me a picture of Gage bent over my knee and me slapping his beautiful hard ass, making me remember the punishment I am supposed to be giving him. When Gage reaches to touch my right side, I swing my head over to shoot him a glare, "No touching, Gage."

He freezes in mid-movement, his eyebrows spike up, his eyes fill with questions and his mouth simply falls open. With a malicious smirk, I turn my attention back to Magennis, leaning down to kiss his lips, getting into the rhythm of his pumping action. Sabre has his thumb making circled passes over my asshole, relaxing the muscles to allow for his girth. Gage slips his hand around my bicep, going toward my right breast. My head whips up, and I snarl at him this time.

"Go, over there," I motion with a jerk of my head to one of the white leather spaceship looking chairs beside the couch. "Remove your clothes, sit in the chair, and watch. If you're a good boy, I will let you touch yourself."

"What the fuck is this?" He barks out, his nostrils flaring as he speaks, he is mad, and I'm good with that.

"Don't you dare question me, now sit in the chair or leave, your choice." My voice has a smoky heat to it, gravelly from all the screaming, but it makes me sound more authoritative.

If looks could kill, Gage's would have me dead. His words now dripping in venom as he asks, "Is that an order, my Queen?"

I turn my head back to Magennis, who has slowed his hip movements for me to concentrate. I wink and give him a big smile. "It sure is."

Magennis almost snorts but covers it with a cough that has his penis jumping inside of me, the sudden pressure of the motion has me groaning again. The sound prompts Sabre to resume his preparations for mounting me from behind and gives Magennis the go ahead to push himself deeper into my tunnel.

I peek over to the chair, Gage has done what he was told, sitting, stripped of his clothes, and not touching himself. His expression suggests he is still quite angry, his body is ridged like he is mad enough to punch something, but it is his penis, hard, standing at attention and ready that tells me he is more lustful than defiant. Apparently, he is less upset with this punishment than he is willing to admit.

"Are you enjoying the show, Mr. Blackwood?" My words come out in a gasp as Sabre rims his girth against my honey hole.

"Mumm, very much so,." he smirks back.

It takes a minute for me to speak again as I work through the painful pressure Sabre is giving to me. The first stroke in my ass always hurts for a few seconds until I relax and allow his mighty entrance. "Show me how much you like what you see," I hiss out.

Gage stands and walks behind the couch to be directly in front of me. With his left hand, he cups his balls, giving them a squeeze before stroking his shaft with his right. "Are you enjoying performing for me, Ms. Rae?" He demands back.

Watching him stroke his length sets me ablaze. "God, yes!" I scream.

The pressure has turned to heat, and that heat is stirring a big storm in my belly. I can feel Magennis thrusting himself against Sabre, a thin wall of delicate but sensitive tissue, separating the two men's cocks. The friction is causing a buildup, my powers flicker out a static charge of energy around us, I am close to another release and if the urgency of which Sabre and Magennis are moving is any indication, I know, they too are close.

Gage grabs a handful of my hair to pull my head far enough back, for him to come over the couch and bury his length in my mouth. This gives Magennis access to my neck, which he sits forward to bite down on my vein to feed while continuing to pump vigorously into me with Sabre still moving in me from behind. Within moments we are one combined power, I feel the crackle of the energy along every nerve in my body. I can't hold on any longer, the orgasm bursts from me triggering Magennis and Sabre to push their seed deep inside of me. My scream vibrates against Gage's erection, he groans, grabbing his shaft and pumping the last of his orgasm across my lips.

Sabre is the first to pull away, instantly the circle of intense power around us breaks. I crash face first into the back of the couch from the surge. "Oaf!"

Magennis tries to catch me in a clumsy hold as my teeth rake across Gage's penis. "Jesus," he swears, jumping away. "What the hell?"

"Sorry," I mumble into the couch cushion.

"Did you feel that?" Magennis asks someone, maybe even me.

"Did I feel her almost bite my dick off, yeah, I did!" Gage grumbles.

Propping my jelly like body up, Magennis explains his previous question, "No, did you feel the shimmer of magic, it pulsed then snapped just before September fell."

Sabre comes back from the bedroom with my robe, handing it to me before tossing towels at Magennis and Gage, "Yay, I felt it, just before I moved, then nothing."

I sit, propped up on the arm of the couch listening to the conversation. I feel cloaked in the magic Magennis is talking about, a warmth that is making my skin prickle, it is like nothing I have ever felt before. I touch my arm with my fingers, and it burns then immediately cools. I examine my arm then my fingers, nothing is on my skin to cause the burning. I try again, this time holding my index finger to the back of my other hand, it burns like I have acid on my skin, and the sensation grows the longer I hold my finger to the skin. I hiss as the pain becomes unbearable.

"Are you all right?" Sabre kneels beside the couch to ask.

I meet his face and he jumps back, landing on his butt and hitting his back on the table. "What the..." He appears beyond freaked out.

Magennis has been standing wrapping his towel around his waist, he looks down when Sabre speaks then watches him fall. "I swear ye two must have been drinking earlier, first laughing now falling, whatever is the matter with the likes of ye?"

"Look at Magennis, September, so he can see," Sabre instructs me.

I don't understand, but I move my head up to meet Magennis in the eye. He too jumps back, and Gage strings together a batch of colorful swear words beside me.

"What the hell is wrong with your eyes? They turned yellow!" Gage is shouting and I sense it is from fear. "Guys, what's going on?"

Sabre recovers first, to approach me, his movements are cautious and his words are soft, "Are you feeling ill, my love?"

"No," I answer then add, "Maybe."

"Talk to me, what are you feeling?" He probes.

Moving my arm towards him. "Touch me," I tell him.

Magennis sits beside me and begins to lecture, "This is serious, September, there's something wrong and we need to figure it out ... not have more sex."

"I'm being serious, Mag, touch my arm, tell me if I'm hot."

Gage laughs. "You're always hot, Baby, but I'm guessing that's not what you mean."

Sabre is the only one on the same page, he reaches out to touch my arm, holding it in his hand. "You're warm, but not feverish."

His hand has not caused the searing burn that my own fingers had. I poke at my leg this time, again, a fire comes from my index finger that I'm holding to my leg. I flip my hand over to look at the skin, still nothing. I look back at Sabre and say, "I'm going to touch you, then tell me what you feel."

Sabre raises his arm in front of me, holding it out with an ease that only comes from trust. I'm scared to break this trust by causing him pain, but I have to know if he can feel this sensation too. My hand hangs in the air as I debate whether to do this or not. Quickly, before I can talk myself out of it, I poke his arm, bringing my fingers down on the top of his forearm.

I watch Sabre's face carefully, bracing myself for what will happen. The room is still of sound, the three men staring at my hand waiting for any reaction. Seconds tick by, nothing, a minute more and I begin to relax. "Anything?" I ask.

"What am I supposed to feel?" He questions back.

"Is it burning or even really hot?"

"Nope, feels normal to me. Want to tell us what's going on?" He takes my hand from his arm and holds it between both of his hands.

"When I touch my skin with my fingers it burns, but not when I touch you. This has never happened before; I think it has something to do with how we were connected during sex. I was a different energy, it was all around us, holding us together, then you walked away breaking the connection," I try to explain the experience.

Magennis puts his hand to my face. "You're not feverish, but your eyes, they are gold or like Gage said, yellow, that's new."

Sabre lifts my arm and turns it over. "I don't see any burn marks either."

I shrug my shoulder. "I can only tell you what happened."

"Try it again, maybe we can see something." Sabre is still holding my arm out, prompting me to try again.

Bringing my index finger down to meet my arm, I wait for the burn to happen. This time my skin heats but not like before, the intoxicating sensation from before is also fading.

My head pops back up to face Sabre. "It's fading, it's not as hot, that's odd."

He nods. "Your eyes are turning back to normal, more brown than yellow."

Gage lets out a breath and walks around the couch to come behind me. I feel him bump the couch as he kneels down, coming in behind my head. He sweeps my hair to the side to place a kiss on my neck. "Don't know about you guys but that scared the shit out of me." His hands come over my shoulders, and he squeezes to massage my neck.

Sabre nods in agreement with Gage, then turns to ask Magennis, "What do you think that was?"

Magennis ponders the question for a minute. "Either our little Minx had a bloody good orgasm or we just discovered some new magic." His quirky smile spreads across his lips as he winks at me.

I'm about to laugh when Gage's hold on my shoulders becomes a death grip. I hiss from being strangled, "Gage, that hurts."

His hands disappear from my back. "Sorry, sorry, um, don't take this the wrong way, but when did you get a tattoo?"

I swing around to glare at him. "A tattoo, I've never had a tattoo, except the paw mark on my back from the pack, if that's what you're talking about."

As I explain Gage is pointing and making hand gestures to Sabre and Magennis. "Well, Darling, it would seem you have one now," Sabre flatly remarks.

"What?" I try to look over my shoulder, wishing for a second to be an owl so I could swivel my head all the way around, and see this tattoo for myself.

Magennis glances at Gage, Sabre, and then me; he seems as confused as we are, not a good sign.

"You have no idea, do you, Mag?" Gage is sounding more concerned than usual.

"No," Magennis simply replies.

Gage groans, "Shit just hit a whole new level of crazy."

I nod my head and mumble, "No kidding."

CHAPTER 10

I'm standing with my back to the large mirror on the wall between the double sink bowls, my robe is a pool of fabric at my feet, hair swept to one side. I'm armed with a compact mirror in hand, aiming it over my shoulder to get a closer look at my newest marking. Even with the overhead lights set to high on the dimmer switch, I am having a hard time seeing this mark. It is like no tattoo I've ever seen before. There is no ink, only a faint outline in my skin like it could have come from tanning in the sun, with an odd shaped shirt on.

At the base of my neck between my shoulder blades, is my wolf pack mark, this looks more like a real tattoo, of an actual animal footprint, a dark paw with four toes and a large pad. In the middle of the pad part is a tiny crown crossed with two swords, the mark of my royal family. I received this mark during my first change into wolf, last November. After the change, a ritual with Gage claimed me as his Beta, and instantly, he became the True Alpha to all the wolves. That's when the crown and swords appeared inside all of our marks, proof to the other packs that I am their marked Queen.

I hop up onto the bathroom counter between the sinks to get a closer view, bringing the handheld mirror in front of my eyes. It helps me get the full visual of my back. I can see the faint white marks, starting at my hairline and spreading down. This part is like an intricate weave, similar to knot work on antique carvings. Its pattern spreads downward on each side of my neck and across the tops of my shoulders. Under the weave part, a separate design begins, this one fills in both shoulder blades then just stops. The design appears leaf-like; a mix of lengths of the leaves growing longer with each row. The mark, tattoo, or design, whatever this is, mirrors identical on either side of my back, leaving an inch of bare space along my spine from the base of my neck at the bottom of my paw mark.

"It's very becoming on you," Magennis announces from the doorway of the bathroom.

I laugh. "If you like an iridescent plant like thing growing out your shoulders, then yup."

He chuckles back while walking towards the sink, leaning into the mirror for a closer look. "Oh, yes, it does resemble a type of plant. That is most interesting."

He turns me sideways on the counter to run his cool fingers over my skin. "There doesn't seem to be any indentation or scaring, quite remarkable don't you think?"

Little hum's and ha's continue from him, that I ignore. I'm beginning to feel like a science experiment. "Do you have any idea what this is exactly, Mag?"

"None whatsoever," he chuckles. "I wish I had more answers for you, but sadly, I do not. I believe this could be something from even before my time, and that's not a good thing."

I turn to face him, worry begins to bubble in my brain. "Why, is that bad?"

He brushes off my concern, "Everything in this world can be bad, my dearest. What doesn't kill us makes us stronger, yes?" His teeth gleam in the light as he smiles, "What I am getting at is, there are only two people still alive today that are older than I. One being Andras, and the other being Lazarus himself. While I doubt, Lazarus will be forthcoming with information, I do believe Andras may have some answers for you, but even he is limited with knowledge of your mother. He is from the Underworld, which limited his time with Livia, and I don't think he ever involved himself with things of this world. Although, he is all we have."

Agreeing with Magennis, I nod my head in understanding. "I will talk with Andras tonight, maybe get some small bit of information out of him to maybe help us figure out what this is growing on my backside."

He laughs again, "If it spreads that far, ye might want to seek medical assistance."

"Ha, ha, not funny." I try to make myself sound upset but Magennis just knows how to lighten my mood.

"That's the spirit, little Minx, if ye can find even a tiny bit of humor out of a difficult situation, then ye have won. Chin up, this will all work itself out. I have a feeling this is not a bad mark, not if it's on you, and I can't wait to see what comes next." Magennis ends his positive words with a hug. Wrapping his arms around my neck, allowing me to return the embrace with my arms around his middle, and my head in the crook of his neck.

We stay joined in the silent bathroom for a few moments, enjoying the embrace before he again begins to speak. "I did come to let ye know the pilot just called, the plane is ready and the sun has set. Time for me to go."

The one thing about being underground is I never know what time it really is. I need to get a clock for the apartment since Sabre doesn't own one. "Oh, okay," I say, sliding off the counter, putting the mirror down and bending to pick up my robe.

Magennis takes my robe from me, shakes it out, then holds it up for me to put on. I turn around to slide my arms through the silk material. He turns me back to face him to tighten the sash then runs his hands up my arms to my back, rubbing back and forth across the new mark. "I wish I had more answers for ye, dearest, and more time to figure out what this is."

"It's okay, one problem at a time, right? We'll figure it out when you get home." I take over the remaining space between us to wrap my arms around his neck. "Let's deal with Lazarus first, and then we will have all the time in the world to discover what this mark means."

I rest my head on his toned shoulder, continuing to hug him tight. "Will ye please consider taking Gage to Toronto with ye?" He pleads and his concern melts me.

"It's probably for the best, but I don't have to like it."

He pulls back to look at me, his grin back in place. "No, I would imagine ye don't. Be kind to the lad, he is trying and if something terrible happens, well, let's just say he will be the better option than the human."

A sudden sadness overcomes me. I can only nod my head to agree with him. With his fingers, he lifts my head so we are eye to eye. "I'll do everything I can to be back home soon, but ye must promise me something."

I glance at him, wondering what he means, what could he need from me, this self-assured man? "Whatever you need, name it, and I'll do it."

His smile fades as he becomes serious for the moment. "So giving ye are, without even knowing what I ask of ye. You have the heart of hundreds, my dearest. I only ask that ye be careful, too. We have no idea where Lazarus is or what he has planned, he will have spies everywhere waiting to find ye. Ye must remain safe, please keep Gage close and try not to bring any unwanted attention to ye'self. If ye want me to make it back home, then I need to know ye'll be here waiting."

"Uh, I'll do my best, but Chris is an international rockstar, people chase him all the time for pictures. Also, you know me with concerts, I don't really have a great track record with them." I joke at first, then I take a deep breath and get serious too.

"I promise, I will do everything I can to be safe. I had a moment today when I thought about what it would be like without you in my life, I didn't like it, and I think it is the same for all of you. However, I too understand my role, and there will come a time, probably sooner than any of us wish, that I will face my ultimate test. Like you, if I am faced with the choice of keeping any of you safe in exchange for my own life, then you know what my answer will be."

I believe that every living thing has a pulse. We quicken and fade. It's a beautiful thing, a life, but it is also that simple. In between we dream, we feel with emotion, from love to hate and back again, some as open books and some in the shadow of a secret curse, until our fade. Each life has its own path of obstacles and mazes it must take, while some mazes are quicker to fade than others, eventually, we all get there, and it's how we choose to live that pulse that really matters.

We take a moment to absorb the magnitude of each other's words, as well as our own thoughts. I realize that the fate of this world is in all of our hands. We must do whatever it takes, even if that means we sacrifice ourselves for the cause. This is why Magennis is leaving tonight to look for Lazarus. We will not be safe until we deal with his threat and why I need to go to Toronto. I have to see Chris, for this could be the last time I see him and I want to be with him one final time before my own fade.

It's hard to say goodbye, and in this moment, that is what I'm doing, with Magennis now and tomorrow with Chris. I'm preparing myself for the worst-case scenario. "Be safe, my little Minx," Magennis says in a knowing tone like he is having the same thoughts.

One last final tight embrace and hard crushing kiss, I whisper back, "You too."

He frees me from his arms, ruffles my hair, and smacks my ass on his way out the door. Not looking back, just walking away.

I try not to read much into it or over think my stress of seeing him go. With a long sigh to clear my mind, I turn back to the mirror. The reflection of the person before me appears tousled, ruminants of my night, or maybe my life. A part of me wants this all to end, today, to just get it over with. I am sick of not knowing what will be next or if I will even have a future. The past couple of months have been a wonderful dream come true. I have a new family, people I love and care about. Gage, Sabre, Magennis, and Chris all make me feel like the only woman alive. I finally understand what living and loving really mean. With our friends, we have built a home and there is no way in hell I will let Lazarus take that from us.

With this thought I relax, knowing I'm ready for the future, however, it may pan out, I am not willing to let Lazarus win. I'm ready for whatever fight comes and I'm betting on myself to win. But first, I have a few other issues that will need my attention, I have bags to pack and a demon to meet with.

I move into the six-man steam shower, walking into the big jet sprayer. Instantly, the day's stress washing down the drain, cleansing me with a fresh outlook. Boy, does it feel good to be ready for anything, until I get to the closet and have to decide what to bring for my trip. Nothing stops a girl dead in her tracks like packing a suitcase. It's like we become someone else, how can it be so hard to plan for a few days away, but there are variables. Weather, events, daywear, nightwear, evening-wear, and don't forget the shoe dilemma, matching undergarments, handbags, and accessories. *Jesus, this is harder than I ever imagined, no wonder people hate to travel.*

I pull out my phone to check the weather, sunshine and hot all week in Toronto with humidity, whatever that means. It even says the nights will be extra warm, something we don't often get in the West. I'm looking forward to that. Zahara has bought me a cute suitcase for my trip, a bright pink cover with different colored polka-dots randomly painted on the hard-shelled case. I'm not crazy about the swirl of color; if I stare at it long enough I might start to go blind, but it does have a cheery vibe to it, and I hope it means this trip will be just as fun as the luggage.

I've never been anywhere except our city, except yesterday when I had gone to Banff, this trip is that times a million. I'm excited for the experience, overwhelmed about the packing, and nauseous thinking about the flight. That last part really has me freaking out, so much so, that I'm glad I will be asking Gage to come with me. I'm going to need someone to keep me from tossing my cookies and he seems like the right person for the job. I take comfort in knowing if I do upchuck, he will be there to hold my hair, since he does like to pull on it so often. Even thinking about that has my mood coasting back into happy-land.

I send a quick text to let Gage know to pack his bag. I'm sure he isn't expecting this change in plans, but I also know he will be on his best behavior. I know he has been doing what he feels is right and I can't punish him forever because punishing him also punishes me. I hate not talking to him or being with him. I don't know how he can do this to me and I make a mental note to not piss him off in the future.

I pull a few outfits from the closet and place them in the bowl of the case, then take out some matching shoes and call it quits. This is only my backup closet in Sabre's apartment, the rest of my wardrobe is at the house, and maybe Lilith will help me decide what to bring from there. I pull my phone from my pocket and send another text to her before closing the bag and zipping it up. I will deal with this later, now I must find a way back home to have a chat with Andras.

Slipping out of my robe, I dress in a pair of deep blue cut-off shorts with brown leather belt, plain black lace tank and a matching pair of black and brown leather flip-flops. Since I'm going to be working and there is no longer an eminent danger, I might as well be comfortable.

Lifting the handle on the case, I wheel it into the bedroom, and out the door to the main room. "All packed up, Darling?" Asks Sabre from the couch. Still, in his robe, he sits with one foot on his other knee, and open laptop on his lap.

"Not even close, do you realize how hard it is to pack your life into one bag?" Leaving the bag by the coffee table, I plop myself next to him on the couch.

Sabre laughs at me and puts an arm around my shoulder. "If it were me, you'd bring an empty suitcase because we'd never leave the house."

"Where's the fun in that?" I play along with his ribbing.

He caresses my neck with his fingers, down the side of my neck bone along my main artery, a sensual spot for a vampire. "There's so much fun in that, do you really need me to tell you."

Almost purring from his caress, my voice sounds more velvety than usual as I answer, "No, I have a few visuals already." I clear my throat with a swallow, "But I also hope to see some of the sights and the concert. I also have to be prepared for the weather and whatever else Chris might have planned."

He stops stroking my neck and moves on to playing with my hair. It isn't sexual, Sabre just likes to touch me whenever we are near, but for me just being with Sabre gets my motor running.

"I forget sometimes that women over think things, see as a guy, I put in one change of clothes and a shaving kit. The essentials are really all you need, Darling."

I find our comfortable banter falling into place, and I am again full of giggles when I tell him, "You'd have me running around Toronto naked. Magennis asked me to keep out of the limelight, but that will put me front and center, silly."

"Magennis has a point. Okay, pack two outfits, if you need more go shopping. It is a city with a fashion district, they must have clothing, and of course, shoes." As he teases his grin grows when he sees my expression over two words, shoes and shopping. "Yes, Darling, you can shop there."

"Oh, I never even thought of that. This will change everything, and you might have something with bringing the empty case."

Sabre's deep barrel laugh fills the room. "Poor Chris, I should send a text to warn him, that I might have let loose a monster."

I poked his belly, "Hey, don't joke about shoes, I take that shit seriously." No longer able to keep my own face straight, I join him in another round of chuckles.

We sit for a while, bantering and laughing, in our own comfortable way. After a time, we just talk, Sabre knows me so well, I can never hide anything from him nor can I ever stay down with him around. He has a way of pushing me to do more, think smarter, be myself but be better, all at the same time.

"So, do you need to get back to the house?" His question breaking my thoughts.

"Um, yeah, I want to talk to Andras, maybe he has some answers about the mark." I sit up to get moving.

Sabre jumps up too and makes his way to the bedroom, "Wait two-seconds, and I'll take you."

"You're busy Sabre. I can take the Jeep home; Lilith can grab a ride back home after work."

He stops at the door and turns back towards me with a serious look, "Darling, I'm never too busy for you."

CHAPTER 11

Our ride home goes by in a flash as Sabre entertains me with details about Toronto. From restaurants and shops to looking out at Lake Ontario from the top of the CN Tower; it all sounds incredible and I'm starting to get more excited for my trip. The band's private jet has already landed at the airport and is currently being attended to at the Blackwood's private hangar. It will be ready for me to leave at a moment's notice, but as excited as I am to go, I still have to chat with Andras first.

Sabre pulls the SUV to the far right of our empty garage and puts it into park before turning off the engine. As we get out, the only sound I hear is the ticking of the motor cooling. I love my home and the property it sits on for many reasons. My favorite being the absence of noise. The silent calm, void of a city's chaos, welcomes me home every time.

"I'm going to go outside to summon Andras," I tell Sabre while climbing out of my seat.

His door closes and he walks around to my door to help me out of the big vehicle. "I'll come with you." He takes my hand in his own after shutting the car door.

We walk in a comfortable silence, out the side door of the garage, towards the back of the property where the big wooden gazebo sits. Last fall, when Andras first appeared, his presence had burnt a black circle into my lawn. Lilith explained to me, and I've even read it on the internet, that under the Earth's surface there are ley lines: alignments of numerous places of geographical and historical interest, such as monuments or in our case, mountains. These ley lines hold the energies of the Earth and what magical beings tap into to use their powers. They also provide a roadway from the Underworld to our world, this is how a demon can be summoned to our realm, by traveling the lines. Being so close to the mountains, my property has strong ley lines underground, humans mistake them for fault lines and often warn us that if an earthquake hits we could be sucked into the lines.

There is a truth to that, we can be sucked into the lines, but it isn't to pull us into the Earth, but rather into the Underworld. There are many stories about people being sucked into a sinkhole or lost forever in the Earth after an earthquake, never to be seen again, but they are not really gone forever. This is the work of the demons, who love to create havoc, and why it is important to summon any demon into a proper circle. Without the circle, they can walk anywhere on Earth and travel back and forth through the lines, taking humans captive to use as servants.

After that night, last fall, Gage set out to make a circle for me to be able to communicate with Andras safely, and not have it look like an eyesore in the yard. His idea had been to build a gazebo over the burnt grass area. After the construction and every day since, Lilith pours salt around the edge of the wooden structure to keep the circle bound tight and prevent Andras from leaving the Underworld. Every time I summon him to our realm, I must first check that the salt has not been compromised in any way, from the likes of rain, the wind, or even foot traffic.

Inside the gazebo is a cupboard we keep stocked with containers full of pure Antarctic sea salt. This salt is made naturally, free of any chemical or industrial process when the Antarctic water travels up the West coast of Africa by the Benguela current. The ice-cold water passes through an underground aquifer and is then pumped into natural drying pans. The intense African sun and Atlantic winds help to sun, and wind dry the salt to purity.

Sabre and I each grab a container and begin to walk in opposite directions around the structure, moving slowly to spill out fresh salt. At the bridge, that goes across the pond, there is enough room for the container to pass under the bridge to continue to pour my contents to meet with Sabre's. Once we are done, we both step into the gazebo, Sabre sitting on the bench-style seat as I begin my ritual to call upon Andras.

Under the wooden floor is the permanently burnt circle with a five-point star in the center. This star represents the elements of magic I will be calling upon in my invocation. On the ledge of the waist high walls and embedded in the center of the floor, sits five candles. Each represents the Earth's direction as well as the different magical elements.

Before I start, I draw a long intake of air to fill my lungs. Then as I let it out, I clear my mind of the usual day to day nonsense to concentrate on my task. With a lit, long wood match in hand, I turn in the north direction and ready myself to start the process.

I begin with lighting a green candle while reaching out to the ley lines with my magic. "I call upon Earth to strengthen me," I say this to the night sky and in return am met with the sweet smell of honeysuckle. Instantly, my body feels revived and full of energy.

Moving counterclockwise around the gazebo, I light the yellow candle next, representing the direction of east. "I call upon air, to fill me with knowledge and help me communicate." As I speak the words, the trees around me rustle from a warm breeze, gently wrapping itself around us. A sense of calm settles over me.

Taking another step to my left, this time lighting a red candle that represents the direction of south. "I call upon fire, inspire me to lead with passion and love unconditionally."

I see the flame on the candle grow, three times in size, before settling back to a natural size flame like the other two candles. Like the heat from the flame, I feel warm all over and full of positive emotions. Sabre is sitting beside this candle, watching me work, perhaps because this candle represents love, it makes me smile at his insight.

Another step brings me to the final direction, west, and I light the blue candle. "I call upon water, guide me with your wisdom and cleanse me of my impurities."

As this flame ignites I taste a tartness similar to that of apples in my mouth. It reminds me of autumn harvest and memories of my past. Suddenly, I'm happy and a smile breeches my lips.

I move to the final spot to kneel in the center of the gazebo, in front of a plain white candle recessed into the floor that represents aster. "Spirit, come forth in the space I have provided. Connect us to all of our elements, Earth, air, fire, and water and help keep us balanced as I ask, Andras Pluto, to please come join me. May he feel free to have an unrestricted exchange in the positive environment we have created." The powers of the elements swirl about until the final white candle comes to life. All around me I feel the harmony of the magic touching me.

I place my hand on the wooden floor next to the candle to be close to the ley lines. My energy, combined with the elements, crackles like the static on a television channel that has gone off the air. This has a different sensation than my usual summons, the norm is usually quicker and free flowing of the magic, this seems off somehow. I glance over my right shoulder to Sabre, he's sitting forward, ridged and uncomfortable looking. He must be feeling the difference too but during a summoning, we cannot speak, I can tell he is jouncing to, though.

After about ten minutes of kneeling on the floor with nothing happening, I try the invocation again. This time skipping only to the part where I ask Andras to come forth, more time ticks away. I think over the ritual as a whole and run it through my head, thoroughly from the start, to see if I might have forgotten a key element. This is standard practice magic and isn't my first rodeo, *what the hell is going on?*

Another fifteen minutes runs off the clock, I stay on my knees not moving a muscle, letting the power continue to wash through me into the ley line as I wait. Just as I'm about to start the process over a flickering ball of red pops up in front of my face. A board on the wooden bench creaks beside me. I hold my free hand up to tell Sabre to stay. This isn't a danger, it is Andras trying to make the connection to the ley lines. Thinking of Andras, I concentrate on an image of him in my head, I picture reaching for him and pulling him up and out of the Underworld. While I do this I also push my magic out my fingertips, down past the wooden floor into the Earth beyond.

The visual helps and soon the sparking ball of red light grows in size to form the man I have summoned. Andras Pluto, the God of the Underworld, fizzles into shape in front of me, from a bright red ball into the black as the night demon. The fireball flashing into his eye sockets, leaving two red eyes to stare back at me. If I was still only human, this would seem like a horror movie coming to life. Of course, I have seen this many a time since the fall and know that as scary as Andras appears, he is nothing I can't handle.

"Proserpine, are you ill?" Andras asks with worry, once his shape finally transforms before me.

"Andras, you made it, what happened?" I ask him back at the same time.

Sabre moves on the bench, I sense his presence closer to my side, he is also worried. When Andras reaches out to touch my face, Sabre stands as a guard at my side, to show himself to Andras. Again, I hold up my hand to Sabre to stay. There is no threat, but no matter how many times I summon Andras, my men are always on edge. Perhaps this is because Andras is the most powerful demon of all, a master at trickery and manipulation. No wonder my mom was so good at getting me to do my chores, she was a demon once herself.

"I have done nothing, Proserpine, it is you who feels different." Andras's words pull me from my thoughts. "Are you ill?" He asks again.

"No, I'm fine, but it took forever to summon you tonight, is something wrong with the circle?" I probe.

His fingers inch forward again toward my face, he wants to connect with my mind to see what has gone wrong. Like with my men and members of my court, I can connect through the mind to Andras, but unlike my court, he needs to touch my face to see the thoughts. In turn, I too get a glimpse inside his head, sometimes that can be worse than a horror movie, demons live in a crueler world than we do.

I let his fingertips fondle my face, once there is a connection from my skin to his, a quick movie like scene plays inside my head, revealing the life Andras lives. Time in the Underworld is different, for every week that has gone by since the last time I saw him has been months for him. So much has happened since our last visit and I am ashamed at myself for making him worry.

The movie stops with him alone, sitting in a chair at what I assume is his home in the Underworld. He's sipping from a mug of some odd shape just before he is pulled towards me in a rough manner. "Oh, that looked painful, did it hurt this time, coming here?" I say in a panic, needing to make sure he is unharmed.

"I am well, my child, but it is you I fear for. Our connection is broken, my visions of you faint, you have been marked by an entity of holy power. I feel it, it is pure and unnatural to me. Touching you now causes me pain, what have you done?" He sounds disgusted with me, causing me to blush with embarrassment over something I have no control.

"September did nothing, this new mark is not her fault, she came to seek your help, not be berated by you," Sabre growls at Andras.

Andras ignores Sabre, but not his words. "You come for my help and what do you offer in return?"

I'm floored by his questions. "I'm not playing that game, Andras. You know when I summon you, I'll share an exchange of power, that is enough. I won't be a part of anything more and you know it. Don't forget you vowed yourself to my service, that includes helping me." I give him a mad poke with my finger to his chest. "The only offer here is, help me out or I send you back and never call upon you again. Which will it be?"

His expression doesn't change, nor does his posture, or tone of voice. "As you wish, Proserpine."

I can't figure out if he is really going to help or only tell me what he thinks is enough. *Damn, demons can be a pain in the ass.*

I sigh out a frustrated breath before continuing, "The new mark I have on my back, have you ever seen one like it? I want the truth and I want full answers, do you understand?"

159

Andras takes a minute to answer, I'm sure he's thinking of a way to outsmart me with half-truths. "I have seen a mark similar to this, on my beloved Proserpine."

I gasp at his answer. "You mean my mom, she had this mark?" I plead, needing to know more about my mom.

He only nods his head, giving me nothing more. "Did she have the same mark or different?" I demand with impatience.

This time he shows me the answer with another movie like vision, and I see then that what he said is true. His fingers touch my cheeks and my mother's image appears inside my head, it is not one I wish to have, though. Andras has indeed seen the mark on her back but he had seen it while he was screwing her from behind. I slap his hand from my face with a hiss then I scream, "That's disgusting, Jesus!"

Sabre's on edge, moving closer to Andras, pulling me a little behind him. "It's okay Sabre, he's not physically hurting me, but I may never get that image out of my head." I shiver thinking about it.

Andras has, however, told the truth and my mom did have the same mark except hers had appeared to be down the full length of her back, whereas mine stops at my shoulder blades. "Have you seen it on anyone else, besides myself and my mother?" I clarify as I ask, you can never trust a demon.

"No." The quick and simple answer from Andras has me thinking there is more he knows, but I'm not asking the right questions.

"What other information do you know about this mark, and I want to know everything," I demand this with an authoritative tone in my voice.

His eyes are on me, he's staring, watching me, reading me better than I can read him. I'm beyond frustrated waiting for his answer, but finally, he decides to give me words. "My beloved was created with the mark, only once did she let slip that there was another like her but she did not tell me more. Your aura and energy are more powerful than hers, even before this mark branded you. Now your touch brings me pain, I fear what will happen the more the mark grows on you."

My head begins to swim with more questions but I know I have to remain calm to get everything I can from Andras. "Why can you feel pain but Sabre and the others don't?"

Andras remains still and void of any emotion as he begins to answer my questions. "As I previously spoke, this is a holy and pure mark, it burns me because I am from darkness."

"Do you mean God marked me?" I'm in shock.

"Not you, no, through your connection to my beloved, yes."

"My mom was marked by God?" I wonder.

"A creature from that realm, yes."

"Do you know who the other person is that was marked, even if my mom didn't tell you, you must have had an idea?"

"No, I have not felt the presence of this mark on anyone else. This is all I know, my child, there is no need for more questions," Andras tries to end our talk.

"You're being honest? You have no other information that will help me figure out what this is?" I push one last time to make sure.

"I do not know more," he says with a bow, meaning he wishes to be released back to the Underworld. I don't blame him for wanting to go, it can't be much fun stuck in a circle with a crazy woman nagging him with questions.

"Fine, but if you remember something on this subject, I order you to bring the information to me. Is that understood Andras?"

With a nod, he answers, "I do, my child, we are the last of the connection between the worlds, you are my Queen and I wish you no harm."

I reach for his hand with my own, releasing some of my power into him before speaking, "Thank you, Andras, I appreciate your help. I know you wish more of me, but I give you what I am comfortable with."

"As you wish, Proserpine." He bows again to end our meeting. I release his hand to be able to send him back to his realm, by pinching out the candle flames, in the reverse order that they had been lit. As I thank the elements for their gift with each pinch of the wick, Andras begins to fade.

I let out a sigh once he is completely gone and the elements have been silenced for another night. I've been given a lot of information but I'm no closer to finding the answers I want. It feels like a loss that I don't want to deal with at the moment.

Sabre is just there, behind me, as if he senses my inner turmoil. He wraps his arms around my waist to pull me to him. "I'm not a fan of demons, especially him."

I turn in his arms to meet his eyes with my own. "You do realize I am part demon, right?"

He snorts then he adds, "Yes, but you at your worst is like dealing with unicorns compared to him. He scares the crap out of me."

"Really? My big vampy-wolf is scared of a demon that can't get out of this gazebo, but me, the one that can cut you in your sleep, you have no problem with. You are far too trusting, Sabre," I lecture, but I'm glad for the change in conversation.

He shrugs his shoulders. "Did you not hear him, he said something that I have always known, you are pure and holy.

There is only good in you, September. It is why I trust you with my life and love you with my soul."

I roll up on my tiptoes, putting my arms around his neck to bring him down to my lips for a soft, grazing kiss. Sabre has a way of melting my heart and if he continues to speak, I know I will start to cry. Whether through beautiful words spoken like today, caring gestures when I least expect them, or sweet little notes left to brighten my day, he is by far the most romantic out of all my men. Every sweet sentiment he offers is a form of foreplay that has me weak in the knees and putty in his hands, tonight being no different.

Moving closer to Sabre's hard body, I press my chest to his rib cage, connecting my hips to his. My lips demand more from his, opening up to him to ask permission to be penetrated by his tongue. He lets out a chuckle, not the response I thought he'd give. "Are you laughing at me, mister?" I glare at him.

"Not at all." His smirk suggests he is.

"I hear a, but," I question, wondering where this might be going.

He shrugs his shoulders. "But, you have a way of changing the subject with the most devilish ways that distract me from the issue at hand."

"Oh, and what is the issue at hand?" My hand slips down his hard chest and ribbed abs, and I realize this is proving his point.

He stops me at his flat stomach, picking up my hand in his own to bring it to his lips for a nibble on a finger or two before he continues. "Well, according to Andras, you have a holy mark, are you not curious about that?"

His question is a valid one. "Sure, I'm curious, but I'm also happy to be in denial for a while longer. I had just started to get comfortable with myself, then Lazarus decides to grace us with his bad-ass self. Now I have to send Magennis away to locate him, and tomorrow I am planning to take my first trip on a plane, away from you for the first time, to possibly say goodbye to Chris forever. So yeah, I am changing the subject because everything has been turned upside-down, again, and I just want a minute to not think about it."

I have never seen Sabre blush before, but there upon his cheeks is a dusting of pink. "I didn't realize, I apologize. I sometimes forget the magnitude of weight you carry. You were born for this role and make it look effortless. Like a Queen should, but the emotional toll you also must deal with is not something I tend to consider."

I step towards the bench to take a seat. "This is one of those women from Venus and men from Mars moments. Don't apologize for something you had no clue about, it's not like I have been forthcoming with information, myself. Trust me when I say, you don't want to hear all of what happens inside my noodle." I stop to tap my temple with my index finger before carrying on. "At times, I wish I could be like you, thinking in black and white answers, but I'm programmed more for gray. I'm female, we over think, over share, over stress, and over worry, every detail of every day." I laugh at my words because of the truth in them.

Sabre, Gage, hell every man I know, think in a cut and dry kind of way. They say men think with their penis, but in life and death situations they don't. For that, they actually use their brains, the problem-solving part of it. Us women, we think with our heart, gut, and the entire brain. We hash out every possible scenario that may arise to be prepared for anything that will almost never happen because we are gluttons for punishment.

Sabre shuffles my way to sit beside me on the bench, leaning back while taking my hand in his and resting the union on his lap. "I'm glad you are from the gray planet of Venus, for what it's worth." He grins at me, lightening the load of seriousness my mind has gone towards.

I give him a small smile. "Thanks."

"You do know all that thinking is what makes you such a great Queen. You think about everyone and everything, never leaving a detail unexplored and finding the ultimate solution that will work for everyone. We men will fix the leaking hose, one pin hole at a time as it arises. Whereas you will fix the first hole, but also figure out how it got there and prevent it from happening again, that's smarter."

"You don't have to butter me up with these compliments, you know. I'm not mad."

"I didn't think you were, I am simply stating the truth."

"Oh." I don't know what else to say.

Sabre turns sideways on the bench to look at me, with his free hand, he brings it to my forehead and with his thumb he massages the frown between my eyebrows. "I am curious," he states.

I look at his face to see questions in his sky-blue eyes. "About?" I hesitate.

He takes a second, seeming to collect his words, "I'm wondering why you said you would be saying good-bye to the human."

Now it is my turn to collect my words and I begin to explain slowly, "I've thought about this a lot, Chris has only been around our world minimally because it's dangerous for him. I have only taken his blood a couple of times, which, I understand, will lengthen his life, but not make it eternal unless he takes my blood. He's a rockstar that parties so that might help get him to a hundred if he's lucky." I smile then

Marianne Maguire

continue. "This isn't fair to him, with his lifestyle, to expect him to remain faithful. It's time for him to go off, enjoy his human life, maybe find someone he can settle down with, and live the human dream."

"September, don't you think that is something Chris should decide?" Sabre blurts.

He shocks me with his outburst. "I would have thought you'd think this is a good idea. You won't have to play bodyguard anymore, keeping his crazy fans away from me, when he comes to town. We will also have one less male in our relationship, and he can be free to do what he wants, not having to worry about our secret world anymore."

This time Sabre's face turns angry. "I see what's going on here. Did you say good-bye to Magennis before he left too? Will you cut your ties with me, tomorrow, when you get on that plane? This is why you didn't want Gage to go with you, you're preparing us, aren't you?" His nostrils flare from his anger; "Were you planning on even coming back, or did you think you could go after Lazarus on your own?"

He releases my hand, I go to grab for it but he pulls away and stands, turning away from me. "Sabre, it's not like that," I try to explain.

I can feel his anger boiling over through our connection, even with my wall block up. He turns back towards me with a glare, his voice calm but deadpan cold. "Then explain, how you can simply walk away, do you not trust us?"

I gasp, "Of course I trust you –"

He cuts off the rest of my words, "Then you must think us too weak to protect you."

I jump in with some damage control, "God no, together we are an ultimate strength, and I know you will do anything to keep me safe"

Again, he cuts me off to continue his assault, "If you trust us and know we will keep you from harm, then I don't understand why you are considering this. Unless," he pauses for a second and I see shock cross his facial features, "You don't love us, is that what this is about? We scared you off by asking for your hand in marriage. We've rushed you and now you're having doubts, enough for you to do the unthinkable, fight this war alone."

The hurt on his face breaks me. My body begins to tremble as a river of tears leak out and roll down my cheeks, this is not what I meant to do, have him think the worst when really it is simpler than that.

"No," I start to say, but my lips are quivering too much to have the words come out audible. I press my fingers to my mouth to stop the movement so I can explain. "I... I'm not sure..."

His ridged frame stands before me, tense as he waits for answers I seem to be having a hard time getting out. He offers me no comfort or support; he is gutted by my actions. I begin to rise from the bench but know I can't go to him even though I need a connection with him. I reach anyway, with my hand to ask for his, he doesn't move nor does he seem to even notice. "Please..." I beg.

"No, just explain this need you have to abandon us as if we no longer matter. As if..."

"Stop!" I shout at him. "Please stop, I'm not abandoning you. I never want to hurt you, don't you see?" I scream into the darkness and the forest echoes back my words.

"Jesus, Sabre, I love you! It's because I love you that I am about to say good-bye. If I say goodbye then I know you can still be out there in this world, safe. You can go on if something happens to me, continue to live. I can't put any more people I love, in a box, ten feet below the ground, not again. I can't do to you what I had to do to my parents. I would rather have you hate me and never speak another word to me, at least I will know you still have emotions and thoughts. Anything will be better than closing the lid on your coffin, and never hearing your voice again."

The tears no longer leak out my eyes, instead, they form an endless stream down my cheek, dripping off my chin to be lost in the night. Breathing has also become difficult but I push through between hiccups and gasps. "With my parents, the disease took them from me, there was nothing I could have done to prevent that. This war with Lazarus, it will mean many will die, for me. I can prevent that. I can keep you, Gage, Magennis, and Chris safe, if you'd just let me go."

Even to my own ears, my words are sounding slurred together and I don't know if he understands them. I open up our connection and pour my heart out, allowing Sabre to witness the pain of my grief. I think about how helpless I was watching my parents die, how isolated I had felt after. Lost and alone, depressed enough to consider taking my own life, for there was nothing else left for me. For the first time, I share my grief journey in the most personal way, mentally spilling out every thought and emotion I had experienced. Allowing him to see my most inner emotions is not only embarrassing but cleansing.

Unless you experience the loss of a loved one, you can never truly understand. The body and mind become exposed nerve endings, every thought, movement, action causes a rippling pain that never really goes away. You never get over grief, you're never the same person after it happens, but somehow you find a way to make it a part of you and go on. Last fall, I had made the decision to go on and it brought me to this world, surrounded by some of the most caring people

I have ever met in my life. I have been accepted and reborn into this stronger person, but I couldn't have done it without my men.

If this war with Lazarus, becomes the epic battle that everyone seems to think it will, I know in my soul, that if just one of my men or even a friend dies, I can't go on. My love for Sabre, Gage, Magennis, and Chris is of a far greater magnitude than what I held for my parents, losing one of them will instantly kill me.

I've been told that Lazarus is a cunning man, able to manipulate my mother from her powers. He probably knows females lead with their hearts, and as I had been thinking before, with Magennis, if he wants to get to me, all he has to do is kill one of my men. If I can just detach myself now, I can prevent this from happening. I can make this fight, over the kingdom, strictly between Lazarus and myself. I might even have a chance of winning if it plays out on a fairer ground.

"Do you really think Lazarus will play fair?" Sabre's voice breaks my train of thought.

I refocus on his face, now absent of his anger and shock to show a softer look of understanding. "No, if he is every bit as evil as you have told me he is, I have little doubt he will make this a fair fight. At least I can go into it knowing you will be safe."

He takes a heavy breath, I watch as his chest grows in size then as he exhales, his tension seems to go with his air. He moves one step forward, "September," he begins while reaching out for me, asking with this gesture for the connection I so desperately need. I wipe my eyes with the back of one hand while grabbing for him with the other. "You are correct in assuming Lazarus is cunning, but do you really think, by distancing yourself from us, he will not still try to use us as pawns in this fight?"

I hadn't thought about that. "I guess he still can, but if I take this fight to him then he will never be able to get to you."

Sabre lightly chuckles. "My Love, sometimes I forget how naive, to war, you are. If he killed you, he will come for us after, knowing we will be out to avenge your death. Without you, we will not care if we die too and this nonsense will be for naught. By separating us now, you're gifting him with the advantage. If we are to win you that throne and gain peace for our kind, our best and only chance is to do it together, where we are at our strongest."

My heart sinks realizing he is right, *how did I not see this.* Without me around, Lazarus will want to eliminate anyone with a connection to me to secure his position and send a message to others willing to fight. It will mean a death warrant for more than just my men, this whole city will be wiped clean. "Oh God, I didn't think of that."

Sabre closes the gap between us, letting go of my hand, but bringing his arms up to wrap them around my body and rest his chin on the top of my head. "I know you didn't think of it, but that is what we are here for. Lean on us, trust us, together we will help you get through the battles, the one with Lazarus and the personal ones of the heart." I feel the warmth from his lips as he presses a kiss on the top of my head. "I'm saddened by the loss you have been through, my Love. I had some idea of the pain you have battled, but not to the extent which, you just allowed me to see. Thinking back, I should have tried to be there for you, race be damned. You should have never had to deal with that alone."

"You couldn't have known back then and I wouldn't have shown you now had you not been so mad, but now you see why I was going to leave." I pull away from him to let him see my face while I speak, "I don't care about the throne, Sabre. I only care about all of you and I'm scared something is going to happen that will leave me alone again. I don't think if I have to go through the darkness that is grief, a second time, I will make it back out. I fear, this time, the darkness will consume me."

His arms tighten around me. "Shh, Darling, don't think that way. We don't have the crystal ball that tells us this is going to happen. You're working up all kinds of images in your head that may not even happen or matter. We haven't even located Lazarus yet, and for what it's worth, we don't even know if he's planning a war with us. We are going on assumptions from his activity, but in truth, Lazarus is acting no different than he always has, he's just closer to us and it has us speculating."

"But, if he could overpower my mom..." I start to say before Sabre interrupts me.

"When he overpowered your mother, it was a surprise, we are quite a bit more prepared than she ever was. Thanks to Magennis, Lazarus will not expect us being ready. He also won't be expecting how much stronger you are, and with us, by your side, we have a chance at winning this. Forget about the darkness, about the what ifs, and believe in yourself, and what will be. The sooner you realize this and start believing in it, you will see that you are unstoppable and Lazarus doesn't have a chance."

I laugh, "You make it sound so easy."

"It can be if we believe it to be."

"Who made you Pollyanna Sunshine?" I laugh and begin to relax because I understand what he is getting at, the law of attraction. I can beat myself up with the negatives, they will probably come true since it is what I had focused on. However, if I think about this in a positive manner with a positive outcome, then is will be my outcome. Give to the universe what you wish to receive and it will provide.

"Yes, exactly, give out what you wish to receive in return," Sabre cheers at me, "and if you get lost along the way, I'll be here to help guide you, only if you don't push us away."

He moves his head to peek down at my face. "You're not still thinking about doing this alone, are you?" His voice is laced with a raw seriousness.

Shaking my head under his chin. "No, I'm not, you're right, it would have been stupid. If there is a war with Lazarus, we will be better together, as long as no one dies. That will destroy me."

Sabre's arms surround me, back into a tight embrace. "We will cross that bridge if we get to it. For now, you have a bag to pack and plane to catch, unless you've changed your mind."

I sigh, "I don't know, what do you think?" I ask him honestly.

Unwrapping himself from my body, he takes my hand to pull me towards the steps of the gazebo and across the lawn to the house. "I can't believe I'm saying this, but, I think you should go. I get the feeling a few days away from reality might be good for you, providing you are not going to run or cut Chris out of your life. He does adore you, September, he won't take you dumping him well."

As we walk, I let Sabre lead us so that I can watch his face as I speak, "I don't think I could have done it anyway, to any of you. Truth be told, I can't live without any of you and I am kidding myself to try to think otherwise. I do really love you all. I just can't go back to where I was a year ago. I hope you understand why I thought of leaving, and that you will forgive me for those thoughts."

His lips move up and across his face while he tucks me into his side and places an arm across my shoulder. "I'm not mad, still a little hurt, but seeing your pain makes me realize where you are coming from. I don't doubt your feelings for me or the others, you were willing to walk away, that takes courage, and shows me exactly how much you do care."

We've reached the downstairs door to the house when he pauses, before opening the door he finishes his thought, "September, I will be the proudest and happiest man the day we marry. I cannot wait for this all to be over so we can start our life together and I can show you that you are the breath that keeps me alive. Please, don't ever doubt my love for you, it burns because you are the fuel that keeps it aflame."

"Jesus, whoever said romance was dead obviously never met you," I gasp out.

He bends down to lift and cradle me into his chest, opening the door he walks us into the house and upstairs towards the bedroom. I'm bubbling with excitement knowing, he is about to show me just how romantic he can be.

CHAPTER 12

Sabre made love to me repeatedly throughout the night. Never letting me sleep more than a half-hour at a time, before gently nudging me awake with amazing foreplay, which led to another round of sensual passion. I'm not sure if he was trying to show me his romantic side, prove how much he loves me or was trying to make up for the days I will be away from him, perhaps it is all three. Whatever the case, by four in the morning, when Gage calls to let me know he is waiting for me at the airport, I am completely exhausted.

With Sabre's distraction, I don't get my bag packed. I decide this is probably for the best since I won't be able to decide what to bring anyway. I do chuck in a toothbrush and makeup for good measure, but the rest I will have to buy while I'm there. Really, it is just my way to justify a shopping spree in Toronto, and not feel guilty for spending so frivolously. Sabre puts the empty bag in his SUV without comment before we head out so I guess this means, I get to get my shop on.

Somehow, Sabre appears more refreshed, from the night's activity, than I do. There is an evil unfairness to that. At least, if he is tired, he can go back to bed while I'm stuck on a plane for four hours. I know people sleep when traveling, but being my first trip, I'm far too anxious to even consider sleep as an option. What if something happens, like a malfunction that prevents the plane from doing its job and we crash? *How's that for positive thinking, not?* Perhaps, Sabre's night distraction had been his way of keeping my mind from over thinking the whole travel dilemma. *Damn, but he knows me too well.*

My tummy does a flip when we turn off the highway onto the airport exit. "Try to relax, Darling, everything will be fine," Sabre reassures while squeezing my hand he holds in his lap.

"Mm, huh," I mumble out because I worry if I try to speak all that will come out will be vomit.

We pull onto a side road and down towards the private hangar the Blackwood brothers own. "Don't we have to go in the airport?" I manage to ask after a couple of swallows.

"Nope, you get the VIP treatment, door to door service and all. They might even have champagne onboard, which I highly recommend to calm those nerves of yours." He's trying not to laugh, but it's quite obvious, he finds my apprehension humorous.

I take some deep breaths, exhaling in slow pants, thinking about how excited I am to see Chris. It has been months since he was home because the band has been touring on the whole other side of our planet. I can't even imagine having to be on the plane for days on end with nowhere to go, and nothing but the inside of the plane to look at. I'm starting to think I might have a claustrophobia problem, the mere idea of nowhere to go has acid churning up into the back of my throat.

Sabre parks the SUV beside a circular building. "September, breath slowly, honey. Jesus, you look like you're about to pass out."

"I think I might puke first," I moan.

Sabre jumps out of the truck and is opening my door before I can even finish my words. He reaches to unclip my seatbelt, then lifts me out the door and onto the pavement. He moves fast to bring my knees up so I can put my head between them. "Slow breaths, in and out. That's it, relax. Think about something unrelated to today, riding your bike, you love to ride. The wind in your hair, the smell of fresh air, the sun on your face." As he talks me off this ledge, he rubs my back with one hand and strokes my hair with the other.

"What the hell are you two doing down there?" Gage asks as he comes towards us from the back of the vehicle. "I'd say a quickie, but that position definitely won't work."

"September is having a bit of a panic attack," Sabre informs Gage.

"Well, hell, baby-girl, we can't get in the mile-high club with you face first in the toilet the whole trip." Gage cracks while bending down beside me. "Although, I guess we can, but it's not much of a turn on for me."

I can't help but let a snort out, Gage is a humorist and his joke gets my mind off what is making me anxious. "That's my girl, we'll have you sucking cock in no time."

Lifting my head, in time to see Sabre rolling his eyes, and it makes me giggle. "It's always about sex with you." I shake my head.

"What else is there, Baby?" Gage's answer sounds too convincing, if I didn't know him like I do, I'd almost believe he's telling the truth.

"Really? You have to go there?" I start in on him.

"Someone is feeling better, okay, up and at 'em." Gage cups my arms to lift me to a standing position. The ground spins under me and I fall sideways into Sabre. "Oops, a little too fast, take a breath," Gage couches.

I cling to Sabre's shirt with a death grip on the cotton fabric. "All good, just give me a second for things to stop spinning."

Sabre braces me while I take a few controlled breaths, I'm beginning to feel embarrassed about my own behavior. I mean thousands of people fly all over the world every day without issues, except maybe a lost bag or two. Releasing my grip on Sabre's shirt, leaving some crinkle lines in the fabric, I'm able to stand up tall, for the most part, on my own. I can do this.

"Feeling better?" Sabre asks with expressed concern.

"I think so," I reassure him with a smile.

"Think you can do this without tossing your cookies?" Gage ribs me.

Turning my head to give Gage an eye roll before sarcastically answering, "I think I'll be fine, but in the event, I do need to toss my cookies, I will be sure to stay clear of your Armani."

"I wouldn't worry too much about that." He begins walking backward to the tail end of the SUV, the grin on his face growing with each step. "My Armani will be neatly stored, next to your Prada, in a nice neat pile on the floor. But, if you do need to vomit, spit me out and turn your head first."

"Just go get my bag, you sicko." There's simply just no way I can stay mad at Gage, especially with comments like that. I know he's only horsing around, easing my nerves with sexual innuendoes, I can't fault him for that. Besides the laugh has helped.

I turn to Sabre, he too has found Gage's comment amusing, for he's smiling in the direction Gage has gone. When I move, his eyes flicker down towards me, they have been shining bright blue from his reaction to Gage's humor, now they begin to cloud over into a gray-blue shade as he focuses on me. His smile dims and I realize he's sad.

"I promise not to do anything stupid and I will come back." I offer to ease his mood.

"I know you will, it doesn't mean I won't miss you any less." Sabre tugs at my dress to bring us together, placing his big warm hands on my hips to lift me so that I can wrap my legs around his waist and arms around his neck.

"I'm going to miss you too." My words get caught in my throat as I whisper them.

Our arms and my legs tangle us together in an embrace, his lips search out for my own for that final long, hard and messy kiss, that will tide us over until we're reunited. I imagine airport cameras capture more shows of affection in a day than what a church will see in a lifetime.

He breaks the kiss first to rub his nose to mine. "You should go, Gage will be impatiently waiting. I want you to have as much fun as possible, within reason of course," he softly laughs.

"Of course," I reply innocently.

He sets me back on the ground so we can walk together, hand in hand, to the other side of the hangar. There awaits my ride, a large white plane with no markings, except some numbers on the backend. I've never seen a plane up close before, and I find it interesting how alien like they seem. A folic tubular vessel with steel bird wings, even the windows at the front on either side give the appearance of eyes. It's kind of creepy, something I try not to think about.

We stop at the staircase that leads up to the side door of the plane to board the aircraft. "I guess this is my stop."

"I guess this means I won't see you for a few days." Sabre sounds sad.

"Think about how much room you'll have in the bed," I joke to cheer him up.

"It will be cold without you," he returns, "but, I will see you in a few days. I love you, September."

I'm filled with my own sadness. I know I will be back by the end of the week, but I also feel like I'm leaving a part of myself behind. "I love you too, Sabre," I choke out.

"Would you two hurry up, I'd like to get to Toronto sometime today," Gage barks down from the aircraft doorway.

"Go, have fun." Sabre gives me a smile then nudges me onto the steps.

My feet are heavy and my heart starts to hurt as I climb away from him. I'm not liking leaving him and I make a mental promise to myself, to never do it again. It has never bothered me when Chris has been away, but I know he travels all the time with the band. It was a given going into the relationship that he wouldn't be around much. With Sabre, he and I have been almost inseparable since the first night of my transition into this world. Even before that, we worked together almost every day for years, he's become an extension of myself to some degree. To not be close to him for a few days, I'm not sure how to deal.

At the top of the steps, Gage is waiting on the platform with his hand stretched out for mine, I grab on to him needing the comfort. Before entering the plane, I take one last look down towards Sabre. He's standing back from the staircase, having watched me go up, he waves goodbye and I return the wave by blowing him a kiss. It's only a couple of days, this one time, and I promise I will never leave without him again.

With that promise to myself in place, I turn on the platform back to Gage and make my first step into an airplane. My nerves begin to prickle again and I squeeze Gage's hand as tight as I can.

"Welcome aboard the private jet of Defeat the Darkness, Ms. Rae," a voice from somewhere inside the plane announces. "I'm Captain Erik Evans, it will be my pleasure to fly you to Toronto this morning."

The more steps I take inside the aircraft, the more a large man slowly becomes visible. He's standing in what can only be the small kitchen galley area of the aircraft. "Mr. Michelson has instructed that whatever you wish is my command. If you have any requests, please let me know by picking up any of the wall mount phones placed throughout the plane." He finishes his speech with a bow of his head.

I take a couple more steps bringing me in front of this large brute. Large is an understatement for his size, though, more like a monster of a man. I'd bet this guy ate gyms in his spare time. I thought Sabre to be a muscled male, but this pilot has to be two Sabre's put together. Standing between the galley of the plane and the open door to the cockpit, his massive body blocks my view of the working end of the plane. I have no idea how he can even fit through the door to fly the plane.

The lack of any hair on his head or face gives me no indication of his age. He appears neither too young nor too old, so I guess he's somewhere in the middle. For a human, this could be anywhere from thirty to fifty and he is human, I sense nothing Supernatural from him. Even though he's human, his extraordinary size, his evil bald look, dark completion, and extremely dark eyes make me not want to have a tussle with him. He seems more like a bodyguard than a pilot, but then again, what do I know about what a pilot should look like.

Erik Evans might make me want to pee a little in my pants from fear, but it's his calm demeanor, confident sounding voice, and a bright gleaming smile that has put me at complete ease. I have every confidence this man will get us to our destination without any distress, all from a simple greeting.

Erik steps forward, offering me his outstretched hand. I've been holding Gage's hand as a security blanket and don't want to let go, so I lift my left hand out to greet the pilots for the shake. Instead of a handshake, however, he lifts my hand to his lips before kissing the back of it then he takes a bow. I glance at Gage but he seems to have the same befuddled expression on his face.

"A pleasure to meet you, Mr. Evans or should I call you Captain?" I hide my social awkwardness with a question.

"I prefer Erik, but whatever you wish is fine, your Grace," Erik says this with another smile.

I now understand his formal gesture. "Okay Erik, now that we have officially met, I'd love it if we drop the formalities and you just call me September," I offer a smile back.

He begins shaking his head. "Mr. Michelson will see that as being disrespectful, I don't think I can do that, Madam. I was also raised to know that when in the presence of a member of a regal family that I mind my manners. My mamma would come back from the heavens just to smack me if I didn't."

I chuckle at his story. "I completely understand Erik; my mom was the same. You're from the south, right?" I ask.

"Yes, Madam," Erik answers cheerfully.

"I tell you what we can do to satisfy everyone, and not have this be an issue of disrespect. I've read that you give women respect, in the southern states, by putting the Miss in front of the first name, how about we do that? That should keep your mamma from haunting you tonight, yes?"

Erik takes a minute to think this through. "I think that might be best, Miss September." His smile grows again across his lips, making his teeth almost glow in the low overhead light.

"All right then, now that we have that taken care of, Erik my good man, let's get this birdie in the air." Gage pushes the conversation to a close and turns to a door opposite of where Erik is standing. "Shall we get to our seats, Miss September?" Gage doesn't say this sarcastically, he's showing his own respect of my decision with Erik, perhaps me being mad at him has done some good.

"Right away, Mr. Blackwood." Erik turns towards the exit we had come through and the starts preparations for closing us in.

Gage tugs me behind him through the door between the kitchen and a spacious living room, not what I expected to see. "What is this?" I gaze around at the room completely awestruck.

"This, baby-girl, will be our palace for the next four hours, shall I give you the grand tour." He gleams his special smile at me when I shake my head in anticipation of the tour.

We start at the door, entering into a long bright area with white padded walls that have a curve to them but are lined with ample windows with pull down shades. From one side to the other we walk on cushy beige carpet and this bare bones part looks like every airplane I've seen in a movie. However, it's the lush parts in the middle that's nothing like a typical airbus.

The first few feet have two rows of airplane seating, single seats on the right and two double seats on the left. The difference with normal planes and this one is, these seats have been steroid injected. The plush white leather lazy-boy recliners with wide leg and arm rests are big enough for two.

Each oak brown and lime-green colored seat cushion comes with a matching fluffy blanket that invites you to sit in comfort.

On the single seating side, there are wall mount tables on the one side of the recliner, big enough to enjoy a meal or get work done. On the double side, the table extends out, to accommodate all four seats that can swivel around to face each other. At every section, there is a small monitor mounted on the wall so that the screen can be viewed perfectly from each seat.

Walking the four or five steps through the first six rows we enter the next section. These two rows have single recliners on each side. The table on the right is already set up with Gage's laptop, his paperwork scattered across it, an indication to where we will be sitting during our flight. I move to the left side to take my seat.

"I'm not done giving you the tour yet, do you want to see the rest of plane?" Gage asks.

I feel my eyes open wide. "You mean there's more?"

Gage smirks, "Of course there's more, and it gets better."

As Gage tugs on my hand to continue our tour, we cross an archway into an entertainment lounge. We are greeted by two square brown leather chairs on the right, these have been set on an angle and swivel to face each other. Behind the last chair is a built-in light maple cabinet, with a variety of glassware behind glass doors and lower cupboards for what I assume is the rest of the bar supplies.

Beside the bar and on either side in the back, before a second door, are big overstuffed couches. A dark brown leather covers the exterior shell while a soft beige corduroy fabric covers the seats. One couch has been folded up to sit upon, while the two in the back are pulled down into beds.

In between each of the couches is another brown recliner, there is certainly enough seating for a small party to happen while making you feel the comforts of being home.

As if the plane is answering my thoughts, I notice on each wall separating the sections, a television screen. Each screen has a detached cabinet decked out with the latest video game console and games. There is almost every type of entertainment tool you can imagine to keep a person amused during a long flight, this trip might not be as bad as I first thought. The simple comforts will allow me to relax from my earlier panic, perhaps this is why Gage offered the tour. I look at him to give him a smile.

He grins back. "Great digs, eh? Just wait till you get a load of this next part," he adds in a flirty wink telling me he's looking forward to this.

He bangs the door open then steps back to wave me inside. I can't imagine what more there will be, the plane seems to have everything you can ask for to make travel enjoyable. I'm excited when I release his hand to enter into this mystery section. What awaits me is something from a dream and I pinch myself to be sure I'm conscious. It's ludicrous to think this is still an airplane, all these extravagant things in such a small space but then to see this room, it blows my mind.

The room has been lit by a foam style fixture on the ceiling, that gives the appearance of sun shining through clouds, and it throws shadows across the bleached white walls. As I walk a few feet inside the door, I confront a king-size bed, it has been made up to invite sleep and relaxation, with multiple sized pillows and two comforters done with light-grey and dusty-blue colors. I want to jump right in, but I also want to continue exploring the spacious bedroom and lounging area, complete with more reclining chairs set off to one side. I venture to the tail of the plane to find an emergency exit between a walk-in closet hidden behind a full-length mirror wall and an amazingly spacious full bathroom with a shower.

I turn around and round, taking in every detail this room has to offer. Gage begins to laugh from his lounging position on the bed, I stop to question him, "Why are you laughing?"

"The look of awe on your face is priceless, Baby. Had I known this would impress you, I would have taken you on my plane long ago," he says with that sexy smirk, inviting me to him.

"Your jet is this big too, are they all like this?" I innocently ask as I continue to wander the room, opening drawers and otherwise being a snoop.

"No, definitely not all jets are like this, depends on what tax bracket you fall into, but Baby, trust me when I say, everything I own is bigger."

Mentally I groan and ignore his comment by walking by the bed to check in the nightstand. Gage rolls back and tackles me, pulling me to the bed with him. I gasp from the sudden tackle, "What do you think you're doing?"

I'm annoyed, but it fades when I see his eyes are smoldering and his lips are curled into a heart stopping smile. "I'm doing what I've been dreaming about since you sent me the text. Having you all to myself on this plane for the next four hours."

He captures both my hands, pulling them up over my head to hold with one of his hands, while the other slides slowly against my skin, down my body. "I want you hot and wanting, wet with desire, spread open here on this bed then bent over that chair. I want you watching me in the mirror as I take you over and over from behind until you beg for me to stop."

For a second he watches me intently, his hand going across my hip and thigh then back up and under my dress. I forget to breathe when he cups my sex in his palm, "But, I won't stop, not until I have marked every inch of your beautiful body. I want you to have love bites on your skin, slap marks on your ass, and a pussy so swollen and sore that when you go to your Rockstar, all you'll be remembering is me."

I swallow what little air I have left into my lungs, my heart races and threatens to leap from my chest from his dirty talk alone. Every part of my body is tingling in anticipation of his promised words. Gage is a vocal lover, he enjoys painting the picture with words before he dabbles on the paint, his form of foreplay. Over the months, he has mastered these verbally painted thoughts, completely unraveling me every time.

I have no words for him now, I can only watch and wait for him to make the next move. The heat from his hand seems to burn right through my panties, when he adds a few circled passes with his palm, I am about to start the begging.

"Miss September, this is Captain Erik, I'd like to let you know we have been cleared to head over to the runway. I understand air traffic control is a bit backed up this morning, but we should be able to take off in the next thirty minutes. I ask that you and Mr. Blackwood take your seats while we taxi to the runway. I'll let you know when we are clear for takeoff." Erik's words have come out of nowhere, I've already forgotten this is an aircraft and not some random bedroom.

I tilt my head back towards the door, "He's not in here, is he?" I whisper.

Gage has stopped playing but continues to hold my pussy in his hand as a mischievous smile touches his lips. "I hope not, it'd be difficult to fly the plane from here."

"Smartass," I say, rolling my eyes then push at him to get up. "I think we should get to our seats."

I commend Gage on his effort of keeping me occupied in the sexy moment, but I'm all too aware of my surroundings now. I know I have to find the safety of a seatbelt before my panic starts to kick back in.

His nostrils flare as he smells my fear but he makes no comment, instead, he rolls off the bed, holding his hand out to help me to my feet. I grasp his hand with my own clammy one and make a quick retreat to the door. As we walk, or rather half jog, down the aisle to the white section and our seats, a high-pitched whine pierces the air. The noise all but has me jumping into the leather cushions.

"What is that?" My frantic question blurts from my lips.

"Is this the first flight you've been on?" Gage asks then shakes his head, "Never mind, dumb question. That sound is the engine and in a minute, we will begin to move forward, there will be a small jolt before we move towards the runway. This is similar to riding in a car as we take some turns and maybe stop and start along the way. Does that explain things for you?"

My head does a speedy bobbing gesture to let him know I understand while I try to keep the threat of bile at bay. I'm still clinging to Gage's hand, knowing I need to let go and grasp the chair arm for him to get to the safety of his own chair. He's holding in a grin as he bends down to one knee before me, he fishes out the seatbelt on either side of my thighs then shows me how to fasten and unfasten it.

"Before we take off maybe I should get you a drink, something strong. I'm sure the boys have something hard in the liquor cabinet." Not waiting for my reply, he gets up to head back towards the tail section, and the cabinet in the couch area.

I don't take my eyes off of him, I'm terribly frightened that something will happen. A silly thought considering we're only at the hangar on the ground, we haven't even moved yet. From the buckled safety of my seat, I follow Gage's every step back to the cabinet and as I hang on to the chair arms for dear life, I pray for him to hurry back.

He opens one of the doors, bending forward to search inside, his head disappears behind the wood while his beautiful hard ass sticks out into the aisle. I watch as his legs shuffle back and forth making his glut muscles flex, I realize he's doing this on purpose. As much as he can drive me crazy, he also knows how to get me to switch gears by showing me his amazing body and that ass, *D-A-M-N!*

With bottle in hand, he stands, closing the cabinet door and reaching for stemware. I lust over his body as he strides back to me, for such a strong and well-built man he certainly knows how to move his mass. He's been able to combine his qualities as a wolf, stealth-like and graceful, into his everyday life. It's how he manages to look as though he's stalking prey instead of casually walking. It attracts my attention, this pursuing strut makes him sexy as hell.

"You seem very attentive," Gage muses, "care to share with the rest of the class?" He chuckles to himself, knowing full well that I've been watching him.

"I was just thinking..." I start to comment but my words are cut short when the plane suddenly lurches.

My eyes, still on Gage, watch as he does a step shuffle to keep upright without falling or dropping the glasses and bottle of liquor. "You need to get in the seat," I blurt in a rush.

"Baby, that's just the plane moving forward, we have some time before we take off, it's like a car, remember." Gage reminds me of his earlier explanation.

"You don't walk inside of a car when it moves, what makes a plane any different? What if we hit another plane on the way to the runway, you could be flung from a window, hurt, or worse, killed." I urge him with my words while my hands and legs hold me to the chair.

"That's a pretty vivid imagination you have, but the planes only move on one-way roads. There's no possibility for a head-on collision and there is no chance in hell I'd fit through one of these tiny windows." He gestures with the bottle at the window to my left before placing the glasses on the table beside me, to pour us each a drink.

The amber liquid pours out the tip of the clear bottle to half fill the glass in front of me. Within seconds a cinnamon and rose aroma hits my nose, from my bartending experience, I know this is probably a scotch whiskey. Gage finishes the pour, putting down the bottle and picking up a glass to hand to me. The plane is rattling along on the rough path to the runway, and even though it does feel like a car ride, I don't believe for a second that something won't go wrong. My white-knuckle grip remains on the seat, drink be damned.

"September, please, have a drink, it will calm you. Besides, holding on to the seat won't help if something did happen." His words are not comforting.

He might be right; a drink might help. At the very least it allows my hand a chance to get the blood flowing in it before I take the glass. The aroma gets stronger the closer the drink gets to my face, but even though it smells of roses and cinnamon it doesn't taste like it. That's the thing with scotch whiskey, depending on how it's aged, which cask is used, and many other circumstances, the smells, and flavors usually range from moss and trees to flowers, or foods.

Raising the glass to my lips and taking the first sip, I instantly taste orange and chocolate, not bad. I hold the liquid in a pool on my tongue to enjoy the flavor before allowing it to drip down the back of my throat. This whiskey tastes smoother than many I have tried and the aftertaste isn't peaty but fruity, maybe from currants or raisins. Not at all what I expected it to be.

"This is good," I state out loud.

Gage chuckles, "You sound surprised."

I nod my head swallowing another sip. "I've just never had a scotch that I liked before. This seems smooth and it doesn't taste like mold or dirt."

Gage steps across the aisle to his chair to sit down, a relief to me and that seems to help relax me. "Yay, I'm shocked the boy band has something this refined in the liquor cabinet too. I did have to dig through bottles of bourbon and tequila to find it, but a single malt Macallan is unexpected."

He lifts his own glass to his lips to take a sip, I watch as his cheeks move from him swirling the liquid around his mouth. Then I watch as his throat moves, Adam's apple going down and back up, as he swallows.

"Mmm."

Gage turns his head to give me a knowing look, "Are you enjoying the drink or the show?" He asks and I realize I have been moaning.

"Both," I mumble into the lip of the glass, feeling embarrassed, not for watching him but for getting caught.

"Dirty girl," He roars then adds, "The drink seems to be helping you relax."

"I guess it is." Among other things.

I happily take another sip and snuggle back into my chair. I'm getting used to the humming noise of the engine, and the rattling of steel or whatever a plane is built from. The up and down bumps don't seem as bad. With the alcohol, I'm able to relax enough to feel that flying isn't all bad.

"Can I ask you something?" Gage asks.

"Of course." I've been daydreaming so I turn in my chair to give him my attention.

"Why are you mad at me?" His question causes my brain to stumble.

"I'm not mad." I start, then think about it for a minute before continuing. "I'm not mad at you, but I am frustrated."

His left eyebrow lifts, he's puzzled by my statement. "Gage, you are a larger than life personality. Everything you do is intense and pushed to the limits. Don't get me wrong, I love that about you, it keeps things interesting. I have done things in these past months, that I may have never even considered trying when I was human, but you make me come alive. I'm more confident being around you because you've shown me I can be, I thank you for that."

I pause for a long minute and he adds, "I hear a but coming."

I laugh, "I guess there is." I lean on the armrest to get comfortable before going on. "I get the feeling that you don't trust me or you don't agree with the way I rule, because you keep hiding things from me, not telling me full details. That questioning behavior lingers with the OSU, I see it at every meeting on every face. If you have no confidence in me, how will I be able to gain respect from our people?"

He places his empty glass on the table to his right and turns in his chair to face me full on. His forehead is creased into a frown; he has not liked my words. "I have confidence in you, I'm proud of you, and I think I encourage you. You may have a point, though, I don't tell you everything, not because I don't trust you, it's my own issues that prevent me from doing so."

The plane engine drops in frequency like we might be slowing down, my body relaxes more. "Then explain to me your issues, help me understand."

He leans back then lets out a breath, it sounds as though he might be frustrated. "September, I don't even know where to start. From birth, I guess. Garo is the oldest, my father molded him, nurtured him, prepared him for Alpha. They had this special bond, I could see it in my father's eyes, his pride for Garo, but when he looked at me, I only saw his disappointment." He pauses to take another slow breath.

"I've never told anyone this, Jesus, I do love you," he lets out a nervous laugh. "I mean that in a good way. You and I have a lot in common, you know."

I give him an encouraging smile. "How so?"

He moves again, mimicking the way I'm leaning on the arm of the seat, it gives our conversation a more intimate feel. "The disappointment burned in me, so I rebelled, I partied, and slept around. It practically drove my father insane. Then after he passed, Garo took over and I thought it would change, but instead of my father's disappointing eyes, I now get to look at Garo's.

"That burning look of judgment makes me want to do better. Like you, when someone tells you that you can't do something or you won't do it right, you make a point of proving them wrong. I see that in you, and it is part of why I'm drawn to you. I think about how you will push yourself every day to be a better person, to help others and to show everyone you can and will do anything you put your mind to. You make me want to do that too, and show everyone I am not what they think, but most importantly, I never want to see that disappointment in your eyes." When he stops to shallow, I see his hands are shaking.

The plane has stopped at this point and I decide to take the chance of undoing my belt to go to him. Moving over the distance between the chairs, I bend forward and hug him, "I will never be disappointed in you, maybe annoyed or frustrated from time to time, but never disappointed. Don't you see how amazing you truly are?" I kneel in front of him, hoping to have a few minutes to explain before needing the safety of my seatbelt again.

"Garo is a shadow of a man compared to you or at least he lives there. You're the one that thought up a way to hide our people a hundred years ago. You built the hotel, then added bars and countless other businesses to employ the subs and keep them safe. You did that, not Garo. All along you were and are the better man, the stronger Alpha, that's why my magic marked you."

I lift his chin with my finger to see a half smile on his lips. "You, Mr. Blackwood, are incredibly thoughtful and the smartest man I know, I wish my brain could be as inventive. Your father and Garo only chose to see faults in your behavior, not your amazing character. The playboy thing you do, that's an act to hide the real person inside. I get to see the real person; he will never disappoint me because I know him too well and I know he loves me. You never disappoint the ones you love but you can piss them off, so stop doing that." I grin at him.

"Thank you," he whispers.

"For what, telling the truth?"

"No, for understanding and believing in me. I will try, from here on out, to always support, trust, and respect you and to do that, no more half-truths." His voice has taken on a serious tone that lets me believe this time he means these words.

"Pinkie swear?" I ask, holding up my hand in a fist with my pinkie sticking out.

He hooks his own pinkie with mine. "I will pinkie swear, swear on a stack of Bible's while standing on my head in holy water, completely naked, if I know it will make you happy." His mood has changed, probably from thinking about being naked.

"That's a visual, but all I want, is for us to be happy."

"How about a really great orgasm?" Yup, he is definitely feeling more like himself.

"Well, there is always that," I snort then go in for a hug.

"Miss September, Mr. Blackwood, I want to update you. We have now been cleared by the tower to take off next. If you will please take your seats and buckle up, we will be taking off momentarily." Erik's voice fills the cabin again.

Instantly, I tense up. I let go of Gage to scramble back to my seat but he stops me by holding my arm. "I have an idea that might help you. Come here."

He guides me in front of him, getting himself adjusted in the seat then turning me around to have me sit back into his lap. I let my legs fall on either side of his and brace my back against his chest. He takes the seatbelt to stretch it out and over both of our laps before buckling it tight. "There, comfy?" He asks.

"Yes, but I think this breaks one of the flight rules."

"That's okay, I plan to break at least a few on this trip." His laugh vibrates through my back while his arms hug my middle, and I finally feel safe and ready for this flight.

CHAPTER 13

We sit for a minute while the engine begins to whirr, the whine is higher in pitch with faster rotations. I have a firm grasp of the armrests at either side of my legs, but I am no longer holding it with such violent force. I'm able to lean back at leisure, resting the back of my head to Gage's shoulder, and his breath on my cheek and neck calms me further. He has moved his arms to rest his hands in my lap and kicked up the foot bar, under the seat, to place his feet, to help keep my extra weight from making his legs go numb.

The plane jerks then it moves forward, which is backward for us since we are facing the tail. I peek out the small window but the skies are still quite dark, making it hard to see anything except a single light here and there. Probably a good thing I can't see, being backward may cause me to become nauseous, especially at the rate we seem to be passing the lights, it tells me we're picking up speed. I take a deep breath then exhale, on the exhale we start to lean forward as the plane lifts from the runway, the belt digs into my hips, and I instinctively look down.

Gage picks up on my nervousness, either from my increasing heartbeat or the sudden change from a relaxed posture to a tense one. "A few more minutes and we'll level out." His words tickle my ear.

The pull forward is intense, especially with Gage behind me. His weight adds to mine pushing the belt deeper into the skin at my midsection, the exact reason why we shouldn't be sitting together. My hands go for the belt, if I can pull the material piece up I'll get relief.

"Don't undo it." Gage stops my hands with his own.

"I'm not, but it's cutting my stomach." My voice sounds higher and panicky.

Gage reacts with quick movements, taking my hands he places them back on the armrests. With a tug, up on the belt, he is able to loosen the strap enough, to bring sensation back into my hips. His hands then move along the belt to my hipbone where he begins to massage the skin, across and over my tummy to help relieve the tingle of numbness.

"Better?" His voice drops much lower than normal.

"Yes, thank you," I sigh, as the tingles fading when the blood flow is restored.

"Mmm, my pleasure," he moans into the side of my neck, nibbling at my earlobe before sucking it into his mouth.

His fingers never stop massaging, back and forth at my waist to my hips and down. "I like this dress, it's cute and practical." His compliment catches me off guard.

I twist my head to try to see a part of his face from out of the corner of my eye. "Thanks, I think," I say, unsure of his motive.

It becomes clear when his hand moves down from my hip and across the outside of my thighs, where my legs have been resting on top of his. From there he reaches for my kneecaps to pull them apart, spreading my legs open to hang down on either side of his, giving him complete access to slip up under the loose pink fabric of my dress. The heat from his hands warms my air conditioned cool skin, and as he sweeps his fingers along the inner parts of my thighs, a shiver creeps up my spine bringing with it goosed flesh.

The plane is still climbing, the momentum keeping us pressed firmly together, where I can feel his cock harden against my ass. I realize, Gage is intent on taking my mind off the flight in other ways, I'd laugh except I'm far too interested in what his fingers are doing. Like his feather touch along the crease from hip to pubic area where he slips a finger beneath my panty line.

With the hand not breaching my knickers, he lifts my skirt and peers around my shoulder. "These are sweet, they match the dress. How attached to them are you?" He muses.

"Very, they do match the dress, as you pointed out," I tease back with an innocent nature.

His hand crumbles the front portion of the cotton undergarment. "Is it string, thong or fullback?" He probes.

"You forgot boy shorts." I giggle at his knowledge of undergarment descriptions.

"These don't come down and across your hip enough to be boy shorts. My guess, string, since they barely cover the front and I can only picture how little they probably cover the back," he growls at the description.

"What's so important... OH!" I squeak when he yanks on the front fabric. "You'll rip them!"

"Exactly," he purrs back, pulling the fabric down and out again.

I feel a pinch, as the string in the back wedges between my butt crease, but the thrill of seeing him accomplish this task makes me not care. The material, stronger than I imagined, won't give, but Gage isn't discouraged. He bunches the fabric tighter and this time pulls it up with a gentle tug, moving the piece over my clit where he begins to make circles back and forth across it, teasing the hood and piquing it with interest.

There's a shuffle of fabric as he lifts my dress up more, "I want you to watch while I get you off with your own panties." His voice is starting to sound commanding.

I'm excited, needing to look down and watch as my panties are bunched up in his hand, and stretched out across my labia. The harder he pulls, the tighter the string gets, cutting hard up the crack of my ass, but the pain mixes deliciously with how well he is playing the front of me. He tucks more of the dress fabric off to the side, to allow for a better view, before running his fingertips over the sensitive area. I never imagined using lingerie as a toy, but I'm thankful Gage has.

The longer he manipulates the area with finger strokes and fabric circles the more I want to cum for him, but there isn't quite enough friction. The intense tease is amazing with the best part being I've completely forgotten about being on a plane. My anxiousness has long since disappeared, and it's all about getting turned on by turning Gage on.

To show my appreciation, I flex my hips back and forth to his slow rhythm, but Gage stops to bunch all the fabric into a ball in his fist then with some additional strength, he gives them a heave. The string pinches my crack; it verges towards painful just before I feel it give way. Gage's hand springs out, not going far since the panties are held together at my hips. A slight brush of air on the right side then the left as he pops the elastic, destroying my pink knickers completely.

"Those are quite a nuisance." He discards the scrap somewhere on the floor.

"Those are the only pair of panties I have with me," I scold him.

He cups my sex with his palm, fingers down, heel resting on my clit. "I'd say I'd buy you a hundred more, but I really think you should consider going commando. I find it to be a bigger turn on knowing I can finger fuck you anywhere, at any time." He shows me what he means, moving his hand down, nudging my legs further apart to insert one of his digits inside of me. "In fact, I promise, if you stop wearing underwear altogether, I will make it my life's mission to either, finger fuck you or eat you out, somewhere other than our home, every day."

I moan, for what he's saying and for him inserting a second finger inside of me. "See, you like the idea too. You're already drenched and once this plane levels out, I'm going to lick this cream out of your sweet hot pussy."

I groan, thinking about his mouth, hot and slick, sucking me off. "Oh God, yes."

His third finger enters me, he works them round in circles to widen my opening, preparing me for his girth later. Gage is as thick as he is long, it takes some work for him to completely fill me, and he's well on his way of making it happen. He presses the heel of his palm back over my clit, continuing to manipulate both areas with the same round movements.

I open my legs as far as the seat will allow, the armrest had once been my savior now it is simply in my way. Though the wider I move my legs, hooking my feet on the inside of his knees, and hands bracing the seat, the more my ass presses against Gage's cock. It becomes easier to rotate my hips around to masturbate him with my ass crack while he masturbates me with his hand.

His free hand starts to wander up, stopping above the halter bodice of the dress. He's in luck with this part of my wardrobe, since I haven't put on a bra and the dress is a light cotton with an elastic weave to it, he'll be able to play with my breasts without having to destroy any more lingerie. I love the idea of him ripping my clothing off, but since I packed so little, I can't encourage him to destroy what I have left.

The dress strap slips down my shoulder, his finger hooks the bodice and pulls, exposing the top of my areola.

He pulls again to allow the nipple to peek out over the ribbing of the bodice. A devilish moan rings from his lips in my ear before he blows air down my chest, to tickle and perk up the tiny bud.

"I like how every part of you practically begs to be played with." His finger grazing the bud to bring it to full attention. "See."

With his right fingers sliding slow, but with purpose, in and out of my opening, the heel of his palm continuing the pressured heat on my clit, and his left fingers pinching and pulling at my nipple, my body melts into his chest. A warmth of heat in my nerve endings spreads like a wildfire, across my most intimate parts. I can hear Gage's breath in my ear, sharp pants with quick intake, he's enjoying working me up.

"You like that, don't you, Baby? You like me getting you off?" He groans out.

I moan out some sort of agreement, but the pressure is beginning to build and I know he is about to make me cum.

"That's right, Baby, let yourself go." His fingers penetrate deeper inside of me, hitting the sweet spot repeatedly to start the flow of the release he's begging me for. "You're fucking sexy as hell when you cum."

I scream into the empty plane in front of me as I watch him milk the cream from my pussy. I've slipped halfway down his lap and realize the plane is no longer pushing us forward. Gage removes his fingers from my opening and lifts them to my mouth. "Taste the pleasure I gave you, Baby."

Opening my mouth, I lick my own sugary syrup from his middle finger, sucking it into my mouth with an anxious vigor. His cock throbs into the small of my back in response. I no longer care about planes, trains, or anything, except tasting him on my lips. My hands move of their own accord, pulling the release on the seatbelt to free us from our binds.

I lift my body, his finger sliding from my mouth as I turn to drop to my knees in front of him.

I have a mission and move with purpose, lifting and pulling to unhook first his belt, then unbutton and unzip his dress pants, thankful for the looser fitting pant. Once the gate opens, his dragon springs forward with gusto, as eager to be in my mouth as I am to taste it. My mouth salivates in anticipation; I clearly can't disappoint it.

With my right hand, I reach out to give his shaft a stroke. His breath catches and his cock jerks, causing a tear of pre-cum to escape his swollen head. Satisfied by this invitation, I smile while looking into his blazing eyes, then slip my lips over his swollen head. Gage loves to watch me and I see the hunger burn in his gaze, whether from getting me off or me giving to him, he loves it when I put on a show. How can I not with such an attentive and intensive lover?

His mouth opens just enough for his tongue to peek out and run along his lips. I mimic him by running my tongue around his reddish-purple head. He licks at his top lip; I follow the action by licking the front of his shaft. He moans his pleasure; I sink him deep into my throat to moan around his hardened flesh and allow him to feel the subtle vibration.

"Oh, Baby!" His voice sounds strained.

I smile around a mouthful, knowing I'm pleasing him. My tongue presses firmly into the back of his silken shaft, the front rides along the roof of my mouth and I guide him in and out of my opening with careful hand strokes. A steady stream of curse words, erotic sounds, and unintelligent words flow from his lips. I cup his balls with my left hand, sliding my index finger across his taint and onto his sweet starfish to massage his whole passage. His breathing becomes labored as a bitter musk taste tickles my taste buds, he is close.

"Miss September, Mr. Blackwood, we have now leveled out at our cruising altitude and we should have smooth air for the next four hours. Feel free to move about, there is a wet bar and a full kitchen, stocked for your connivance, but please use caution as we do sometimes hit pockets of turbulence. If there is anything you might require, please use one of the courtesy phones to let me know. Relax and enjoy the comfort of the flight."

As Erik's voice crackles in the speakers, Gage let out a low growl, cupping my head in his hands and holding me in place. My mouth around his cock, his fluids dripping down my chin. "Stop!" He growls.

My eyes flicker up to his face, there I see some frustration and bits of annoyance, mixed with the heavy desire that still burns bright. Erik has just cock-blocked him and if my mouth wasn't full, I might laugh at the situation.

Gage pulls himself from my mouth then briskly removes his tight black shirt to wipe at my chin. "September, in all my life, I have never had a reason to be a jealous man, but then again, most of my dates lasted only mere hours."

He slips from the seat, tucking himself gently back into his slacks as he rises. Once up, he extends his hand to help me to my own feet. "Then I met you, sassy and smart, but shy at times." Gage kisses my hand, leading me to the back of the plane, stopping before the next section. "But also, sexy as hell." He gives me a heated glance from head to toe.

At the archway, he pushes me into the padded wall, filling my personal space with his mass, holding me in a position to be controlled. "Baby, you were made to fuck, everything about you. Your eyes remind me of Bambi's, open to the world with a sweet innocence, yet they also burn wildly for something dark and dirty when you look up at me." His fingertips outline my eye socket then move down my cheek. "Then there are these pink pouty lips that look perfect on the end of my cock." His fingers cup my cheek as he slides his thumb over my lips and into my mouth for me to suck.

He doesn't linger long, instead, his hands slither down my body, moving over every inch with careful consideration. "And this body, so beautiful, every curve, etched perfectly, so when placed in the right position it can be gripped for a hard pounding. Legs, long enough to wrap my waist, an ass firm enough to hold or thrust against. This here..." He bends on one knee with his head at my waist, hands gripping my ass cheeks. "this is why I get jealous; I have the perfect woman."

He takes my hands this time to place them on his shoulders, then he lifts my left foot to balance it on his bent knee. From there he unbuckles and removes my pink wedge platform sandal. Once done with both he nudges my legs apart to begin the slithering hand exploration again. As he searches for some secret braille across my skin, he also kisses and breathes me in. Being wolf he often does this, maybe to see if I have been with someone other than my court.

"Do you know how intoxicating you smell, like a flower from the desert but so much better. I'd say you changed your perfume, but I know you don't wear any. Your scent does things to me, and I want to mark you," He runs his nose up my thigh, across my pelvic area then stands, putting himself back into my space. "I want to bite you like you do to me, but I want to leave an indentation to stake my claim and show the world I own you."

He takes my hands again, raising them above my head to hold them with his left hand, with his right he slips it down underneath my crumpled dress. Again, he cups my sex with his palm, dipping his fingers into the slit and rubbing my cream around the opening. "Here, in this spot, I want to mark you, with my seed, over and over until it drips down your thighs and makes you full with my child."

He continues to rub circles around my clit and slit, dipping his fingers in after every pass, working me up as he talks. "I want to collar you, with a jeweled neck ring, to declare your worth... but mostly I want to marry you, have you for my wife, mine and only mine."

His eyes burn with an intensity that pierces right through me, this is how Gage expresses himself, with sex, it's how he understands his own feelings and how he explains them for me to understand. "You wanted to know why I don't tell you things... this is why; you are mine. Mine to protect, mine to cherish, mine to care for, and mine to control. The wolf in me knows no other way, it's my nature, I've never been jealous because I never felt for anyone, what I feel for you. I'm learning to switch the jealousy into other emotions. I'm learning to get more turned on when you're with Sabre, Magennis, and even Chris. I want to be everything they are to you, but better."

He has taken his hand away from my sex, as he speaks he's undoing his own pants again. With his cock in his hand, he strokes it to release some pre-cum lube before leaning his hips forward to rub himself along my slit. "I'm even learning how to relinquish my dominance by helping you build your own, it turns me on watching you become verbal and demanding. So, you see, I am learning to be a better man, not because I need to, but because I want to, for you."

The whole time he speaks, he steals my breath away with his raw honesty, it shatters some part of me. I know he has been trying, but I never really thought how or why. I've been too wrapped up learning my own new world to notice the others around me might be doing the same. I want to say something, to tell him I appreciate what he is doing, that I love him more now than ever and how amazing he is for sharing his emotions.

His left hand moves away from holding my arms up and his fingers press against my lips. "Shh, I know Baby-girl, I feel it all too, but for the next three-plus hours, I want to pretend that it is only us in this world and that you are only mine. I want to hear you scream because I know just how to make your kitty purr. We're going to christen every inch of this plane as my way of dealing with you spending the next few days with your human toy."

He grabs for my hands again, pulling them up higher to stretch out my body, giving him better access to masturbate me with his cock head. On his next words, he pushes his swollen head into my more than ready opening, "Most importantly, I'm about to bite, scratch, pull hair, bruise, pinch, mark, and cover you in my semen. So, in the next couple of days, when you're with him, you'll still remember today. It will have him questioning if he's as good and I'll be able to see my mark and smell my scent to know you are and always will be, only mine. This is my way of contending with the difficulties of our world, I don't have to do it often but occasionally if I ask, will you please play along."

How can I say no? Later I might over think it three ways to Sunday, and have some issues. That is how us girls think, we over think. Right now, his words make me putty in his more than capable hands, I want to be just his too, for the next few hours anyway. Pushing up on my tiptoes to meet his burning stare with my own, I whisper, "Then be my Alpha, and take me like a bitch in heat." I bite at his lips to start a kiss.

His nostrils flare against my cheek right before he pulls himself out of me, flipping me round, slamming me into the wall, and inserting himself back into my opening with a rough push. In this position, it stings going in, partially because I'm clenching from being manhandled, and partially because I'm not quite as ready for his mammoth size as I thought. I hiss then squeal at the discomfort.

He slides himself back, allowing the combined fluid to slick me up, then bit by bit he moves in circling motions to massage the inside muscle and relax it enough to take on more of him. This time I moan at the warm feel of him sliding against my inner wall. The sting of pain fades into the heated dampness.

He takes my hands to cross them behind my back like he's arresting me, holding them with one hand while the other has a firm grasp on my neck. With my right cheek pressed against the wall, I can only see a sliver of him in my peripheral vision. His mouth slightly open, tongue just peeking out from his lips, the eye I can see has darkened with his desire. I know his nose will be flaring, the closer he gets me to the orgasm, this is the face of my dominate Gage.

Every circled thrust makes it easier for him to inch further inside me until I'm engulfed. I can feel every solid inch of him as he rubs the special spot deep inside, over and over, it tickles and teases me, building up the endless dam. He steps in closer to my back, allowing his final inch to press up onto the trigger. I have been moaning until he hits the button, letting loose a violent scream that shoots from my mouth, allowing the heavens around us to know I just orgasmed.

Gage lets my arms fall forward so I can grab for the wall, he pulls me into his chest, one arm holding me at the waist the other across my chest like a bear hug. In this position, my toes just graze the floor, I am totally trusting of his control by letting him hold me. His hips slow to grinding motions, using his full mass to fill the deep darkness inside of me. Again, he works me up but this time he teases me, keeping me on the edge, pulling back at just the right moment, changing the motion or direction. My moans turn to frustrated grumbles that have him chuckling behind me.

Kneeling forward, he places me back on my feet and steps away, detaching us, for what I hope is only a moment. Still behind me, he shuffles us to the next area while pulling down the zipper in the back of my dress. He picks one of the long rectangle leather couches, kicking the pillows to the floor before spreading a blanket over the cushions while shaking the pants from his body. "Come, stand before me and remove the dress. I need to see you and feel you without the restrictions," he orders.

I obey by stepping towards him, he is sitting on the edge of the couch, and I move between his legs, knowing this is what he will like. With the dress zipper, already down, I only have to slide the straps off to start the fabric tumbling into a pink pool at my feet.

Gage's nose does a dog like thing, flaring and moving seemingly on its own. "Did I hurt you?" He asks with concern.

I shake my head. "I'm a little sore but that's what you were going for," I joke.

He pulls me close to him, running his hands down my stomach to my hipbones. "You're sure, I can smell blood."

"Well, this conversation just got weird." I start to laugh but seeing his serious face, I add, "Gage, I'm fine, it was a little rough, but shit, I am immortal, it's not like rough sex will kill me. If that was the case, I should have died in my backyard the first time we had sex."

He seems to think about this for a minute, then takes another sniff.

"Would you stop doing that." I push him back against the cushions while climbing on top of him. I decide it's my turn to take some control. I pull at the magical energy inside me and shoot it at him. "The clock is ticking and we haven't even christened half of this plane yet. You're slipping, Mr. Blackwood. I guess it's time for me to take over."

He shivers as the magic absorbs into him, and I feel his Mr. Happy spring forward from his hips to slap into my Ms. Excitement. "That's more like it," I giggle.

He seizes me in his arms, eyes wild with lust, his lips meet mine for a violent takeover. He seems possessed, his lips eat at my mouth, suckling my tongue, and taking my breath from me. His hands grope every curve and stroke every surface of my skin. I am stretched out with his body, which allows even his legs to be part of the entangled madness.

Everything shifts, as he swings us around with quick supernatural speed, his sudden sexual reaction is sheer animalist. I have never seen Gage this voracious, not that I am complaining. I too feel a shift, I'm a sudden jezebel, filled with a wanton need that I have no intention of fighting. I want him, need him, buried deep inside of me.

My arms, now pressed between the mounds of cushions and Gage, making it hard to maneuver my hands. I manage to wiggle them between us and down, seeking him out, hard, ready, and still slick from our earlier session. Wrapping one hand around his shaft, giving it a squeeze and half stroke, with the other hand kneading his heavy sac. He moans into my open mouth, sucking deep on my tongue with a sharp nip, I taste my own coopery blood, signaling my fangs to join in the fun.

Gage lifts his hips, breaking our kiss to look down to where my hands hold him. Beads of juice escaping the tip as I stroke him with a strong grip, his hips rotate to my rhythm, he's getting close. With a hiss, he pushes against my hand and stops. I see his Adam's apple bounce in his throat as he tries to swallow, and his heart flickers against his chest as he tries to calm himself.

His head goes up towards the ceiling, eyes closed, lips pressed firmly together, he's concentrating on pushing the orgasm down. I move my hand ever so slightly, his head snaps down, and eyes flash open; his irises have turned a deep turquoise color with very tiny pupils. His mouth opens and his husky voice whispers, "Fuck."

His obvious discomfort has me confused to my next action. I don't want to move but I oh, so, want to watch him cum. I smile with the most wicked of grins and inch my hand closer toward the head of his cock. I hear the rumble of a growl deep in his throat. I love how much I seem to be affecting him. A tiny voice sings out this sweet victory inside my head as I think about who has the control now.

It is a short-lived victory as I watch the restraint fade to wickedness on his face. The evilest of smiles breaches his lips, and I know he has regained his control. I am in for something feral.

He jumps back, away from my outstretched hands, which he pulls back up over my head, locking me into a controlled position. Nudging my legs further apart, he then lifts my left leg to rest on his right shoulder. With an eager jerk, he enters my glistening abyss with an aggressive swiftness. Even though he has worked me up to a heated need, I still feel the string of his size as he penetrates me. I hiss from his assault, pushing against him, this only makes him sink deeper into my wetness and allows his head to tickle the sweet spot.

My hiss turns into a pleasant but muffled cry on each hard thrust he takes, making my body heavy with desire. His yearning eyes watch me with keen sharpness, I'm his open book, filled with a story of passion that only needs to have its pages tickled to tell the tale. He knows with each broken pant to move at a faster pace, each moan suggests the right position has been achieved and the open, round, but void of sound mouth, means the release is near.

Gage's hair is damp and tousled around his head. Beads of sweat drip from his body to mix with my own, pooling in the dips and valleys of my curves before trickling off. I can smell our lust, thick and musky in the air as it fills my lungs on every deep inhale. He is a hot, sticky, delicious mess, and he is all mine.

The thought of me claiming Gage, has me dancing on that delightful edge, but what pushes me over is how he has possession of me too. I realize how much I enjoy Gage's hold on me as I scream out a cathartic release. We wage a war back and forth on who reigns in this relationship, almost daily, when the truth is simple. We both need to be controlled as much as we need to be in control, together we balance each other out. He is the yin to my yang.

This release is intense as it bursts forth, coating Gage's manhood with a slick cream. His rhythm changes, growing even more forceful and with purpose as he rides my hips with plunging grinds. Within seconds, his breath hitches at the start of his own release.

"F-u-c-k!" Gage draws out in a loud grunt.

That's when, the ecstasy of the release, turns into a violent excruciating pain. It explodes like a bomb blast through every nerve ending, out toward my skin and has me screaming in agony.

Moments before a blackness takes over, I wonder with fear, *what fresh hell is this.*

CHAPTER 14

I'm standing at the end of a narrow-unmarked asphalt road, surrounded by miles of barren dirt fields. I seem to be at the end of some sort of journey with only traces of old footpaths on each side of me. I try to think of what led me to this place and what I'm in search of, but nothing comes to mind.

The darkening gray sky rumbles far up in the heavens, a storm is brewing and I will surely need some shelter soon. Turning myself around, I search for options.

Behind me the road goes on for miles with no end in sight, to my left, the footpath is through an open dirt field, it too stretches out towards the horizon. Before me, lay more fields and to my right, the other footpath seems to lead to a tree line miles away that looks like it extends into a forest beyond.

Going back down the road of where I must have come from, doesn't feel like much of an option. I have obviously come down this road for a purpose, which leaves the decision of which of the two footpaths to take, and before the clouds overhead burst open on me. The problem is, which path will lead me to where I need to go?

As I stand, contemplating my next move, the wind kicks up, tossing about particles of dust and dirt, with the whirl of the air a voice carries whispering words. The wind is blowing from out of the forest on my right, but the words seem to be floating in from all around me.

"Where are you?" It asks, then answers, "I'm coming for you." The words continue on a loop reel, over and over.

I turn around in a circle, searching for who the voice belongs, hoping it will lead me to where I need to go. "Hello," I yell. "Is someone there? I'm lost and need help."

The only answer I get back is a crackle of thunder from out of the heavens. I must find safety before the nasty storm brewing dumps a whole lot of moisture over my head. I scan left and right, weighing the decision out. The forest might provide protection, but who knows what might be lurking in the depths. However, the open fields hold no safety, nor do I feel right about that direction. Some odd sixth sense is telling me not to go that route and I feel inclined to listen.

My decision is made; I turn right and take a step towards the footpath. "I'll find you, I'll come for you," the wind whispers again, stopping me from going any further.

Had coming this direction been a mistake? I look back over my shoulder, to find the other path gone, so too is the road. My mouth goes dry, realizing there is no going back. I'm trapped in this strange wasteland, and I need to figure out fast, what I'm looking for, to get out.

I head back towards the forest, which is now just a few feet ahead of me. *How'd that happened?* I have no idea, but I'm somewhat relieved that the forest will shield me from the storm.

"September, baby, wake up. Please, wake up for me," this different voice calls out to me from deep inside the forest. It's familiar and I want to run to it.

"I'm coming for you, I feel you now, soon I will find you." This is the voice in the wind, closer now.

I freeze, unsure what to do, run to what is familiar or run away from what might be hunting me. Something in the shadows of the trees moves, my heart jolts inside the cage of my ribs. "Who's there?" I ask, but the words barely come out.

A figure steps along the edge of the shadow of the forest, a tall and wider person that I assume to be male. His face is cloaked by the dark, but I can definitely see he has yellow glowing eyes. "There you are, I can feel you now. You can no longer hide from me. I'll be coming for you soon."

I bolt in the direction of the forest, the familiar voice, and away from my hunter. I'm engulfed by the forest, trees whip by me and branches hit my face, leaving a sting in their wake. On my heels is old yellow eyes, I can feel his presence so close like I haven't even moved. "You can't run, not anymore, you're one of us, I'll always find you."

I close my eyes and scream, praying for someone to help me.

"Jesus Christ, September, baby. I'm here, you're fine, calm down." Gage's sweet words sound panicked but so wonderful to my ears.

My eyes flash open to find myself still on the plane, still with Gage, but we've moved to the bedroom section down by the tail. The sick panic I just experienced has left me covered in a sheen of sweat, my heartbeat is racing, and I'm gulping for air from the run. Then I realize it could also be from the extreme pain I am in, my skin is on fire from the inside out. I had been fine seconds ago, but that was a dream and this reality is a nightmare. More screams escape my mouth when I have a chance to collect enough air.

"September, shh, baby, talk to me, tell me what's going on. Let me help you." Gage, sounds crazed from worry, and frankly, I don't blame him.

"Burning!" I shriek as my back arches from the sheer fire on my body.

Gage understands, he picks me up into his arms and rushes me into the tiny bathroom shower of the plane. This is not the way I imagined us using it, but I'm damn grateful it's here when he places me on the cool tile floor of the stall and pulls the water lever out and to the right.

I curl into the fetal position on the floor, praying the cool water trickling from the ceiling will give me some relief. The shower stall is much smaller than average, there is no room for Gage, but he never leaves my side. He sits down on the floor, outside the stall and leans into the door to stroke my hair. I grab his hand while he whispers soft words of love to help ease my pain.

Tears leak out of my eyes, making my vision blur, I'd close them except I'm too scared I'll go back to the dream and to whoever had been chasing me. Instead, I stare ahead at Gage, finding a comfort when I see his deep-blue eyes. The scorching fire within my body has started to sizzle out, either from the water or my shivering goosed flesh.

I have no idea how long I spent in the tiny square stall, in the dream, or even how much time has passed since we had finished making love. I am exhausted like I haven't slept in weeks, and my muscles ache, like I've spent the day working out at the gym. I do, however, feel relief as the burn dissipates and I'm able to finally sit up.

Gage has been clinging on to my hand as though it's his life support. I move closer to him to keep our hand connected, giving him a tired smile. "Is the burning gone?" He asks, hopeful.

I manage a nod of my head to let him know it is indeed gone. My only wish is to know what the hell it is. He gets up on a knee to reach for the lever, "You look frozen, should I turn up some heat or do you not want to chance it?"

I think that over, and decide there are worse things than being cold, "Off, please." My teeth chatter between words.

The water disappears and towels appear. Gage wraps me up after helping me to stand, then marches me back to the bedroom where he pulls back the comforter and climbs in to help me in. He sits propped up against the headboard and pillows so I can snuggle in between his legs and on top of his chest for warmth.

His arms wrap around me in a tight hold, and he begins to rock me in his arms. "Don't ever do that to me again."

A snort comes out of my mouth. "Like I had any control over it."

"I know." He kisses the top of my head before continuing, "What happened?"

I fill him in, on the burning, the dream, and the figure from the shadows that spoke to me. I have no idea what his words meant or who he could have been. Gage then lets me know I have been out for almost an hour, that my eyes, while in the shower, had been yellow again and the mark on my back, has grown down to almost my hips.

"Gage," I say through tears, "I'm scared."

I hear him hiccup as he pulls me to him in a tight hold, for a few minutes he doesn't say a word. I can hear his breathing is ragged, but it's only when a drop of water hits my cheek that I understand his silence. He's crying too.

I push up with my arms to look at his tear-streaked face. "I'm sorry, Baby," his voice cracks out.

"Why?" I ask, wondering.

"I'm supposed to protect you, but I don't even know what happened and that scares me too." His arm moves so he can wipe his hand down his face. "I'm petrified that I'm going to lose you to this craziness, and there won't be anything any of us can do to help you."

Gage's words stop me, he's right, this dream is a sign that I'm vulnerable and none of us have a clue of what's going on, or how to stop it. "We need answers, someone must know something," I almost plead.

Gage sits quietly, his brow creased as he stares at me, deep in his own thoughts. "I'll find out," he says this with certainty.

"How? The only person who might know is Magennis, and even he has no ideas."

"There has to be someone," his voice grows louder, more urgent. "I have to figure this out. Don't you see, Goddamn-it!" He's almost frantic. "I can't live in a world without you, not now, not ever. You are a part of me, you complete me."

His hold on me becomes painful, I can tell he's determined and means his words. I can also feel how scared he is. There isn't much we can do, though, until we land, which is about another hour away. We have to remain calm and I don't even dare to try to sleep. The only thing I can think to do, to keep both of us sane, is to speak the language of Gage.

Pushing myself forward to reach his lips, I kiss him hard. I need him to understand that we both need this. "What are you doing?" He mumbles against my kiss.

I lick at his bottom lip. "The only thing we can do right now, make love to me."

His eyes bug open. "You're crazy, that's what started this whole thing. Now that I think about it, it also happened the last time I was involved."

I think about that too. "Huh, that is interesting. We should test that theory." Brushing my breasts across his abs, peaking the nipples. "To be sure, of course." I wiggle my eyebrows at him.

Gage looks determined not to move a muscle, unsure of my sudden change in mood, but I feel like I've gained some sort of second wind that has me seriously wanting. I blame it on being exhausted and needing to refuel, sex and blood are what I want. Even the thought of both has me horny as hell, a flush of heat hits my intimate parts.

"Please," I purr. "I think I need to feed." Explaining to him my sudden change in behavior.

I don't wait for his answer, I'm too desperate, and begin my attack. I lean in to lick at his nipples, my hands play with his long locks, and hips dry hump his leg. When his cock bounces into my belly, I know I will have his full participation. I smile into his nipple then bite down while looking up into his eyes, there are lingering questions in the blue depths, but there is also a spark and that is all I need to start my motor.

He flips back the covers and pulls me up his torso, my legs lock into the sides at his hips like they belong there. I place my hands on his chest then guide myself back to sit upon his cock. I moan with what seems like relief as his dick pushes into me. Somewhere in the far back corner of my mind, I question what I'm doing. I feel oddly different and I'm acting crazed like I'm an addict, but my drug of choice is cock instead of crack. It reminds me of the first night of my change, but more intense. I care enough to think the thought, but not enough to think it over any further.

"Jesus, are you ever wet." His fingers stroke my wet clit rubbing the cream over the nub.

"Mmm." I whimper, rotating my pelvis in long slow bucks, feeling his inches move in and out of me.

The hand he isn't using to stroke my sex is kneading at my swollen right breast. Looking down at his fingers pinching at the nipple, I swear my tits have gained a cup size, another thought that flickers through my mind but again doesn't stay. The images and feel of our bodies together do stick in my mind, and in response a barrage of sounds and words stream out my lips.

"Yes, more, oh, harder, ummm, yes, God!" I scream and mumble out as the first orgasm hits, but it doesn't seem to satisfy and I keep pumping my hips over him.

I've been watching Gage's face when I see his nostrils flare, and a hint of something takes over his mind. He howls sharp and low like he does in wolf form, right before he kills some prey. He bolts up to reach my breast with his lips and bites hard on the nipple.

I scream, "Yes!" in pleasure as he sucks away the string.

In a flash, we are flipping, this time in a more appropriate doggie position, since we're already rutting like wild animals. I've balanced myself on the edge of the bed on hands and knees, Gage grabs my hair in a ponytail, locking me into a position he can control and he thrusts into me from behind, burying himself deep inside me. With his free hand placed over my tailbone, to keep me from falling, he uses his thumb to enter my rear.

"Stroke your pussy, make it purr," he orders.

I obey, rubbing my fingers across my puffy clit, it's sore, swollen, and sensitive. I moan.

"All you need now is a cock in your mouth, and you'd be full." His voice is a velvet growl. "Do you know how fucking sexy you are? How fucking turned on you make me?"

"Yes," I cry. "More," I beg.

He tugs at my hair, pulling my neck back. "Cum for me, Baby, cum on my dick."

I love being told to cum, him giving me permission to be greedy makes me want to eagerly obey, the dam bursts and I release another flood on him.

"That's my girl," he praises while his hips slow to ride out my convulsing waves. "That's it, I know you're not done, greedy girl, keep fucking my cock until you've had enough."

I love how his words make me tingle in all the right places, his sexy voice drives me mad, crazy, and I love how the rough tone gets me completely worked up. "You're my dirty girl, right, Baby. You want more don't you, dirty, dirty girl." He's practically making love to me with the words.

My fangs drop, I need all of him now, and I try to swing my head, but he's got a death grip hold of my hair. "Feed," I get out between pants.

His stops to turn us, he sits and pulls me down onto him, he spreads my legs and plunges himself back into my opening. As he sinks himself in, I think of what he had said earlier, how I'll be sore from our vigorous rutting, and I'll be feeling the ache later during the simplest of tasks. My muscles are screaming and other parts ache, but it's an incredible hurt.

His body, covered in sweat has coated me with his musky scent that I welcome to smell for the rest of the day. I can feel bite and bruise marks all over that will remind me, for the next few days, of this union. He has indeed claimed me today, as his own, and cared for me as his one true love. It doesn't change what I feel for the others, but he makes me see how alive I can be with him and that I too can't exist without him.

My gums begin to ache, begging for the drink. I watch his face; he is lost to me. I open my mind connection, letting him feel what I do, see my intimate thoughts before I sink my fangs into his neck to suckle from his vein. His warm blood hits my tongue and fills my mouth with the most amazing taste, woodsy and masculine. As I drink to quench my thirst he marks me as his mate, filling me with semen. The warmth of his seed heats me, spreading a fire through me, the same fire that burned me before. I jump back from him but he pushes me to his vein, the blood hits my tongue, and instantly cools the fire on my skin.

Somehow Gage figured out his blood will help. The more I drink from him, the more the burning fades to a fizzle. He continues to stroke himself in my vagina, over and over, working on the trigger deep inside. The tingle starts as the great dam breaks apart, releasing a powerful orgasm. I lick the bite closed in time for the scream to explode from my lips.

He grunts as he pushes into me as far as he can go, his hips changing into his signature stroke, signaling his own orgasm. With an urgency, he grabs my hips, pushing himself into me, balls deep, so he can fill me with his seed. I cry out in pain from the force of the action and wonder what the hell he's doing before he collapses. We end up at the edge of the bed, bodies resting on the mattress, but legs dangling off the side, still attached as we catch our breath.

I can't bring myself to move, I ache from head to toe. My breath, labored, hard to catch. My heart beats violently trying to break free from my chest, but I also feel happily satisfied.

"I do what I can," Gage mumbles into the sheets.

I forget our mind link is open, but I really don't mind, there isn't much in my head that Gage doesn't already know. Right now, I'm too out of it to care.

He rolls to my left, but not enough to pull out of me. "You'll have to give me a second before we start another round." I smile letting him see I'm somewhat joking.

"You have to be crazy if you think I can go again." He laughs back.

I touch his arm to give him a tiny spark of my magic. "I give, no more, really. I know that sounds shocking, but seriously, I think I might have sprained the bone," he says with his hands up in surrender.

I snort, "We need to mark this down, the day Gage broke his boner." This has to be a first.

"Ha, ha, as you can see I'm not laughing, but I do think I figured something out." His tone becomes more serious as he props his head on his arm to look at me.

"Let me guess, you obviously figured out that position isn't a good one."

"Nope, that position was perfect and at just the right time to."

"You're not joking, are you?" I ask, giving him my own questioning look.

He smiles. "Nope, not at all."

"Oh, I'm sensing something serious is about to be said." A sudden wave of anxious energy washes over me.

He gives me a minute to prepare then lets the words flow. "I vowed to tell you everything from this day forward, no matter what. I'm not sure how you will react to this but here goes nothing."

He pulls in a breath and begins, "I think I do have something to do with, whatever this is, that is happening to you. Your eyes went yellow just before you fed, but my blood calmed you. That gives us maybe the cause and a solution, but not the why. Not until I realized..." He stops himself.

"Until you realized, what exactly?" I press him, excited that he may have found some answers.

"You're bleeding, you're in estrous or heat. That might be why I effect you, I'm the only one that can potentially impregnate you, and to be honest, because I promised to tell you everything, I just gave it my best shot." He cringes back waiting to hear what I might do or say.

No words find me, though, I'm stunned. I'm staring at him, blinking, trying to think.

"Okay, that's not quite what I thought you'd do, but I can see the shock. I'll give you a minute."

I resemble a fish as I open and close my mouth, thinking of what to say. "I'm, and you, but I thought, oh, OH!"

There's a long moment that only the sound of the whirring engine fills. This whole thing with the yellow eyes and marks might be because I'm in heat. Heat, like a dog, that disgusts me until I really think it out. I mean, I am a dog, sort of, in the werewolf sense. I'm also human, and we have all agreed there's a possibility I can get pregnant, but now that the possibility is right in my face. I don't know how I feel about it.

I see Gage read that in my mind. "I'm sorry, I just, I'm not prepared. I thought we'd get more time or I don't know. Please don't think I'm not happy about this, I am, I think. Oh, fuck, shut me up!"

He leans over and kisses me, eating up my words so I can't make a bigger fool of myself for saying them. He lets the kiss linger then pecks at my lips in our signature three quick pecks, or as I like to think of it as our lips saying I, love, you.

"I wasn't expecting this today either, but what's done is done. I can't say I'm upset because I have wanted this for some time. It does explain both of us being extra promiscuous today, and it also might explain some of the other stuff, but not all of it."

"Like the dream," I add.

"Yes, that still worries me but we'll figure it out, all of it, I promise. I will do anything to keep you safe and hopefully, our child too."

"Our child." I swallow that down like it's a mouthful of glass. "How do we know for sure, that I'm pregnant or not?"

"Um, I'm not sure because you are human too, but for a wolf, the estrous lasts about a week, and the most fertile point is within the first forty-eight hours. I think we are in the midst of that window, and normally to be sure, a mated pair will breed several times in that first couple of days to make sure it takes."

He stops, grinding his teeth for a minute while I wait for him to continue. "We should be able to tell with one of those pregnancy tests at the end of the week."

I wait for more but nothing else comes from his mouth. "Something's bugging you, did you want to wait to have a baby?" I ask, trying to understand his mood shift.

"God no, more the opposite, I have been hoping for this, but I know you needed to want it too." His face lights up as he talks.

"Then why do you seem upset?" I probe, wondering if I want to hear more or not.

His expression darkens. "I want the baby to be mine," he says through clenched jaws.

"Um, I'm confused, I'm almost positive that it's your dick inside me right now," I joke in hopes of making him laugh.

He doesn't even budge. "We still have a day maybe two, in which to get you pregnant."

"So, we all know you are the only one that has the best shot at reproducing. Besides, Magennis is who knows where, and Sabre's home, and Chris. Oh, right Chris," I gasp, realizing my mistake.

"Yeah, that guy." Gage curses out a few choice words under his breath, but I get the meaning.

He's been wanting to mark me all day; this jealousy is because we are going to see Chris, his only real competition. "Look at it this way, we'll have a better chance with Chris around. Think about it, twice the sperm count with a fifty percent shot from both of you." I try for a tease then add, "Also, remember that I wasn't going to let you come with me today, so you wouldn't have even been part of this if I hadn't changed my mind." In my head, I also realize the reason for us butting heads lately, might be some supernatural PMS thing. I should keep that in mind for the future.

Gage growls, "Fine, but if the kid comes out with green eyes, I am not going to be happy."

"First, we don't even know if there is a kid, and second, I really think we need a shower. This talk has me feeling dirty, and not in the good way." I start to move back but Gage grabs me.

"Then you're all right with this?" His eyes burn into my face as he watches for my answer.

I blow out a breath. "We really don't have a choice now, but yeah, I think I'm good with it. We won't know until the end of the week, that will give me time to mull it through my head, but I have been thinking about it. I've never been against the idea. Long story short, yeah, I'm cool with being a mom."

Gage hiccups and I see the tears building up. "I love you so much, September."

He rolls me on top of him to get in a full body hug. "I love you too, Gage."

"You're going to be the most incredible mother."

I laugh. "How about we take it one day at a time, besides you guys haven't even got me to the altar yet, for crying out loud. Now we'll probably have to have a shotgun wedding like we're some kind of hillbilly rednecks. God, I can almost hear the banjo music now."

Gage looks at me for a minute, rolling his eyes. "Oh Baby, sometimes you're such an idiot, but you're my idiot, and that's what matters."

CHAPTER 15

We start the descent into Toronto. We've already come back to our seats after a poor attempt to clean ourselves up in the telephone-booth sized shower. No longer as anxious about our flight landing, I choose to sit alone, but within reach of Gage across the aisle. He taps away at the keys on his laptop, catching up on some business emails. I should be doing the same, but instead, I sit contemplating the last few days.

I'm getting a familiar sense of déjà vu, reminding me of how I had been introduced to this world. I don't know what it is about me and this Otherworld, but when shit happens, it hits the fan quick and crazy. Only a couple of days ago I celebrated my twenty-seventh birthday, in the mountains, on a motorcycle, happy and carefree. Now, Jesus, my brain is spinning out of control with my new reality.

Looking around the plane, I see my glass from the beginning of the flight has rolled off the table, along the floor, and is now resting halfway down the aisle, propped up between a wall and a seat. We've made a mess of the plane, pillows have been tossed, blankets thrown, and not to mention the sheets in the bedroom. It's been fun though, while it lasted, but the outcome might be life changing, in the biggest way. *I could be a mom, holy shit!*

My body presses into the back of the seat as we close in on the landing, the engine has gone from whirring to a loud whoosh noise. I pay no attention, mulling over life seems to be my new debate. In mere days, I have gone from being the Supernatural Queen, commanding a kingdom from my small corner of the world to a Queen in possible danger, from a mystery supernatural that ultimately began the destruction of my parents. Then add, some freaky unknown marks and eye color changes, that may or may not, have something to do with a werewolf version of PMS. Though this can be calmed by vigorous sex and the blood of my wolf mate, it just might cause the side effect of impregnation.

Let's not forget the imminent danger from a dream state stalker, that has me not wanting to fall asleep again, probably not a great idea for someone in a possible motherly way. And for good measure, we need to add all the small stuff in too, like my mate's newly ex-wife's father that has gone missing, this can't be a good. Oh, and don't forget that I'm extremely horny, bleeding, and without underwear. I swear there has to be something about me that attracts this weird and wacky, but I do know, I'm close to my limit with it all.

The plane hits pavement and lurches, once, twice, three times until it levels. A loud screech starts that I assume is the break being used since we slow to a normal car-like speed. During the whole landing, I feel nothing, numb, not a good sign. I think I'm suffering some sort of shock, and overload. I need a hot bath and a glass of wine, stat.

Our plane stops with another quick lurch, the engine whines down to a quiet purr then turns off, the overhead lights switch on and a steam-like hiss leaves us in a silence. My first flight has come to a dramatic completion. With a sigh, I unhook my seatbelt and stretch before standing up. Gage is already packed up, standing in the aisle with his hand ready to help me to my feet.

"You've been quiet, everything okay?" His voice is light, but I know he's concerned.

I smile at him. "Nope, not yet, but I'm optimistic."

He smiles back but doesn't laugh. "That's hopeful. Let's get you to the condo and once you've had a hot shower maybe we can figure this out."

I'm mildly frustrated when I whine, "This is supposed to be a vacation, a fun vacation."

Gage shakes his head. "Stop being so dramatic, it still is a vacation. You'll have fun, but you are also a Queen, and that means duty calls, even on vacation. Suck it up, buttercup!"

"Is that my pep talk for today?" I grumble but he's right, I am being a bit of a suck.

"One of them, but the day is still young," he jokes with a small snort.

He gets me chuckling and it makes the difference, we will figure this out, we always do. We'll call Sabre, and maybe Magennis, and we'll work it out, then we'll go shopping, because damn-it, I am getting in some retail therapy on this trip if it kills me.

Together we walk to the front of the plane where Erik is already waiting for us, "Miss September, did you have an enjoyable flight?" His glowing smile greets me.

"Yes, I think we did, Erik, and thank you for taking such good care of us." I like Erik, he's down home, and warm baked rolls, inside a big giant teddy bear body.

"Mr. Michelson asked that I take you to Mr. Blackwood's condo, I am waiting for the car service now," Erik informs us.

Gage butts in, "Not necessary Erik, I'll be driving Ms. Rae and myself to the condo."

Erik seems confused when he relies, "But Mr. Michelson has requested I stay with Ms. Rae for the duration of the day until he finishes his press junket."

"Change of plans, thank you, though. I've already made Chris aware of the situation, I imagine he'll be calling you soon." Gage seems off as he speaks and it seems odd that he used Chris's first name but then again, Gage doesn't think much of my human.

Erik looks from Gage to me. "Is this comfortable for you, Miss September?" He asks and I'm warmed by his concern.

"Yes, Mr. Blackwood can be a grump, but he can also be a gentleman. Don't worry, I'll be in good hands, Erik, you go enjoy your day." I wink at him over my stab at Gage.

Gage, however, doesn't seem nearly as amusing, when Erik goes to open the outside door to the plane he slaps my ass. The hard-unexpected sting shocks me, but sends a quick text from my lower region, letting me know other parts do like it. A warm heat spreads between my legs and I cough out a groan. Jesus, I am a walking hormone today. I give Gage an evil stink eye in warning, but he only smirks back. He's playing with me to lighten my mood and he knows which buttons will work best.

Thankfully, the outer door opens with a squeak from the metal and I can finally get a breath of fresh air to clear my head. Erik steps aside to allow me to walk out to the platform staircase. A wall of moist hot heat meets me at the door frame. It feels like I've walked inside of a fish tank and I'm trying to breathe in the water with each wheezing breath.

Gage notices my struggle. "It's the humidity, a lot different from the dry heat we get at home. Relax and breath slower, you'll get used to it."

I try what he suggests, taking slower deep breaths, immersing myself in the wet air as I climb down the steps. By the time we reach the bottom, my body has a sheen of wetness clinging to it, I'm unsure if it's from the wet air or sweat. Either way, my first few minutes in this new place is not as enjoyable as I would have thought, and I have a feeling I'm going to be needing more showers in my future.

A few feet from the bottom steps is a black Audi with dark tinted windows, awaiting our arrival. Gage strides ahead to the driver's side in time to meet a man coming out. They speak a few words, shake hands, and the man heads off towards a building on the other side of the car. Gage throws his briefcase in the backseat of the car before he hurries around to the passenger side to open the door for me. As I settle in the car, Erik brings down our luggage and places it inside the trunk of the car. With a wave, Gage jumps into the driver's seat and cranks the air conditioning before heading off.

We exit the private hangar section of the airport onto some sort of four-lane highway, bustling with an abundance of motor-vehicles. Humanity is everywhere in this city. The mostly car traffic is heavier than what I'm used to. My city has a rush hour, but this is midmorning and already far greater than our four o'clock grind.

I notice Gage is relaxed, one hand playing the wheel like a race car pro, the other shifting gears with a smooth even transition. I know Gage comes to this city about once a month for both personal and OSU business, but seeing him drive with a confident ease proves he is just as home here as he is in our city.

I, on the other hand, am a nervous Nellie. Cars rush up and pass three lanes over, some don't even bother signaling. The aggressive nature is more than this country girl can handle. I grip the armrest and edge of my seat, even play with an imaginary break on the floor of the car with my foot. *Christ on a cracker, I won't survive a day in this steel and concrete jungle.*

I try to somewhat calm myself by enjoying my first views, I notice that everywhere around us is a bustling metropolis. Warehouses give way to shopping malls, car factories sit next to car dealerships, suburbia spreads like a disease everywhere in between. There's no end to how far this city stretches and I'm already missing my mountain views and sprawling forest.

Gage slides over a lane to an exit announcing some expressway. He shifts into the curve then speeds off the ramp, merging into another packed roadway, this one only two lanes, which causes, even more congestion. Our surroundings also change, from warehouse industrial to lush greenery, in a blink, we are suddenly between a wall of trees and beautiful brick houses. There's no transition from one to the other like the engineers ran out of room and just threw buildings in wherever they could find a spot.

I'm in awe of the whole thing, so unlike anything I have experienced before. I'm used to big open skies and flat prairies with a city somewhere in the middle, with much room to grow and roam. I wonder how the subs can exist in this place, with no real room to run, and the hunting limited to squirrels and birds. Magic users won't have much of an Earth element with so much cement and steel. Though I can see the vamps doing well, with so many people everywhere, a snack would be easy to find.

We come into a more open area, up and over a bridge, there before me, stands the skyscraper world of Toronto. I see the famous CN tower, looking down from a yellow hazed sky, not the picture-perfect postcard view I hoped for.

To my right, out as far as I can see, the sun sparkles off the murky waters of Lake Ontario, one of the many great lakes. Again, I think of home and our small man-made reservoirs, valleys flooded out for agricultural purposes, puddles in comparison to this vast mass of water. There is no end to it, stretching out for miles, and not a boat in sight. *How can no one be enjoying such a gift?* With all these people around, surely someone owns a boat.

As if in answer to my question we pass an area with a dock, lined with boats of all sizes and shapes, the tops closed up with no one in sight. Somehow, that seems sad, to have such a luxury at your front door, but obviously, no time to enjoy it. Instead, everyone speeds along the great roads, rushing from one place to the next, oblivious to what jewels they have in front of them.

I look at Gage, still relaxed at the wheel. "Do you like it here?" I ask out of curiosity.

Not taking his eyes from the madness of the road, he smiles. "Um, yeah, I guess I do, why do you ask?"

"It seems so crowded; how do you find a moment of peace?"

He laughs, "You don't, not really, at least in the city. Some people have cottages, though, up north that they run to every weekend." He shifts the car and slows us to a crawl on top of another bridge.

Large high-rise apartment buildings encase us on either side, we are in the heart of the city. "I think they have it backward, they should live at the cottage and come to the city on occasion."

Gage shrugs, "Not really possible, cottage country is at least two hours away, and the jobs are in the city, that's a long drive every day."

"I think these people have their priorities messed up, I'm already missing our backyard," I speak the truth.

Gage shakes his head to agree. "I understand that, after a week here, I am more than ready to come home, but I like the rush of this place from time to time, too. I guess I live in the cottage and travel to the city on occasion," he laughs.

Our car inches off the bridge onto another ramp, this one goes down beside the bridge and under to a road going into the downtown core. As we drive between shops and office buildings, the population grows as the sidewalks fill with even more people. *How is this even at all possible?* Bicycles, scooters, motorcycles and pedestrians, all moving at a rushed pace, places to go, things to do, everyone is in a hurry.

There are signs to the important tourist type places, including Chinatown and the University. Gage passes them until we come to a street named Bloor, where he hangs a right and drives another three blocks, making a left into the side of a glass four-story building. He lifts his hand to his visor to press a button in the roof of the car. A garage door, on the building, winds up and we head into the dark abyss.

My eyes adjust quick to the well-lit underground lot and I see about ten parking spots in total, half of them empty. Gage rolls to the end of the row, pulling into the empty spot beside a car with a big tarp over it. He puts the car in first gear and pushes a button to turn off the engine. "Here we are, our home away from home."

I glance out my window at the parking lot, the cars are high-end, BMW, Jaguar, even a couple that could be on a race track, not in a parking garage. I get the feeling the people living in this building might be on the Fortune 500 list.

Gage, already up and out of the car, opens my door to help me out. I've been so busy gawking; I haven't even undone my seatbelt. I move with speed, to not keep him waiting, taking his hand and lifting myself from the seat. Walking to the back of the car, he pops the trunk and takes out our bags, stacking them on top of one another to wheel them to an elevator door.

"This building used to be an old housing unit for the University. I bought it a few years back because of the prime location in the downtown core and for the history factor. I like the older buildings; they hold so much character." He explains while we wait for the elevator car to arrive.

"How many people live here?" I wonder, thinking about the size of the building.

"There are just two condos, one is mine and the other belongs to an old friend."

I look back at the parked cars in shock. "Who owns all these cars then?"

"Two are mine, the rest are his but he must be out, one of them is missing," he explains this like it's normal for a man to have several cars.

"I will never understand boys and their toys," I mutter, just as the elevator pings and the doors slide open.

"Think of it like your shoe collection, I don't understand the infatuation... No, never mind, I get that too," he chuckles. "How about this, a car to a man is about the benefits, it gets us laid."

"My vibrator does that, but you don't see me flaunting it," I say dryly.

Stepping into the waiting lift, Gage bursts out laughing, "You got me there." He pushes the bags to the side to allow us some room. "So, what you're saying is, I don't need the cars and material stuff to impress you."

Now it's my turn to laugh, "Seriously, you think that's why I'm attracted to you, because of your car and money. Wow, and I thought you knew me so well."

He pushes me into the back wall of the car, invading my space to press against me. His muscles flexing as he moves in to grab handfuls of my ass to guide me into his hips. A small gasp of air rolls out my mouth, but he catches it with his own and sucks it in along with my bottom lips. He holds me to him, his left hand securing me by the hip with the right hand, cupping down around the crack of my ass, two fingers sliding along the divide, spreading my cheeks apart until his middle finger glides over my puckered hole.

The stress of the trip, the anxiety of the day, the teasing words escape my brain, giving way to thoughts of Gage and what he will do to me next. I'm filled with an excitement and anticipation as we make out in the elevator. A hum starts in my body and spreads as the magic pulses through me. My demon nature is overjoyed with the heightened hormones, and I'm practically begging, with each moan, for him to fill me.

The elevator pings again, letting us know we reached our chosen floor. I don't remember Gage hitting a button, but then again, I'm not even sure of my name at the moment. He pulls away from my lips, a smile spreads across his mouth, showing me his straight even teeth. "No car in the world can get me as worked up as five minutes with you can, but you have to admit the luxuries are fucking awesome."

At first, I don't really hear him, my libido working overtime, but the words sink in and make me smile. "Yeah, I like fucking you in cool places."

His eyes widen and his mouth opens then shuts, turning into the biggest grin I've ever seen on his face, "Christ, a week with you like this is going to kill me, but I will die a very happy man."

I dig my hands into his long locks to pull him back to my lips, *enough talk ... more action.* I suck at his wet lips, licking my tongue across the opening to introduce it to his in a slippery duel of tongue tag. He groans pulling away,

"Baby, we have to stop, I am already late for a meeting and I fear if we continue, I may never get there. The city council will not be happy."

I let out a disappointing gruff and pout my lips. "God you're killing me, I'll be back in an hour, less if I can beat the traffic." He sounds as disappointed as I feel.

Stepping back, he takes the handle of the luggage and waves me out the door, making sure to keep his distance, much to my chagrin. I take a breath to clear away the frustration then step forward. The elevator opens into a large brightly lit foyer done in smoke gray walls and white marble tile floors. A table sits on my left before an open doorway, on it is a beautiful glass vase filled with birds of paradise flowers. The multicolor blooms have opened to fill the hall with the most amazing tropical fragrance.

At the end of the hall, on the other side of the doorway, is a wall made of natural looking glass stones. As we move closer I notice the wall shimmers from a flow of water cascading down from the ceiling and over the stones to collect in a trough at the bottom near the floor. This elegant and classy start to the condo has me wondering what the rest will look like, and worried I might break something.

We move to an archway to the main room, between two limestone columns that have me thinking of Greece, Roman gladiators and mythology. The powerful statement is a running thread through the apartment as I get my first glimpse of Gage's world. The stunning room opens into a large bright room with windowed back walls, allowing the room to glow in the afternoon light. Everything is colored in gray and white, including a baby grand piano in the center of the room.

"I didn't know you played music?" I glance at him in question, sliding towards the gleaming instrument.

He turns away like he's shy, taking the bags to a steel spiral staircase that goes up through the ceiling. "I don't play for crowds of thousands, but I know a few songs," his humble answer has me wondering if he's jealous that my human is better at something than he is. I store that little nugget of information away for a later date and move on.

"As I said, I do have a meeting, make yourself at home, I had the fridge and bar stocked, the master bedroom is on the second floor. The third is the guest rooms where the boy band has been staying, and the fourth floor is a gym, sun patio and pool area. If you need anything send me a text, and I'll check in with you after the meeting." He strolls to the piano and where I'm standing. "I won't be long, but promise me something."

"Sure, name it," I say without hesitation.

He smiles, satisfied that I am so willing to do what he asks, "Don't fall asleep until I get back."

I understand his worry as I'm on the same page, I nod my head, "Don't worry, I have no intention of it, but I might snoop, if you don't mind. This is a whole other side to you I've never seen." Waving my hand around the elegant room.

On the left side of his head, his hair is tucked behind his ear, and I see his ear tip turn red. Something about this side of him, embarrasses him. I'm determined to figure it out.

"Help yourself, it's your home, too." He gives me a hug. "I really do have to go, please don't fall asleep," he warns one last time before giving me three quick kisses then rushes back through the door and the waiting elevator.

As he leaves my mood shifts, as his presence leaves, so too, does my heightened sexual emotions. All that's left is my excitement to explore. I turn, wondering where to start first. Gage mentioned the master bedroom on the second floor, which also means a master bathroom. I want a shower in the most desperate way, and hopefully, I'll find something of Gage's to put on.

With my decision made, I head over to the staircase to collect our bags, each weighing next to nothing, and I'm grateful for packing light. The stairs remind me of the ones at the hotel, black rod iron with mesh see-through grate steps. The only difference to these are, the steps are smaller and the circle is a lot tighter, which leads to me being dizzy by the time I reach the second floor. I can't imagine doing it drunk or in a hurry.

The iron bars keep going up with openings at each level, I get off the spiral ride at the appropriate second level. The staircase sits in between a spacious office and a media viewing area. The office, on the right, has a large antique dark wood desk and matching ornate chair, like a throne. The back wall is lined with shelves that hold volumes of old and new textbooks from medical to law, and everything in between. Including some wood carvings, of naked bodies in different entwined sexual positions. This discovery does not shock me; I am after all inside Gage's home.

On the left of the staircase, the wall of windows continues and in the center of them, a double door can be opened out onto a patio. I notice the windows have an opaque coating to keep prying eyes from seeing inside this building from the one across the way. The furniture in the room, simple and casual, but yet, quite elegant. A white canvas material covers oversized puffy cushions, with black rope like ties on the armrests that make the couch appear as though it can be closed up like a sack.

On the wall, a big plasma screen sits like a picture over the built-in fireplace. There's a gray wood panel decorating the walls, but no other knickknacks or pictures fill the space. I find it odd that everything appears so clean, sterile even. It has the feel of a show home, staged to look just right for entertaining, not living. This shows someone of a wealthier background, with great taste but void of emotion, not the Gage I know, but the Gage I have heard stories of. I wonder if he entertains a lot in this space, showing women of a higher class a good time. I immediately flush that thought from my head before it drives me insane with jealousy.

I carry on in my search, moving forward from the staircase to a short hall. On the right are two doors, the first opens to a standard laundry room, the second is a simple bathroom. This one doesn't give me the impression it belongs to a master en suite since the two bedrooms across the hall are void of furniture. This means the room I want must be on the other side of the staircase.

I head back, pulling the luggage down the marble tiles, past the media room to an offset doorway. No door hangs from the opening, instead, the walls on either side create a maze opening. Entering the zigzag, I come out at a short flat wall, to the left is the bathroom and on the right the bedroom, I take the right direction out of curiosity.

The white marble floor carries forward into the room, a light gray throw rug adorns the center with a low king size bed at the top side of the carpet. The bed takes up the back wall, behind it the gray panel is cut out to create a headboard with shelving, and above the shelves is a large mirror, tilted down towards the bed. Only Gage would think of having a viewing screen above the bed.

On the adjacent gray panel, wall is another plasma television above another insert fireplace. The glass wall in between, looks out at the park across the street, from a well-furnished patio. This leaves the wall behind me, which opens into a square walk-in closet connecting to the bathroom. There's a simplistic feel to this room too, no decoration except a framed picture on a table at the right side of the bed. I move to the bed to see who is in the picture, happy to find it's one Gage has taken of me. I smile at the sentiment, considering the lack of personal things so far in the apartment, this one small token speaks volumes.

Setting down the frame, I turn back to the closet. More than the average sized walk-in, it reminds me of the dream I had only a few nights ago. The back and two side walls have rods, shelves, and drawers for clothes, and on the bottom, are many racks for shoes, a whole lot of shoes. In the middle of the room is an island with a gray granite top, and more drawers and cupboards surrounding the sides with beautiful wood cabinet doors and copper handles. With so much space, I'm shocked at how little hangs in the closet. The left side is all menswear, mostly suits and dress shoes, on the right is a small selection of female wears.

Setting the luggage by the door, I'm a moth to this light, heading straight for the silk, satin, and leather fabrics. My little green monster rising, as I rip the articles from the rack to check the size, popping the tags from the lining of a dress, a pair of pants, with each one comes price tags. Upon further inspection of every last piece, I find the same thing over and over, all of it is in my size and brand new. I'm feeling silly for thinking otherwise, and thankful to have no one witness this mild freak out. Of course, I mentally blame my hormones, and only hope this is not a sign of a week full of similar outbursts.

Counting to ten with slow even breaths, I make my way to the doorway into the bathroom and the anticipated shower. My first glance is more than I expect. Sure, the apartment so far has elegant flare everywhere, but this room, I feel like I died and have gone to luxury heaven. The long, but wide room, has the same gray panel and white marble, the wall on the left has two sink units, connected by yet another fireplace and television. *Who needs that much channel surfing in their life?* Thinking about it, in the last eight months, Gage has almost never watched a television. It seems odd for him to have so many in this space.

The mother load of this room, is the right side, starting with a shower about the size of the closet. My men love their showers and love to have an abundance of knobs and buttons in them, this one is no different. A floor to ceiling glass door shows a wraparound bench with nozzles at every angle, and buttons or levers to turn them to life. Even the floor and ceiling have tiles in them that shoot or propel water, I can't wait to try them all out.

I sidestep to the middle of the room beside the shower stall, to a giant oval freestanding porcelain tub. The tub itself has more than enough room for two. The best feature, though, similar to the front foyer, is another stone wall with cascading water. To be surrounded by the warmth of a bath, in front of a roaring fire, listening to the sounds of a trickling stream, that's a wonderful slice of heaven.

I debate between the shower and tub, both have equal perks, but in the end, the relaxation of the tub wins me over. I turn on the taps and go in search of bath oils or foams. I hit the jackpot at the farthest sink unit, it is set up with all my favorite soaps, shampoos, makeups, moisturizers, and hair products. It makes me laugh, I spent so much time stressing about what to bring and in the end, I needed nothing. My men take care of me well.

I busy myself pulling out everything I'll need while I wait for the rise of water. When the level is perfect, I shut off the tap, stripping down, and stepping into the heat of the foaming water, allowing myself to sink in to enjoy every moment of the experience. I roll up a towel and place it behind my head, leaning back against the porcelain with a deep breath. I let the day drift away as I listen to the relaxing sounds of water dance down the stones.

Finally, I am on vacation.

CHAPTER 16

An hour later, I am exfoliated, moisturized, primped, and dressed. The closet has several amazing outfits, but once I find a kick ass pair of soft leather pants, I quit searching. The pants are like a second skin as I slither into the low hip huggers. Feeling insecure about my belly, I find a thick metal and chain belt with skull-head buckle, this will take eyes away from my not so flat tummy. In one of the drawers, I dig out, a matching chainmail tank and pair it with a sexy black lace bra. I leave my hair loose to dry natural, which makes it a wild wavy mess, but with the outfit, the hairstyle is fitting.

Gage has not yet returned but he's always good on his word. While I wait, I check out the rest of the apartment. The third floor is straight forward, four bedrooms and two bathrooms where Defeat the Darkness have been staying since their arrival in the city. I don't bother going into any of the rooms as they are full of their personal stuff, and not my place to be snooping.

Instead, I check out the fourth floor, which I have a feeling I might spend most of my time. A sliding glass wall divides the outside pool, hot tub, and lounge from the inside gym, wet bar, and social area. With all the sun shining in, I'm excited to spend some time around the pool to work on my tan lines. My mood has switched again, now upbeat with the possibility of seeing what this city has to offer.

I don't spend long on the fourth floor; I will enjoy it later. I go back down the staircase to the main level, confirming that when you go fast, you end up dizzy. I giggle to myself while clinging to the bottom handrail; I like to try things at least once, even if they are silly.

Once my eyes have adjusted from the spinning, I wander around the main floor. In the back along the wall by the glass windows, is a bar with a beautiful view from the patio. I can see large elegant parties taking place here, with plenty of room for mingling. There is also a den behind the bar where I can see myself curling up with a book by the fire.

I step out to a patio off the enormous kitchen, to finally see the views from the main level, when I hear muffled voices and then someone calling my name.

"September, you here?" The smoky voice is familiar, but I haven't heard it in a couple of months.

I twirl back towards the windows at the bar, seeing Alex and Samuel walk by, on the way to the kitchen. I take more steps to see Phoenix behind the bar fixing himself a drink. Then I see him, my rockstar, instantly my heartbeat accelerates, my palms get clammy as Chris, swaggers out through the door. His gorgeous face is lit with a smile to greet me, I squeal like an idiot as I run. I leap into his open arms for a great big bear hug.

He swings me around laughing. "You, Kitten, are a sight for sore, tired eyes." His smooth velvet voice slithers in my ear, I shiver with delight.

"I missed you too." My own voice shaking from my excitement.

He continues to hug me but moves his head to find my lips. I welcome his embrace, especially the kiss, it has been far too long since our last visit. Sometimes I have a hard time remembering the small details about him, like the way his goatee tickles my chin as his warm lips dance across mine, or how he always has a hinted taste of herbs and liquor on his tongue.

His body, thinner than my other men but toned against mine, and strong from many nights of strumming guitar on stage. His calloused fingers, rough on my skin; I've missed the way they feel, but glad to have them sliding down my back to settle on my ass so he can hold me to him. I wrap myself around his waist; surprised my leather pants are soft enough to allow the stretch. This moment with him has been worth suffering through the rest of the shit of the day, and I don't care if we're in a mansion or a tour bus, I finally feel whole again having him with me.

Chris became part of my court after the crazy night with the members of the vampire council. At the time, I didn't have full control over my different magic's and needed an extra feeding because Gage, Sabre, and Magennis had been too weakened to provide. Chris stepped up, a brave response for a mere human, but he proved that night he was more than worthy. By taking his blood, I made him part of my court, forever bound to me, which makes it difficult when he's always on the road. It feels like a part of me is out there with him, missing.

Since Chris is human, I lengthen his life with every feeding I receive, but we don't know how many extra years he will gain. Over the months, I've tried not to take from him at all. He is a famous rockstar, people will notice if he never ages, and I have left it up to him to make the choice. At any point, if he wishes, I will make him one of us, by letting him drink from me, he'd go into transition, and finally be mine forever. Not something easily decided upon, and I'll never push him into it.

I never realize how much I crave him, though, until a moment like now, when we've been reunited and today, my body is working in overdrive. The craving desire to have him deep inside me is overwhelming and my body reacts on its own accord. My magic flares, it ripples out of me like a wild storm, I gasp as it overpowers my senses.

I grab at handfuls of Chris's shoulder length curls, pulling him into me with a rough force to melt our lips and taste our need. My legs pull him into my hips to bridge the gap at our most intimate connection. His body mimics mine, his hands entangle in my hair, his legs moving us forward to brace me up against the balcony railing, we are like a couple of lustful teenagers rutting each other.

My lower parts start to chaff in all the wrong ways. My damn leather pants causing a heated friction, I want to stop but the urge is too strong. Chris pulls at my hair to get me to move away. "God, Kitten, what's gotten into you?" His breath comes out in heavy gasps. "I know it's been awhile but shit, this kind of hurts."

I try to pull him back to me, using his hair, but while I tug I hear his words and they freeze me in my tracks. Chris isn't like the others, I can hurt him, even break him. I slide off his hips, standing on my feet to move away from him. "Sorry, I'm not really myself today."

Still holding my hair, but no longer pulling on it, he grins. "No need to apologize, I like that you miss me, but sometimes I forget how strong you can be. I think my dick got blistered." He shifts his hips to adjust himself with a pained expression.

"Should I kiss it better?" I bite my lip and bat my eyelashes.

"God damn, Gage told me what's going on, but I didn't expect, well, shit, you're fucking horny!" He steps back unsure of how to handle the situation. "Even more than usual."

"Mmm, very," I purr.

I see him think this over, debating his next move. I try to help him along, cupping his obvious erection, giving him a squeeze. "No, no, we need to switch up here, get you going in another direction." He takes my hand from his groin and places it on the railing behind me. "I have the day planned for us anyway, this might be what you need, out in public, although, that might not be such a good idea either." He seems to be thinking more out loud than speaking to me.

He thinks these words over too then adds, "Yeah, that's the best plan right now, we can come back to this later when I get some backup."

His reference to having Gage help him later has that crazed heat bubble up inside me again. Many flashes of Chris and Gage, in different positions, pleasuring me, has me going out of my mind. My succubus nature always craves sex, but I've been able to function like a normal being. This new feeling is altogether different and seems to be getting worse as the day progresses, I'm unsure of myself. *Can I keep it together or will I suddenly be dancing naked through the streets of Toronto, looking to spread my legs for any willing male? I have to get a grip.*

I turn away from Chris and focus on the park across the street, if I can't see him, then maybe I can clear my mind. I take deep breaths, calming myself, and try to remember my earlier thoughts of exploring the city. It takes some doing before the burning need between my legs starts to fade. Chris stays behind me, but not too close, and he remains quiet, he seems to sense that I need the space and I'm thankful he's an observant kind of guy.

It takes me a few more minutes before I mentally have this new part of me wrestled to the ground. I take one last cleansing breath before turning back towards him, "So what do you have planned?" I ask, my voice somewhat husky sounding, but controlled.

His eyes travel over me, assessing that I have a grip before his face lights up and a big smile spreads out, stretching his goatee. "It's a surprise."

My heightened sensitivity to emotions has my mood shifting with his. "That sounds fun!" I cheer.

Lifting his hand up, hesitating for a second before entwining it with mine, he glances down at my face, checking to see if I'm on the same page or if I flipped again. He seems satisfied and pulls me to the open balcony door. "Samuel, we're heading out, hurry up," he calls out.

Samuel, the drummer of Defeat the Darkness, comes strolling out of the kitchen, half a sandwich in one hand, beer in the other. "That was quick, I didn't even finish my sandwich. You do know you have to get the chick off too, right?"

"Fuck off, Sam," Chris barks back. I can't quite tell if he's playing or annoyed.

"Hey, Foxy Lady!" Samuel catcalls out to me as we head out to the foyer. "If he can't take care of you, I'm in the second bedroom on the right, call on me anytime."

I giggle but Chris answers, "Dude, trust me, you can't handle her, she'll eat you alive."

I turn to wink at Samuel. "It would be a good way to die."

Samuel places his empty bottle on the front foyer table. "It sure would," he roars, as Chris holds the door for the elevator.

The three of us enter the square box, Chris hits the button for the main floor below and steps back beside me, but giving me some distance. Samuel leans back into the small front corner beside the door. "So, Queenie, what's going on in the paranormal realm? Still kicking ass and taking names?" Samuel jokes.

I laugh but don't get a chance to answer when the door opens for us at the main level. A security guard is sitting behind a beautiful stone desk and Samuel gives the big man a head nod as he passes, while Chris speaks to him, "Hey James, we're going sightseeing, we'll be back in a few hours."

The burly man, James, looks me up and down then glances at his desk for a minute, seeming satisfied with something he says, "I'll let Mr. Blackwood know you are out with Ms. Rae." As an afterthought, he adds, "Have a pleasant time." This time he smiles, but it looks awkward like maybe he doesn't do it often.

As we exit out to the street, I have a thought, when big Jim had looked at his desk, he must have glanced at a picture of me to know my name. His demeanor changed in that instant, which must mean Gage set up security, in advance to my arrival and warned them to be cordial. It never stops surprising me and continues to warm my heart, at how well my men take care of me. Even now, walking down the quiet street, I sense Chris has asked Samuel to come with us, to help keep me safe. They have both taken up guard at my sides, keeping close and somewhat alert to our surroundings.

Our walk takes us east down the street, it is quiet at first, both with the three of us and the foot traffic around us. It gives me time to play tourist, taking in the large skyscrapers, the big tower to our right, and the quaint shops along the way. We only get a few blocks when everything starts to speed up, the shops becomes plentiful, restaurants galore, and the people crowd the streets, making it a bit claustrophobic.

We hit a main artery, a street called Younge, and head south, that's when the madness begins. Chris clutches my hand tight in his, dragging me with him as we continue around the crowds. On some street corners, there are musicians playing instruments, on others, there are people doing skits from plays, hocking jewelry, or painting art. With every step, we hit bulk groups of people, human, and subs, from all walks of life, it amazes me to see such diversity. Not that my own city isn't diverse, just not on the same scale, this is larger than life and in my face at every turn.

I keep bumping into people when Chris isn't tugging at my hand. He blends in with the crowd, going with the flow like he knows the unwritten street code, that I don't get. Samuel stays behind us, chattering away at pedestrians he passes, completely at ease with the world around him. Both Sam and Chris have put on dark sunglasses and hoodie jackets to hide their identity and it seems to be working, not one person looks at them with recognition, but they blend with half the crowd.

We have traveled a fair distance, the heat of the sun burning down on us as we go, making my skin stick to the leather pants. The discomfort doesn't stop there, with this number of people at such close range, my emotions flip all over the place. Most of the emotions are easy to dismiss, just everyday stuff, but when we pass a person that checks us out I get hints of lust, flickering the heat inside of me. I stop a couple of times when the heated need becomes almost painful. Every time we stop, Chris backs me into a wall of a storefront, and let go of my hand to break our connection until I get a hold of myself.

"I should have taken Gage's car," Chris says at one stop, in front of a coffee shop, his brow pinched in worry.

"It wouldn't be so bad if you two weren't so damn sexy." I try to joke to ease his mind.

Samuel picks up on my joke. "What can I say, I'm sexy and you know it."

We keep the conversation going with the same light humor as we cross the street at Wellesley and head east again. Getting off the main route and onto a less crowded one, seems to provide some relief. We hike another few blocks before turning south down Church. Finally, we stop at a storefront with plenty of stickers and colored posters plastering the door, but no noticeable name to give any indication to what is on the other side.

"Ready?" Chris asks while bouncing on his toes, he's excited.

"I'm not sure, what is this place?" I ask, with apprehensive.

Samuel goes to the door, turning back at me to say, "What's the matter, Queenie, are you chicken? Come on, step out of that secure bubble for a minute and live a little. Have some fun with the boys for a change."

His tease hits a cord, he's kind of right, I do live in a bit of a bubble, but I don't think I'm dull. I know how to have a good time. I'm annoyed, even angry by this statement. After all, this is why I've come here, to have some fun, and spend some time with Chris and his friends. Then I realize, Sam isn't being mean and I'm just overreacting, again.

I mentally shake myself to change my mood to match theirs. "Well, what are we waiting for, let's go."

The door opens into a short hallway, the only things to see are a few plaques on a beige wall. At the end of the hall, the room opens to an older wooden staircase going up. Samuel hits the steps two at a time, we climb at a much slower pace. At the top of the stairs is an empty waiting room, reminding me of a doctor's office, complete with uncomfortable plastic chairs, tables with stacks of magazines, and a greeting desk. Though the person staffing this desk doesn't look anything like a doctor's assistant, but more like a hippy.

"Hey, Darin." Samuel goes over to the ear-pierced, tattooed, and thick dread-locked man to give him a handshake, complete with knuckle bump and fist pump.

"Samuel, Chris, been a long time, good to see you," greets a smiling Darin. "What can I do for you?"

I stand back by some chairs to have a snoop about while the boys touch base with their old friend. "We came, cause this guy is getting hitched, and wants a special tat for him and his bride," Samuel explains and my head jerks up.

Flipping through some pages in a book, Darin says, "Sure, but it will have to wait until I finish up with my next appointment."

Chris turns back at me and with a wink he explains, "We are the next appointment, it's under September Rae, I had to use my fiancé's name so your staff wouldn't call the paparazzi on us."

"Wait, what?" I blurt, "You brought me here for a tattoo?" I stare at him, trying to understand.

"Where else did you think we'd take you, Queenie, a spa? Come on, it will be a cakewalk, especially for a tough chick like you."

I ignore Samuel's ribbing and continue to stare down Chris. He rushes over, bringing me back towards the staircase as Samuel tells Darin we probably need a minute to work out a tiff. I'm about to have a major tiff all over both these guys.

Chris moves us out of view of the other two men and begins to explain in a whisper, "I didn't mean to upset you, September. This is supposed to be a gift, between the two of us, something that says we belong to each other like you have with the others."

I catch on quick, "You mean the paw marks?" I ask, understanding what he's getting at.

"Yeah, I thought maybe we could get our own mark, something they wouldn't have, and the only way to do it is with a tattoo." His green eyes shining with hope.

Sabre had told me Chris adored me, and until now, I haven't really considered how much. I had been ready to let him go, thinking he would be better off, happier without our drama. Since I don't see him every day, it's easy to forget he has similar feelings as the others, and I realize I adore him too.

As far as the mark, I consider it a curse for the men, bonding them to me for all eternity. They have proven to me they don't see it that way, and now Chris is doing the same. As much as I have mentally fought to understand my world, I am still learning and the one thing that always comes back to me is, love has no boundaries. With love, we all have a common ground and will do anything to keep it.

Chris waits patiently for me to make my decision, as one thinker to another he understands my need to work stuff out in my head, *if he only knew the half of it.* "All right, what did you have in mind?"

Chris explodes, "Yea-haw!" He shouts while he picks me up in another of his bear hugs, but lets me go quickly so he doesn't flip my turned-on switch. God only knows, what a complicated creature I can be, but I'm thankful my men seem to get most of it.

Chris grabs my hand and hauls me back into the shop, where we spend the next few hours in the chair, while Darin gives us our special marks. Chris's thought behind the tattoos comes from him wanting something special for just us, personal, but also showing our bond as a couple. Since I already have a ring from Sabre to show my engagement,

Chris thought the tattoo should be placed on the same finger, to indicate that he's an equal in the group of men.

The design is simple, a Queen and King of hearts, like the playing cards. Chris explained that he is a King of rock music, at least I have always thought him as such and he's also the human sovereign in my court. I am, of course, the Queen to the Supernatural, but also his little rocker Queen, and the heart is simple, it's for our love. I think the idea is brilliant and can't wait to show it off. Even after I'm almost brought to tears by the surprising sting of the application. I can't imagine how painful the wolf tattoo Chris has on his shoulder must have been, or any of the other twenty colorful images he has on various parts of his body.

The tattoo gun is more like a sander, it scrapes along the skin, making me think Darin is trying to rip my flesh apart. I hiss, jump and fidget after every dipping of the needle to ink. "Squirm much, Queenie," Samuel mutters to me.

"Dude, zip it," Chris scolds his friend.

Darin laughs, "Don't worry, September, these two cried like a couple of babies last time I inked them. Though, I'm wondering if I'm hurting you since you have experience and all."

I look at Darin confused. "I'm sorry, but I don't have experience."

Now it's Darin's turn to stop and look at me with confusion. "The tat on your back, or is that fake?"

Oh, that, now I get it, he's referring to my marks, but how can I tell him how I got them... not without looking like I belong in a mental hospital. Instead of trying to lie, I look to Chris for help. Judging by his expression, he's searching for a believable story too.

Thankfully, it's Samuel that comes to our rescue, "Queenie doesn't remember much about those, we took her into Van one weekend and got shit-faced. Next morning, we all woke up with some pretty questionable memories, if you get what I mean." He winks at Darin like there's more to the story, in a kinky way.

Darin appears satisfied with the lie if his grin means anything. He turns back to me, "If you can survive a weekend with these boys, then you're all right in my books." He goes back to drilling into my finger with his gun, keeping up a steady flow of chatter while he finishes the detailing of my new tattoo.

The boys chat, about parties of the past, girls they bedded, crazy stunts they pulled on and off stage as Chris and I switch seats. While Darin is getting to work on Chris's tattoo, I realize he knows quite a bit about his clients, which opens me up to a whole other world. One of adventure with a rock band, and the people they meet along the way. It is a different side to Chris, a wilder side that creates questions, for me that is a never-ending problem, but I let them go. Quietly sitting to admire my new ink and to take in as much as I can, to learn more about my rockstar.

My Rockstar, who is confident, relaxed, and comfortable as he kibitzes. He laughs freely with every ribbing and it's infectious, soon we're all holding our sides from the comical stories Chris and Samuel describe. Chris is animated and full of personality; he loves to have fun and he loves being with people that enjoy a good time.

I appreciate learning new things about my men, with a cornucopia of personalities, the knowledge is endless. I wonder how they don't clash more as they are all so contrasting. Yet, as Chris takes my hand to play with my bandaged finger in the middle of another tale, I realize it is through their shared affection for me, they work out their differences and keep a civil manner towards each other. It makes me smile, if not for our connection these four, Magennis, Chris, Gage, and Sabre, would never have become friends, and they'd never have felt the close connection of having someone at their backs through thick and thin. It's moments like this that ease my doubt of our polyamory relationship, without our connection I wouldn't be the strong person I am now, and I'm not the only one that gets something out of it.

As the last of our hour ticks by, Chris and Samuel's cell phones begin to make dinging noises, the longer we sit the more frequent the chimes. Samuel's the first to dig into his pocket and check the commotion while Chris gets the finishing touches to his ink.

"Oh shit, we got a problem," Sam announces while scrolling through his phone.

"Trouble with one of your groupies?" Darin teases with a laugh.

Sam's face pales as he explains, "Ah, no, how about every social media site posting our current location."

"Quit screwing around, Sam?" Chris snaps.

"No, for real man, there is a Twitter feed going with hashtags. There are a couple hundred people talking about either being out front or on the way." Samuel turns his phone screen to Chris for confirmation.

Chris digs into his jeans for his own phone, scrolling through the feeds, his face pinches up in worry with each thumb flick to reveal more posts. "Kitten, you got anything on your end?"

I reach in my back pocket for my phone, touching the screen to wake it, I have one new text but no other activity. I touch the text app to read a message from Gage, saying he's running late at the meeting and to enjoy my day.

"Just a message from Gage. I take it your fans have no idea I'm with you," I answer.

Chris nods his head, placing his phone back in a pocket. "D, you got a back door to this place? We got to split."

Darin jumps out of his chair to go to a window, looking out over the street below. "Downstairs, other end of the hall from the front is a door leading to the dumpsters in the alley. So far it looks clear, need me to run interference for you?"

Samuel's fingers are flying over his phone keypad and he doesn't look up to answer, "Na, thanks my man, but I got a plan." He stops typing, turning to look at Chris. "The boys are on the way, they should be here in fifteen. You take September out the back way, go south, towards the lake. We'll head off the herd so you can make a break for it."

Chris turns to me, I can see his hamster wheel going full speed. "Can you run?" He asks with a nod at my heels.

I glance at my platform shoes, comfortable for walking, but not so much for a hard pounding run. "Not really, but I think I got my own idea." I give the boys a wicked grin.

"That smile tells me Queenie has a backup plan," Sam replies with his own grin. "Should I even ask?"

With Darin in the room, I can't say much but I can say just enough for the boys to understand. "You could say I'm a wizard with escape plans." I wink at Chris.

He shakes his head in understanding then turns to Sam, "I think we got a plan." He fishes out his wallet, pulling out cash to pay Darin for the tattoos. "Thanks, D, great work as always. Sorry, we got to bail on you, but we'll be at the Shoe later for drinks if you can make it."

The money and handshakes are exchanged, "How can I pass that up, it's already looking like a gong show?" Darin laughs out.

"True dat," Sam agrees while giving Darin his own fist-bump handshake. "You haven't partied until you partied like a rockstar."

Chris takes my bandaged hand in his own and leads us to the staircase. "Later D," he yells back and we hit the stairs.

At the bottom, we all turn into the hall away from the front door, but stop before the exit to the alley. "Are Phoenix and Alex close?" Chris questions Sam.

Samuel works his phone again, tapping out a message and waiting for the response. "They just turned down Church."

I'm up against the alley door, Chris and Sam blocking me in. "Okay Kitten, we have to get you out of here before your picture is splashed all over the media, and Gage kills me for drawing attention to you. Whatever you have planned, now would be a good time to do it."

"Work your voodoo, Queenie," Sam adds with a wink before stepping back to check the hall. "We're clear."

I reach for both of Chris's hands with my own, I sense his nervousness and give them a squeeze to let him know I got this, "This shouldn't hurt, but you will feel a tingle."

"Damn, why does he get all the fun." Sam snickers over his shoulder, still blocking our view to the front door.

Ignoring Samuel's ribbing, I take a deep breath and let it out slow to ground myself. I have practiced this spell with Lilith a number of times and know with confidence I can pull it off for myself, but I've never done it with another person before.

I close my eyes to concentrate, digging deep into the magical part of my mind, feeling the heavy reserves I have stored away. I mentally search out a ley line and ground myself to the Earth's magic. Toronto, like Calgary, is covered in ley lines. Before the ice age, this area was part of the Laurentian River that flowed from Lake Superior to Lake Huron. Since then, the area has dried up and created separate Great Lakes, but the aquifers are still very active, deep in the Earth's core. These are what provide the ley lines for us magical subs to tap into.

Tapping into a ley line is like what I imagine would be connecting into a party phone line back in the day. Many magical feelings from different magical creatures cause a buzz of activity, like hundreds of hummingbird wings buzzing in the back of my mind. The magic connection is strong but foreign, much like Toronto is to me from my home.

Once connected, I allow myself to become comfortable with the flow of energy before creating the spell in my head. This spell will be similar to a cover spell, but instead of completely hiding us from the public eye, it will create a type of blurred costume that will allow us to blend into the crowds of people. We'll appear as an average couple at a distance and when a human looks our way we won't register as anyone of importance.

I visualize the spell in my mind, whispering the Latin words Lilith taught me, to bring it to life. It becomes a bright ball of light in my mind that I push out of me to wrap around both Chris and myself. As I mold it to our forms, the magic tingles my skin, feeling like the pins and needles in nerves when asleep. I feel Chris's hands shake and know it's working on him as well.

The magic coats us like mud, thick and with a quick snap, like an elastic band breaking, the spell is locked in place. I open my eyes to Chris; a halo of yellow is attached to his aura and I know I have done it. Lilith will be a proud mama witch when I tell her, and that has me feeling proud of myself.

I grin from my success. "We're ready." My words sound perky because I'm giddy about my accomplishment.

Chris, however, is confused, "What did you do?"

"I created a costume for us, we should be able to walk the streets and not be recognized," I whisper back, in case Darin can hear.

"You aren't in a costume; how do we know it worked?" He asks a fair question.

I throw a glance over his shoulder at Samuel. "Sam," I say a little louder than my whisper.

Samuel turns toward us, his face switches from his normal expression to complete shock. "What the hell?"

"See it worked," I brag in a cocky tone, full of confidence. "You can't see it because you are a part of the magic. Other magical beings will be able to see through it too, which means, I hope you don't have too many witches hot for you, or we'll get busted."

"Well done, Queenie. Shit, you are one scary chick," Sam praises my work, but still has a shocked expression on his face.

"I guess we're covered," Chris decides with a nod. "Sam, you ready to feed yourself to the proverbial wolves?"

Sam hasn't taken his eyes off us, he stares until Chris asks his question. He shakes his head as if to clear it. "Yup, sure, I'm up for being the sacrificial lamb. The guys should be out there to give me a hand, I hope. Once we ditch the crowd what's the plan?"

Chris shrugs with a questioned brow turn at me. "How long will this last?"

I think over his question. "As long as I'm topped up with magic, so maybe a couple of hours then I'll need to refuel." I use air quotes on the refuel part.

"Then we need to meet with Gage, back at the apartment, so you can recharge." Chris being a smart guy, knows I'll need to feed to build my magic back up. He can normally deal with my feeding of sex and blood, but with my recent condition, he's using caution by including Gage.

"Then we'll meet you guys later for drinks, once we hook up with Gage. Do you mind staying clear until then?" He means clear of the apartment to give us privacy.

"Ah man, just when it's going to get kinky we get the boot. Why does he get all the fun?" Sam winks at me.

Chris rolls his eyes, "Dude, there's a crowd of hot and horny at the front doorstep, have at it. This one's off limits."

Sam puts his hands up in surrender as he starts to walk backward, towards the front door. "Yay, but nothing out there could ever compare to Queenie."

"Ah, Sammy, I love you too." I blow him a kiss and he mock plays dying as he catches it.

"You are such an idiot Sam, just go before the crowd figures out there's a backdoor." Chris takes my hand, giving it a squeeze. "Ready, Kitten?"

"Sure, but I think we'll be clear, and Gage will probably be a while. His text said he was stuck at his meeting."

"So, what does that mean?" Chris asks reluctantly. I sense his apprehension since I will need to refuel and Gage is running late.

"I'm thinking," I grin at him, "since we're already downtown, that maybe we make a couple of stops along the way."

He has been going for the door but stops with hand on the doorknob, groaning he says, "You want me to take you shopping?"

Running my free hand up his back. "I'll make it worth your while." Feeling a flare of heat raise up my body.

His mouth twitches while trying to hold back a smile, playing with me. "Hum, tempting, but there is really nothing you can buy that will look as good as you naked." His eyes travel down my body as he says this, and I swear, I can actually feel the heat from the glance on every inch of my body.

The heat from his stare takes my hormones from a simmer to boil in seconds, "We either go shopping or I take you here," I pant out.

Chris's eyes widen. "Shopping it is then." He pushes at the bar to open the door, pulling me through it to meet that wall of humidity. I welcome the hot muggy mess as it dampens my mood. I'm teetering on a slippery slope, and I'm not sure how much longer Chris will be able to play keep away.

CHAPTER 17

Defeat the Darkness is Chris's hard rock band with an edge. He and his mates live what they sing, the bad boys of the rock and roll world, living large and playing hard, a fantasy dream for many. The songs Chris writes, tell stories of hot women they bed, getting high, playing in clubs, and having fun. When I really stop to listen to the lyrics, I sometimes hear the pain from a lonely sadness, born from broken hearts.

The band has fun but they also work long hard hours, day in and day out. Many bands break up from a clash of personalities that don't mesh. DTD has a great mix, the right combination of attitudes, and the perfect talents to make it work. They also have a strong drive that has helped them get to the top and stay there for the last ten years. It says a lot about Chris, his drive and determination are not only for the band, but he puts the same effort into our relationship.

This afternoon with him has been a learning experience, opening my eyes to the one man I don't often get to spend time with. When we first met face to face, backstage at the concert in Calgary, I had been drawn to Chris. I often thought it was from years of obsessing over the group, like every other groupie out there, then my magic had bound us together to make that obsession stronger. Today, I realize Chris is much more than an obsession.

For the rest of the afternoon, we stroll through the busy Toronto streets, ducking into many of the local boutiques to cool off from the summer sun. We eat lousy street-vendor hotdogs, have a beer at a local pub, and laugh, at everything and nothing all the same. We talk for hours to get to know each other in the same intimate way I know Sabre or Gage, and I discover, Chris also wants a stable home and loving family. No matter how complicated or different it may be, as long as we all make it work.

I notice Chris also takes the responsibility of keeping me safe as serious as the others. He constantly checks over our shoulder, scans the street for threats or groupies like a watchdog. Never once does he let me out of his sight when he isn't holding my freshly tattooed hand, but he does keep our day as far from sexual as possible. Much to my chagrin, he plays the gentleman, for a Rock God that can get a piece of tail in a finger snap, this speaks volumes to me. I realize my love for Chris is as great as it is for my other men. There is no way I can cut the cord that binds us, not now and not ever. Our relationship might be different, but we all have a place in it and one common thread, we need each other and that is what makes us a strong unit.

As we head back towards the apartment, the late afternoon sun fades in the sky, cooling down the day. We are debating my need to have another shower, and how it can't be good for the environment when I suddenly feel an unusual magical presence. I let go of Chris's hand, swinging around to put him at my back and me in front of this new magical force. I've never felt anything like it before, a mix of the elements that seems familiar, but foreign all the same.

"What is it, September?" Chris asks from behind me, his voice drops down to a soft deep whisper.

"I'm not sure," I answer while scanning the empty street behind me. We are only a half block from the street entrance to the apartment, a quick run to safety if trouble brews.

Chris turns, I feel the flat of his back press into mine, he grabs my belt in his hands and starts guiding me backward towards our destination. "Let's get you back and find Gage."

He's playing this smart, helping me get to the apartment, and he knows if shit goes down I have a better chance of defending us than he does.

I hear the squeal of tires behind me, we stop a few meters from our building, I swing towards the sound to defend us from the new threat. I push Chris towards the door to get him out of harm's way and crouch in a fighting position. A black Audi pulls up in front of us, parking on an angle in between me and the street. The door swings open and Gage jumps out of the car, rushing to my side.

His nose crinkles with his nostrils flaring at the sides. He sniffs first the air then crouches down to the street. "What's wrong, September?"

"I'm not sure, there's a presence, it doesn't feel like any I know, and yet, it's oddly familiar like all the elements combined." I look back down the street towards the wave of magical energy.

"Is it still here?" He stands to step in front of me, protecting me.

I open up my own magic to do the sensing for me. "Yup, still there, it hasn't moved. In front of us, not more than a couple of blocks."

The front door to the apartment building opens and our security friend, James, comes out, "Problem, boss?" He asks while doing his own sniff of the air.

"Ms. Rae can feel a sub but can't identify the race." Gage's eyes are scanning everywhere, but his head is pointed in the direction of the threat.

James glances towards me with a smirk. "Sure it's a sub? Maybe Ms. Rae is confused, given her condition and all."

Gage growls in rage. Turning on James, he grabs him by the front of the shirt and slams him up against the brick building. "She is your fucking Queen, you asshole! Don't ever doubt her, and don't ever let me hear you disrespect her again!"

James is strung up, his feet dangling in midair, and his face starts turning some funky shades of purple as Gage chokes him out. "Stand down, Gage," I order in a quiet but firm tone. "We are being watched, don't show any weakness or this might become a bigger issue."

Gage drops James, not giving him a second thought, but the anger is dripping like smoking acid from his entire body. "Sorry, my Queen." His voice is deadpan and empty. "You need to get inside before whoever this is attacks."

I glare at him. "No, you need to get a grip on your temper before we go check this out."

I watch the anger spike in his eyes before his body turns away from me, facing the magical threat. Through our connection, I sense him calming himself before he answers. "As you wish, my Queen."

"Chris," I call to the open door of the building.

Chris comes forward and to my side and I instruct, "Take Gage's car to the underground parking garage, then go upstairs, and wait. We'll be back after we check this out."

Chris gives my hand a squeeze and nods his head, before he goes he looks to Gage, saying, "Take care of her." An agreed message passes between the two men before Chris follows my order, getting behind the wheel of Gage's car and driving it away.

"James, are you okay to check this out?" I ask the security guard, noticing his face has gone back to a more normal shade.

"Yes, my Queen." He bows his head to show the respect he didn't seem to think I needed before. A lesson learned the hard way is a lesson never forgotten.

Satisfied with James being onboard, I direct my question to Gage, "How should we approach this?" I speak to the back of his head while we both watch the street for any magical being.

"Anyone else in the area?" He asks for more information before making a plan.

I search out again with my magic, this time nothing comes back. "Wait," I try again, expanding my search further as Gage swings around at my word.

His face is clouded with worry. "What?" He practically begs of me.

I say nothing while I stretch my magic even further this time, reaching out towards Younge Street, and back around in a circle. "Nothing. It's gone."

"Which direction is the sub heading?" Gage presses, not understanding me.

"It's not… It or they just disappeared. One minute I felt them maybe two blocks away, and the next they are nowhere to be found." I keep trying to locate the energy I had sensed, spanning further and further with my magic to track down the being. "Nothing in ten kilometers, how is that even possible?"

Gage's face has completely changed from anger to concern and is shifting into panic. "I'm not as good with tracking magically like you, but I know nothing can move that fast. Can you search further?"

"I am, maybe twenty-five kilos, still nothing. Whoever that was has vanished."

"Demon?" I see where he's going with this question.

"Maybe, did you smell sulfur, we are close enough."

He shakes his head, "If someone summoned it inside a building, we won't be able to smell it."

My magic has pushed out to about fifty kilos, and still there is no trace of the magical creature. "I've never met another demon, other than Andras, and I know he doesn't feel like that ... but I guess it could be a demon." I continue to push my magic hard, as far as I can get it to go, covering a few hundred kilometers. I sense hundreds of subs, from every race, except the one I am searching for. I max myself out, digging deep into my stored reserves and blast it forward, and with a slap like a mental backhand, it comes shooting back at me.

"Oaf!" I scream from the backlash. A fierce pain hits my head before I fall to the concrete.

"Ms. Rae," James calls from behind me, making Gage move in a cat like flip.

"Jesus Christ," he swears, falling to his knees to check me over. "September, talk to me."

My head spins from the magical head punch and the collision with the hard surface. I close my eyes, trying to make the buildings stop dancing in my vision. This does not go over well with my stomach, it does a flip and a roll, churning the bile before shooting it up and out my mouth. I don't need to see where it lands, I can tell by the swearing coming from Gage's mouth.

"Sorry," I think I whisper as the world fades around me.

The darkness has become an annoying friend as of late, one that comes for a visit, and just won't get the hint to leave. As it sucks me into its deep void, it coats me with a black inky substance. I'm numb in body, and I feel no presence of beings around me, but somehow, I know in this dark place, I am not alone.

Like my dreams before, I sense someone is with me, but before I can think much on it, a crack of light opens above me, like the inside of an egg when a chick is ready to bust into the world. The crack allows a piercing white light to shine down. With the light, I see two arms reach out to wrap around me.

"There you are. I knew I would find you, Angel." The voice is the one from my dream, this morning on the plane.

The mystery man lifts me up into the brightness, blinding me for a time as I'm brought from the dark into light. I can't struggle or move until he lays me on a soft surface. His hand sweeps a lock of my hair behind my ear, and with his fingers he caresses my cheek. It's not a sexual gesture, but it does seem intimate like we have a connection.

My squinting eyes begin to adjust to the light, around me a picture starts to form. I see the soft surface I've been placed upon, is a white sand beach that stretches out in front of me, meeting an incredible turquoise blue ocean, spanning out into forever along the horizon. I have seen travel websites for tropical paradises, but this view is pristine and perfect. A place clearly never touched by anyone except this mystery man, his own hidden island sanctuary. I'm not sure how I know that but I do.

Turning my head, I find the man standing in a comfortable pose by the shade of a tree, a few feet away. His massive size is draped by a white robe, belted then bloused at his waist, his legs from the knee down and feet are bare. "Welcome home, Angel," his smooth voice greets me.

Unlike the dream on the plane, where I felt afraid of the mystery man, this time I'm at ease. "Who are you?" I ask, pushing myself up into a seated position.

My head spins again and when I touch the back of it with my hand, I feel a large bump from where I hit it on the sidewalk. I realize I remember that, and somehow, I know I'm not dreaming this time. "Where am I?" I wonder to myself and to him.

Mystery man inches closer, allowing me to finally see his face, he looks like no one I have ever seen before, but I sense I should know him. My heart accelerates, not from fear, but from his incredibly attractive exterior. His strong chiseled Godlike features have me salivating. My fingers tingle to touch his ink black, medium-length hair, that shines almost blue in the light. I can envision his perfect plump lips brushing against my own, but my body ignites when our eyes meet. He's watching me like a predator watches its prey. I can almost see his thoughts through the deadly black windows to his soul, he is good and evil; sin and salvation all in one.

"Livia, my angel, this is home, have you no memory of it?" He speaks with confusion, but his eyes never leave mine.

He thinks I am my mother and this odd island is our home. Perhaps this is why I feel a connection to him, "I need to go back, please, my men are waiting. They will be worried about me."

He cocks his head to the side, "You may come and go as you wish, Angel, I do not control you. I only lost you for a time, but now I have you back and you will no longer need those men."

"I think you have me confused with someone else, I don't belong here, I don't even know where here is. My home is with those men and a couple of more, who, right now are probably freaking out. So, if you don't mind, give a girl a hand and shoot me back there." I stand slowly as I speak, moving away from him, preparing myself, for what? *Temptation or fight.*

"Livia, what has gone wrong? You are not yourself." He steps towards me, but I counter with another step back.

"Dude, I am not Livia, she was my mother. You got the wrong girl and I am in the wrong place. So please, I am begging you, send me back."

He halts, his head snaps up to stare at me, I'm struck with a bad feeling. "Your mother?" He says calmly, but his eyes get darker, "You are Livia's daughter? How is that possible?"

"It's a really long story," I say with a shrug, looking around for a way out.

"How?" He shouts, his fists starting to clench.

I put my hands up. "Whoa, okay. If I tell you, then will you send me back to my home?" I negotiate with him.

He growls at me, "You will tell me, now." I get the sense this is an order and I better start spilling, or this might not end well.

"I only know what I've been told and what we found in all the prophecies. Livia is my mom and David, my father; together they were the Queen and King of all the Supernatural beings. Thousands of years ago, they were kidnapped by an unknown creature named Lazarus." As I speak he stares at me, showing no emotion in his coal-black eyes. I prattle on, "He apparently wanted world domination, and couldn't do it with my parents around. I'm told that he used a black curse to make them humans so that they would suffer from hardships until death. What Lazarus didn't know, and the prophecies tell us is that as humans, my parents could have a child."

"You," he adds, then he falls back into the tree, sliding down the trunk until his ass hits the sand.

I realize he has not been a threat, he is only wanting to understand. I move towards him and the shade from the tree, sitting down to join him in the sand to finish my account of how I was born into the supernatural world. As I tell him my tale he rests his head on the side of the tree and closes his eyes. By the time I finish, I think I have put him to sleep. His breath has slowed to an even pace and he's quiet for a long while.

"There is only one problem with this story." He finally opens his eyes to look at me.

I have been watching him rest and his words make me jump. "What's that?" I ask with a squeak.

"I'm Lazarus, and I can honestly tell you, I did not try to have Livia kidnapped, killed, or otherwise."

I freeze, panic rushes through me. I slowly try to slither away from him. He moves in a blur to capture my knee with his hand. "Stop, I didn't hurt Livia, and I certainly won't hurt you," he speaks quietly, his face softens, and a small smile touches his lips.

My heart skips a few beats, and I have to shake myself to speak. "Sorry, but you have to understand my wanting to run away from you." I don't move any further, but I do remain alert, this might be a trap. I have been told Lazarus lies. "You have done some seriously evil shit to our kind."

"I've done none of what you say. Livia and I, we are the last of our kind, we were put here to keep order, between good and evil in this world of which we created. Your creatures, they have not been as saintly as you have been led to believe," he says with disdain.

"This all doesn't make sense." My head, already hurting from my fall, now has a dull ache from this new information. "Look, I don't know what the truth is, but I do know that I need to go back. My men will be worried sick about me, and if what you are telling me is the truth, I also need to call off a search party." Thinking about Magennis.

"Ah, yes, the vampire on my tail. That, was you?" He smirks.

"Yes, I'm guilty. You didn't do anything to him, did you?" I glare at him with my question.

"Of course not. I had been investigating some strange deaths in South America when I felt a magic presence. I suspected it to be Livia, calling out for me. She has been lost to me for some time." He pauses, his eyebrows pinch as some thought brushes him, for a second he appears sad.

As I watch him, I see a slight tremble in his body then his eyes meet mine and he continues, "When your vampire began to follow me last night, I noticed he was covered with your magic, though I thought it was Livia's, and the vampire one of hers. I let him follow me, knowing he would eventually go back to you. So, I led him straight there, I am sure you will see him at dark."

I nod, thankful for the news. "Wait, you said there have been many strange deaths ... We believed you killed them, then stole the powerful magic for your war. I think you need to help me here because none of this adds up," I press him for some history.

"None of this makes any sense, that I agree, but your questions will have to wait until I, myself, seek out the truth. You are right, your men will be worried, it's time for you to go back. I will come to you when I have answers." He rises to his feet, cutting off our conversation. He extends his hand to help me up. "These men of yours, they need to keep you safe. What happened to Livia," he pauses with a sigh, "If this doesn't get sorted, I fear it will happen to you as well."

I shake my head to agree and it throbs in my skull. The weight of what I have been told is heavy, and it leaves me exhausted. I rub my temples and sigh, "Send me back before I don't want to go." I'm close to happily spending the rest of my life on this beach, and not dealing with any more of this.

Lazarus puts his hand on my shoulder. "I know you don't trust me, little one, but I will figure this out to prove to you I am not the enemy."

I nod my head, "I'm not the only one needing proof, you know."

He grunts in agreement. "I have been away for far too long. I was clouded by pain, ignoring my responsibilities killed your mother, for that, I am sorry. I promise you, I will not let it happen to you. If you need sanctuary, use your magic, think of this place, and you will be here. If you need me, do the same." His words are full of sadness and I wonder why.

I'm no longer sure of much anymore. My world has just been completely changed, but I do believe Lazarus is telling me the truth. "Thank you," I tell him, "you can send me back now."

He chuckles. "I didn't bring you here, nor can I send you back. As I said, use your magic, think of where you want to be and it will happen. Now, go to your men and be safe. I will be with you soon."

He gives my shoulder a final squeeze then steps back, and stares at me for a few more seconds; that sad expression never leaving his face. He gives me one last smile, and then just vanishes. I realize this is why I couldn't locate him earlier; he has this disappearing trick and now I do too. I glance out at the ocean, wishing I could stay here a while and not have to deal with any of this, but that's not me. I don't hide from my troubles, I face them with the support of my men, men I need to get back to.

I'm excited to use this new travel tool and decide it will probably work best if I close my eyes so I can concentrate. I envision a picture of home but remember Gage will be going out of his mind for me in Toronto. I think of my tour of the apartment earlier: the elegant main rooms, the winding staircase, and the big open office, where I know Gage will be pacing the tile floor. I need to get back to him.

As suddenly as I think of his apartment, I'm there, with only a slight ripple in my magical energy to tell me it has happened. I open my eyes to find myself in the lounge across from Gage's office. Gage is indeed pacing the floor in front of his desk, shirtless and shouting like a madman into his cell phone. "I don't know where she is, she just fucking vanished. How can this even happen?"

It takes him a few seconds to feel my presence, but once he does he lets out a string of curses a sailor would be proud of, "Holy fucking fuck!" The phone drops from his hand as he comes running towards me. "September, is that you?"

He doesn't wait for me to answer, instead, he picks me up into his arms and hugs me tight to his body. "Yes, Gage, it's me," I sigh into his ear, enjoying this minute of calm before he creates a verbal storm.

"Jesus Christ, do you know how fucking crazy you made me?" He tightens his hold around my body until I can feel his heart pounding wildly against my chest.

"I'm sorry, I had no idea I could even do this until Lazarus told me." I realize my mistake seconds after I say the words.

His arms flex me into a hard squeeze, and I can barely breathe. "Did you just say, *Lazarus*?"

"Gage, please ... I can't, breathe," I puff out around his tight grip.

Sliding away from me, but keeping his hands on my shoulders, his cool-sapphire eyes burn daggers at me. I take a slow breath to prepare myself for his reaction. "I did just say Lazarus," I whisper.

The room gets so quiet; I hear Sabre swear on the other end of the phone on the floor. "Is Sabre still on the phone?"

Gage blinks, but it's the only reaction he makes before walking over to the desk, bending at the waist, he picks up the phone, "We have a situation," he calmly speaks into the phone, before pressing the button to hang it up.

He turns back towards me, not raising his head, but taking a long slow breath. "I have no words." His hands rise to his head and sweep through his hair as he drops to his knees on the floor. "I'm sorry, my Queen. I failed you."

At first, I'm unsure of what he's doing, but as I think it through I understand. I had disappeared on his watch, in front of him. Gage and Sabre take their positions seriously, and when it comes to my safety, nothing else matters or gets in the way. In Gage's mind, he failed to protect me. Usually, this would be handled with a punishment of death, and he's waiting for me to hand it to him.

I walk over to stand in front of him, debating what to do. The fact he awaits death shows his honor and courage. I place my hand on his head. "How could you ever think you failed me?" I whisper, my heart breaking with hurt for him. "We had no idea I possessed a power that makes me disappear."

I slide my fingers into his thick dark locks and drop to my own knees in front of him. "There is no blame, nor is there any fault. I'm not hurt, nor am I in danger." My hand moves down towards the side of his face where I lift his chin to look into his eyes. "How can you expect me to carry out this punishment when I don't believe you failed me? I am humbled by your honor and blown away by your courage, but until you do something really fucked up, I can't and won't be the one to take your life."

There's no panic in his eyes, he is willing to let me extinguish his pulse and I shiver at the thought. What I do see in the deep sea of blue is a man willing to die for the one soul he loves most. As much as Gage can be a pain at times, I know I will never take his life because I can't live without him. "God, I love you," I say through fresh tears.

"I love you too," he whispers back. "But, please, don't ever do that to me again."

A snorting sob comes out of my mouth, and he leans in to wrap his arms around my body. "Now that you aren't going to end my existence, can I get mad at you for scaring me shitless?" He jokes, but I detect more than a hint of seriousness.

I laugh. "If you start yelling, I will reconsider."

With a slight chuckle, he adds, "I can't make any promises."

Our hug continues for a few more minutes, giving us both time to let the severity of the moment melt away. "We will need to talk," he finally says.

He backs away bringing us both to our feet. "Sure, where's Chris? He should be included, and we can Skype in Sabre and Magennis."

Gage lets out a curse then grabs the phone. "I sent Chris downstairs to watch the block in case you reappeared." His fingers fly over his keypad as he sends Chris a text. "Sabre is on the jet; he should be here in less than an hour."

"How long have I been gone?" I wonder how long I've been missing if Sabre has already been on a plane for over three hours.

"About two hours," he mumbles while concentrating on typing.

This means Sabre had left while Chris and I were shopping. "Why is Sabre coming?"

"Well, initially I had called him after I left for my meeting. Your hormonal situation had me concerned; we both felt that him being here would probably be safer than you chewing Chris to shreds." He laughs about me taking out Chris, then composes himself when I show how not amused I am. "But then some shit went down this afternoon at the meeting that confirms I need backup ... and now this." He puts the phone on the desk and sweeps his hands through his hair again. Gage's telling tick when he is stressed.

I walk behind him to rub his shoulders. "What shit went down this afternoon?"

His head falls back, and circles around as I relieve a knot of tension in his neck. "I think the pack here is moving to challenge me for Alpha. They tried to scoop my contract with the city for a major high-rise project and the word is they don't believe the whole royal story. They want to break my business, then come after me."

"Of course they do, when it rains it pours. It wouldn't be a normal day if one of us isn't being challenged or tested," I grumble in annoyance.

Gage turns into my hips closing the gap between us, bringing us face to face. "Hey, this shit I can handle. What I can't handle is you disappearing outside and reappearing in my office two hours later, telling me you talked to Lazarus. Want to fill me in on that?"

"I do, but Lazarus also informed me that Magennis followed him here. We should probably fill him in, and while we are at it, we might as well wait on Sabre too."

"Don't forget about Lilith, she's on the plane with Sabre."

"One big happy family."

Gage grins, "Yeah, we are, aren't we?"

I kiss his nose. "Yes, we really are."

His head tilts up so he can brush his lips over mine. "I like the sound of that."

Meeting his soft kiss with my own, I stop to nibble briefly on his bottom lip. "Me too."

With just this small touch I can feel myself being drawn to him, needing him. My magic fizzles, but my reserves are low from the massive amounts I have used throughout the day, I will need to feed. Instantly, the switch in my head turns on and all I want is Gage.

His hands travel up my back and into my hair, where he plays with the strands. "So, what do we do for an hour while we wait if we aren't going to talk about what just happened?"

God only knows what will happen next, and I am not looking forward to finding out. A distraction with Gage right now will give me time to clear my mind and prepare. I smile into his kiss, "We can work on extending our family."

His fingers stop mid-glide through my hair. I watch as his eyes brighten to a shine as his palms press into my shoulder blades. The mark instantly heats from his touch and as he drags his nails down the length of my spine my entire back starts to tingle.

His wandering hands scoop down around my butt where he grips some ass cheek. His whole face lights up and his lips spread into a grin, wide across his whiskered cheeks. "Mmm, I really like the sound of that more," he groans out.

"Good, then tell me your thoughts on shower sex..." I don't finish my words before they turn into screaming giggles, when he swings me up and over his shoulder, making a quick beeline down the hall.

CHAPTER 18

The steam from the shower fogs the large bathroom up in the mere minutes it takes for Gage to strips me of my leather and lace. He's leaving crumpled piles of discarded clothes like markers on a trail, all the way to the shower. An hour isn't much time but he doesn't appear to be in a hurry, leading us into the giant misting glasshouse, and turning on most of the spray nozzles. Once he sets the stream of the spray to a warm temperature, he turns his focus on heating me up.

He gets down to business, walking us into the spray to soak our bodies, then makes quick work of washing my hair before soaping me up. His touch is gentle while massaging the suds on a cloth over every inch of my body, stopping at trigger spots along the way to tease me until I think I'm about to go mad. When he presses the cloth between my legs and works the soap into a lather over my clit, I cry out. I'm so close to a release that my downstairs aches for his penetration.

"Easy Baby, I'll take care of you." I shiver from his whispered words in my ear.

He pivots me to face the back wall, allowing the above waterfall to cascade down, taking with it the remainder of soap suds. He moves around me, spreading my legs apart and placing my hands on the wall for support. He then positions a few nozzles before turning them on and aiming the pulsating jets to hit my sensitive buttons.

"Ahh." A small squeak of joy escapes my mouth.

The intense pressure of the water's pulse provides an incredible sensation across the lower part of my ass and hits hard enough on my clit to spark the coals to a roaring flame in my basement furnace. I give into the urge to buck my hips and ride the water jet, like a cowboy on a bronco at the rodeo. Other jets are aimed, one on my left breast and another hitting slightly on my ass crack. While each jet provides stimulation and feels amazing, it doesn't hit collectively to complete the task. The spray is strong enough to keep me teased, dancing close to the edge, providing I continue to move around, but it does little in the way of pushing me into what I ultimately want, a satisfying orgasm.

"Please, oh God, please." I plead to the water and to Gage, as I wiggle my body back and forth from one jet to another, playing some kinky game of shower twister for one.

Gage sits on the long granite bench, lounging back to watch the show. His eyes blaze with a hunger and his cock grows erect as he strokes it in his hand. "You want more, Baby?"

"Yes, please," I beg while shifting to another position.

"Tell me what you want..." I can hear enjoyment in his voice.

After our day, I know Gage needs to have this control, this is how he is wired from whatever happened in his life, and I'm completely accepting of that. Another shit storm awaits us on the horizon, we both know it, and when it hits, I believe he'll let me take the wheel. It's that give and take that makes us work well together; it has just taken us a while to figure it out.

"I need you, Gage, desperately," I cry out in frustration, continuing my attempt in getting myself off, through water manipulation.

He chuckles, "Sounds bad, but not at all descriptive enough, you know how I love details, Baby."

I pound my fist up against the wall. "Damn it Gage, get over here and fuck me. Hard!" I swing my head in his direction to give my best come hither look.

He has one of those cocky smirks on his lips, he's leaning back on the bench, looking like he won't be going anywhere anytime soon. He has a bad boy confidence, and it's sexy as hell. That look does more to turn me on than all the water jets combined. My biggest turn on is turning him on and right now, the only thing I want is for him to bend me over and bang me, hard like a screen door in a hurricane.

I give up trying to get off by artificial means and slither towards him, hips swaying and hands kneading my own beasts, putting on a show to entice him. Stopping inches in front of his knees, I drop my right hand down to dip a finger into my cream, then lift it to his lips.

I bend at the waist to put my face in front of his to paint him a picture, "Taste how ready I am for you." I push my finger into his mouth and it's met by his moan. "What I need, is for you to take me hard and deep until this cream is coating your cock from my release and then, I want you to fill me so full of your seed, that it drips down my thighs." I pause to let the words sink in. "Is that descriptive enough?"

His smirk turns into a beautiful smile. "As you wish, you are my Queen, and my cock is your throne, please sit upon it."

His hand comes up to grab a fist full of my hair so he can pull me to him. Our lips collide in a hungry crash, all lips and tongue suckling, and tasting. His other hand pulls me forward to help position me over his hips where I can wrap my legs around his ass as he stands us up and pushes us against the wall. I feel the bulge of his cock head, licking at my entrance seconds before he drives up and into me in a hard thrust.

"Sssshhit," I hiss, eyes opening wide from the aggressive stretch to my sex.

He freezes. "Too much?"

"No, not enough. Give me more." My voice is husky with need.

I lick at his bottom lip and it draws back into a smile. "That's my greedy girl." His hips thrust forward, allowing in another inch.

"Yes, more," I groan. "Harder," I beg.

His firm hands squeeze my ass cheeks apart, allowing for his final inches to bury deep inside of me. I grip the long length of his hair at his neck to use as a handle, dragging him into me with every urgent thrust of his hips. My legs hug his waist, crossing over his ass, where I feel his muscles clench, and my vagina responds like a vise milking his length. My toes curl, body tense until the heat that has been burning in a low simmer, explodes, along with the blood-curdling scream from my mouth.

Instead of relief a good orgasm usually brings, a fire spreads wild through my veins, causing my fangs to drop from the scorching pain it leaves in its wake. Our mouths are still connected. I nick Gage's lip, causing him to look at me with a questioning expression that quickly turns to understanding.

"Eyes," he mumbles into my mouth.

That one word, tells me everything, my eyes have changed color again, to what, yellow, red, I don't know. Nor do I care. As he had pointed out earlier, I'm a greedy girl, for his blood to quench my thirst, and his body to satisfy the burning ache that will not go away between my legs.

"More, please Gage, I need more."

"Jesus," he swears but doesn't lose focus. He tilts his head to the side to give me access to his artery, I strike like a cobra attaching myself to his vein.

He hisses then moans as I suck with a voracious appetite, taking what I need, which includes more sex. Letting my hips do the talking for me, I wiggle them with circling strokes over his. He gets what I'm throwing down, meeting my grinds and stroking with rapid motions over the sweet spot.

My magic flares, my thirst grows, and my desire is out of control. I've never felt this alien before like someone else is driving my body. The only clear thought in my head has been my insatiable necessity for Gage: his scent on my skin, his touch on every inch of me, his taste on my lips, and his seed deep inside of me. He is all I want, and I open our connection to make sure he can read it in my mind.

"Oh God, Baby, I'm going to fill you so full," he screams and shakes as the orgasm hits him. The slick warmth it creates helps me follow him into bliss.

Gage wobbles seconds before his legs give out, we tumble down, my back scraping the tiled wall as we fall. We hit the hard floor with a whack, him on his knees and me on my butt. He reaches out to the wall, trying to balance himself, but loses the battle as he goes horizontal, water spray hitting his face.

He rolls, groaning while trying to regain himself, "I think you broke me."

I grab for the levers, shutting off the spray. "Are you okay?" I ask moving towards him to check for damage.

"Nope, I think you damn near drained the life out of me," he moans out, rolling onto his back to look at my face. "They're still yellow."

I wipe at the water around my eyes. "Is that bad?" I ask, unclear on the problem.

He laughs then coughs out, "It depends."

"It depends on what?"

A smile spreads across his lips. "It depends on whether or not you still need my cock, cause frankly, Baby, I think you sprained it." As if in response to his statement, his cock twitches then jerks forward, causing Gage groan in pain.

"I can't keep doing this," I mumble to myself. Getting up to walk to the glass door, and reach out for towels.

"Hey, the mark grew again." Gage drags himself up to a sitting position to get a better view.

I turn my head to the side to catch a glimpse of the white mark, not far from my hips. "That's it, I'm never having sex again. This is ridiculous."

"Yeah, whatever," he snorts, climbing the wall to his feet in slow motion. "Like you can stop yourself ... or us for that matter."

"Gage," I say, throwing a towel at him, "this is serious, everything is going sideways, again, and it scares me."

He lets the towel drop to grab my arm. "Hey, it's going to be okay. The guys will be here soon and we'll figure it out, we always do."

This time I run my fingers through my hair in frustration and let out a sigh. "In moments like this, I want to go back to being normal again."

He wraps his arms around my shoulders, hugging me. "Don't kid yourself, September, what's normal for the spider is chaos for the fly. Besides, that's not you, to give up, you're my fighter."

I laugh. "Says the guy that completely checked out of this world and ignored his responsibilities for years. I get why you did it, but you can't be the pot calling the kettle black, you know."

He's silent for a time, resting his chin on the top of my head. "I wish it had been that easy, I was blindfolded then, but now I see."

I step back to look at him, his eyes have clouded to an aqua-blue color. "What do you mean?"

He takes the towel from my hand to rub it across my back and arms while walking us towards the door, and back out into the bathroom. He hands me the towel to finish the job and goes for the robes.

"Gage, what's wrong, you know you can talk to me," I offer, taking the robe he is handing me.

He tosses his towel on top of my crumpled leather pants on the floor then wraps himself in white fluff before sticking his hand out for me. "Come, let's go sit," he says, guiding us back to the lounge in his office.

He motions for me to sit on the couch while he goes to the wet bar for a couple of drinks. I make myself comfortable, pulling my legs up and wrapping the puffy robe around them, waiting patiently for him. He comes back to the couch, handing me a glass of amber liquid, from the smell I know it's bourbon, one of Gage's favorites. He settles in next to me, crossing his left foot to his right knee to balance his glass, and draping his right arm across the back of the sofa around my shoulder.

Taking a sip from his drink, he lets it coat his throat before he speaks. "I want you to know, I will never do anything to hurt you or our child if we are fortunate enough to get you pregnant this week," he says with a sad smile.

"I've never doubted that, Gage." Placing my hand on his knee for comfort. "It's one of the reasons I decided to try to get pregnant, I know we can make this work and I think you'll be a wonderful father."

"I know you do, Baby," he sighs, sitting for a minute before taking a bigger gulp of his drink. "I'm going to try to be what my own father wasn't for me. He blamed me for my mother's death, she died due to complications giving birth to me."

"How was that your fault?" I ask, feeling irritation for a man I've never met.

He snorts. "It's not, but Jacob Blackwood was a righteous bastard, and when he made up his mind about something, there was no way anyone could change it."

"He sounds like a douche, what happened to him anyway?"

"I killed him." His words have no feeling or remorse.

"You, but then why is Garo Alpha?" I ask, feeling confused.

"That's what I'm trying to explain." He shifts sideways to be able to face me, his fingers absently playing with my wet hair. "My family, our pack, has been around since the continents were connected, but as wolves. After the ice age, we found ourselves on a mountain range in southwest Germany called, Schwarzwald or the Blackwood Forest.

"It is said that Livia came across the pack one day, along the French border in the West. What she found, she was impressed by, our brute strength, courage, and loyalty made her want us for her own protection. That was when she touched us with magic and created what we are today, but the adjustment had been difficult, some even felt it was a curse. Mothers that died during birth were believed to be carrying evil, and the fathers would kill the young to prevent misfortune to the pack.

Our kind was the last of the races created and not long after, your mother disappeared. The older generation, like my father, believed that when Livia eventually died as a human, the curse would be lifted; this is why my father spared me from death, but he certainly didn't spare me the cruelty of his hand." He stops to take another drink, allowing me to digest his story before he continues.

"When I was old enough, I ran and didn't look back. I searched the world for a place to fit in, and I came here, to this country, it was not easy, but I made my way. Then one day, the bastard tracked me down, he could never be happy for me, and tried everything he could to destroy what I had made for myself," he growls the last part, the words ripping open the wounds of his past.

"Garo was there the night he died, it had been an accident, but we both knew the damage my father had caused would mean no one would believe my story. I would be hunted by the pack and killed for my actions. Garo stepped up and took responsibility for what I had done, he was well liked and easily accepted as Alpha, but he couldn't do it alone; so, he made sure to remind me of what I did, quilting me into helping him." He pauses to take the last gulp of his drink to douse the hatred that spits like venom from his lips.

He turns his burning blue eyes on me. "For over one hundred years, I have lived in the shadows while my brother successfully pulls the wool over the eyes of our pack. From my own, more humble successes, I was able to bankroll our move to this land and eventually build the hotel, and the Underground, for the safety of our people. Letting Garo take all the credit while he made me out to be the slacker."

From Gage's account of his life, I understand the man beside me a lot better. I finally understand his need to be in control, his embarrassment when asked about certain things, the cover-up about his ex-wife, and the way everyone treats him.

"Why have you never told me any of this?" I ask, feeling hurt that he doesn't trust me with his story.

His eyes dart down and he shifts a few inches to the left, "I've wanted to, God, you have no idea how much, but I've been living this lie for such a long time. A part of me worried that once you knew, you'd hate me too."

I'm shocked he can think I would hate him. I move my hand to take his chin, turning it to meet my face, "Gage, when I look at you, I don't see your past or the mistakes, nor do I care."

His lips crack open a small smile, "Today, I realized I finally know what it means to let someone in, to see this side of me that no one knows, or ever will. I knew I finally needed to be honest with you because I can no longer have you thinking I am a lesser man."

"Do you think I would have chosen you if I thought you were a complete fuck up? Please, give me some credit." I tease a little before getting serious again. "I think of you as my rooted tree and I am, the blossoming leaves. We all have an unfortunate past, but I need the Gage I fell in love with to continue to help me grow, and with the others our future will become a forest."

He leans forward to brush his lips to mine in between his words. "I'd crawl across this world for you," He begins to crawl across my lap, "I'll fight for you, even give my life for you, do anything you ask me to." He presses me back into the cushioned couch, "If it means I spent the rest of my life loving you."

I sigh into his passionate kiss, his words melting my heart. This day has brought us both to a place where we need some reassurances. He has provided me that and then some.

"September, Gage, anyone home?" An untimely, but familiar shout comes from downstairs.

Gage groans at the interruption, "I think the cavalry is here." His hand has been surfing under my robe, stopping the caress of my breast with a squeeze, he adds, "I'll get back to worshipping this beauty later." He winks then shouts out a greeting to our intruder before helping me to my feet.

When I left on the plane this morning, I had been sad that I'd be leaving Sabre behind, but now an excitement fills me knowing he's only a few steps below. This day has been a start and stop of my hormones, with small adventures in between. It's hard to believe a mere sixteen hours have passed since I left my home, bound for a relaxing getaway. It has been anything but relaxing to this point.

Gage and I go to the stairs. I hit them running, circling only partway down until I crash to a halt into Sabre's hard chest. "Oaf!" I blow out.

"I missed you too, Darling." Sabre steps down one stair to regain his balance before stepping back up to give me a hard hug. "I hear I can't let you out of my sight, for trouble seems to know where to find you."

Gage comes down in behind us. "Easy Sab, this isn't September's fault and to be fair, it's been a day."

Sabre has been standing with me in a hug, his body tense. Once he sees Gage, I feel him begin to relax. "Good to see you're in one piece."

"Glad to be in one piece. Are the others with you?" Gage asks, gesturing for us to move the rest of the way down the steps.

"Eric dropped me and Lilith off, he said Chris has gone to pick up Magennis. Has he been here with you?" Sabre glances at me in question.

I shake my head, "No, I was told he came before dawn."

"Who told you?" Sabre directs this question at me but looks to Gage for help.

"Let's wait until we are all here to have a meeting so we don't have to explain everything twice," Gage offers.

Sabre seems annoyed with the answer but nods his head in understanding. We make it to the bottom of the stairs, turning into the massive entertainment room, where I search for Lilith. Of course, it's not until we move into the kitchen that we find her getting comfortable with the surroundings, a true witch. I laugh, knowing Lilith couldn't care less about the rest of the house as long as she has a kitchen.

"September!" She shouts when she sees me, leaping the length of the island to give me a hug. Thankfully, Sabre is standing behind me to brace our collision.

I respond with my own embrace, "Lilith, I'm so glad you came."

"I couldn't let Sabre come alone, he was a wreck getting on that plane. He'd never have survived the four hours without me." She steps back to wink at Sabre.

I freeze, thinking of the plane, and what I had done on it with Gage. I know Sabre will never cheat on me, especially with my friend, but I'm overly sensitive today, and my mind has no problems playing havoc. A deep growl escapes my mouth as I shoot Lilith a cold look.

Gage's arm appears between us. "Easy, September. I'm sure Lilith only bored Sabre to tears by talking his ear off about spells, or worse, fashion."

Lilith's initial reaction has been to jump back, with hands up, ready to defend herself with a spell. Then the fear in her eyes changes to annoyance, "Don't you growl at me, Missy!" She begins to scowl at me, wagging her finger in my face, "And don't give any of this hormone bullshit either, you damn well know I would never do anything inappropriate with any of your boyfriends. Now, step back and tell me how sorry you are, or I will zap you." Her fingers wiggle out a warning.

The room filled with instant tension from my growl, now it sits silent from Lilith's words. Both Sabre and Gage stand as frozen warriors, awaiting the battle of the next explosion. As Lilith's frown line pinches and her lips purse together in annoyance, I realize this isn't normal for my usual smiling friend. Her combination of lecture style comments and defensive stance, make me feel like I just got worked over by Tinkerbell.

An uncontrolled eruption of giggles escape my lips, and the surprise from them causes me to snort. I clasp a hand to my mouth, but the laughter won't stop. The events of the long day, worry about our future, my unusual emotions, and the quick riff with Lilith, sets me off. No one is prepared for this and as I giggle myself into tears while holding my sides for relief, the others join in. Before long, Lilith and I are holding each other in a happy hug, forgetting only for a minute the severity of our future.

"What the bloody hell have the lot of you been smoking this time? I swear, I can't leave you loons alone for one second," Magennis announces from the archway to the kitchen.

I have a sudden relief from hearing the heavy Irish accent. I turn to find Chris, standing with Magennis by the door. I hurry towards them, jumping into Magennis's open arms while reaching out to take Chris's hand. I'm complete again having all of my loved ones together, and I know in my heart we can deal with any situation, as long as we remain together.

"I'm glad you're back," I cry with happy tears into Magennis's neck. Chris squeezes my shoulder before walking into the kitchen to give us our moment.

Magennis squeezes me tight to his chest. "Me too, little Minx, me too."

My hands slide up his neck and find their way to his shoulder length locks. My fingers grasp the strands, and I clutch his head to bring it forward to meet my mouth, allowing our lips to melt together for a long overdue kiss. Having Magennis and Sabre back fills in the pieces of my puzzle that I haven't even realized went missing.

I want to get this reunion underway, my body tingles with the anticipation of sharing myself with all four men. The atmosphere in the room changes as quickly as my mood, a crackle of energy that calls my men to me.

"No, no, no, I did not just fly all this way to watch some big orgy. Magennis, step away from September, and September, girl, cool your damn jets. Jesus, you're worse than a pubescent teenager," Lilith yells out from behind me. "I don't know how any of you get anything accomplished in a day, if you never get out of the damn bedroom, yeesh."

Magennis smiles against my lips, giving them one last peck before obeying Lilith and stepping away. "As you wish, Ms. Lilith," he chuckles out.

When I turn back towards the kitchen, I see Lilith nudging Sabre and Gage towards the island. "Chris, Magennis, come sit, at that end with Sabre and Gage. September, you sit at this end, maybe some distance between you all will help."

At the far end of the counter, I hear, "Someone took her bitchy pills this morning." I try not to giggle at Gage's comment while moving to my assigned seat.

Lilith ignores the comment by busying herself in the kitchen, preparing drinks for us before sitting beside me, I'm sure to keep me in check. "Now that we're comfy," she turns her attention my way, "Let's catch up on current events before your mood gets crazy again," she says with a wink, but I get the point.

My eyes travel down the island in search of Gage, "Where do I start?" I ask him since he's been with me most of the day.

Sabre pipes in instead, "From the beginning, which seems to be from the moment you left home this morning." As Sabre speaks, I see his guilt for not coming with me this morning in his eyes.

Moving my head down the line to Magennis, Gage, and Chris, I see the same guilt-ridden look on their faces too. Each man blames himself for the latest bit of drama in our lives and not being able to protect me from it. In truth, no one can be blamed, this day has had to happen, just as months ago I had to go through my change, and they need to understand that.

I take a sip of water from the glass Lilith has brought to me, I get comfortable in my chair, then begin to unravel the day.

CHAPTER 19

After what seems like hours of me rambling on like a crazy person, I finish my account of the day, with Gage filling in the areas I had been either out cold or missing for. My tale starts with the incident on the plane and ends with my introduction to Lazarus on the island. During my explanation, my audience is attentive, not one person makes a comment, sound, or gesture to show me they disbelieve, or even think I'm on the crazy train.

Once my update is complete, I watch as my court processes the data. The expressions on the faces range differently from one person to the next, but behind their eyes, their minds churn up the information at rapid speeds. I can tell they have questions and I know they will be of a similar nature to my own. What does it all mean, and how will we deal with it?

When we all have a few minutes to get our thoughts in order, the discussion begins with Magennis, Sabre, and Gage doing most of the talking. They determine my newest change must be the last of the curse being lifted and may have been triggered by my going into heat since the two happened simultaneously. The marking still mystifies Magennis, he knows of nothing similar in any of the histories in our world or the Underworld. This leaves even more questions and the more we talk the more I realize none of us have any answers.

I sit back in my chair, allowing my own thoughts to twist about inside my head. On the island, Lazarus had told me if I needed him, he would be there. If ever there was a time to need someone it has to be now, but how will I find him? He told me how to travel from place to place by only thinking of it, can this work to find him too?

"Earth to September, where are you?" Lilith shakes my arm bringing me from my deep daze.

Her touch startles me, "Oh!" I bring my focus back to the room, "Did you ask me something?"

"We did, but apparently, ye went on vacation." Magennis smiles, leaning into the counter. "Care to share, a penny for your thoughts and all."

I laugh at his comment. "I happened to be thinking, sometimes I go into my head for that, but I might have come up with an idea." Cautious of my group's reaction, I continue, "I think I can call on Lazarus to help us figure this all out."

I'm not surprised when Gage pushes back his chair to stand, "You want to ask Lazarus here, in my house?" He's outraged and I don't blame him.

"I think it might be our only option, Gage. He said he'd help me if I need it, why not ask?"

"You spend fifteen minutes with the guy and you think he's going to solve our problems? That's hard for us when we know him as the guy that has been trying to destroy our world since the beginning of time. Have you forgotten what he did to your parents?" Gage throws his hands in the air like he can't fathom my words.

Sabre rolls his eyes like he too expected this reaction from Gage, "Maybe we should hear this out, G, it sounds reasonable to ask the only person who might have a clue. Besides, he tried to help September, not harm her."

"I have to agree," adds Magennis. "September said, Lazarus knew I was following him and yet, he led me back to her, instead of trying to kill me. I'm not saying we trust him completely, but I also think we should give him a chance, to prove we have been wrong all these years."

Gage is pacing the floor behind Magennis, he stops abruptly to glare at him. "You've got to be joking, of all the people at this table to say that, I'd never expect it from you. You were there when the shit happened with the Originals, how can you say you misjudged him?"

Magennis turns to Gage, "I never said I was there when Livia was taken. I heard about it like all the other commoners. There was much speculation and turmoil at the time, many names had been brought to the table to blame. It took centuries for our kind to piece it all together and I don't think we have the whole story, even now... in the end only Lazarus was left and by default, he took the fall. Like ye, Gage, I have no other option except to believe he is evil, but, there is a difference between believing something is true and knowing it is." I have never seen Magennis get on a soapbox before, it even shocks Gage, who takes a step back.

Magennis swivels back to me, his eyes finding mine, softening immediately, "I wish I had all the answers for ye, September. I don't, but I also know when to ask for help. This could be a trap, we don't know, but we also can't sit and wait for a better plan. If ye trust Lazarus and think he'll be helpful or at least shine some light on this, then do what is needed to get him here."

I look at Sabre for some guidance, he has always been my voice of reason. "What do you think?" I ask him.

He leans back in his chair, stretching his arms out in front of him and exhales a breath, "I'm not sure what to think." He pauses to ponder, then continues, "If Lazarus is telling the truth then everything we've been led to believe is a lie. For us to have believed in this lie for as long as we did, it means we have a patient and cunning sub amongst us. One that has been waiting all this time to get what they want."

He looks over to Magennis to continue, "Lazarus has been the easiest to blame and sometimes the easiest solution is not always the correct one." He then turns to Gage as if to make a point. "We've run into a wall with this and Lazarus seems to be the only option left. If he's a friend we keep him close if he's an enemy we keep him closer."

Gage stands still, taking in Magennis and Sabre's words to chew on them. I see the struggle on his face and know his need to be in control, battles with letting me lead my court. His eyes flicker around the faces at the table finally ending on mine. With a nod of his head, he says, "I understand what it's like to live with the lies that others create. Maybe Lazarus is telling the truth, maybe he's setting a trap, the only way to know for sure is to call him out."

He steps around the island and walks towards me. "You believed in me even when no one else did, maybe we need to do the same for Lazarus. You have shown me there is still good in this world, perhaps he isn't what we thought." His feet stop beside my chair where he reaches for my hand, he pulls the bandage from my healed finger to rub his thumb over my tattoo. "Everyone at this table loves you, not just because you are our Queen or mate, but because of the person you have become. It has taken me a long time to wrap my head around this and to find my place. It hasn't been easy for you, I know, but you stuck it out and trusted me, even when I didn't give you any reason too. I don't like this idea of asking Lazarus for help, but I trust in you, and know if there is anyone that will get us through this, it will be you."

I don't get a chance to respond because a loud clapping of hands rings out behind me. "Bravo, wonderful speech," says the voice I recognize from my dreams.

There is a clutter of chairs scraping across the tiles as everyone at the table jumps to their feet. Sabre and Magennis run forward towards this threat, Lilith puts her hands forward as her lips begin to move into a spell with Chris falling in behind her, knowing he needs to stay out of the way but safe. Gage, still at my side, moves fast to pull me up into his side, his arms wrap around me for protection.

"Halt!" Commands Lazarus, and as a group, my people just freeze in their forward positions like statues frozen in time. "I am not here to cause harm; I am answering the call for help from your Queen."

I try to move in Gage's arms but he is as hard as a rock and my fight to get loose is futile. "What have you done to them?" I turn my head back to glare at Lazarus but can't see him in this position.

"I merely prevented them from attacking me, they can't move, but they can see and hear us just fine," he says smugly.

"This isn't proving to them that you mean them no harm and in case you haven't noticed, I'm a little stuck here. Care to lift the spell and talk with us like a normal supernatural?" I say in an angry tone while trying to wiggle myself from Gage's grip.

Lazarus makes a huffing sound but Gage's arms relax around me, dropping down to his sides. I'm able to stand and face Lazarus and see he has not allowed my people to be free of their statuesque state. "Lazarus," I growl out a warning to him.

He walks through the archway making his way around the kitchen, opening cupboard doors and drawers, seemingly fascinated by what is in them. "Little one, I have come because you called me. I do not wish to fight your people and for that reason, I keep them in this state until we are done." He counters my warning but acts uninterested in our conversation.

I look back at Gage, his eyes have darkened from the rage inside of him. I sense the others are just as mad, but I have a feeling Lazarus will not cave. I touch Gage's cheek, cupping his jaw in my palm, his eyes flicker down to mine and I whisper, "I'm sorry, but hang in there for me, I'll work this out." I watch as his eyes close and he takes a breath, I hope this means he will be patient.

I make my way around Lilith, touching her shoulder for comfort as I pass, walking over to the far side of the island to where Lazarus is standing. He has a bottle of wine in his hand and glass in the other. "Would you like a libation, little one?" He asks while pouring out some of the red liquid.

I can't believe his carefree attitude, I'm furious but I got the sense on the island, Lazarus works on his own schedule. If I want answers, I will have to remain calm. "No thank you, but I would like to know some answers, starting with who you really are?"

He places the bottle on the counter, swirling the wine in the glass with his other hand, he lifts it to his nose for a sniff before dropping it to his lips for a sip. "This is lovely," he states, taking another draw from the glass. "Sure you don't want some?" He smiles, completely ignoring my questions.

I am about to snap and I let out a growl in frustration. He smirks at me. "Temper, temper. Oh, but the demon is deep within you. You must learn to control it, little one."

My vision starts to haze in shades of red from irritation. "What I need to do is not rip your fucking head off your shoulders and the best way to do that is for you to start talking," I snap at him, pounding my fist on the top of the counter.

He turns his black eyes on me and cocks his head to the side, watching me for a minute before he sits in Sabre's chair. "I see you have inherited your mother's dislike of humor, my niece. Very well, you have asked for my help, I am here to give it. What do you need?"

I blink my eyes a few times to clear the red, realizing what he called me. "I'm your niece, you're my uncle?" I sputter out at this strange piece of news. "I don't understand." I'm so shocked I fall into a chair across from him.

"Yes, I see that you don't. Perhaps we should start from the beginning." He snaps his fingers, causing the others to move like robots around the table. They file in a single line towards the chairs and take seats. They still do not have control of their own bodies, but at least Lazarus has included them for our discussion.

"Thank you," I say while watching them all sit.

"As I said, I wish you and your people no harm. Now, shall we have our talk?" He asks this in a softer tone.

When I pull my eyes away from my paralyzed lovers, I can see he is watching me again like he is trying to figure me out. I guess he probably is trying to get to know me, in his own strange way, I am after all his niece.

I sigh, I'm about to get the biggest history lesson of my life, and I'm not entirely sure I'm ready for it. Whether I am or not, I think for the benefit of our kind we need to know the truth, so that maybe we can finally stop living in fear and just start living.

I reach for the wine bottle and he slides over an empty glass. I pour a splash in the bottom then pour a lot more for good measure. I don't bother with swirling it or even giving it a sniff, instead, I bring it to my lips and tilt it back in one big gulp. I let the wine slide down my throat, burning as it goes, helping me relax for what I'm about to hear. I fill up my glass again then settle in.

"Okay, let it rip," I tell him.

He seems somewhat amused by my actions; a smile breaches his lips, but he doesn't say anything about it. Instead, he takes his own sip of wine before setting the glass off to the side to clasp his hands in front of him. "Do you know of religion?" He simply asks.

This question seems to come from far out in left field, I wonder where he is going with it. "Ah, sure, I guess. I've never been to a church or anything, but I get the idea of it." I'm confused but wait with all the patience I can muster for him to go on.

"It's probably for the best, as it is not what is written in any scriptures on this Earth. You see, long before humans walked this world, there were only spoiled, selfish, bastard Gods. They used this world as a toy, playing with creations to satisfy their boredom, and just like small children they fought. The feuds caused the destruction of many beautiful creatures, from fires, floods, an ice age, and even a few plagues were part of their perverse idea of fun. This constant war of the Gods is how your mother, myself, and ten others were chosen as the fallen, to be put on this realm to keep peace, between the Gods. Cleaning up the messes they created and to help keep the Earth beings safe." He stops to study me again, testing the waters, I'm sure, to see if I am able to hear more.

When I don't respond, he nods his head, satisfied by my acceptance and begins to go on, "The war has been going on for many millennium, splitting the Gods in their twisted beliefs. It was your mother that named this the battle of good and evil, and it was also her idea to create a new world, to separate the Gods. She named that new world the

Underworld, and in it, she created the demons for the evil Gods to play with. They were the first of her children and she wanted them to survive the God's brutalities, so she made them strong, eventually they fought back against the Gods to claim the Underworld as their own."

He pauses to clear his throat, reaching for his glass to take another sip, after his taste he goes on, "Your mother was an incredible problem solver. She was able to keep the chaos contained by keeping the Underworld controlled by the demons. This worried the Otherworld Gods, that she was getting too powerful and she would try to control them as well. They sent more fallen down, this time to rid the Earth of her and the rest of us brothers and sisters. We were hunted like animals, some of our siblings were simply slaughtered. Your Mother was laced with guilt and began to create an army to help protect the rest of us.

She started with an earthly demon, a cousin to the Underworld demons called the elven, but somehow, they were taken out. She created the magical beings, they were strong, able to stop the fallen with spells and curses. The Gods were not happy and became relentless in their pursuit, they countered with the creation of humans and the wars that humans fought as a distraction. We busied ourselves trying to keep away from the humans, but also stay alive while wars and plagues took out a few more of our siblings.

Your mother was strong and kept us alive by creating more beings, like vampires to try to control the humans, and werewolves to protect us. She also created the island to hide us when we needed it, that is where I had been when your mother and her David disappeared." Lazarus becomes quiet after his story, his eyes stuck in a stare as he recounts the tale in his head. I understand his pain of having witnessed so many of his siblings murdered, but I also have a sense of pride that I came from a woman as strong as my mom.

I never knew this side of my mom before, having only seen the human sickly version of her. I'm intrigued and eager to learn more but to also figure out how this gets back to me and my people. "So, my mom and you are angels from heaven, who battled the Gods by creating the supernatural races. How does this get to her becoming human and me being born, and then reborn to take her place? And, how do you fit into all of this?" I ask, bringing him out of his trance.

I see that tremble in him again before his eyes flicker back to me. "You are very accepting of all this, strong of mind, like Livia. She would be proud of you, as I am." He offers the compliment with a genuine smile then continues, "I had been almost killed when Livia put me on the island to heal, hidden from the Gods and humans for my own safety, but also keeping me from protecting her. When I was able to come back to this realm I could not find her, I searched for centuries, but knew she was gone. I heard the rumors like your people told you, first her men were suspected of killing her, then Andras was thought to have kidnapped her, and finally it was decided that I must have built an army from the magical beings and cursed her. I swear to you that none of these are true."

I move forward in my chair, my patience wearing thin. "Then what happened?" I almost beg him to tell me.

He goes to tilt the glass of wine to his lips, realizing it is now empty and discards it on the counter. He wets his lips with his tongue, looks at the bottle then back to me. He smiles seeing me, maybe he senses my eagerness for more details because he forgets the drink and carries on. "I believe Livia cursed herself, I believe she had been out of options in the war. We were the only two left, the Gods had started to kill her more powerful creatures and we were losing the battle. I think in order for her to remain alive and to allow the war to subside she felt she needed to disappear for a while. I think she knew that becoming human would kill her, and she put in a safeguard to have the curse pass to you once she was gone because she knew the war would never be over, and that you needed to continue to fight in her absence."

"You mean my mom knew all this and she never thought to warn me, or even prepare me for it?" I feel betrayed by my own mom and I'm left with questions of why.

He reaches across the table for my hand, squeezing it in his grasp. "Do not blame her, little one. Whatever spell Livia put on herself, could only be passed to you once she died and only if she did not tell you. That is how magic works. If you knew, you would not have been protected for as long as you were, and the Gods would have searched you out to kill you. Since Livia disappeared, the Gods have been quiet, except for a few unexplained incidents here and there, until recently. I can feel the shift of the world around me, the humans are unsettled and war is upon us again. This could be from the Gods sensing you or the cycle of the human race, either way, I believe you are still not safe."

A shiver of fear trickles over me, visions of CNN reports of chaos around the world flash into my head. "So, I can never be safe as long as I am alive, the Gods will try to destroy me and this world."

His face goes into a frown. "No, I think they would have killed you by now had they considered you a threat. You are inheriting your wings, if I can sense you, so too, can they, but you have such power that perhaps even the Gods fear you. I believe, for now, they are waiting, watching you. I did some listening, your people think highly of you, you are changing the supernatural world. You have more of the good, than evil in your heart, that will appeal to the Gods, and your disconnect of the Underworld will help you win them over. Livia wanted to control the Gods, you seem to want to only rule your races. Perhaps you will be able to find a peace amongst us all."

"But I don't want to fight Gods, I don't even want to rule the races. I only do it because I thought that is what I inherited. That I have to protect the races from you, but if you mean them no harm, then why should I continue? This is not my war." I'm angry, not at Lazarus, but at the whole idea. I don't want this, to play the middle man for Gods and the beings that were created.

His hand grips mine harder as he senses my pain. "No, this is not your war, but because of Livia, you must be a Queen for these people and protect them from whatever wrath the Gods want to bring down on them. This is a great responsibility to be asked of you. I sense your anger, but I feel your strength. You can do this, and maybe together with your court, you can change how the Gods behave in the future. Perhaps this was Livia's plan all along, to create you, a being made from her flesh which contains all the races. One that will be strong enough to bring peace to all the worlds."

The weight of this responsibility is heavy and I groan, "This sucks! I thought I had only inherited a kingdom, but in reality, I inherited a whole universe of bad history. Now, I have to play schoolyard referee to some spoiled Gods while keeping the rest of the worlds safe from their bullying. What about me, and my friends and family? How will we be able to live happily knowing that at any minute the Gods might get pissed and kill us?"

"I know this is a lot to absorb, but think of your future daughter, you can build a better world for her." He says this so casually that I almost miss it.

I gasp, my head swings to Gage, across the table, two seats down, on Lazarus's right. His eyes are practically bugging from his head as my glance meets his. There is no way Lazarus can even know what's been happening, but he is an angel, and he would have no other reason to say it other than it might be true. An *oh my God* moment, passes between Gage and myself, before I turn back to Lazarus. "Are you fucking with me?" I snap, unsure of his intentions.

He chuckles, "No, little one, I assure you that I am not. You and the wolf will have a child, a girl. I can see it in your near future. Perhaps this will give you all the more reason to make the world a peaceful place for her to live in."

I pull my hands from his, one clasps my mouth to stop my lips from quivering, and the other to my belly. I'm numb from the shock, overwhelmed by of what Lazarus said. I have anger and hate, but it dissolves when I think about a baby. Our baby, Gage's and mine.

Lazarus's chair brushes the floor as he stands then moves around the table to my side, he places his hand on my shoulder to bring me into him for an awkward hug. "I know this is not how you envisioned your life, as I know Livia did not wish to burden you with this choice, but this is your destiny whether you want it or not. I will always be here to help you; I will do everything in my own power to help keep you safe, as I know your men will do the same. They have fought valiantly today, to break from my spell, you should be proud of them. They are true warriors, with many hard battles ahead of them, some sooner than others."

I look up at him. "What do you mean?" I ask, wondering what more is about to come.

"Your wolf, for one, will be challenged to an Alpha duel to the death. You must not interfere, little one, he must do this to restore order to your kingdom from all the doubters. You will forever be tested on your morals; it is the Gods' will. Choose your moves carefully by following the good within your heart." He looks towards Gage and nods his head. "I know you all will have much to discuss and prepare for. I will leave you to it. I do hope I have given you reasons to trust me so the next time we meet, I do not have to spell you." He grins while ending his glance at Lilith, "Though, I'm quite enjoying the mental battle of power with the witch, you, my little gem, are a feisty one. I look forward to many more encounters with you."

I watch as he winks at Lilith, when I turn toward her, I notice her cheeks have a bright shade of pink on them. I'm amused by the exchange, yet oddly weirded out that Lilith and my angel uncle might be flirting. I store that uncomfortable nugget somewhere in the back of my brain for a later date.

As I stand from my chair, I block Lazarus's view of Lilith, "Are you leaving?" I ask the obvious for lack of anything else to say.

He smiles. "For now, yes, but I am never far. You merely need to reach out to me with your mind and I will come, I even encourage it. I do look forward to getting to know you and your people, you are all my family now, too."

I realize since my mom disappeared, he has probably been alone. Spending his time searching for her or away on the island with no one to talk with. We stand for a minute, staring at each other, neither of us sure how to say goodbye. I feel like I should hug him since he is my uncle, but as I think of it, he just simply vanishes.

The room erupts behind me, as the suspended animation lifts. It sounds like the pond in my forest at home in spring when the frogs come out of hibernation. Except, instead, of the sweet sounds of frog chirping, there is a heavy amount of swears and curses.

I turn back toward the chaos, happy to see them up from their chairs and moving about. Chris has gone to make sure Lilith is okay, a sweet gesture, showing his loving heart. Magennis and Sabre are standing down at the end, rapidly hashing out Lazarus's information and formulating plans for our future. I know I should be right there with them, it is my future too, and I am the Queen. But it is the last thing on my mind at the moment.

My eyes go to the chair Gage had been sitting in, the rod iron stool is empty. I have a quick thought that he has been taken or worse run for the door by Lazarus's news. No sooner does the fear of either option start to flicker in my head, that his arms wrap around my waist, his hands settling on my stomach.

"Are you okay?" He asks in a hushed voice.

A shaky breath of relief leaves my mouth and I lean my head into his shoulder. "I'm not sure, you?"

"I don't know. Do you believe him?" His voice is super low in my ear, keeping our conversation private for now.

"I can't see him lying, it would give him no advantage. There is no way he would have known about our issue. So, yeah, I think I believe him," I say, then turn in his arms to face him, to see his reaction. "We will have a baby, Gage."

Our eyes meet and in that moment, nothing else matters. I don't care about the Gods and their wars, about good or bad, about ruling a kingdom or being an angel. None of it compares to the reality of this moment, of Gage and I, knowing in our hearts what Lazarus has said is true. I know from his big dopey grin and tear filled eyes, Gage is feeling the same way.

I watch him swallow a lump in his throat while his lashes do a rapid blink to prevent the drops from escaping his eyes, "We are going to have a baby," he practically sobs the words out. "You have made me the happiest man in all the damn worlds," he laughs, from making a joke.

"Hold on, he said our future child not that we have a bun in the oven, yet." I smile, but don't laugh as another thought enters my head, "If you believe Lazarus about this, then what about the other thing he said?" My hands tighten on his forearms as the fear trickles in.

"You mean the Alpha fight, please, Baby, I got this. I knew before you disappeared this afternoon, that I will have to prove myself. I never got the chance to tell you before, but I say bring it on." His chest puffs forward and I can see he is ready for this.

"He didn't say you would win, he actually made it sound like something bad will happen and I can't interfere." There's a shake to my voice as I stress, "Don't start getting cocky, not now."

He rolls his eyes. "September, this isn't cocky, this is me being confident. I'm holding in my arms, all the reasons in the world to fight and I promise you, I will win."

"You two okay?" Sabre asks, coming up behind me to embrace my back.

"All is good, my friend, better than good." Gage gives Sabre a wink and steps back to accommodate for Sabre's arms joining our hug.

"Someone took their happy pills," Magennis says to Gage, from across the table, noticing his shift in mood.

"How can we be anything but, you heard the angel? We are going to be fathers. I think we need to celebrate," Gage announces.

The impact of the day has my brain doing double time, flipping from positive to negative with each heartbeat. "I think you're jumping the gun." I sputter out, getting completely worked up, "You're fixated on this one point when there is so much more that Lazarus told us. There's Gods to appease, a kingdom to rule with you having to prove yourself as Alpha, and in case any of you missed it, I'm apparently a fucking angel."

Gage looks at me during my ranting burst, his smile hasn't faded. "So, we are in about the same place as we always are. Someone's riding our ass, making threats, testing our loyalties and again, we wait for impending doom. The way I see it, we have two options, one, we sit here and work ourselves into a frenzy, which it would appear you are well on the way to. Or two, we say fuck it, and live a little, maybe celebrate that we made it this far, we must be doing something right to still be alive and kicking."

Magennis chuckles. "I can't believe I'm about to say this, but I have to agree with Gage on this one, my dearest. We just found out our whole lives, and the stories of our existence, have not been what we thought. Gods created this world, Livia created us to help her keep the peace and protect the humans, so far, we have done not a bad job of it. It would also appear we no longer need to worry about Lazarus being a threat, I say that alone is a reason to celebrate."

"What about the impending doom, as Gage put it? What will we do about that?"

Sabre turns me to face him. "September, darling, we can hash this out all we want, but until these Gods present us with some situation, it appears, for now, there isn't much we can do. As Gage said, it's situation normal. We will always be tested, we will always have threats, and we will deal with them as they come."

"Yeah, I think you need to take a chill pill too, Sep. We've had a really long day and our emotions, especially yours, have been on high alert. We can use a little break to unwind, it's not like the problems won't be there tomorrow, but maybe a change of pace will allow us to deal with it more clearly when it does happen." As Lilith adds her peace I start to realize they might be right.

All eyes are on me, they wait to see what my reaction will be, as their Queen, friend and mate. I never asked for this role as Queen, but thanks to my mother I don't have much of a choice. Unlike her, I won't hide or disappear when the next shit storm starts, because I have these amazing people who believe in me and together we will deal.

For now, I see they are right, we can't sit here waiting for what ifs, we should celebrate the small victories. We have made it this far and we're still alive, I just found out I have an uncle and he told us I will be a mother myself, at some point in the future.

"Fine," I say, making my decision. "Break out the champagne, but if the world ends tomorrow when I have a hangover, there will be hell to pay."

CHAPTER 20

As a collective group, we decide to forego the stay at home champagne celebration, for a night out, to clear our heads after such a heavy day. Chris recommends we join his band downtown at the bar he's been talking about all day, called the Shoe. Gage shocks me by agreeing to the idea and before I can get my say, we are rushing around getting ready to go out.

Since this Shoe place is a live music venue, it might be more appropriate to dress in something other than my bathrobe. Lilith takes it upon herself to nudge me up the stairs to change. She finds for me, in the back of Gage's closet, a little red number made of rubber with crisscross straps that barely cover. The outfit screams more bondage than bar. With the day being so up and down for me, between sex and stress, to anger and anxiety, somehow this kick-ass outfit seems to suit not only the mood of the day but who I am, sexy and strong.

As usual, everyone is ready long before I am. Coming down the stairs I am met by my four handsome men, dressed in a range of styles showing the individual personality of each. While they all have on casual jeans, Magennis has gone with a bright green shirt with some cartoon figure on the front, while Sabre's has on his signature plaid collared dress shirt with rolled sleeves, and Gage stuck with what looks good on him, business casual. He has a crisp light blue dress shirt with a navy dress jacket that highlights his eyes but says romantic dinner for two and not loud bar party. It is only Chris that has gone with a grunge leather style that is more in tune to my outfit and a bar, then again, this is his area of expertise.

"You all look so good that I'm rethinking this going out idea," I say with a purr in my voice as the lust starts to settle in while I ogle my men.

"I have to agree, darling, I would rather see that outfit on the floor of the bedroom than parading through a crowded bar." As Sabre replies the others chime in with approving moans that suggest, we skip the going out and head straight to bed.

Lilith steps down the stairs, coming around me with hands held up. "Hold up, I am not sitting here all night alone while the five of you play some freaky game of sex twister upstairs. You can do that later, once I've primed myself up with enough liquor to pass out, so I don't have the audio sex track playing in my head." She makes a disgusted face and shutters, "I had to live in your house for a couple of months and it took me forever to get those noises out of my head."

There are a few chuckles, but thankfully Sabre steps forward to cut off any comments. He puts his arm out to Lilith to escort her down the last few steps. "You all heard Ms. Lilith, let's go get her primed."

"And maybe laid." I hear Gage mumble under his breath, and a few more chuckles follow.

Chris walks behind Sabre to meet me at the bottom step, giving me a wink before escorting me towards the elevator. We somehow manage to pile everyone in and make our way down to the lobby and a waiting stretch limo.

"Now we're talking," Lilith cheers as she climbs in and sees a fully stocked bar. As the rest of us join her inside the limo she begins serving up refreshments.

"Thank you for getting us a ride to the bar, Gage. My feet will be happy we don't have to walk. I will be sure to show you my appreciation later." I say with a smile, accepting a champagne flute from Lilith.

Gage gives my stiletto-clad feet an approving look then sighs, "Unfortunately, I can't take credit for this one." He actually appears disappointed.

"My record company sent the car," says Chris with an amused smile. "Not sure how they would feel about your idea of a thank you, though."

We have a laugh at Chris's comment and continue to kibitz as the car turns south on Spadina Avenue. The ride is a few short blocks to our destination on Queen Street, and our conversation is cut short as we pull up in front of an old warehouse district, cut into store fronts that connect down the city block. The Shoe is on the top half of the block in what looks like an old farmhouse, smashed between an ancient stone structure that has obviously been a bank for the last two centuries, and a modern glass and metal structure promoting a dress sale.

As we exit the car in front of a short iron gate, and lonely umbrella suggesting this to be a patio area, I marvel at the diverse architecture on the street. "Wow, this is kind of cool," I comment.

Chris climbs out of the car behind me. "Yeah, there's a lot of history in this area. The Shoe used to be a blacksmith shop in the eighteen hundred." He points to the bar.

"Really?" I ask with fascination.

"Well, that's what the plaque inside says," Chris laughs. "The bar itself has been open for about sixty-five years, and every Canadian band that has ever wanted to make it in the industry, has played here. Even a few big-name bands from around the world have graced the stage, this place is a big deal in my world." He looks proud to show it off to me.

His excitement is contagious and I want to know more. "Did Defeat the Dark play here?" Wondering out loud if they got their start in this infamous club.

"We did, and we still do, every time we come to town. Many bands play here even after they have made it big, it's how we say thanks for giving us the opportunity. If this place wasn't around, DTD would still be playing gigs at the local community halls back in Alberta and we'd all be working at the mill to make rent." Chris seems somewhat humbled by his words. It gives me a glimpse at how hard he and his band have worked to get where they are today.

"Come on, let's check it out," he says with a gleam in his eye.

We file through the blackened glass doors and into the dark bar, the only word I can think to describe it is, dive, and that's being generous. The first thing I notice is not the run down exterior complete with hanging ceiling wires and decade old band poster wallpaper, but the pungent stench of a bar that has been fermenting for sixty plus years. The mix of stale beer, sweat, and even cigarettes – though you can't smoke in bars anymore – is overpowering. Not one thing about this venue, including the ancient looking bartender, has seen an upgrade since the hippie revolution.

I might be revolted by the nasty smell, the mishmash of decor, and extremely loud music, but the fully packed house of partygoers, having a grand time, don't seem to care. The crowd is squished in like sardines, but they have enough room to bang their heads and jump around to the screeching death metal coming from a back section. As the horrifying sound invades my thoughts and renders me paralyzed to go on beyond the entrance area, Chris grabs my hand to drag me into the vast meat market. I want to pull him back, except Gage is behind me gently nudging me on.

We weave through the bodies, I dodge a few grabbing hands, making our way to a displayed old motorbike with the word, Triumph, on the side, and dust an inch thick on the seat. We go to a doorway with a couple of steps that take us into the loudest part of the club. Chris steers me over to a bar on the far-right side, where Samuel, Phoenix, and Alex are already sitting amongst a crowd of fans, which includes our tattoo artist, Darin. As we approach the crowd opens a gap for us, once they notice Chris. Within seconds we are sucked into the fandom void of flirting bimbo groupies and air guitar want-a-be musicians.

I look behind me for the rest of my group. Gage and Sabre have taken their usual bodyguard posts on either side of me, while Magennis and Lilith are on the outside of our circle. My eyes meet Lilith's between the bodies, and I can tell she is about as thrilled as I am to be here. This place is nothing like our Silverclaw nightclub back home, that is way more millennium modern, and a great deal cleaner than this, shit-hole, another generous description for it.

"Six double Jack and cokes," Chris yells out to a man that appears to be in his late fifties but hasn't got past the eighties.

The bartender is dressed in a metallic silk dress shirt and snug white jeans, that kind of go with his long flowing mullet and hoop earring. He is the walking epitome of business in the front and party in the back. I know there are many older rockstars out there, Steven Tyler comes to mind, as well as Mick Jagger, so maybe this club is some sort of retirement facility for once cool, but now aging bartenders.

"Queenie," Samuel calls out, breaking me from my musings. "Wow, leaving the bubble again, twice in one day. I'm impressed to see you living on the wild side." I can't hear him laughing, but I see the joy on his face as he teases.

Chris turns back to hand me a short thick tumbler, filled to the brim with ice, but with very little mix. The streaks on the side of the glass have me wondering if it has even seen the inside of a dishwasher or if the glass is as aged as the property. I take the offered drink and give my best smile as Chris winks at me.

"Please tell me I'm just being a bar snob." Lilith loudly whispers into my ear, after wiggling her tiny body through a wall of bleach blonde Barbie's. "This place is beyond gross, my shoes are stuck to the floor."

I giggle at her over dramatic response, then shut my yap when I realize, I have been just as judgmental. I turn myself around in a standing circle to get a full view of the room, one of the things I notice is, not everyone around us looks like a serial killer or stripper. There are groups of all different types of people, much like the streets earlier, there is diversity everywhere. On one side of the stage next to a large pillar, which I imagine is an important part of the structure and likely holds up the roof, there is a well-dressed group of maybe office workers.

I nod my head in their general direction, "Not everyone here looks like an escaped convict, we should try to give it a chance." Even as I loudly say the words, I feel the mix of high energy in the room. Most of the emotions, except mine and Lilith's, are happy and positive ones.

Samuel hops off his barstool, grabbing one of the drinks from the pile Chris has ordered and squeezes himself around a few people to approach us. "I know those stuck-up looks, you two have no sense of adventure. Here," he hands the glass to Lilith, "after a couple of these you won't even notice that you're standing in a puddle of vomit." He laughs as we both jump back to look at the floor. "Oh, you are both so easy to get going."

If looks could kill, Samuel would have died, on the spot, in his make-believe puddle of vomit, but he does have a point. The bar might not be the classiest of establishments, but every person in it is having the time of their life. We came here to forget our day and mingle with the mortals, they do say when in Rome, do what the Romans do. I take my glass and raise it up. "Cheers," I say to Sam.

"That's the ticket." He grins at me then clinks my glass before we both shoot back the contents of the drink.

Lilith watches us, her face crinkled up in horror of what she is witnessing. Once we finish swallowing, I see her think it through, and as if she's dared herself, she takes a big breath and knocks back the drink. "Whoa," she yells out and wipes at her mouth with her hand, "that was strong. These are like shots, not drinks."

Sam shuffles towards her. "If you think these are strong let me buy you an actual shot. It'll straighten your pubic hair." I hear Lilith snort as Sam guides her towards the bartender.

Behind me, I hear a couple of girls complain about Sam's choice in drinking buddies. I smirk knowing these pop-tarts will never be in the same league as Lilith, and I hope maybe tonight she and Sam will have some fun together. They both deserve it.

My own glass now empty, I look to the bar for a refill, Chris is sandwiched in between a gorgeous brunette and a voluptuous blonde, with no room for me to get close to him. I'm more annoyed that his female fans are taking up his time than I am jealous. I know when he's presented with a chance he'll find his way back to me and until then, I can find company with my other men.

I turn around to face Gage and Sabre to find them with their backs to me. They are keeping me guarded, but someone has also taken them away from me as they both seem locked into conversations. I look around for Magennis, who has also been pulled away by a gang of girls dressed in head to toe black. The goth girls have no idea how perfectly fitting they look next to the vampire. *If they only knew.*

I laugh at my own musings and at the idea of been ditched by my people. I should be upset, but I know they didn't ditch me on purpose, they are just playing politely with the humans, and as Lazarus said, this could be why the Gods have kept us around, we are indeed pleasant people. I leave them to mingle with the mortals on my own and stay in the good books, while I head to the bar for another drink.

This is easier thought than done. I'm not used to being on this side of the bar and the four-foot trip to order a refreshment has given me a whole new respect for the patrons. By the time I get to the service station to place my order, I am covered in sweat from the workout I didn't quite expect.

"You look like you could use a drink," says a male voice to my right.

"Or a shower," I mumble to myself.

"Are you offering?" He's got my attention, having heard my quiet words, I know he must have exceptional hearing, of the supernatural kind.

I don't need to look at him to sense he's a wolf, but I swing my head to get an eye full anyway. The wolf is handsome; I'll give him that. A massive rugged exterior draped in leather and decorated with chains, has me thinking biker. His short cut brown hair is even flat on top from wearing a helmet, and his dark brown eyes are circled with a white sunglass tan line, probably from riding in the July sun.

"I don't think my mate would like that much." I smile politely.

"And which one of the four, you walked in here with, is the mate, cause from where I'm sitting, they don't seem to be too worried about you," he smirks back. "If you were mine, I wouldn't let you out of my sight, especially looking that hot." He gives me a flirtatious scan and a heated stare while his nostrils flare.

I laugh. "Nice try, but I'm not interested, I do appreciate the compliment, though." I wave my hand to get the bartenders attention.

The grandfatherly man comes over. "What's your poison, Honey?" He asks.

"May I get a couple of double Jacks and one for my new friend here?" I gesture to the wolf. "Please," I add.

The bartender looks at the wolf and gives him a wink like they are sharing some male bonding moment, then he shuffles off to retrieve my order. "Thank you," says the wolf.

"It's the least I can do, considering I'm declining your offer." I give him another polite smile.

"You're really not interested, are you?" He sounds shocked, but I bet not many women turn him down, he is incredibly attractive.

"No, I'm not," I reply then decide to soften the blow, "I'm sure you'll have no problem finding someone special, but you might want to look for her somewhere other than here. The pickings don't seem that great unless you like the goths and strippers. If that's the case, I doubt you're planning on something that lasts longer than a quickie in the bathroom."

He chuckles out loud. "Zander," he says, moving forward and extending his hand in greeting. "I'm Zander

Paine, or as my friends call me Zee. It's a pleasure to meet you..." He trails off waiting for me to shake his hand.

I look back through the crowd, my men still look preoccupied and I decide I have time to make a new friend. I grab his hand for a shake, "Pleasure is all mine, Zee. I'm September Rae."

He stops our shake mid pump; his eyes go wide and his mouth opens into an, oh, "You're the, oh shit, sorry, I didn't..." He stumbles out and it makes me laugh. I love having this effect on people.

"Don't sweat it, no harm done."

The bartender comes over and drops the drinks. "The band has requested I put you on their tab." He gives me a strange sneer then turns to Zander, "Brother, I'd leave this one alone, she seems to get around, if you know what I mean."

Zander turns to the older man grabbing him by the scruff of the neck, with a low deep growl he says, "I suggest you be politer to the Lady, you have no idea who she is. I recommend you give her respect or I will be happy to rip out your throat and shit down your neck. Capisce, brother?"

I watch the bartender pale and swallow before he nods his head. His eyes flicker over to me and I offer him a shrug, I am not explaining myself to this human. He mutters an apology before Zander pats the side of his neck before letting him go. I glance down the bar at the patrons, no one has noticed the assault, but Zander's quick movements made it appear like two people talking, instead of the grilling.

Zander turns back to me, "I apologize, my Queen. I didn't realize..."

I put my hand up to stop him, "I said don't sweat it, but thanks for coming to my rescue, although, I would have enjoyed giving old Woodstock there, a piece of my mind."

He gives me a questioning look, "Uh, Woodstock?" He asks with a smile.

"Oh, I am referring to the bartender. I mean, hello, the seventies called they want their hippies back." My joke seems to break the uncomfortable moment as Zander breaks out in a snort that turns into a full barrel laugh.

After a minute, he contains himself. "I have to say, your Highness, you are more than just a looker, that shit's entertaining."

"Why, thank you, Mr. Zee and you can call me September, so the humans don't start to ask questions." I take one of the two drinks in front of me and knock it back.

"Oh sure, I guess you have to think about that." He watches me swallow and adds, "I see you also handle the liquor well." He looks amused.

I set the empty glass down on the bar top, replacing it with the full one. "You could say it is the Queen's little helper." This time I only sip, knowing the bartender is going to stay clear of me for a while, I'll have to make this one last.

"How so?" He asks then his eyes widen again, "You don't have to answer, I should know better than to pry." He turns slightly to retrieve his own drink, taking in a mouth full to shut himself up.

I watch as his cheeks flush by his ears, he's gone from being confident like he's going to get laid to being nervous. "You know I don't mind questions, our people should know more about their Queen. You don't have to be nervous either, I don't bite, well, strangers anyway." I snort at my own joke. "The liquor helps me control my cravings for blood, lust, and power, especially when I'm in a crowd of horny, happy humans."

He gives me another chuckle. "Yes, I can see how that might be a problem, given the estrous and all."

It is my turn to blush, it's a bit unsettling knowing that some people can smell that I'm in heat. "Yeah," I mumble, taking a big gulp of the Jack.

"Sorry, but I did smell it as soon as you entered the room. It's also why I have this unrealistic urge to mate with you." He blushes an apologetic pink.

I nod my head. "That and my power makes you desire me more than any other wolf in heat. I draw men to me because I'm a succubus, and right now, that draw is more powerful because of the estrous. But, if you don't mind, I really don't want to talk periods with a someone I just met."

His hands go up. "No, I totally get it, this has to be the strangest conversation I've ever had with a chick, in a bar or anywhere for that matter. I'm a nomad biker, I live alone from the pack and from rival bike gangs. I don't have personal conversations with anyone, so I don't even know why I am now." He seems a bit confused.

I place my hand over his on the bar top. "It's not you, it's me. I bring the weird out in people. Don't worry about it. How about you tell me about you? You said you are a nomad, I have not heard that before, what is it?"

He takes a breath and I watch him relax as I change the subject, "A nomad isn't a what, but a who, and thank you for changing the subject." He smiles and begins to talk more freely, and as he does his confidence comes back.

He tells me a nomad is a person that doesn't conform to one side or the other, in a bike gang or in his case, a pack. He has a few home base locations and travels between them, picking up work with either the gangs or the packs as they have need of him. It sounds lonely, but as he tells me about himself I can see he is quite comfortable with being by himself. I find the more he tells me the more I like him, and

I hope maybe I can find a position for him somewhere in the OSU. As a hunter, perhaps, since I see a bit of Gage in him.

While we talk, I notice the noise level in the room has changed. I glance behind me to see the stage is being cleared of the metal band and DTD is setting up. I'm curious as to why they are setting up to play, but Chris did say they like to do so anytime they are in town.

"Is something wrong?" I hear Zander ask.

I turn my attention back to him, "Uh, no not really, I just noticed one of my mates is about to get on the stage and I don't know where the other three have disappeared to."

"Oh, the four men you came with are all your mates? That makes sense." He shakes his head, "I had heard rumors but... okay all true. Is there something you'd like me to do, maybe help you locate them?" As he asks I see him scanning the crowd.

"No, they are probably making sure I am safe by walking the crowd. If I stay here I know they will be able to find me if something goes wrong." I try to sound casual while my mind wonders where the hell my men have gone. It is not like them to leave me alone, especially with a complete stranger.

I search them out in the crowd with my magic, finding them immediately. Chris is on stage with Lilith and Gage, that's a strange combination, but I move on. Magennis is with Sabre close to the front door, and I pick up a couple of other wolf auras with them. "It's okay, I found them." I sigh, relieved they are just socializing.

"Ah, pardon?" Zander asks, giving me the, *this chick is nuts,* kind of look.

Laughing I say, "I have magic that helps me find our people, especially those in my court. I can also talk to them through a mind connection, but I don't need to, they seem to be chatting up the locals, a couple of wolves that just walked in," I explain.

Zander gets tense from my words, "Did you say a couple of wolves just walked in?"

Seeing his sudden change in posture makes me uneasy. "Yes, it that bad?" I ask while I mentally prepare to notify my people of potential trouble.

"I'm not sure, one of the reasons I frequent this place is because not many of our kind like to come here. Hearing a couple of wolves showed up is out of the ordinary strange, especially with the rumors floating around about an Alpha duel." As he explains, his demeanor changes. His eyes darken as he watches the crowd and his body seems to grow as he stands up to show his massive size.

"You mean the Alpha duel with Gage?" I ask, wondering if it is the same rumor Lazarus had told us earlier.

His eyes flicker down to mine, "I am seriously off my game today. I should have known who you were when I saw you come in with Gage. I smelt wolf and assumed he was traveling in a pack tonight because of the threats. I never thought you were his Beta." He offers an apology, but I wave it off with my hand.

"You know Gage?" I ask then add, "He's never mentioned you."

"Gage and I go way back, we were nomads together before there was even a name for it. Then one day his Dad showed up and things changed, but we have always remained friends. The reason I'm in Toronto is because I heard rumblings of a power shift and figured he might need some help."

This explains why my men haven't come to check on me, Gage probably saw me talking to Zander and felt I'd be safe. I'm happy they have left me alone; I can find out information on my own. "So, the rumors are true, someone wants to challenge Gage," I mumble this to prevent anyone from hearing our conversation.

His voice drops low, "Yeah, from what I've been hearing, someone has the wolves doubting Gage is even your mate. Some of the older packs think he's just hiding behind your apron strings, but that bullshit stems from his Dad's lies. Gage's dad did some real damage that many have not forgotten."

I hear some feedback from a mic on the stage, but I'm too interested in what Zander is saying to pay attention. "Do you know who's challenging Gage?"

His head pops up and swings over to the stage. "I don't know who wants to challenge him, I only know many doubt his position as your Alpha because they don't see Gage as anything but weak. A wolf's memory is long, and we don't change our minds very often, even when we are proven wrong, it's a pride thing."

I understand, especially after hearing Sabre's story about the wolf's treatment of him for eight hundred years. "I think the politics in the sub world is sometimes worse than in the human one," I say, shaking my head.

We don't get a chance to say more on the subject as a kick drum pounds twice followed by a quick sound check. "I see your witch making her way over, I'm going to wander the crowd and see who those wolves are. I will be back in a few." Zander says loudly, then strolls off in the direction of the door.

I watch him go just as Lilith makes her way towards me, she motions in the direction I've been staring, "Making new friends?" She asks with a laugh.

I blink then look at her, there's a megawatt smile spread across her face, telling me she is super excited about something. "He's an old friend of Gage's, but I have a feeling you didn't come over here to meet him. What's up?" I'm suspicious of her excitement

She is practically wiggling out of her skin with joy, "Oh, nothing." She sings out then let's loose a giggle, "A little birdie just told me something I know you are going to love."

Even though I'm intrigued about Zander, worried about the wolves at the door, confused about the God stuff, and everything else that has happened today, this piques my curiosity. We did come to have some and it's about time I get with the program.

CHAPTER 21

The bass drum pounds out again, followed by a snare and tom, the beat repeats a couple of times before it's extended, and joined by a guitar cord sliding up in scale. DTD comes alive on the stage, starting off with one of their classic hits to instantly wake up the crowd. A loud roar erupts as people recognize the song. The ear-piercing screams closely follow as the crowd rushes up towards the stage.

Today has felt like the longest day in history. So much has happened in such a short period, it's like a lifetime has passed since I stepped on the plane this morning. With one strum of his electric Fender, Chris reminds me why I came here in the first place. I wanted a break, a vacation from my life, except that's not possible because my life is all consuming and follows me no matter where I go. This might be normal for life as the Queen, but it doesn't mean I have to be so damn serious all the time.

I give myself over to the crowd, letting the hyper level of energy in the room roll into me. It feels amazing as the jolt hits, and my heart skips double time to the heavy beat of the music. My body is buzzing like I drank hundreds of espressos all at once. I have no choice, but to move. My foot begins to tap, my legs shuffle side to side, my body sways, and before I can stop myself, I'm dancing. I've caught the contagious bug of music fever, and when I turn with a bounce, Lilith is dancing right along to the same groove.

We take over the space in front of the bar, grinding our hips, and shaking our money makers. Our moves look seductive, and before long we gather our own crowd. I usually love the attention that reminds me of days behind the bar, back home not long ago, but with this crowd comes a spark of sexual desire, making my demon perk up quicker than normal. I fall against the bar as my magic flares inside of me with a brute force and I almost drop to my knees from the heat it provides.

"Ah, fuck," I curse while grabbing the bar edge, turning my body away from our audience in an attempt to look like I'm stumbling.

A small hand grabs my arm to hold me up. "Hey klutzy, you okay?" Lilith asks with a laugh. "Maybe you should start wearing flats or you're going to break your neck in those damn heels."

I shake my head then twist to look at her. "I don't think the heels have anything to do with it."

Her eyes widen in shock as she takes in my face. "Holy shit," she gasps. "I think you might be right, your eyes ... oh my God."

I watch her do a quick mental flip out, then she kicks herself into action. With great strength for such a tiny girl, she hauls me up off my knees and turns me back towards the bar. She puts herself at my back and I sense her using her magic to call out for help.

I hear a few people ask Lilith if I'll be okay, she responds with a laugh, "Someone is just a lightweight with her liquor. I'll get her some water and she'll be fine."

"Causing a scene, little Minx?" Magennis asks, sliding a glass of H2O in front of me.

My magic flares from Magennis's presence, then I start to pant when I feel Sabre come near too. My fingers grip the bar ledge, turning my knuckles white as my nails dig into the wood, all from an insatiable desire.

"What's wrong with her?" Lilith whispers, her voice cracking with concern.

"I believe, she's horny," Magennis says with a serious candor, like a doctor telling a patient they have a life-threatening disease.

Our conversation is drowned out when Chris screams out over the mic, "Good evening, Toronto."

The crowd erupts into a cheer, helping to switch my mood. Thankfully, it's enough to lessen the burning desire to strip off my clothes and screw my men on the disgusting floor.

"How's everyone doing tonight?" Chris pumps up the growing crowd.

Sabre shifts to my side to close the gap between me, the three of them blocking me into the bar to keep me protected until I get myself under control. My grip is locked on the bar ledge and my back to the room, while I try to concentrate on anything but what my body is screaming for, sex.

"Do you know we are playing tomorrow night at the ACC?" Chris keeps up his banter with the crowd, and I wonder if he knows I need the distraction. "It is our last stop on tour before we head into the studio to record a new album." Some of the crowd screams while some let out rounds of low boos.

Another switch in emotions, this time I sense disappointment and I try to cling to it with my mind. My shoulders slowly relax as I feel myself gaining a morsel of control.

"I know, we hate coming off the road too, but don't you guys want some new music?" He asks, the crowd answers with more cheers.

"Well, we have a treat for you tonight, our way of saying thanks to the Shoe and all of you for hanging with us. We thought we'd play a little something we've been working on, with a friend, for the next album." Chris gives the crowd some time to work itself back up into hysteria. "We need you all to put your hands together to bring this guy out. Gage Blackwood, my man, come help us out with this one."

Hearing Chris's announcement, I swing around to face the stage. The sudden news knocks my mood into complete shock and wonder, as Gage runs up the steps, and goes to the right side of the stage. I spin to glance over at Sabre then Magennis, but I see they too share my look of surprise.

"What the hell?" I comment out loud, and they both shrug.

Lilith turns around at the sound of my voice. I take it by the relief on her face, my eyes have gone back to normal. "I told you before you would love this." She hesitates as she watches me then flashes me a big grin.

Gage settles in behind a keyboard and I think about the piano at his apartment. I'm about to see him play, something I have been waiting for. My eyes start to prick as tears form in my eyes, and I get overwhelmed with new emotions. God, I feel bipolar.

"Gage wants to dedicate this song to a special person, that we all hold near and dear to our hearts. This one is for you Kitten, it's called Share."

As the first note on the keyboard rings out, a tear rolls down my cheek. A beautiful soft melody begins, it sounds sweet and slow, but as Gage plays the notes, I hear the volume increase with intensity. Chris lets out a deep low vocal riff with Sam backing him up with a higher note. It sounds haunting, as they repeat it a few times, I notice they have the crowd eating this up. As the intro builds, so too does the level of excitement.

On the fourth vocal riff, Alex jumps in with a low bass note to lead in Sam, together they bring the beat. On the first drum beat, Chris jumps in on his guitar and begins to sing a slow tale. "I'm waiting on the full moon light, only when the time is right, then I will know when to strike."

With Gage and Sam on backup vocals, they chant in, "I don't want to scare you." They harmonize the word, you, while Phoenix strums his rhythm guitar to build the overall sound.

The dark room begins to glow as cellphone lights are clicked on, leading Chris right into the second verse, "I saw your eyes blaze my dear, and my hair raised in fear, then I had to fight him here."

"I don't want to share you... but I'm going to share you..." As they sing the story, I realize Gage wrote this about me or rather our relationship. Not only am I blown away by his talent in writing this rock ballet, but him playing it for the world, putting his own emotions on display for everyone to hear. I'm absolutely stunned.

A faster part comes up that is harmonized on repeat, signaling the chorus break. "A she-wolf with a wicked desire, devours sex in the witching hour." Chris might be doing the singing but these words are all Gage. I laugh and cry at the same time. "I got to share you, I'll only share you."

There is a guitar break with Chris and Phoenix battling it out, building the song up, for the epic explosion of the crowd's applause, in a second of quiet air. Gage jumps back in, playing his quiet melody again until Chris starts the third verse. "Didn't care if I lived or died, I can't stand to live this lie, I'd rather we live our life."

"I might want to share you." The backup voices sing softly.

"I just want to share your place, howling with you into space, you're my Queen and it ain't no race," Chris growls out the last verse and holds the note.

"I'm ready to share you, we're going to share you."

As they jam it out leading back into the chorus, I hug Sabre and reach for Magennis to join us. "Don't tell me you're enjoying this dribbling nonsense," Magennis teases, making me laugh through tears.

"I think it is so romantic," Lilith sighs as she turns back to us and I see she has tears streaming down her face too. Sabre extends his free arm to let her join in on our hug before Magennis breaks off to grab us more drinks.

We stand, lining the front of the bar, listening to the boys end the song and jump into another. This one has a funky blues beat. I watch with pride as Gage plays right along as if he has been a part of DTD from the start. His body grooves to the beat as his fingers dance across the keyboard with the confidence of a seasoned player. His eyes are fixed on his hands, and there is a serious frown of concentration riding his brow, but the smile on his lips says it all, he's having the time of his life.

One blues beat turns into a rock anthem, that turns into four more of the band's big hits. The crowd is jumping along, bringing out the club's security, to break up a group trying to body surf. Magennis keeps a steady stream of drinks coming, which keeps me on level ground, but after a few, I notice Lilith is getting tipsy. She seems plastered enough to pass out and not hear us in the bedroom and after another hour, that's where I'm longing to be.

As if Chris read my mind ... *okay, I do send him a mental message*, he cues the band to wrap it up. The drums drop, and the guitars and keyboard fade with only the bass still keeping a beat. "We hope you had as much fun as we did tonight. Thanks for coming out. Good night!"

They jam out one final song, ending with Sam throwing his sticks out to the crowd. There are some screams as a couple of girls fight over one of the sticks. The stage lights flash off and the guys exit towards the back.

"That's our cue," Sabre says, taking my hand. "We'll meet them outside."

Sabre leads our way, keeping his grip on my hand to weave us around the drunk patrons. Magennis is behind us, his hand securely clamped onto a stumbling Lilith, as we make our way out the front exit.

"I love that bar," Lilith slurs as she trips over the threshold, and falls into Magennis with a giggle.

"We'll see how much she still likes it come morning," Sabre chuckles to me, as we watch Magennis try to get Lilith to climb on his back, so he can piggyback her.

I, for one, am glad to finally be outdoors, even the wall of moist heat thick in the air, is a welcome. Once the door closes behind us, it's as though a weight has been lifted as the extra energy I've been soaking in is locked safely away.

"Can't say I'll miss this place much," I say to Sabre with a sigh.

His eyebrows pinch with concern. "Are you okay?" He asks.

I nod my head. "I'm a bit drained and hungry, but I'll be fine once we get back to the apartment."

His attention is behind me and he smiles. "I can help with one out of two." He tugs my hand still in his grip, turning me in the direction he's looking. "How about some street meat?"

I giggle when I see a hotdog cart halfway down the block. "I could go for some strange meat, as long as it's hot." We walk towards the heavy BBQ smell.

"What's hot?" Gage asks from a dark alleyway beside the building.

I turn to see him, Chris, and the band coming out of the shadows. "Well, I was thinking the street meat but seeing you guys, I might have to change my order."

"Really, Baby, you're comparing me to ground feet and beaks... I'm insulted. I mean, I can see how you might be confusing the human with that, but me? I'm prime cut grade A." Gage plays it up, sliding into my arms for a hug.

His body is warm and his shirt is wet from sweating on stage. "You might be right; you definitely feel hotter than street meat." I give him a big hug then whisper in his ear, "Thank you for the song, I loved it."

He squeezes me tight. "And I love you."

"You'd think the guy performed some miracle or something," Sam barks out.

"I know. Where's the love for us? We had to carry his ass in there," Alex adds his jab.

"Come on guys, go easy, for an old dude, he rocked it, not too bad. Although, he did slow down towards the end and he'll probably need a nap soon." Chris slaps Gage on the back.

Gage turns his attention toward Chris, in a serious voice he says, "Choose those words wisely, buddy, this night is still young, and we have some entertaining to do. We'll see which one of us is begging for backup then."

"Oh, burn," Sam laughs, then high-fives Phoenix.

"Before this turns any uglier than it already is, how about we let September eat some food, or we will all be begging for backup." Sabre hands me two large sausage foot longs, covered in ketchup and dripping with cheese. Just the way I like them.

"Good call, feed the beast before the beast feeds on us." Gage jokes while placing his own order.

"Hey Magennis, what's with the monkey on your back?" I hear Sam tease, getting some laughs from the rest of the band.

Magennis gives a chuckle then explains, "Ms. Lilith has fulfilled her goal of getting intoxicated this evening."

I listen to the banter as Lilith slides down Magennis back, stating she's not nearly drunk enough. "Well, Lily-girl, you've picked the right guys to help with that." Sam takes Lilith's hand and gives Magennis a nod that says, he's got her.

"That's a big smile," Chris says to me, looking back at the others where my smile is directed.

"I think Sam likes Lil, it's cute how he's taking care of her," I say, hoping that maybe they will find companionship with one another.

Chris turns back to me, meeting my smile with his own. "Yeah, he digs her, a lot, but don't tell him I told you. He likes to play the tough guy, and he'd hate it if you thought he had a soft side."

I shake my head at the absurdity, of course they have big hearts, I wouldn't be standing here otherwise. Men, they think they have to play it tough, when really, us women, fall for the soft side every damn time.

"We should probably grab a cab; it will be safer." I hear Sabre say to Gage, and I don't have to look far to see my soft-hearted men taking care of me.

Gage shakes his head, digging out his phone. "I'll call my car service; it will be better to stick together in one car." Sabre agrees with a grunt.

As we munch away on our late-night snack, we start walking up towards the main road, keeping ourselves grouped together. Even at this late hour, the street is full of party goers filtering out of the clubs and taverns we pass on our way. Most of the people we pass are human, but on occasion, I sense a sub in the crowd. Our quick walk has taken us to the corner of University Avenue and our car has not yet appeared, but judging by the number of people coming out of bars, this doesn't surprise me.

"This walk is taking forever." I hear Lilith grumble.

Alex pulls a flask out of his back pocket, "Here, this will help." He hands her the metal flask that she twists open to take a sip.

She takes a swallow and starts to cough. "Oh yuck, what the hell is this?" She pushes the flask back to Alex, making more coughing sounds.

Alex takes the tin and sucks back his own swallow. "Smooth, isn't it?" He too coughs out, "It's called samogon, a Russian moonshine I got when we toured there."

"That's awful," Lilith says, reaching for the flask for another sip.

"They say the cars are backed up and it could be another fifteen minutes," Gage says to Sabre, bringing my attention back to them, and away from Lilith signing her death warrant with homemade hooch.

Sabre turns back down the street; a worried frown crosses his face. "We will need a few cabs to get back, and it will split us up."

"You four should go together," Chris joins in the conversation, nodding his head at Gage, Sabre, Magennis, and myself. "Keep September safe, the guys and I will get Lilith back to the apartment."

"I hate that I'm saying this, but I agree." Gage gives Chris an approving head nod.

"Well, we can agree all we want, the only problem is, I haven't even seen a damn taxi since we left that flea infested mouse trap," Magennis chimes in.

I look back down the street we just walked up. I see many cars driving by but not one is a cab. "Well, at least it's a beautiful night for a walk." I turn back to my men to see faces full of worry. "Hey, we'll be fine, it's only a few blocks."

Magennis drops his head down at my feet with a shake, "Perhaps I need to piggyback ye, my dearest."

I grin. "I can take my shoes off, but a piggyback ride does sound fun." Magennis comes at me, grabbing me around the waist to pick me up in a hug. "I think you got this backwards," I giggle out.

"Hey, we should race," says Lilith, tackling Sam. They stumble, and both tumble onto the sidewalk.

"Oh," I gasp then cover my mouth to stop myself from laughing, the others are not as polite.

Chris leans over to help Lilith to her feet, and more laughter ensues when somehow she brings him down too.

"Jesus suffering fuck, ye all are a flaming bunch of eejits," Magennis scolds them, and this starts another round of laughs.

Someone lets loose a loud whistle down the street that has me covering my ears. Sabre and Gage swing around, crouching into a fighting stance, while Magennis walks us forward away from the possible threat. Being in Magennis's arms, looking in the direction of the caller, I notice Zander coming down the street waving his arms.

"Gage, it's your friend, Zee," I say, and pat Magennis on the shoulder to stop him. "We're good, he's friend, not foe." Magennis stops and half turns but doesn't let me go until he's sure Zander isn't coming to harm me.

Zander jogs the rest of the way down the block to meet us, once he's close Sabre backs up to be closer to me. Chris and Sam finally get Lilith to her feet and pull her back towards us, while Alex and Phoenix stand closer to Gage as a front line. I'm not sure if any of them know they are building a wall of defense or if they had some meeting beforehand on what they should do, whichever the case, they all unite as one.

"Hold up," Zander calls out. "I didn't realize you left the club. I have something you need to hear."

Gage walks forward to greet Zander. They shake hands, but Gage doesn't let him get any closer. "What's up?" He asks, keeping himself in front of Zander.

"Earlier, when I was talking to our Queen, I promised her I would check out the wolves in the Shoe. I wanted to tell her what I found out," Zander explains to Gage, his eyes searching our group for me.

I wiggle myself out of Magennis's arms, making my way towards Gage. "It's okay Gage, he's telling the truth. Who were those wolves?" I place my hand on Gage's ridged shoulder, he steps off to the side but stays in front of me.

"As I told you, I go to the Shoe because other subs don't." He turns to Gage to explain himself, "I like being alone, always have."

Gage shakes his head in understanding as Zander continues, "I didn't recognize them when they were talking to you two." He gestures to Sabre and Magennis, now behind me. "After you guys finished talking to them, they went to the bar by the pool table; so, I joined them for a beer."

"They said they were from the Buffalo pack. Mag and I talked with them, they seemed to check out." Sabre sounds unsure of his words and when I look back, he and Magennis are sharing an uneasy glance.

"Yeah, they're from Buffalo, but they came here for the same reason so many others have, over the last few weeks." Zander fills us in then turns to Gage. "They heard the rumors about you, my friend. The same ones putting questions in everyone's minds, and have made you lose local business."

I watch Gage get tenser, he's practically vibrating from his stress. "What are you saying, Zee?" Gage asks in a demanding tone.

"I'm saying, no one believes you are the Queen's Alpha, and when you hit the stage with these guys, the wolves took off, but not before they made some comments about you not being fit for the role." As Zander explains, I finally understand.

Wolves are about the strength, especially for the Alpha, they have to show their dominance with everything they do. This is partially why Gage and I have had so much trouble in our relationship, and it all goes back to his father. The old ways are deep in the wolf culture, Gage's dad hated him because he wasn't masculine enough. He plays music, decorates homes, has a soft loving side, and has allowed me free reign, for the most part. For the wolves, he's showing weakness, and they don't see him as someone that can lead all the packs, especially if there's a war.

"This is stupid," I spit out as my temper starting to surface.

Sabre reaches out to place his hand on my shoulder. "September," he says in the tone he has that tells me to calm down.

I turn to face him. "Well, it is. They are judging him on words said by a dead man. A dead man that wasn't strong enough to win a fight... against his own son."

"It doesn't matter, the wolves have their ways." Sabre tries to settle me.

"I don't give a rat's shit about their ways. My magic picked Gage, not their beloved Garo. All these rumors and lies about Gage is a direct reflection on me as their Queen. It means if they don't believe in Gage, then they definitely don't believe in me."

"September." Gage comes over to stand in front of me. "What are you going to do, take them all out?" He smirks at me, "Baby, I love that you're getting worked up to defend my honor, but this is my fight. One I should have had a long time ago. I've hidden for far too long because I believed what everyone, especially my father, said about me. It has only been through you, I realize I'm a better person, that's what I tried to tell you earlier. You made me believe in myself, for the first time in my life, and because of that I will prove my worth in this challenge."

"You don't have to prove anything to anyone, Gage, I picked you."

His hand cups my cheek. "I know you did, Baby, and that's why I have to do this. The only person I need to prove anything to is myself. I need to know in my heart, I am worthy enough to be your mate."

I grab for him, throwing my arms around his neck to bring him to me. "Jesus Christ, Gage, why must you always be so damn difficult."

He laughs. "You bring out the best in me."

I roll up on my toes so our eyes are level. "You are lucky you're my favorite pain in the ass." I lean forward to capture his lips with mine. I convey emotions through the kiss that I know I can't say out loud, I'm scared.

Through our connection, I hear him tell me everything will work out and I will never be rid of him. After a few minutes, we part lips but stay in our embrace. "So, what now?" I say, bracing myself for the answer.

Gage turns his head towards Zander. "Have they gathered?"

Zander looks around at our group, nodding his head. "I followed the two from the bar, they met with a large rout at Queen's park. I heard they fixed it so you'll have to walk home and they will ambush you on the way."

"Dirty buggers," Magennis swears.

"Does anyone else notice how ironic it is that they are in a park called Queen?" Alex comments.

"Oh, the irony is not lost on us, I assure you," says a soberer Lilith.

Sabre turns to Gage, "How do you want to play this out?" He then adds, "I'm with you, whatever you decide."

Gage thinks for a minute, his eyes flicker from me then over to Sabre. "Don't even think about not including me." I wave my finger at them.

"It will be safer if you go home, Baby," Gage pleads with me while Sabre adds, "They may try to go after you too, Darling."

I huff, putting my hands on my hips. "I dare them too, no one messes with my family. Lead me into these wolves and I will show them my special brand of badass."

"I don't doubt that, Darling," Sabre agrees and Gage adds, "Not for a second."

CHAPTER 22

University Avenue is only three city blocks from Gage's Apartment, with the park cutting through the center of the third block. If we stroll along at a human pace, exploring the dark shop windows, the walk will be about twenty minutes. As supernatural, with the ability to move at a much faster pace, and now having an ambush to walk into, we can make the trip in less than five minutes. This can give us the upper hand against the wolves waiting to attack us, but Gage is adamant and feels this duel needs to happen, whether I want it to or not.

Before we set out or even make a plan, Samuel runs off to a twenty-four-hour connivance store, for supplies of coffee and energy drinks to sober up Lilith, and the human half of our group. We all need to be on our toes for whatever is waiting for us in the park. We know Gage is the main focus for the wolves, but there is always a possibility for this to be just another test for me by another group of subs.

A plan is difficult to formulate since we don't really know what we will be walking into, but when push comes to shove I know we work better under pressure. All we can do is be ready, alert, and willing to roll with punches; as we start our trek down the sidewalk, I sense an overall confidence in our group.

Most of the first block passes in silence while we're lost in our own thoughts. I don't even need my magical abilities to know what we are feeling. There is worry written on the faces of my court, and their bodies move with an anticipation of nervous energy.

Halfway down the first block, I realize how far we have all come. Not even a year ago, we were either strangers or just acquaintances, and now we have become this strong family-style unit. Willing to put everything we knew or were before, aside, to support one of our members in trouble, and we do it without judgment because we care.

At the start of the second block, we pass a couple of wolves. I watch as they cross the street and double back towards the park. "They have people watching for us," I quietly tell Sabre.

"I don't doubt they had eyes on us most of the night," he says then adds, "The two from Buffalo were probably sent into the bar to keep tabs on us until we left. I should have thought of that." He sounds angry, and I know it's at himself.

"Hey, this isn't anyone's fault and it won't be the last time someone comes for us." I reach for his hand, saying, "Especially now that we know what Lazarus told us. I have a feeling tonight will be a walk in the park in comparison."

Magennis laughs, "No pun intended, I presume."

A few of us chuckle over my slip of words and it lights our mood as the banter begins at the start of the second block. "I have to tell you guys, hanging with you is always an adventure, but it is starting to become hazardous to my existence," Sam teases.

"Don't worry, if anything happens to you, I will happily bring you over to our side," says a sarcastic Magennis.

I turn back to smile at Samuel. He does not have the expression of someone worried about becoming an undead. Instead, he seems to be debating the idea and when his eyes glance over to Lilith, I realize he might not mind becoming a more permanent part of our world.

Turning my head forward I notice Chris is watching Sam too, he sees me looking at him and shrugs his shoulder. "It's his life," he whispers.

I frown at Chris. "He better not do anything stupid."

Chris smirks. "Like becoming one of the Queen's mates, you mean. That's not stupid, Kitten, that's doing the right thing because you love someone."

"This is different," I try to explain.

He chuckles. "No, not really. Face it, we men will do almost anything if we know we'll get the girl."

I hear Gage, Sabre, and Magennis mumble agreeing words around me. I glance to each of them in surprise. "Really, you would put yourself in a position that may lead to your death or becoming something other, all for a girl."

As a group, my men all say in a quiet whisper, "My life for you, my Queen."

I sputter out, "This is a totally different thing."

Gage puts his arm around me. "No, it isn't, Baby. If the kid wants to convert to our side because he loves the girl, then I won't stop him. I think we all can understand the allure of the right woman, human or other."

I huff, "Well, that's silly." I roll my eyes.

Sabre squeezes my hand. "Is it Darling, because none of us would even be here if we thought it silly?"

"And before ye go off saying something like, we men think too much with our penis and not enough with our brain, and that we might not be going into another situation had none of us been involved," Magennis says in a tone to emulate me talking. "I will remind ye that on our own, we three, were a bunch of hollow shells, merely existing and now we have a purpose."

"I agree, Mag. I didn't even belong to a pack before I met you, Darling, and now I'm walking towards a park to defend my Alpha and my Queen. I'm worried, but I'm ready to fight for us," Sabre announces.

"See what you created, Baby." Gage hugs me. "You have given us all a reason to go on, so don't discourage the kid's decision. It's his to make like we did, and if I had to go back to do it again, I'd walk through the gates of hell to find you."

I love my men, they put up a great argument, and I would have to be a selfish and narrow-minded creature to not understand their points. "You're right, all of you, if that is his wish when the time comes, I will do everything in my power to make it happen." I say with a nod.

Gage jolts beside me. "Holy shit, I guess there won't be a need to walk through hell since it just froze over."

"What, I can't agree with you?" I ask with a grin.

Magennis laughs. "It's so rare for ye and Gage to agree on anything. I'm inclined to wonder who ye are and what did ye do with our little Minx?"

"This trip might have been a good idea after all," Chris adds, clapping Gage on the shoulder.

Again, they have a good point, Gage and I have come to a place in our relationship that works. It just figure that it happens just before he is going into something that might take him from me.

"Hey now, no sad faces." Gage stops us at the mouth of the park, turning me to face him.

Ahead of us lurking in the shadows of trees, I sense many wolves waiting for us. I lower my voice to not be heard, "I understand why you need to do this. I support your decision and I have no doubt that one on one with any wolf, you will be victorious. My only concern is the other few hundred lurking in the trees, I'm getting an odd feeling this isn't going to be a fair fight. Maybe we should regroup, or, I don't know..."

Our group moves in, creating a tight circle around me and Gage. He has been holding my arms as I have my little freakout when I'm done he trails his hands down my arms until they rest at my hips. He grabs my waist and pulls me to him, "September, you are not the only one that gains strength from this union. If they want to fight dirty, then let them. I think we're all ready." He looks around our group; at the heads nodding in agreement he adds, "See, we all stand together and that is how it will always be. Nothing is going to happen to me tonight, I promise."

I roll my eyes. "Stop being so damn cocky, you can't guarantee that."

His eyes light up with a sparkle. "Oh, but I can, Baby." A wicked grin spreads wide across his lips. "You heard the angel, he said *we* will have a child, our window of opportunity is closing, but we still have time. This means, I will come out of this tonight and when I do, I will make damn sure by week's end, you're pregnant, and that's a promise you can take to the bank."

There's heat to the stare he lays upon me, for a brief moment I catch a hint of his desire. He's holding it back because there are more pressing issues, but it is there, and it's enough to melt my panties off if I had any on. A tiny moan escapes on my exhale of breath as my switch is flipped, yet again. I feel myself light up from the inside, every nerve in my body springs into action, craving touch. My magic sends out a signal to my men, screaming all systems are good to go, and like magnets, I feel them being drawn towards me

"All right then, on that note, enough of this. We came here for a purpose. Now, let's get this show on the road."

Lilith moves in between me and Gage, pushing us apart. "You two need to learn to keep it in your pants, for God's sake."

"Puppies, picnics, pickles, and beer," Chris chants over and over to himself, moving away from me as fast as he can.

"What the hell is that?" Gage throws Chris a questionable look.

Defeat the Darkness break into a laugh. "It's our blue balls chant," Phoenix spits out. "And by the sounds of it, the dudes got a heavy set, waiting to burst."

Lilith groans and sends me a disapproving sneer. "Boys are disgusting. I don't understand how you can deal with so many of them."

"Knock it off the lot of ya. Ms. Lilith is correct, we came here for a reason, and it is not to look like wankers. Let's tuck our bursting sacs aside and get on with it, shall we?" Magennis's scolding helps me calm down. "Now, my dearest, let's get ye focused, tell us how many of the beastly bastards are hiding in the trees?"

I've been standing with Lilith in the center of our circle, which has moved out and away from me, but still close enough for us to communicate. Magennis's question has done what he intended it to do, focus me on our goal and not on them. I close my eyes and take a breath, meditating to concentrate on our surroundings. Using my magic like earlier today, I force it forward, searching for other sub energy. Unlike this afternoon, when I couldn't find Lazarus, I do locate what I'm searching for here.

The park isn't that big, a city block that has two sections. The first starts down by us with a stand of trees on either side of a walkway, leading to some large building. "I sense a half dozen at this end before a building, with a few on the side paths around to the back," I tell my court.

I stretch my wave of magic further, towards the second section, another area equal in size to the first, but this one has more trees. In the center is another structure where all the footpaths lead to. "The other part of the park has way more... I'm sensing close to a hundred, maybe. It's hard to tell, there's a lot bunched up, especially in the middle," I explain.

"Then that's where we need to be," Gage announces.

"By the statue of King Edward, I wonder if that has any significance?" Magennis ponders out loud.

Sabre turns to Magennis. "Wasn't he the king that chose to abdicate?"

Magennis slaps on his worry grin. "The one and the same."

Sabre swings back towards Gage, his head swivels between me and Gage. "Mag, back me up here, but I think we just figured this whole thing out." Sabre's face has gone blank and I can't tell what he's thinking.

He moves between me and Gage as Magennis says, "We have indeed."

I'm lost, I have no idea what Sabre and Magennis are getting at, and I have no clue what it has to do with some old king. I do feel both Sabre and Magennis shield their thoughts from me, and their moods shift like they are bracing for something bad.

"I'm not going to like where this is going, am I?" I glare at Sabre.

He turns to me, reaching out for me to come to him, "Sorry, Darling, but no, I don't believe you will."

I sigh and reach for his outstretched hand with my own. "Well, fill me in, the suspense isn't going to kill me, but I have a feeling someone else might be in danger."

Sabre pulls me into his arms, turning me away from Gage towards Magennis, who steps closer to us. "Mag, you want to do it?" Sabre asks Magennis.

His worry smile sits on his lips. "Yes, I believe that will be best." He turns his head at Gage to give him a hard stare. "You, my boy, better brace yourself."

I'm not sure what Gage does because Sabre hugs me to his chest and places his hand on the back of my head so I can't move. All indications pointing to me about to go into a massive red moment.

I get what they are doing, shielding me from the waiting wolves and protecting me from possibly killing Gage. "King Edward the seventh ruled in England for a very short term, I believe it was less than a year. He chose a relationship with a woman over his crown and that is why he abdicated," Magennis explains.

"I don't get it, kings are allowed to marry, what's the big deal?" Asks Chris somewhere close behind me.

"Yes, of course, they can marry, and it is encouraged to continue the bloodline, but they cannot be a king and marry a woman that has been divorced if the ex-husband is still alive. It is simply forbidden, so he chose to give up the throne."

"So, what does this history lesson have to do with me being challenged?" I hear the annoyance in Gage's words.

Magennis smirks in Gage's direction. "My dear boy, are ye daff? Think it through, there is symbolism all over the place."

I hear Gage gasp and Magennis nods his head. "Now you see?"

"I would like to see too." I'm annoyed with this dance, "Magennis, what the devil are you trying to say, spit it out."

Magennis purses his lips then takes another small step closer to place his hand on my cheek. "Gage, unfortunately, had a wanker of a father that emasculated him. The dick, made the poor boy out to be a poof, and since he never consummated his first marriage, the Kelowna pack believed the rumors. Now, their missing Alpha has reappeared to stir the pot rotten and is waiting for us to join him by the statue of an abdicated king. Where I have no doubt, the bugger is going to want your Alpha to either abdicate himself or die while they beat him to a pulp."

Sabre's arms tighten even more around me. "Jesus Christ, Magennis, you could have said it a bit more delicately."

As I stand pinned to Sabre's massive chest, I'm glad Magennis tore the band-aid off the way he did. I much prefer having the information slapped in my face. That's what this is, a slap, not only in my face, but Gage's too. That redheaded bitch, Cassandra and her father, Leland Kline, have been the catalysts behind dethroning Gage, ruining his business and challenging him as Alpha. I'm sure while they were at it, they put doubt out there about me too. I should have taken the cow out when I first met her, instead, Gage let her walk away, probably with a large chunk of change, even after she tried to blackmail him.

The more I think about the smug faced little twat, the more I want to smash her into perfect bite-sized bits. Not only is my demon peeking out, but the twitch of a change coming on too, that will turn me into my she-wolf form, so I can catch my prey and eat her. A low dark growl vibrates up my throat, as the hairs on my arms start to rise from the prickling of nerve endings starting to shift.

"Shit, Gage, she's changing, help me." Sabre calls Gage before he begins to plead with me, "September, darling, please talk to me, tell me what you're thinking."

I growl again, as my vision slides into shades of red, everything else around me fades. "Lift her legs, help me carry her into the trees." Sabre orders someone, who, I don't really care. I only want to hunt; I only want to kill.

My world tilts.

September!

My name is screamed inside my head and my wolf perks up to listen.

September, stop!

Him, just one word but when I hear it only one person comes to mind. My Alpha. He is commanding me; I must listen but I don't want to. I want to hunt.

Hunt who, September?

The red one, Alpha, she must die first. I want to kill her for threatening my territory.

September, no! No kill and no hunt.

But Alpha, she has wronged us, I won't allow it, she will be brought down.

September, stop, now!

I feel my Alpha at my back, he has grabbed me, pinned me down, and is biting my neck. I fight him, but he bites harder, pinning me in place.

Enough!

I freeze, my Alpha is angry. I've done wrong and as his Beta, I must submit. I relax my body going limp, giving myself to him to punish. I'm sorry, Alpha.

September, stop the change, now!

I must listen to my Alpha, but the change has started, too hard to stop. I can't stop.

Yes, you can, you are strong. Do it, stop the change.

My skin is already ripping; my bones have begun to shift and are starting to pop to move into new shapes. The all-encompassing pain has blinded and paralyzed me. How can I stop this; it has already begun.

You will stop, don't make me say it again!

He bites my neck hard, in warning, I understand. I scream as I fight myself to stop, my lungs burn as I vomit the last of the air from them. I will my body to reverse the order of events, re-break the bones, set them back, shorten the spine and align. I convulse, the violent shake takes control of me, flips me back and forth like a fish out of water. My vision has been gone, lost in a sea of darkness, but ever so slowly a flare of blood red color glows around the edges.

The pain is indescribable; I want to die just to make it stop. Then I smell a scent reminding me of my home and the forest surrounding it, dirt and pine, musk and fresh water. I concentrate on the smells, I know them, they represent home, family, and all that I love. This triggers another response, this time lower and makes me want my Alpha, in ways only he can make me crave.

Instantly, my vision flares again, the reds dim into pinks that turn orange and finally settle into yellow. With the change of colors, I can also make out shapes, long and thin, bushy, square, they don't make sense at first until the yellow begins to clear. Finally, as my head becomes more lucid, the shapes become objects, people, trees, garbage bins.

The world starts to take shape before me again, the pain is nearly gone, except for my lungs that beg desperately for air. I gasp a breath and a few more. I wheeze and cough, like a heavy smoker as my lungs begin to work again.

"Ssh, Baby. Take slow breaths, just relax, it's almost over." I hear Gage whisper in my ear and I can feel his hand stroking my hair.

Once I gain my bearings, I realize I'm face down in grass, behind a thick bushy hedge, tucked off to the side of a stand of trees. I hear car engines, so I know we are l close to the road, but hopefully at this late hour, the darkness hides us from the view of anyone passing by. I also notice I am surrounded by people; Gage has me pinned with his body pressing into my back, Sabre is in front of me loosely holding my arms. There are more hands on each of my legs, and I see several feet standing around me. I don't even want to know how many of them it took to hold me down.

My breath has leveled out, but there is still a bird-like-peep sound when I breathe in. I'm sure if I can get the weight of Gage off my back and sit up, the chirping noise will go away. "I'll let you up, but you will remain calm, do you understand?" Gage speaks in my ear, exactly how he had in my head. *He's my Alpha, I get that loud and clear.*

"Good girl," he praises me, lifting his body off of mine.

I suck in a bigger lung full, already the chirping noise is gone. Sabre lets go of my hands, staying crouched in front of me, he offers his own hand to help me up. I roll to my side, noticing Magennis and Chris standing on either side of me. Lilith is behind them, her back to us and her hands out in front of her, she has spun a spell around us to keep us hidden.

I take Sabre's hand and he stands up, pulling me with him. A dizzy feeling, probably from lack of oxygen, and I stumble, but Sabre is right there to catch me under his arm. "Move slow, your body has to be exhausted, give it some time to recover. Just don't ask me how much time, because I have never seen anyone get that far into a shift and be able to stop, then reverse it," he says, with pride in his voice.

I smile up at him to say thanks since my throat won't allow me to speak just yet. It feels like I ate a bowl full of glass, and then the bowl for good measure. Gage, walks back with his jacket in his hand, opening it for me to step into. Looking down, I understand the gesture, the shift had been so close to complete, I shredded my outfit. *I am sad for that loss, I really liked the dress.*

I walk myself into the jacket, turning to put my arms in the holes. Like Gage, this jacket is huge, it covers more of me than the dress had. I snort at how comical I look, but with a few rolls to the sleeves and with the buttons done up, it doesn't seem that terrible. I give Gage the thumbs up sign as he finishes dressing me. Then I notice Alex, Sam, and Phoenix lined up across the hedge, their heads just high enough to peer over the leaves into the courtyard of the building. I snort again, knowing Sabre would have made them look away from my nakedness, and they probably stayed there knowing I was shifting. No one wants to see that, it's repulsive.

"How are you feeling?" Sabre steps in front of me to ask.

I swallow. "Okay," I rasp out.

"Don't talk, not yet. Gage, she will need to feed soon, she looks pale," Sabre stresses to him.

"I know, but we still have a roadblock to get through," he snaps at Sabre then adds, "Baby, can you please hang on for a bit longer." His tone much softer as he speaks to me.

I nod my head to let him know I can, but to be honest, I'm not sure for how much longer. I am starving, in every way, if we are going to deal with the Kline family, we need to do it fast.

"Zee," Gage calls out towards the hedge.

"Yeah man." Zander's head pops up on the other side, making Alex jump.

"For fuck's sakes, dude," Alex screeches.

Gage ignores the exchange, "How we looking?"

"The crowd is growing and we got company." He tips his head sideways toward the courtyard.

"Okay, I guess it's now or never. Everyone ready?" Gage asks.

I feel Lilith drop her magic wall around us, as a few chime in on getting this over with, and the band does some more swearing. "Sab, you stay with September, if shit goes sideways, get her out of here. Chris, you and your boys work together, don't be fucking heroes. When this is over, we'll meet at the apartment to celebrate, got it?"

They all nod their head in response except for Zander. "Uh, Bro, you do realize our Queen has to be there, right?"

Gage turns back to face Zander, his head tilts to the side, "Why does she have to be there?" His voice is dead calm.

All eyes are on Zander now; I see him fidget under the pressure. "This is a challenge for Alpha, a duel to the death. Whichever wolf survives, must take a mate as his Beta, in front of the pack. In the event the Alpha is already mated, like you, he must perform the ceremony again, so the pack will respect the Beta. And, Gage, if he beats you, your Beta will be given to the Alpha, to do with as he sees fit."

There's a string of curses from almost everyone, a few hell no's, a couple of fuck that's and one, not fucking going to happen. Magennis slaps Gage on the back. "My advice to ya is, win."

Gage says nothing, his body says it all for him. As he takes a shaky breath in, I watch his shoulders roll back as his spine straightens, his jaw clenched, and his eyes darken into a deadly glaze. He doesn't look at any of us as he stares off at the courtyard. Mentally, I sense his anger and outrage, he's feeding himself from his own emotions, and it makes my demon happy.

I muster up some of my magic and send it to him, he closes his eyes and shivers as the power soaks into him. After a quiet minute of us all preparing for what awaits, I watch Gage open his eyes and look at me.

The person I see is not the Gage I know; he's void of any emotion. In a low deep gravel sounding voice, he speaks with a deadly tone, "Let's kill this mother fucker."

CHAPTER 23

Gage doesn't wait for us to respond. I feel his determination, he's more than ready for this fight. I glance at Sabre and see a mirror of the same expression on his face too. He reaches for my hand to guide me around the bush and straight towards the building's steps. Behind us, everyone breaks into pairs of two. Magennis is with Chris, Lilith walks beside Samuel, and Zander follows both Alex and Phoenix. There's a confidence to our small but mighty group, I can feel it radiating off of us, and I'm proud to call this my family. If we fight together, we will stay together because once we deal with this, there is nothing that will break us apart.

Gage makes it to the long stone steps first, he stops a few feet from the bottom to face up the top. As Sabre and I near, I finally get to see the wolves, not all of them seem as though they are here for a fight. I also notice the ones hiding, in the trees, and along the sides of the building, have not come forward. I think like many of the subs, they are curious, of me and my court as well as the outcome of the fight. Whatever happens tonight will have an effect on all of our lives. If my life had turned out differently, and I was just one of them, I'd be here watching too.

Sabre and I stop behind Gage, I slide into his left and Sabre takes a spot to his right, but we give him plenty of room in case he has to move fast. As the rest of our group arrives, we seem to fall into a pyramid shape of hierarchy. Behind Sabre on his right, Magennis takes his spot with Zander hovering behind Magennis. Behind me to the right is

Lilith with Sam to her right. On my left is Chris with Alex and Phoenix both standing on his right.

I realize the right of a person, is who stands for your protector or right-hand man, whereas the left side stands for your heart and the one you care for. As I think of how we have placed ourselves subconsciously, we all know our position within this court. Even if I stand at the head of the line, Gage and Sabre have been known to stand on either side of me, as I consider them equal in every way. Yet the rest of the pyramid stays the same.

Looking up at the door, to the castle-like building, stands a man that could pass for forty, but I imagine he's much older. He's not as tall as Gage, maybe more Magennis's height with a tree trunk build that is bulkier than Gage, but smaller than Sabre. This puts him somewhere between my men in size but doesn't come close to any of them in the hair department. His big cue-ball dome creates a glare on top from the glow of the security lights hanging on the building. He has on a short-sleeved collared shirt that is unbuttoned to show off his smooth chest and six-pack abs. The only hair he seems to allow is on his sun-kissed face, dark black eyebrows sprinkled with gray with matching goatee to shade his face and dark brown eyes. Looking at this man, Leland Kline, I find it difficult to believe he's related by blood to Cassandra.

"Well, would you look at this boys and girls, it's a special day. Better break out the tea set and sex swing, the Queen, and her hybrid are here with their cuckold," Leland announces in a loud baritone voice.

The wolves around him, and a few hidden in the shadows of the park chuckle out. My hackles rise, while beside me, Sabre, lets loose a low growl at the insult, but Gage remains silent in front of us.

"Oh look, the hybrid is angry." Leland laughs out from his soapbox, "It must be difficult to hear the truth, eh mongrel."

Sabre steps forward to align himself with Gage. "You show our Queen and Alpha disrespect with your words." Gage grabs Sabre's arm, holding him in place.

"Ah, yes, our Queen." Leland comes down a couple of steps to stand just above us. "I do find it intriguing how so many have accepted this human as their leader. We would be better off with the Overlord, at least he has shown his worth, and he doesn't surround himself with lesser beings. Really, my dear, a court of humans, do you think they will save you from the big bad wolf?"

There is another round of laughter from the tree line, Gage stiffens up in front of me. I imagine this is like a haunting image of his past, coming back to life. I touch his back for support, sending him another spark of energy as my demon begins to stir. If Gage doesn't rip off this asshole's head soon, I know I will.

Gage moves his hand up in a halting gesture to me then aims his words up at the wolf, "I presume you set up this ambush for a reason, Leland, why don't you tell us what you want?"

Leland has been laughing at us until Gage speaks. His smile, now absent on his face, replaced by a distasteful sneer, "What I want is what every wolf wants, a true Alpha. One strong enough to lead us when the war with the Overlord comes, and it will, now that you and this Queen have announced to the world that you exist. You bring the war to us, but you are not man enough to protect our race," Leland spews out.

Gage steps forward to offer his own speech, "That is where you are wrong, Leland. There is no war with Lazarus or one our race alone can win. Yes, war is coming, but not one we have ever seen before, and it will be this Queen, who will win it. We must be strong enough to stand with her, to protect all the subs. You seem to have forgotten we were created to be her protector, not feuding amongst ourselves for our own gain."

Leland steps down another step, only one remains between the two Alphas as they stare each other down. "This girl holds our curse, if she dies, then we are free. Let the other subs deal with whatever war, with or without the Overlord, by themselves. We will no longer subject ourselves to being a part of this world, you and your human army cannot stop that."

Gage levels the field, taking the last step up to meet Leland eye to eye, a devilish grin breaches his lips, "Is that a threat I hear, Leland?" Gage asks with malice.

Leland makes the final step down, coming just below Gage's chin, "No pup, that's a promise. I hereby challenge you, in front of these witnesses, to an Alpha duel and when I win, your Beta will be mine to do whatever I wish with. I might just keep you alive long enough for you to watch, as I first rape this she-wolf before I gut her, and pull the human heart from her chest."

Sabre growls out beside me, "Rip him apart, Gage." He then turns to step in front of me, moving us back into the rest of the court, making room for the duel.

Gage steps back down the step to the grass, he gestures for Leland to join him on the level ground. Leland just smirks at Gage, walking along the step he's on, slowly moving away until his back is to Gage. I'm sure this is some test to see if Gage will take the cheap shot of attacking Leland's from behind, but Gage is not the coward they think he is.

Leland, on the other hand, is not above a few cheating shots of his own. As he gets out of reach of Gage, I watch as he signals up towards a group of wolves. I sense the sudden rush of excitement in the air just before these wolves come bounding out to pounce on us.

"Protect the Queen," Gage yells at Sabre before he jumps forward to meet Leland's advance.

I don't have time to watch Gage's next move as Sabre is pulling me towards the hedges. Leland's wolves are advancing on our group and he is getting me out of the way.

"Sabre, wait." I place my hand on his chest to stop him. "I'm not running, Gage will be left alone. We have to protect his back, as well as each other's, we are stronger when we stick together."

Sabre meets my eyes with a wild glance. "I have been ordered to keep you safe," he's demanding that I comply.

"Safe, from what, these wolves," I laugh. "You and I both know they are no challenge for us, not after what we have been through." I give him a reassuring smile. "Besides, I'm Queen, and I out rank our Alpha."

He meets my smile with one of his own. "True enough." He swings his head back to check on our situation, taking in as much of the perimeter as he can, then turning to face me. "Alright, let's go win this, my Queen."

Knowing we are about to fight, Sabre turns off the worry and turns on his warrior. With a commanding confidence, he begins to shout orders to our court, "Mag, you and Lil take the others and go up the left side. Keep the wolves away from Gage's fight, let's keep it fair for him to win. September and I will take on the right side with Zander. Everyone clear with that?"

"Am I setting my spells to stun or kill?" Lilith asks, her hands already up to defend us from the wolves closing in.

"No, don't kill anyone, not unless you have no choice, we can't fault them for being misled." Sabre is right, even though my demon doesn't agree. This confrontation is not the fault of these wolves; it's only too bad Gage's father isn't here to answer for the injustice he did to his son.

I nod my head in agreement. "He's right, let's do this the right way. We can knock them out, but not off."

"The beasts are coming, are we ready?" Magennis asks the group, but his eyes are locked on me and full of unease.

I hear a few mumbles, but there is a lack of enthusiasm that worries me. We need to be fighters right now, and I know how to help. I dig deep into my magic; my pool is desperately low, but I have enough to get through this fight. I pull it out to sprinkle on my court to give us a bit of an advantage. Once I'm done wrapping them with strength, I can already see the confident expressions on everyone's faces, "Now let's kick some ass!" I shout and this time, I'm answered with equal cheers.

Sabre breaks off first, rushing back towards the building's steps, immediately tackling a wolf, getting him in a headlock to put him to sleep. My eyes flicker to Gage and Leland, dancing on the grass like two fighters in a boxing match, and in the quick glance, it appears to be a fairly equal round. The wolves, perhaps from Leland's pack, have circled around them, they appear ready to move in at any moment if Leland fails. Our objective is to clear up the field and protect Gage's back, but we first have to get through the dozen or so wolves coming at us.

Sabre knocks out another wolf then heads closer to Gage, while Zander splits off to the far side of the lawn to hold off any new advancing wolves from the trees. This puts me in the middle as a swing hitter, keeping their backs protected so they can do the important fighting. My demon is not at all happy, I can fight as equal as any of my men, and I crave the battle. All around me I can hear fists meeting flesh, a whiff of a copper tang in the air, and the sense of aggression from emotions, it has my demon practically doing backflips. My vision is clear, but there is a slight red haze starting to build on my peripheral vision. When I scan the stairs towards the big wooden door, I notice this is not a red moment coming on, but a red-haired annoyance instead.

Cassandra Kline stands on the top of the landing, looking down upon us. If I didn't already hold the title of Queen, I would swear she is auditioning for the role with her regal poise. I want to wipe the condescending expression off her face, as she watches her father and Gage beat each other, with blow after blow of heavy punches.

I glance at Gage; he's holding his own, but he's bloody from his beating. A beating that doesn't need to happen, a beating that started because of this she-devil. My demon jumps to attention from my anger, a growl escapes my throat as I stalk up the stone, toward my target.

A wolf comes at me from the left side of the platform, he jumps down to punch at my head. I duck then swerve with a super speed, allowing him to fall beside me. I twist down then around behind him, grabbing at his head with my hands. I pull up on the sides of his melon, extending his neck, with a quick jerk of motion, I feel the pop, an audible snap as his neck break and his life is extinguished. His body sags as it falls from my grasp. With a thud, he rolls down the steps, and I don't give him another thought.

Staying crouched low, ready for another attack, I scan the area to see two more wolves coming my way, they halt to a stop as they watch me kill the wolf. I grin at them, making sure to drop my fangs and let them be shown in the light. I'm running on reserve power, I'm hungry for everything that starts with an F: fighting, feeding, and fucking. Maybe they see this in my face since they both turn and hightail it back towards the trees.

I snort at the cowards while they beeline it to safety, noticing Sabre and Zander have knocked out quite a few of the wolves themselves. There is now a clear view of the Alphas from my vantage point on the steps. Gage has Leland down in a grapple, and it appears he has the upper hand. It won't be long before their fight is over and my window of opportunity to kick the she-devil's ass will be closed.

I swing back to the pastel princess, climbing the steps with a slow stealth like a cat does towards a mouse. She has not taken her eyes from the fight, the stupid girl. I will take her by surprise, it will be an easy kill. My eyes seek her out and everything else fades into the red haze. I will kill her, I can see it in my mind, taste it on my tongue, and hear every bone crunch in my ear. This will show her, and any others, you don't mess with what is mine.

A hand clasps my shoulder, and the grip pinches a nerve to bring me great pain, it stops me from going forward. I fall down on one knee to twist and kick at my captor's legs to get free. Lazarus stumbles down hard on top of me, but keeps his hard grip on my shoulder, pinning me to the stone surface. "I can't let you do this, little one, they are watching."

I don't understand what he's saying, who is watching and why do I care? The only thing I see in my head is taking down the skinny bitch, that's what matters to me right now. "Do not give into the jealousy, it is just the evil talking. The Gods will not like you killing an innocent," Lazarus reasons with me.

Somewhere in my head, the light breaks through, a golden glow, stopping me for a second to think over his words, from now and earlier today. The internal debate I'm having is one of good and evil. My demon half is wanting, craving, practically begging for the blood of Cassandra. All because of jealousy? Perhaps. It doesn't see any other path but the one that will take me to her. There is no rationalizing with this part of me, except when my men have shown me there is something better. From them, I have discovered this new part of me, the yellow light representing my angel, and the good that can come to us, if we believe in ourselves.

A sudden thought hits me, this is another test of my will. By taking out Cassandra, I prove to the Gods the darkness and evil win. If I step away, I prove there is light and hope for us all. My mom made these supernatural, and the Gods created the humans. In all of us is both good and evil and my job, like hers, is to instill this order. She might have lost hope, but I am stronger, and together with my family, we will make this world better.

As I teeter on this slippery slope of right and wrong, debating my existence, all of our existences, I wonder how will I make this work? "Trust in yourself and those around you, little one. The answers you seek will come from the hearts of those that matter most. This is only the first test you must survive, there will be more, and they will get harder as you become more powerful."

I blink, trying to clear my thoughts, letting the cold stone under my cheek cool me down. "I don't think I can handle any more power, Lazarus. I think I'm pretty much at my limit now, and I don't seem to be doing so well with controlling it."

He eases off my back, testing me to see if I have my head on straight again. When he's satisfied, I'm done with my hunt on Cassandra, he offers me his hand, "I think you are doing quite fine. Remember, your mother had a lifetime to build all this. You have had but a breath of that time."

I turn to him, "Yeah, but she failed and she knew what she was doing." My words come out angry, I know it is for her and not him.

Lazarus crouches beside me. "She did not fail; she knew she needed to create something even more powerful than herself. It was from her own sacrifice that you have come to be, and you will be greater than us all."

I roll my eyes, I don't mean to but come on... "Really, exactly how do you see this playing out because right now, I've about had it with the mood swings, the hormone spikes, the responsibilities, the need to make everyone happy, and keeping the races from killing themselves. And, if you're keeping track, I'm not even doing that well." I shout my anger at him and point to the lawn where Gage is standing over Leland's body.

For a second, I wonder if it's over, but then I remember the part where an Alpha has to die and I have to be claimed. A part of me shutters at the repulsion, and the other part shivers with anticipation. "Christ, I'm fucked up."

Lazarus sighs. "No, not fucked up, but you are original." He laughs then gets serious, "September, you are the true Queen, of light and dark, of all the races from all the realms. I know this can't be easy to navigate, but I assure you, it is for the good of all the worlds that you don't give in to either side. I promise to help you, but you also have to try."

I take his offered hand to bring myself up to a sitting position to survey the park. My court has done a number on the wolves. There are a few bound to trees from Lilith's magic, and many more who will be needing some icepacks, and Advil, come morning when they awake.

"I'll try for all of them, but what about me?" I ask with a sigh.

Lazarus rolls back on his bum to kick his legs down the step, sitting next to me. "You?" He says as a question, making me turn to him. He grins at me and gives me a wink, "You, my little bird, will one day be known as the most infamous Goddess of them all. You will find peace and happiness with those men, and you will go on to become the greatest ruler of all time."

I snort. "Now you're just shitting me." Whether he is or isn't, the man knows how to motivate a person. I feel better already.

He shrugs his shoulders. "We will just have to wait and see."

We sit on the steps, quiet for a time. I watch Sabre calmly talk to the wolves that have not attacked, and realize they all haven't come with the same opinions as Leland. Maybe there is hope for us after all. "Since I didn't kill Cassandra, does this mean the Gods will leave us alone or is there some other test they have waiting for us?" I ask out of curiosity.

He turns his sad eyes on me, offering a tiny smile. "I am sorry, but you must be challenged, a ruler cannot become powerful without being tested occasionally. For tonight, take the small victory; however, don't celebrate just yet. You still must do your job as Queen, gain respect from the wolf race by allowing this ritual to be performed."

He doesn't need to remind me; I've been watching Gage circle Leland's body for the last few minutes. I can tell Gage has not killed him yet, for Leland's chest continues to rise and fall, heavily with each breath taken. Gage is waiting on me, giving me time to prepare mentally, but I don't need time to think this over.

As I look to my people, I know where we stand and what is expected of us. Sabre showed me earlier, we all have a job, a title, but ultimately, I hold the cards and they will do whatever needs to be done for me. I am the Queen, and I accept this will not be easy, but I have support and unlike my mother, I will not run or hide.

I also accept each role I have within the individual races and tonight, I must become a Beta to my Alpha. Something I would had fought only a few days ago, but now, I understand. This time spent with Gage has given me a new respect for him and his role. I can see, by him waiting to kill Leland, he might have a new respect for me too.

I wonder why my lessons must be done in such a dramatic fashion and always in public places? I used to think the supernatural community was just a bunch of wacky perverts, always having to watch their leaders have public sex. I have obviously come a long way, or it's the estrous talking, but I'm kind of turned on about doing this.

I shake my head, *yeah, I'm fucked up.*

CHAPTER 24

All eyes are watching me: the wolves, my court, and especially my men, as I ascend the stairs then cross the lawn. I hold my chin up, my shoulders back, I am proud to be walking towards my Alpha and I want everyone to see that. Gage doesn't need to fight to show me his worth, he has already proven himself to me, since our first mating. However, I will gladly allow him to claim me in front of our followers to prove conclusively, my magic knew then what my heart knows now. Gage is our one true Alpha.

I'm thankful for losing my shoes back at the hedges, the cool grass feels amazing on my naked feet, and is keeping my mind grounded, while my body heats, the closer I get to Gage. From my moment of acceptance back on the staircase, I began to feel an incredible magnetic pull towards him. He is my light and I walk towards him in search of my need to recharge my magic, feed my hunger, and mate. With each step, my stomach flutters and my heart races with the anticipation of our union.

As our eyes lock, I'm drawn in by those beautiful sapphire globes guiding me to him and everything else around us becomes just a blur. A few feet before him I stop, to drink in the mere sight of him. His shoulder-length hair is covered in dirt and leaf litter, as it frames his striking, but blood smeared face. His left eye is swollen, his top lip is cut wide open, and his nose is a little more bent, but underneath the mess, is the cocky confident smirk I love. *Damn, he is sexy as hell.*

As I stand before Gage, any modesty I might have left, drifts away with the breeze as I remove the jacket from my body to present myself to him. Some natural force seems to take over, and I find myself bowing down before him. "I am yours, Alpha, if you see fit to claim me." I offer him, with a boldness in my voice.

Leland's body lays between us and I hear him groan out, "Kill me now."

Gage slams his foot down on Leland's chest, I hear a crunching sound before the older man screams in pain. Gage waits until the screams turn into gasps of breath, then with a deep booming voice he announces, "Let it be written in Werewolf law, that I, Gage Blackwood, am victorious in the duel against Leland Kline. For his defiance of my authority, he will be punished for his crime, by death. Anyone seeking to challenge this decision or the title, come forth now."

I stay on my knee, facing Gage, but with a peek, I can see many of the wolves in front of me. They have come from the trees to show their respect to Gage with a bow. Behind me, I hear the shuffle of bodies as many take a knee to the ground. Sabre is suddenly at my side, he watches the gathering with a keen eye, waiting for any wolf willing to take on Gage or me. He has stepped into the role as Gage's second in command, which is funny since, as my Vampire King, Sabre's second in command is Gage. They have truly become brothers in arms.

Once Sabre is satisfied the wolves are accepting Gage as Alpha, he too drops into a kneel. "All hail our Alpha," he shouts then adds, "Long live our Queen."

The group chants Sabre's words back, as acknowledgment for what has taken place on this early morning, is given. There is then a silence, except for the car traffic on the outside of the park and Leland's wheezing sputters. Beside me, Sabre rises and moves towards Leland, where he picks him up under the arms and drags him back.

This allows Gage to step in front of me, I don't look up, not yet.

He places his hand on top of my head, my body instantly recognizes his touch with a jolt of heat sinking low in my belly. "September Rae, do you accept me as your Alpha?" He asks loud enough for everyone to hear, and the deep rumble of his voice vibrates inside my head.

I swallow the part of me that usually fights him for control because it is now a small voice in my head while the louder one cries for his dominance. "I do," I answer in a purr.

His feet step to my right side where he cups my chin in his palm and brings my head up to meet his blazing stare. "Will you honor and obey me?" He sounds amused with this own question.

My body screams yes, it wants him to ravage me, but my brain screams no, this is a trick question. I take a second to think it over before I give my response, "As my Alpha, I will." This gives me the loophole of being able to continue to rule, as his Queen, when I need to.

His top lip splits open, a drop of blood forming in the center, as he smirks at me. The tangy scent has me salivating and my fangs drop down, craving his taste. "Will you allow me to provide for your every wish?" He draws his thumb across my lips and dips it into my mouth.

"I will," I jump to answer, my words are a mumble as I suck his thumb. The expectancy of his promise to provide what I need has my pussy pulsating.

His nose twitches as his smirk grows into a full-blown grin, he can smell how aroused I am and is enjoying my reaction. "Will you allow me to protect you and our future offspring with my life?" He asks, and this time I glare at him, knowing he is keeping the foreplay going to sneak in extra questions.

His left-hand moves fast to grab a fistful of my hair to pull my head back then he bends at the waist to bring our eyes level. His right hand is still cupping my face but he's removed his thumb from my mouth for me to answer.

"Fine," I growl a whisper. "I will," I say louder.

Again, a grin appears on his lips, "Will you respect my decisions for our race and support me in my role to rule?"

This time I roll my eyes, bringing his smirk back because he's about to play dirty. He drops his right hand under my breast, I feel the heat of his palm as he cups a handful to give it a squeeze. My nipple perks up, hardening by just his touch, as the areola pimples out, so too does the skin on the rest of my body. As a bit of extra torture, he blows down across the puckered nipple and I whimper at how unbelievable it feels. "Yes, yes, I will," I sputter out.

His palm curves up my breast so he can pinch the nipple between two fingers. He gives it a rough roll with the pads of his fingers. A spike of heat shoots from my breast along my nerve endings and down into my pussy. My muscles go into a voluntary spasm and my back bows, had his dick been inside of me, I might have just orgasmed.

I no longer notice the crowd gathering around to watch our interaction, I don't even care if they see I am putty in his hands, his bitch to control. My magic pulls to Gage, but it also pulls to my other men too, I want to give myself freely to them all at this moment. I ache for more touch, I crave their scent over me, I want to be bathed with their affections, and drown in their lust. I have waited too long, I need to recharge, I need to feed all the creatures that make up who I am. My demon, my vampire, my werewolf, my witch, and even my angel craves some sort of special pleasure.

Gage has been watching his fingers roll my nipple, I choke out a cry and he glances up to my eyes. His pupils expand in shock at what he sees, either my eyes changed color or I look shamelessly sinful; whichever the case he begins to move fast. "As the true Alpha I claim, September Rae, as my Beta and she will be forever respected as our Queen. Any harm done to her, our offspring, the members of her court, or my second in command will be a punishable offense of my choosing. I hereby acknowledge this as written law."

As he gives his speech he pulls me to my feet, once he's done Sabre shouts, "All hail our Queen." The circling crowd repeats Sabre's words and begin to bow.

The words of the ritual have been spoken and we can finally get to the part I desperately desire. Gage has bowed to me but cuts it short to stand at my back. I hear him unzipping his pants before he pulls my back into his chest. In my head, he tells me to concentrate on Sabre in front of me and to try to control myself, he's going to be quick so that they can get me out of here before I lose it.

The only problem with this is, I already lost it the moment he put his hands on me. My engine is in maxed rev, locked into the highest RPM it can go, and if he doesn't get his foot off my brake, I will implode in what I fear will be an epic crash. I reach back to grab a fistful of his hair, spreading my legs and tilting my ass at the same time. I lean back and with a low purr to his ear I growl, "Damn-it, just fuck me already."

I hear him gasp as he realizes I'm beyond a quickie, thankfully it prompts him to continue with a forced speed. Grasping my hip with his left hand to hold me in place, he guides his cock with his right. He begins to stroke himself between my ass cheeks for a couple of pumps, milking the pre-cum from the head of his cock. A drop drips down onto my asshole and continues to fall until it sails past my opening and falls away. I'm torn between wanting to turn around to suck him off with my mouth or bend forward to let him plunge deep into my abyss. The images of both burn in my mind and before I can decide, I'm moaning as Gage slips down to push himself into my wet opening.

The combination of our lust, allows me to welcome his cock smoothly into my opening, but he has to work at getting his girth in further. His left arm clutches me around my stomach so I can lean over without falling. This frees his other hand to spread my pussy lips open, with his middle finger he can rub my clit, and get it into a happy place. The combination of clit masturbation with his slow circling hip thrusts provides the perfect sensation I crave for a release. It doesn't take him long to get the pressure to build and with a shameless zeal I let go.

The moment the release starts, the burning in my skin returns and just like earlier on the plane, I feel like I'm on fire, from the inside out. The pain is much more intense than it had been hours ago and my eyes seek out Sabre's to plead for help since I can't find a voice to scream. In my head, I send pictures to both Sabre and Gage, of char burnt meals and bonfires to get my point across.

Sabre bolts forward but stops once he reaches me. "What do I do?" He asks aiming his gaze at Gage for an answer.

Gage pulls out of me to stand me up, the loss of contact increases the pain until I can no longer see and my body begins to convulse on its own. "Before, when she fed off of me it helped." I hear the panic in his voice while his hands spin me round.

I'm lost in my head, a bright glow of light is all I can see, it's harsh, blinding, and I feel sick. I force myself to concentrate on my other senses, and as quick as the thought,

I am engulfed in the scent of my man. "Baby, take my vein." I feel a hand cup my head to pull me forward until the scent of the woods and Gage fills my nose. I'm unable to see to take his vein, though, so I whine in my throat.

"Sab, cut me open, I don't think she can find my vein." I feel Gage shuffle back and Sabre's musk scent is added to our mix. I realize Sabre is about to dig his own fangs into Gage to allow the blood to flow for me to make contact. That image plays out in my head, and the burn sinks down between my legs until I'm dripping with a heated desire I have never experienced before.

My mouth is salivating from the scent of coppery goodness. I want Gage's blood but I also want so much more. A string of erotic thoughts and sexual explorations play in my head like a gif on a Tumblr site.

"Oh fuck!" Chris swears from somewhere behind me.

I hear Magennis chuckle, "What a dirty Minx." I think he likes this the most and I'm thrilled to have him so open to my ideas.

Against my back, I feel Sabre's voice boom, "This is something very powerful September is fighting. She will need us all, body, blood, and spirit to get through it. We're out of time to get her to a safe place but if we work together we can help her."

"Zander, take Alex and Phoenix to circle the wolves, block us in so I can spell the perimeter while these guys take care of the rest." Lilith starts organizing our team, knowing my men are busy at the moment.

"September, lead the way, whatever you need, my darling, we are here for you." As Sabre gives me the go ahead, I lick my lips with an anticipation of what is to come. I'm hoping it's all of us.

Sabre is right, whatever is happening to me, it's a powerful force craving something from every part of me. I strike at what I know is the strongest of my cravings, it happens to be Gage's vein, thanks to Sabre biting him open for me. I feel him jump then tense from my violent bite, but as I begin to suck in his life force he slowly relaxes. I don't even notice his usual amazing flavor. I have been starving for too long and the thirst doesn't seem to be going away.

I know I need to quench the other cravings within to get through this. I lean against Gage and let my hands explore down his body until I find what I'm looking for. I grasp his cock in my hand, it is still coated with my release and my fingers slide up and down easily. He didn't get to release earlier so every stroke I give, has him throbbing in return. He's dripping pre-cum from his swollen head, telling me he's close to letting go. I think back to one of his comments about filling me so full of his seed it drips down my thighs, I know this is what I want to give him. To be so full with not only Gage but all my men, that connection is what will get us past this.

I don't know how to get us there, but I trust my Alpha to take care of us. I lick his neck to close the wound, then in my head, I relinquish my control to him. He presses a kiss to my forehead where I feel his lips spread on my skin from a smile, "I got you, Baby, we all got you."

Our lips meet, he winces from the cut Leland gave him, but I suck on the wound to close it up too and make him feel better. He returns the favor by lifting me up so my legs can wrap his waist. I feel the air around me shift as he pulls us both to the ground. He adjusts my legs so he can lean back, then he lifts me to my knees. From behind, I feel his cock head brush up and down on my slit, yet his hands are still on my legs.

A spark in me flares when I realize another man is jacking Gage's cock against my slit. I moan into Gage's mouth when I sense this is Sabre, then I groan when Magennis begins to knead my heavy breasts, and Chris's hand connects lower, to manipulate my sensitive clit. By touch alone I know they are all here, all my men, together to please me, like only they know how. I sigh into Gage's mouth as the burning on my skin is shifting into a lighting of passion deep in my soul.

I close my eyes and allow the light to fade until I have only images of their faces wrapped in passionate expressions in my head. In my ears, are our groans of ecstasy and pleads for pleasure. I sniff and smell the air, to find a mix of their intoxicating scents laced with a thick mix of our lust. My body responds from each tantalizing touch, causing a deep fever to rise and coat my skin in a sheen of sweat.

"Please, oh God, please take me," I beg into Gage's mouth over and over.

Giving me what I ache for, Sabre pushes Gage's cock head into my aroused opening. As Gage lifts his hips to enter me, I accept the intrusion with a greedy need by sitting back and allowing him to take me deep. A deep groan of appreciation rings out into the air as his thickness engulfs me. I can no longer hold myself back, I begin to ride his length with a wild bounce, grinding my pelvic bone to his.

Gage grips my hips and meets me, slam for slam, creating a loud skin smacking sound. Magennis grasps my breasts in a hard clench, using the plump pillows to guide me up and down. Chris and Sabre also help by taking my arms so I have something to push on for leverage. My body hammers into Gage's nail, the harder the better, each pump creates the deep fire to spread until my dam let's go again.

I scream out my release, but it quickly turns to another shriek and my back bends as the burning returns. "Ah, aww!" I yell, drawing out the vowels into a howl.

Sabre's hard chest pushes up against my back, his thick arms fold across me in a hug. "We're going to try something new, Darling," he whispers in my ear, "but, you have to trust us."

I nod my head once to let him know I understand, "Trust us to take away the pain, my love." His sweet words are enough to make me weep, of course I trust them, with my life, but it still amazes me he is such a gentleman to ask. Again, I nod my head and try to make some noise to let them know I'm good with whatever they decide. If they can take away the violent pain, I will do whatever they ask.

Sabre tilts me forward until I can feel Gage's breath puff across my face, he's panting heavily from the first vigorous session. I'm still blinded by a bright glow in my eyes, I search out the cool grass on either side of Gage's head with my hands. Once I am forward, he pulls me up his chest, where I feel his cock slip a little out and I whine in protest.

"Hang on, Baby, you'll feel better in a second." He tells me but sounds distracted.

I realize why when; Sabre's cock runs down my ass crack and over my hole. I think he's about to take me from behind until he bumps past the puckered bud and continues down to meet Gage's cock. Gage pulls his out a fraction to allow for the meeting, again, I whimper. They mash their meat together, pushing the entrance open and with an ease, they both slip inside my pussy.

"Ohh," I squeak, as this foreign pressure stretches my vagina. Gage and Sabre are equal in many ways, including penis size. Having them both in the same place, all at once, is difficult to get accustomed to.

They are patient while they work together in a calm rhythm, letting the natural juices lubricate us with each steady draw out and push back in. Each pump gets easier when my muscles begin to relax around their combined excessive girth, helping them to push just that much farther inside. The allover burning of my skin shifts back into my belly where a furnace fire grows. My shoulders twitch and my back feels like a million ants dancing across it.

I pay no attention to the change while they rock me back and forth, Gage is our guide, directing me with his hands at my hips. Their steady beat slowly turns from foreign feeling into almost painful madness, as they tease me. They don't quite push all the way in to hit the sweet spot, and Gage's hold won't allow me to move to do it myself. They keep me on that fine edge of bliss, denying me what I want, while also keeping away the pain.

I dig my nails into the hard ground from my frustration and growl down at Gage in warning. "Mag, shut her mouth up," Gage orders.

Instantly, my head is pulled back by a grip on my overgrown bangs and Magennis fills my mouth with his sausage. I smile as I accept him into my throat, letting him pump my face while I suck him deep to the root. I work him up with my tongue, swirling the head on the out and sliding it against his growing shaft, on the return. My mouth salivates as a sample taste spills out his head, I flick my tongue into the hole to suck out the flavor. "Such a dirty girl," Magennis moans out, "So very naughty."

A hard open-palm whack stings across my ass, as Sabre reminds me with a slap, that he will not be ignored. I moan a response, causing Magennis to groan and pump my mouth again. Another slap to my ass and we repeat the process until I can feel the veins on Magennis's shaft bulging against my tongue. With all this going on, Chris jumps at the opportunity to take care of the last available position. His finger starts a slow massaging around the opening. Sabre gives me another slap, Chris adds a digit, pressing it into my ass and scissors his fingers open, playing with the entrance to prepare it for another cock.

I'm teetering on a line of, absolute pleasure, and *dear God, they can't possibly think I can take more.* I have never taken them all at once, not like this and my anxiety level has my heart pounding violently in my chest. *Is this even possible? I should really watch more porn, for the pointers.*

These thoughts are mere blips in my mind as we play, slap, suck, and fuck. Flickers of concern easily melt away with every incredible sensation. My magic dances to life, happy to be so close to a natural setting. I feel a strong connection to a ley line, I let the power course through me and wash over us, intensifying our physical connection. Gage and Sabre begin to work at a quicker, yet mismatched pace, when one pulls out the other moves in, there is a constant beat of pressure being applied.

My demon is overjoyed by this new daring situation. It craves more, the kinkier the better. I feel myself feeding from the lust around us, not only from our union but also from the excitement of the watching crowd. As the hunger in me grows, so too does the crawling sensation across my shoulders and down my spine. The tingling ripple only seems to add to my desire and I begin to push back against the pressures.

Magennis gives my mouth a quick long pump, pausing deep in my throat until I gag. Every muscle in my body contracts and clenches. Gage, Sabre, and Magennis moan in unison then Magennis pulls away. The pain springs forward causing me to gasp but only for a second, we shift until I feel a heavy weight above me, Magennis has mounted me from behind. Chris's fingers, now spread inside my back door, dip and stretch then disappear, at the same time Magennis pushes against my rear with his saliva drenched swollen cock.

The pain on my skin jumps down to my ass as Magennis moves to a halftime beat, between Gage and Sabre's, to bury his size into the darkness. The pressure is incredible, I've never been this full and even though it hurts, it also feels so, fucking, good. A screaming groan shoots out my mouth when the rippling tingle along my spine starts to spread.

"Chris, now," Gage instructs Chris, and right away, I feel his presence in front of me just before he slides his length into my mouth.

My gasps turn to groans while they all work to bring me the pleasurable high my body and being screams for. The pull is complete as we are joined into one incredible force. All the pain I had endured is switched into something so amazing, no words can even begin to describe it. I lose myself in this new discovery, I can't tell which touch turns me on the most. Pleasing Chris with my tongue, suckling his length until he is fully erect. Having Magennis slide his vessel in my ass, stretching me so full, while Gage and Sabre sword fight inside my pussy.

Somewhere deep in my soul, I hear a click and the beauty of the world around us comes shining into my vision. The first color I see is so incredibly blue, it is like the skies in heaven, as Gage looks up at me. He offers me that special smile he only reserves just for me and it is the trigger I need. The pressure is great and when the dam explodes, a rush of electric force whooshes out of me and shoots out into my men, as well as the people watching in our circle. I taste the bitter salt on my lips as Chris fires his release into my mouth, Magennis, Sabre, and Gage follow him.

As my men fill me, the electric charge returns like a boomerang, hitting me with such a jolt I bow back into Magennis. I knock him and Sabre over as I bend backward, almost folding in half. A loud ripping sound comes from my back, like sheets being shred. A gut curling scream bleeds from my throat as my fangs lengthen to hit my lips. This pain is nothing like any before, it comes from within and makes me its bitch. I'm frozen in place by its torture as I'm lacerated open, first with tiny pinprick stabs that quickly turn it into machete slashes.

All I can do is watch above me, the dark night has started to turn into the glow of early morning, then I realize the glow is not coming from the heavens, but from me. A golden shimmer of light cascades up from my body and illuminates this part of the park and all that is in it. Including the tight circle closed in around me and Gage, with Magennis, Chris, and Sabre rising to join hands with Lilith, and Zander, holding a beaten Leland beside Alex, Phoenix, and even Lazarus.

My eyes flicker to each of their faces, but there is no time to read expressions before another bout of tearing begins. This time, my skin bulges down the length of my torso then it burps bursting pockets of air. From each of the burps, a flicker of softness emerges, one tiny pocket at a time. As it bubbles along the skin I feel it take shape, and I finally get what is happening. I have just inherited my final powers, being gifted a beautiful set of iridescent white wings, to mark this grand event.

As I feel the wings spring forth, spreading up and out of my back, Lazarus calls out over the crowd, "Behold, your Queen, and witness the birth of miraculous power, she holds.

Only one with pure divinity can be called upon to represent the heaven." Lazarus's voice booms over the crowd to be heard and as he speaks, he unbuttons his dress shirt.

I watch the white linen falls from his shoulders just as a black set of wings shoot out from behind him. "I am the Angel Lazarus, and this is my sister Livia's daughter." His wings spread up and flap, causing a rush of air to push down. "Kneel subjects and pay respect to our Goddess of light, September."

A wicked sense of déjà vu hits me; this is just like last year when I became the Goddess of Darkness to Andras. Lazarus's words now make sense to me, I am both good and evil, the balance of all the worlds; a being made from all the creatures of this realm and together with my court, we just became the Supernatural equivalent of the Justice League.

"Well, crap on a cracker," I mumble and look down at Gage, he's leaning back on the grass propped up on his elbow, watching the show.

As our eyes meet, he gives me an amazing grin. "I kind of think the wings are a huge turn on."

I roll my eyes and snort, "Only you would."

He looks up to Sabre, Magennis, and Chris for help, they move forward to help me stand. "Sure, in that position they have appeal but the buggers damn near took me eye out." Magennis teases with a wink.

"Yo Goddess, that was some show, what do you do for an encore?" Samuel jokes, then Chris slams him in the ribs with a backhand. "Watch it, that Goddess is my soon to be wife."

They all huddle around; the wolves are still kneeling. I seek out Sabre. "There's a good question, what's next?" I ask.

Sabre comes forward to take my hand, he places a kiss on the knuckles. "I say for tonight, we go home, tomorrow is another day with a whole new set of challenges. Let's take it one small step at a time."

Lazarus stands behind Sabre, I watch his wings flap up then back before they fold in on themselves and disappear. It is my first lesson and I think the process out in my head. I hear the whoosh of air as my shoulder blades move the extensions. The wings go up and back then I think of them folding until they are no longer there. I'm surprised they tuck away a lot less painfully than they come out, but the first time I became a wolf that hurt like a bitch too, and now I can change into a wolf as easily as changing clothes.

Chris appears with Gage's jacket, he looks from me to the garment, confused whether to put it on me or not. I help him out by taking it to put on and thanking him with a kiss.

"The Gods are appeased, for now, little one," Lazarus congratulates me.

"What does that mean, Lazarus? Are we done with them?" Magennis asks the angel.

"For now. The warrior said, take it one day at a time, I agree. Enjoy the victories when you can, lick your wounds when you get defeated, and in between cherish the moments. You are immortal, there will be plenty of time for the Gods' games, until the next battle, keep your kingdom, and your Queen, safe."

Lazarus nudges past Sabre to press a kiss to my cheek before he continues with a whisper, "I'm sorry I couldn't help you go through that. Only someone truly pure of heart can survive the winged gift. However, you are of my blood, and your mother's daughter; I knew you would be strong enough. I must go now, but I will be back to check on you soon, my beautiful niece." He turns toward Lilith and gives her a smile before he simply vanishes into the air.

Lilith's cheeks turn a few shades of pink. I give her the lifted eyebrow questioning glance. Her eyes dart around, making sure I am the only one to see their exchange then she jumps forward to start her diversion, "I guess this means we move on to the next pressing matter."

Magennis perks up, "And that would be?" He says a little panicked, like maybe Lilith knows something he doesn't.

"Well, duh," She slaps his forehead with her palm and lets out a giggle. "We do have a wedding to plan."

A chorus of laughter and good cheer breaks the mood of this notoriously long day. As I look around at the flurry of activity, I reflect for a minute, and what I get from my thoughts is so simple. Today, we won in a fight with Gods, and a battle with the wolves. Today, I won a little more respect as a Queen, as a Beta, and as a woman, but I couldn't have done it without this incredible group before me. My people, my family, my heart.

ACKNOWLEDGMENTS

My first book was a dream come true, but this one was my, can I believe in myself to do it again, moment. There were days when I had all kinds of doubt going on, and if it wasn't for the following people, Inheritance, might not have happened.

I owe my sanity to my beloved, Scott. There are not enough ways to say thank you but I hope I have created a few to show you how much I do love you.

To my most generous and beautiful friend, Marie, you inspire me with your inner strength like no other person I have ever met. I am so proud of how far you have come and how you never give up. I am honored to call you friend, and I think I get way more out of our friendship than I could ever give. I heart you.

To Shannon, the most refreshingly honest and confident woman I have ever met. I cannot express how thankful I am to have such an open, candid and truly thoughtful person on my team. Thank you with all my heart, and I look forward to this growing friendship.

A special nod to Eniko, for being my beta reader this time. I appreciate all the hard work and thoughtful suggestions, thank you. I must also add a big thank you to Heather M. and Theresa for being my first beta's, sounding boards and dealers of my cray-cray, not only for book one but every step of the way. You sista's rock!

To my remaining family and extended family, thank you for the endless cheers of support, now will you all just read the damn book! To all the friends I've met along this life's journey, I believe our paths were meant to cross so that I could collect all these amazing memories that inspired me to create this world, and hopefully much more.

And finally, to all my readers, every comment, review, spoken word, and story shared have made me learn and grow, as a writer and as a person. I write because I have stories I want to share, and you all make me feel like it is worth sharing them. I heart you all!

ABOUT THE AUTHOR

Marianne Maguire is your sister in sin, and the bestselling Paranormal Erotic Romance author of the Legacy Series. She lives outside of Toronto, Ontario, Canada on her critter ranch with her husband and four-legged fur-kids. When not entertaining you with her devious mind, you can find Marianne beautifying family pets, helping the bereaved in her community, or out in her backyard jungle taming the wild landscape and saving the woodland critters.

Learn more about Marianne's books and where to follow her at:

www.mamaguire

www.ingramcontent.com/pod-product-compliance
Lightning Source LLC
Chambersburg PA
CBHW060149260626
47160CB00001B/184